THE
WISDOM
OF
STONES

BRIAN PEYTON JOYNER

The Wisdom of Stones © 2017 Brian Peyton Joyner

Golden Rule Omnimedia
2244 Sunshine Way
Palm Springs, CA 92264

FIRST EDITION

Book design by Gwyn Snider, GKS Creative, Nashville

Library of Congress Cataloging-in-Publication Data has been applied for.

978-0-9981467-1-3 (trade paperback)
978-0-9981467-2-0 (mobi)
978-0-9981467-3-7 (epub)

*For my grandpa who inspired me with his stories
and with his faith in Christ, and*

*To my husband who inspired me
with his story ideas and his faith in me.*

I wish the two of you could have met.

1

December 11, 1983 (Sunday)
Benji (13 years old)

People like me will have our own ghetto in Hell. And by "people like me," I'm not talking about other husky kids with blond hair. Or boys who step on girl's toes while dancing at the junior cotillion.

Satan will jam-pack my kind into his hottest area where the temperature and humidity are gonna make August in South Carolina feel like iced tea. For me, the brimstone will be worse than the fire. Spiked with extra sulfur, it will make my skin itch like I ran nekkid through poison oak. But no matter where I scratch, it won't help. The itch will jiggle around, always moving until it settles in the middle of my back. I'll stretch my arm over my shoulder, grabbing my elbow with the other hand and pushing to get to that spot. But no matter how hard I try, I won't be able to reach it.

I could cry out for help but that won't do any good. I'll be alone. No one I can count on will be in Hell.

I'm Southern Baptist and have gone to church my whole life, so almost everybody I know will be in Heaven. Momma's been there since I was seven. My dad is still alive, but he's gonna end up in Hell. Or at least that's what Momma told me after that Thanksgiving Day in 1976 when he walked out on us.

We thought Mee Maw was going to Heaven earlier this year, but I prayed and made a promise to God. And he healed her. When she does go to Heaven, Grandpa says she will have a reserved section, with a monogrammed golden gate and an attendant like at the Greenville Country Club.

Grandpa says he wants to come back and live another life. The first time he told me that, I quoted Preacher Dale, "Life ain't like shampoo. There's no lather, rinse, repeat. You got one chance on this earth to do things right."

But Grandpa don't care too much for Preacher Dale and even though he appreciated a clever remark, he wasn't persuaded. "Ain't you always saying through God everything is possible?" he asked me.

I nodded.

"Then I think God's gone give me a do-over on a couple things."

While Grandpa's living his other life and everyone else is enjoying Heaven, I'll be in Hell. I want to think that because I've accepted Jesus Christ as my personal Lord and Savior, I won't be going there. But according to Preacher Dale's sermons, I'm too broken. Because of this condition, hellfire and damnation are waiting for me.

And to make matters worse, Mee Maw and Grandpa know.

During dinner tonight, Mee Maw was looking at me all funny, and Grandpa wouldn't look at me at all. When I told them that I was heading up for bed, I heard Mee Maw tell Grandpa to go talk to me.

And he followed me upstairs and stood at my doorway for a while. I asked him if there was anything he needed to chat about, but he shook his head. And he said that he loved me no matter what. At the time, I had no idea what he was talking about. I told him that I loved him too, and then felt the need to add "no matter what."

He left, and then the little voice in the back of my head started up. *Just take a quick peek. You'll feel better after you look at your magazines.*

I ignored the voice at first. I'd been taught at school by my science teacher to be careful. My body was hitting puberty, and it was full of something called "hormones" that would make me crazy. But in that moment, the little voice was right. I wanted . . . no . . . . I needed to look at that magazine. I lifted up the edge of my mattress, expecting to find the latest *Sports Illustrated.* This issue had articles on all the top college football players, and I couldn't wait to look at their pictures. But that magazine wasn't on top. None of my magazines were in the same order where I'd put them under my mattress.

And then I realized why Mee Maw and Grandpa were acting so strange at dinner.

They knew.

My stomach ached, and I ran to the bathroom. I threw up and then rested my forehead against the cool porcelain. Vomit burned my throats and nostrils, and I threw up again. I splashed cold water on my face and tried to shut out the little voice. *All your magazines are still there waiting for you. Remember the one with the picture of the guy doing bicep curls? He's shirtless.*

They were always shirtless.

And that's why I have nightmares about Hell and the brimstone spiked with the extra sulfur. I've already got an itch I can't scratch.

I don't want to spend eternity like that.

2

December 30, 1977 (Friday)
Benji (7 years old)

Momma died because of my love of snow ice cream, and Dad left me for a half-baby who hadn't even been born. And everybody in my life kept lying to me about two things. It wasn't my fault and I was gone be okay.

The day of Momma's funeral, it wasn't cloudy no more. Just a little bit of snow hiding in the shadows of the tombstones. Preacher Dale stood in front of the coffin, right next to the mountain of dirt that would fill Momma's grave. Me, Grandpa and Mee Maw sat in fancy chairs with gold backs and black seats. Grandpa was wearing Class Stan, a gray hat with a red feather. The wind kept about blowing it off his head so he held it in his lap. His white hair stuck up all which away, and his being so skinny, he looked like a Q-Tip. Mee Maw was more cotton ball. Her hair was white, and she was as wide as she was tall.

The wind about froze me, and I tried to keep my hands warm in my pockets, but I couldn't on my right side. A cast runned from my elbow to the end of my fingers. I pulled a little bit of the padding from the cast to cover my fingers. The sun shined and hurted my eyes, but I kept looking around. I counted thirty-four people, but not my dad.

I kept thinking Dad was gone show up places. At Grandpa and Mee Maw's house where I stayed after Momma died. At the funeral home last night when everybody came and told me how sorry they was for me. At the funeral service this morning. But I shoulda knowed better. Momma always said Dad had left us and wasn't coming back.

Last night, I had gone down to get a glass of water, and Grandpa and Mee Maw was in the kitchen. I heard Grandpa tell Mee Maw that my dad wasn't gone come. Miss Julia was about to birth his child.

"What baby?" I asked. They both jumped about two feet, which is a lot for old people. Mee Maw run up and hugged me and told me to be excited. I was gone have a half-brother or sister.

I didn't know what a half-baby was, and I liked people to think I was smart so I wasn't gone ask her. I went back upstairs to bed. I fell asleep quick, but I had nightmares. One about a little brother with a body but no legs. Another about a little sister with just a left part of a body trying to crawl around on her side.

And they was calling me, "Benji! Benji!" And I knowed babies can't talk.

I woke up screaming.

Grandpa came in, and I told him about my dreams. He told me what a half-baby was, and he also said that my dad loved me. But I didn't believe nothing he said.

Not that Grandpa hadn't tried to get Dad to come back after Momma died.

Over the past few days, Grandpa had gone in his office downstairs and shut the door. I didn't know what he was up to until I had picked up the phone in their bedroom upstairs to call my friend Craig Allen. Grandpa was on the phone with my dad, and I listened in.

"A boy should be raised by his father," Grandpa said.

"You and Lilly are much better set in life. Julia's going to give birth soon, and we just can't afford another mouth to feed."

"Another mouth to feed!" Grandpa shouted so loud that I could hear him both on the phone and from downstairs. "That boy's your own flesh and blood!"

"I want to start a new life with Julia," Dad said.

"Richard." Grandpa huffed like he did when he was madder than a wet-setting hen. "I ain't really liked you from the first time we met, and you just gone downhill from there. Maybe he should just live with me and Lilly."

"If you wouldn't mind," Dad said, and then there was a pause. I could hear both Grandpa and my dad breathing. And I wanted to say something. To tell my dad that I'd be a good half-brother.

But before I had a chance to say nothing, Grandpa shouted, "You didn't do right by my daughter, and I'll be damned if I'm gone let you treat my grandson like some red-headed stepchild! Benji is gone live with us. End of story!"

Grandpa slammed down his phone, but Dad and I was still on the line. I wanted to say something. To tell him I was sorry for what I did to make him leave me. Promise him that whatever I'd done, I'd never do it again.

But he hung up, and then I just heard a dial tone.

"Ben, you upstairs?" Mee Maw called out. Then I heard her

and Grandpa coming up the squeaky old stairs so I ran to my bedroom. I pretended to be interested in the stack of baseball cards they'd bought me the past couple days. I hadn't opened any of them. It didn't feel right going back to doing normal things just yet.

Grandpa sat on the edge of the bed. "We've got some good news for you," he said, and patted the spot beside him.

I sat down, and he put his arm around me. I smelled the lime of his Old Spice.

"We want you to live with us permanent," Mee Maw said, and took her place on the other side of me so that I was squeezed between them.

"Just like last year?" I asked. Momma and I had moved in with them for a couple weeks after Dad had moved with Miss Julia to Chicago.

"Yes, but even better," Grandpa said, and stood up. "You won't be staying in this room. You get to have your Momma's old room. The one she had when she was your age."

Mee Maw looked at him with her eyes wide, like she hadn't heard him right.

He nodded. "It will be the best thing. We'll donate Dot's old furniture, put in some new carpet and paint it a real pretty blue color." His eyes got all wet, and I thought he was gone cry. "Or any other color Benji wants."

Mee Maw's eyes got real shiny too, and she got the sniffles. She stood up to head to the bathroom, but Grandpa stopped her. He put his arms around her. "Lilly, we've got to all move on. We can't leave her room as some sort of shrine."

"Charlie, I don't care about this room or Dot's worldly possessions. I just always wanted a son." She got a box of

Kleenex wrapped in a macramé cover I'd made at Vacation Bible School. She handed me a tissue.

I started crying again and Grandpa waved his hand for me to come over. "We gone be our own little family," he said. I hugged Mee Maw and Grandpa and they hugged me back real tight.

Now, as Preacher Dale finished up his sermon at the cemetery, I realized we was in that same position. Grandpa had his arm around me. Mee Maw was leaned over and holding me.

I reckoned that maybe I was only being told one lie.

Maybe I was gone be okay.

Dad and Miss Julia might not want me, but Grandpa and Mee Maw did.

The breeze kicked up, but for the first time since the accident, I didn't feel cold no more. Me and Grandpa and Mee Maw was a family.

I listened to the rest of Preacher Dale's sermon, and I felt a little better. Preacher Dale said that God had a special way of taking care of kids. And he told everybody there to watch out for me and help my grandparents if they ever needed anything.

After the service ended, Preacher Dale came and kissed me on top of my head. "You're a very brave boy, Ben." He shook Grandpa's hand. "Sorry I've got to run, but I need to get to the hospital before visiting hours are over."

Mee Maw grabbed him and threw her arms around him. "Bless you for everything you've done. I'm so grateful to you for staying with us at the hospital every night."

"Helping others is my favorite part of the job," the preacher said. "Y'all holler if y'all need anything."

Everyone came up and said their goodbyes, but me, Grandpa and Mee Maw didn't want to leave Momma's coffin. We just stood there until we was the only ones left. The folks that worked there was ready to lower the box with Momma's body into the grave.

"Can I say goodbye to her one last time?" I asked Mee Maw. I wanted to give Momma one last hug and kiss.

Mee Maw took me over, and I tried to get my good arm around the top of the coffin. The dark brown wood was colder than I expected. I kissed the side of the box like Momma would kiss me when she put me to bed at night. I wanted to cry one last time, but all my tears had runned out. Mee Maw put her arm around me and tried to get me to go, but I didn't want to leave. The wind blew up the fake green grass covering the mound of dirt beside her grave.

Made me think about a movie I seen one time. Everybody at the funeral took a handful of dirt and dropped it into the grave. I didn't know why they did that, but it seemed to make them feel better. I grabbed a big ol' clod of Georgia clay and chucked it into the empty grave. My insides hurt a little less so I grabbed another handful. Mee Maw moved to stop me, but Grandpa held her back. I throwed fistful after fistful of the red clay soil as hard as I could into the grave. And each time I felt a little bit better.

I didn't know whether I'd throwed dirt for one minute or ten. But when I grabbed one last bit of the clay, I stopped. They was something sharp in it. I dropped the clod on the ground and reached to pick up a stone. It was as long as a pack of gum but the shape was more like a triangle. It had a rough edge like a knife.

Grandpa let go of Mee Maw, and they came up to me. Mee Maw gave me a hug, but I held my hands out so I wouldn't get mud on her dress.

"What you got?" Grandpa asked.

I was breathing hard like I'd runned a mile and couldn't answer him at first. I gave the stone to Grandpa, and he rolled it over in his hand. It was a pinkish rock, but I wasn't sure if that was its color or if it was from the red clay.

"That looks like a gen-u-ine Indian arrowhead." He held it up to the sunlight. "I think it's pink quartz."

He had a look in his eye. A sparkle that I hadn't seen since Momma died. Grandpa and I was always walking around in the woods hunting for rocks. And we was always on the lookout for arrowheads to add to his collection of stones.

"You want it?" I asked.

He really liked it. I could tell.

But Mee Maw said, "Charlie. Give the boy back the arrowhead. You've got enough rocks already."

Grandpa frowned but gave it back to me. "It's yours," he said.

"But I want you to have it," I said, and I meant it. It was the best stone I'd ever found. I pushed it back into his hand.

"Well, I'll have to give you something in exchange." He rubbed his chin and squinted his eyes like he was thinking real hard. "See this arrowhead like this?" He moved it so the point was up. "That was the logo for the Atlanta Crackers. Best minor league baseball team of all time. Seeing you throw that dirt made me think of watching them play. They had some of the best pitchers in baseball." He turned the arrowhead over and over in his hand. He scrunched up his face and then started nodding.

"But this story is about a runner. The best base stealer in history. His name was Climax Clinton."

And while they lowered Momma's body into the grave, Grandpa told me the funniest story I ever heard.

3

January 7, 1978 (Saturday)
Benji (8 years old)

For my birthday, Grandpa took me to the 31 Flavors. I wanted to get vanilla, but he insisted I get anything else. I had him pick so we each had a sugar cone with two scoops of Rocky Road. Grandpa also bought an ice cream cake for later. That night, as Grandpa brought out the cake with eight candles, he and Mee Maw sang. "Happy birthday dear Beeee-eeeennnnnnn. Happy birthday to you!"

I made a wish, sucked in a big ole breath and blew out the candles in one shot. I just knew Dad would call at some point. They was a few hours left in the day.

Grandpa cut a whopper of a piece and handed it to me. Mee Maw shot him a look, pooching out her lips.

"It's his birthday," Grandpa said.

He cut an even bigger piece for himself and then a teeny-tiny one for Mee Maw. She rolled her eyes.

"Is it raining?" I asked Grandpa, and when he looked I grabbed one of the whole cherries that was in his piece of cake.

"It that lightning outside?" He pointed, and when I turned my head, he took his fork and ate half the brownie bottom of my cake. We got to giggling, and Mee Maw got up to cut herself a larger piece.

I tried to make Grandpa turn around again so I could take another bite of his cake, until I got to laughing so hard I about got choked.

"All right, you two," Mee Maw said. "That's enough." She took our plates, even though we wasn't finished. "Wash up your hands, Benji. I got another present for you." She rinsed off the cake knife. "And your grandpa says he's got one last thing for you, too."

I washed up and then sat back at the table with Grandpa. Mee Maw brought me a wrapped present and a card.

"The card's from your dad," Grandpa said.

"Did he call today?" I asked.

Mee Maw started to answer, but Grandpa interrupted. "He did call, but it was while we was at the 31 Flavors. He told Mee Maw to wish you a happy birthday."

Mee Maw gave me the card, but didn't look at me. I had a hard time opening it because my right arm was still in a cast. On the front of the card was a monkey in a baseball outfit. Inside, it said "Ape-y Birthday!" and contained money. Dad had written, "Sorry I couldn't be there. Love, Dad." I looked at the ten-dollar bill and realized it had black smudges on one side. "It's got ink all over it," I said. I rubbed where Dad had written "Happy Birthday" and the card smeared.

"Your Dad must not have used a very good pen," Grandpa said, and took the card from me.

Mee Maw handed me a box the size a shirt would come in. "I can't wait for you to open this, Benji. Your Momma bought this for you."

The box was heavy as a dictionary, and I couldn't even hold it. I set it on the table and didn't want to open it. Momma had got this for me, and I felt like I should keep it just like it was.

The room got really warm. And bright. Like I could feel her there with me. I squeezed my eyes shut and imagined her wrapping the present, making sure that the paper was cut just the right size and folding over the creases so that they were even. And creating the bow. Momma always made the best bows.

I opened my eyes and looked at the package. The paper on the bottom didn't line up. The corners was all crooked where it was folded over. And the blue bow was store-bought.

Mee Maw realized how much I was studying the present. "I wrapped it, but your Momma bought it for you. It just came in last week."

Knowing that Momma had nothing to do with the wrapping, I tore into the package. Inside was a black leather book. My full name, Benjamin Thomas Stark, was written on the bottom in curly gold letters.

"It's the King James Bible," Mee Maw said. "Your Momma wanted to get you one of those new translations, but I talked her into getting you the real thing."

I ran my fingers along the edge. The pages looked like they was made of pure gold. I could smell the new leather.

Momma had bought me a real adult Bible.

I cleaned out a whole drawer in my nightstand for the Bible and couldn't wait to go to church the next day. I begged Mee Maw and Grandpa to take me to Jordan Baptist, the same church Momma and I went to.

Even though it was a farther drive, they agreed. When we got there, I took Grandpa and Mee Maw to the pew where Momma and I used to sit. The service started, and the whole church sang my favorite hymn, "Onward Christian Soldiers." I sang louder than normal, and the woman in front of us kept looking at me. Every time she did, Grandpa would start singing louder too until she turned back around.

After the choir sang their second song, Preacher Dale got up and asked us to turn to Genesis, Chapter 10. Using the same steady hand that I would apply to a game of Operation, I opened my Bible. The paper was thin, and I feared that ripping a page, even on accident, would be a sin.

Preacher Dale read the story about two angels that went to visit Lot in the city of Sodom. Lot didn't realize they were angels. He just thought they were out-of-towners, so he invited them in for a big feast. While the party was going on, all the men in the town stood outside Lot's house and wanted to "know" the strangers. Lot wasn't having none of that, and he told the angels he'd send out his daughters instead, but the townspeople really wanted to meet the two angels.

That made the angels real mad, and they told Lot that God was gone destroy Sodom. I followed along in the Scripture as Preacher Dale got louder and louder. "Then the Lord rained upon Sodom and upon Gomorrah brimstone and fire from the Lord out of heaven."

He went on and on about sin and God's judgment and ended his sermon with some even harsher words. "And know that the sodomites of today face a similar fate." He let those words wash over us, and I worried for them sodomites. I didn't know who they were, but they probably slouched in church so I sat up straight, feeling my tailbone sharp against the wood pew.

After the sermon, Grandpa said something to Mee Maw about

how he had heard enough sermons in his lifetime about hellfire, but she disagreed. "People need to hear about these things, Charlie. How else will they know right from wrong?"

I kept worrying about the sodomites. I'd heard Preacher Dale use that word for years. That was the first time I'd read the story, and I still couldn't figure it out. I needed to know. When we was leaving, I made Mee Maw and Grandpa take me out the center door where Preacher Dale thanked people for coming.

He took Mee Maw's hand. "How y'all holding up?"

"Each day gets a little easier," she said.

"Y'all are in my prayers," he said.

"Well bless you heart," she said.

A long line had formed behind us, and Grandpa and Mee Maw was halfway out the door when I grabbed Preacher Dale's hand and pulled him into me, like I was gone tell him a secret. "What's a sodomite?" I asked.

Preacher Dale let go of my hand like he was holding a snake, Grandpa stepped back, and I heard Mee Maw suck in air.

"Benji," Grandpa said, "There's some things you learn about when you're young and other things when you're older. This one's for when you're older." He put his hand on my back to push me out the door, but Mee Maw squatted down in front of me. She looked me in the eyes and her face got real serious. Her lips, eyebrows and nose all pushed together.

"There's some boys who are wrong," she said. "They like other boys instead of girls."

Preacher Dale put his hand on my shoulder. "Your grandma's right. These boys call themselves gay, but they're the farthest thing from happy. They're sick molesters of children and God will punish those sodomites."

Grandpa grabbed me by the arm and jerked me away from Preacher Dale and Mee Maw.

I wanted to ask more questions, but Grandpa high-tailed it out of there, dragging me through the parking lot.

"Hope to see you next week," Preacher Dale called out to us.

Mee Maw had to run in her high heels to catch up. "Charlie Phelps!" she yelled. "What's gotten into you?"

She caught up with us and grabbed my arm, causing me to drop my Bible on the pavement. Mee Maw let go, but Grandpa kept his grip on me. I squirmed away and picked up my Bible. I dusted off the tiny rocks and looked at it real good. There was a scuff mark on the black leather right above where my name was. I felt the tears starting, but Grandpa hugged me.

"We can fix that," he said.

I looked into his eyes and they was watery just like mine. I thought we was both gone cry, but then he smiled. "It's gone be okay. Just needs a little black shoe polish."

I smiled too, but as we walked back to the car, I could tell Mee Maw was real mad. She had her lips pushed together and was walking real fast.

I ran up to her. "I'm sorry I dropped my Bible," I said.

"It wasn't your fault," she said. "I shouldn't have grabbed you like that. I'm just frustrated with your Grandpa."

She didn't say nothing the rest of the way home, and as much as I tried, I couldn't stop thinking about them sodomites. Finally, I just had to ask again. "Grandpa, when am I gone be old enough to know about sodomites?"

"One day, I'll talk to you about that," Grandpa promised and looked at Mee Maw. "One day."

4

I "listened" to everything my wife told me about how we needed to raise Benji. But sometimes I ignored what she said. As much as I liked being right, Lilly hated being wrong, so avoiding fights with my wife was better than winning them.

I had let her be as strict on the boy as she wanted to be, and only on rare occasions did I say something. But finding us the right church had been one of them few times I'd put my foot down. Lilly had not cottoned to going to a church that wasn't all hellfire.

"By the time Benji is a teenager, we'll be too old to keep a good eye on him," she had said. "We've got to mold him now."

"He's a good boy," I had told her. "And you got him worried so much about what's gone happen to him in the afterlife, he ain't enjoying the time he's got in this world."

"Charlie. We can't have the boy end up like his father: A worthless cheat who is guided by his nether regions instead of his head."

Because we couldn't agree, we had bounced from church to church for years, until we met Brother Steve, the assistant pastor at Galilee Baptist. Lilly liked him because he was smart. I liked him because he was a good man who followed the principles of Christ and didn't just pick Bible verses at random to suit his need or make a point.

For the past three years, we'd taken Benji to church there, and Benji had matured in a way that made me and Lilly proud.

It was a dark day when Brother Steve announced he was gone leave us and move back to Chicago to take a job at a seminary. To say goodbye, we invited him to supper, and Lilly was gone make her famous vegetable soup with okra, tomatoes and colored butter beans. She'd run out of buttermilk to make corn bread so she sent me to the grocery store. When I got back, she wasn't in the kitchen, and the beans was boiling over on the stove.

"Lilly?" I called out, thinking she must be in the bathroom. When she didn't reply, I shouted. Still, no reply.

I found her upstairs asleep on the bed with her shoes on. "Lilly," I whispered so as not to scare her. It was hot in the room with the afternoon sun coming in. "You okay?"

She blinked like she wasn't quite sure where she was. "I just need a couple Bayer." She sat up, and her face was redder than Tim Taggert after drinking a bottle of Turbo Stomper moonshine.

"You sure it's still okay to have Brother Steve over?" I asked. In the past few weeks, Lilly had been real tired.

"Everything is almost ready," she said, and propped herself up in the bed. "I've brined the chicken all night. It just needs to be breaded and fried." She groaned and shifted to get more comfortable. "And I need to make the cornbread."

I helped her up from the bed, and put my cheek against her forehead. "You feel a mite feverish. Why don't you mix up the cornbread? I'll fry the chicken so you don't have to stand over the stove no more."

"I love you, Charles," she said, and pulled me in. I could smell her hairspray. Good ol' Aquanet. Even though she'd been laying on it, not a hair was out of place. I hugged her tight.

"Ouch," she said, and pushed me away.

"What's the matter?"

"Just a little tender," she said. "Nothing for you to worry about, dear."

At 6:02 p.m., Brother Steve arrived at the door with a bunch of daisies.

"I declare those are the most elegant daisies," Lilly said. "Benji, make room for those on the table."

She put her hand on Steve's forearm and led him into the kitchen. He helped her bring the food to the table, and we held hands while Benji said grace.

Lilly was a good cook and no one said nothing for a few minutes. After I finished my first piece of chicken, I asked Brother Steve how he was enjoying being at Galilee Baptist.

"It's great work. I get to spend time with the kids every Sunday, and then on the weekdays, I work with the elderly." Brother Steve helped himself to another piece of chicken. "I'm going to miss it, though," he said.

"What do you mean?" Benji asked. I forgot that we hadn't told him that Brother Steve was leaving.

"This fall, I'm heading to teach at seminary in Chicago," he said.

"What's Chicago like?" Benji asked. He was always interested in learning more about the city where his dad lived.

"It's the greatest city in the world," Brother Steve said. "Chicago has the best people you'll ever meet, outside of South Carolina, of course."

Benji peppered him with questions about the Windy City and gobbled up every word about the same way that Brother Steve ate all the fried chicken. But when Steve started talking about all the snow from Lake Michigan, Benji's face changed. His mouth drooped, his eyes dropped down, and he sniffled. He was about to think about something he didn't need to think about so I jumped in.

"Benji, Mee Maw tells me you found a new stone down by the creek bed."

Benji dug in his pocket and handed it to me. I took the stone and scratched it a little with my fingernail. Tiny amounts of talc flaked off. "You know what they call this?" I asked.

"Steatite," he said without hesitation.

I studied him. The boy was smart but not a geologist.

"I looked it up in the encyclopedia," he said.

"Most folks call it soapstone," I said, and handed it back to him.

He scratched at it. "It's like hotel soap."

"Reminds me of my days when I was a hobo," I said. "I met one of my best friends in the whole world because of soap."

"You were a hobo?" Brother Steve, Lilly and Benji all asked at the same time.

"I did a lot of things before settling down," I said. I looked at Benji. "I ain't ever told you about how I got kicked out of the house by my maw when I was sixteen."

"I've never had much respect for a parent who would abandon a child," Lilly said, and then caught herself. She checked to see if Benji had noticed her slip-up.

"My maw did the best she could for us." I gave Lilly the stink-eye. "I don't blame her one bit."

Benji had been so nervous as a kid that he was gone be abandoned again that I hadn't told him this story when he was younger, but by the time he was thirteen, I reckoned he was old enough to hear it.

"This is a nice stone, Benji." I put the rock on the table. "In 1931, Pa died, leaving maw with seven kids."

"What happened to your father?" Brother Steve asked.

"He was unloading hay from the McPhail's barn when the stacks fell over and crushed him like a penny on a train track."

"That's terrible," Benji said.

"It wasn't coconut cake," I said, and picked up the stone again. "I was sixteen and as the oldest boy I needed to get work, but I couldn't keep a job because of the trouble I got into."

"What kind of trouble?" Benji asked.

"Women," I said. "I've always been this good-looking, and two of Mr. McPhail's daughters took a shine to me."

Lilly kicked me under the table, wanting me to stop, but I had Brother Steve and Benji hanging on each word. "Suzie was the purdier one, but Bessie made me laugh so I liked her better. Problem is, I kissed them both, which was real forward for that time. Bessie started bragging to Suzie, and when Mr. McPhail found out, he blackballed me from finding work anywhere in town."

"And that was after your dad died working on his farm?" Brother Steve asked.

"I couldn't believe it myself, but I'd sullied the reputation of his daughters. At that time, I did more thinking with my. . ."

Lilly kicked me again, this time so hard I stopped.

She said, "You were talking about how you got throwed out of your house by your maw."

I got back to my story.

"A couple months after that, Maw insisted that the whole family be present at Sunday dinner. She cooked up a meal the likes of which we hadn't seen since the Thanksgiving before Pa died. We had cornbread dressing, congealed salad and sweet potatoes topped with marshmallows. While I was taking a bite of fried okra, she announced that she was expecting a baby in six months and with winter coming, she couldn't afford me or my sister Gertrude no more. I had a week to get a job or move out, and Gertrude needed to get married. And she wasn't kidding. We had Gertrude's wedding the next Saturday in the McPhail's barn, and I had to leave the house the next day."

I stopped for a moment because just the thought of that moment made me tear up a little even though it was sixty years ago.

"Why didn't your sister get married at church?" Benji asked. He never missed a detail.

"We didn't exactly have a building, since ours was burned to the ground by a Klan group from the Baptist church over in the next county."

"Baptist Klansmen burned down your church?" Brother Steve asked.

"Case of mistaken identity," I said. "The Second African Methodist Episcopal Church was gone have a marriage ceremony for a white man and a black woman. Wudn't gone be legal, just symbolic, but the Klan wasn't gone tolerate their union. Those idiot coneheads decided to burn down the AME church before the wedding could happen. But they got so drunk before setting out that when they got to our church, Second Baptist, they just saw the word "Second" on the sign and didn't read the rest. Next morning, our church was a pile of ashes."

"What did you do?" Benji asked.

"Some church deacons argued that we should seek an eye for an eye and go over and burn down they church, but our preacher talked them out of it. Pastor Jacobs said you could find a Bible verse to prove any point you wanted, but it was more important to think about what God wanted. No way did God want another church burned down."

No one said a word so I started to grab the last piece of chicken again. Lilly gave me a look so I asked Brother Steve, "Can I get you anything else to eat?"

"I'm stuffed," he said, and patted his belly. "Just saving room for a piece of that coconut cake I've heard so much about."

Lilly chuckled and pushed up from the table. I'd seen her clear the table a thousand times, but it was like she was in slow motion. She picked up Brother Steve's silverware and set it on top his empty plate. Her thin fingers grabbed the edge of his plate, causing purple and bluish veins to bulge in her hand. Her whole body shook. Then she fell like a skirt dropping to the floor.

"You okay, Mee Maw?" Benji jumped up, his reflexes much faster than mine.

He and Brother Steve helped her back into her chair. I felt my stomach knot up. About the same feeling I'd had when my maw told me that I had to leave home. I had to tell myself to breathe.

"Just a long day," she said.

"Then let me help you clean up," Brother Steve said.

"But you don't know where all these things go," she said.

"Benji can help me, won't you?" he asked.

Benji nodded. He had a look of panic on his face. His mouth fell open, and his eyes got so wide I thought they was gone circle around his head. He and Steve cleared the table, but Benji didn't stop looking at Lilly. "Y'all making too much of a fuss," she said.

"Let us make a fuss." Brother Steve handed a clean plate to Benji to dry.

I got her a glass of cold water with some ice.

"I'm taking you to the doctor tomorrow," I whispered so Benji wouldn't be able to hear me. I felt a scratchy feeling in the back of my chest, like a teeny tiny mouse was gnawing at my nerves.

Something was very wrong.

5

August 12, 1983 (Friday)
Benji (13 years old)

Grandpa was gone take Mee Maw to the doctor, and he'd asked Brother Steve to watch me. We was gone visit shut-ins, and I was super excited. I hoped at least one lived in a bubble.

The first woman we visited was Mrs. Kimpton. She lived clear across town, and along the way I quizzed Brother Steve about what it was like to be a pastor. He was glad to answer any question I had, and I'd never met anyone who loved his job so much. Before I knew it, we pulled up to the trailer where Mrs. Kimpton lived.

We stayed at her place for about two hours, reading the Bible. She even had costumes, and we acted out some passages. Wearing a long white beard, I pretended to be Moses, and in a thunderous voice, I read the Ten Commandments like I'd just come down from Mount Sinai.

Before we left, Brother Steve went to the bathroom, and Mrs. Kimpton told me I could take a piece of butterscotch candy from the glass bowl she had on the coffee table. I reckon she seen I'd been eyeing that candy. She got up from her chair and sat down beside me on the sofa. I unwrapped the candy and listened as she told me a secret. "Now, you don't tell Pastor Steve, but I'm not nearly as sick as I used to be. It's just that no one in my family . . ." She turned her head away from me.

"Ma'am, your secret is safe with me," I said. I wanted her to be sure so I pretended like I had a lock on my mouth and twisted a key and then tucked the key under the candy dish. I sat for a moment and then realized I needed to say something. I got the key and unlocked my mouth.

"Brother Steve knows you're better. The whole way over here he talked about how much he enjoyed visiting."

She stopped frowning. "I don't know what I'm gone do when he moves to Chicago."

"I'll tell you what. I'll come over and visit you again." I patted her hand, and she looked at me. She tried to smile, but it wasn't real, and I saw pain in her face. Her forehead was all wrinkled and her mouth turned down.

"I've seen the pictures you got on your mantel. I know you got a son. I'm gone pray that whatever issues y'all have between you, the Lord will see fit to fix them. Mee Maw says I've got a special line to God, and he's gone listen." I squeezed her hand, and this time she smiled. A genuine ear-to-ear, teeth-showing grin.

"If I close my eyes, you sound just like a preacher." She leaned over and gave me a kiss on the forehead. "And I mean that in a good way. You ever thought about being a preacher?"

"No ma'am, but I know it'd make Mee Maw proud."

Brother Steve came back from the bathroom. "You two look like you're up to something."

"Just talking," she said. "You've got a good one here." She patted my head.

"Don't I know it. I should just chauffeur him around and let him visit people while I wait in the car."

We all had a good laugh, and I wondered if Grandpa had a chauffeur hat. Brother Steve looked at his watch. "We better head out. Mr. Luckadoo gets irritated if I visit too close to his lunchtime."

After a fifteen-minute drive, we arrived at Mr. Luckadoo's small, dark, second-story apartment. He had crazy eyes that were so blue they looked fake, and wild white hair that went every which a way. Plus, I think he was the oldest person I'd ever seen.

"Benji, this is Mr. Luckadoo," Brother Steve said.

Mr. Luckadoo just grunted, and we followed him into the den. Brother Steve talked to Mr. Luckadoo for a while about all the things going on at church. I just stared around the room. He had two whole shelves of different dipping birds. The ones where you push their head into a glass of water and they keep moving back and forth drinking water. On his coffee table, he had a bowl filled with all different rocks.

After about a half hour, Brother Steve had finished sharing all the church news. I was about to ask Mr. Luckadoo about his rock collection when Brother Steve stood up. "Could I use your phone?"

"There's one in the kitchen," Mr. Luckadoo said. "I'll show you where it is."

"I'm sure I can find it," Brother Steve said, but Mr. Luckadoo insisted on following him in there.

"I don't like people in my things," he said, as if Brother Steve was gonna take something. They started to go, but then Mr. Luckadoo halted. He turned around and crooked his finger at me, like the witch in the Hansel and Gretel story. "Now you be good out here. I don't want you breaking my stuff."

"Yes sir," I said. With all those dipping birds, he was right not to trust me. To avoid temptation, I was gonna join them in the kitchen when I noticed that one stone in the bowl looked like a purple diamond. I thought Grandpa had something similar in his collection, but I couldn't remember what it was called.

And then I heard a voice in my head, like a whisper. *Just take a closer look at it. No harm in that.*

I picked up the stone and took it over to the window. I was inspecting it close when Mr. Luckadoo stuck his head around the corner. "Boy, what are you doing?"

"Nothing, sir." I meant to put the rock back in the bowl, but Mr. Luckadoo didn't take his eyes off me. I slipped the stone into my pocket and went into the kitchen, figuring I'd put it back later. Brother Steve was hanging up the phone, being as careful as if the phone was made of glass.

He put his hand on my shoulder. "They need to do a few more tests on your gramma," he said, "but the good news is that you and I get to spend all day together."

He smiled but showed too much teeth. He was hiding something. He'd gotten some news about Mee Maw that he wasn't ready to share with me. I felt a tightness in my stomach and the hiccups coming on. "Could I please get a glass of . . . *hiccup* . . . water?" I asked.

"Yes, but then you best be going," Mr. Luckadoo said. "It's time for my lunch." He said "my" like a little kid does when he's got a toy he doesn't want someone else to play with.

"Thanks for having us over," Brother Steve said. "We need to head out anyways."

"Nice meeting you," I said, and went to shake hands, like I'd seen Grandpa do all the time, but Mr. Luckadoo grunted and waved us towards the door. He went back into the kitchen, and before I realized that I hadn't returned the stone to his collection, we were out the door.

Brother Steve went down the stairs, but I stopped. "Wait a minute," I called out. "I forgot something." I'd never stolen anything in my life, and as much as I was freaked out by Mr. Luckadoo, I had to go back. I was gonna drop the stone on his doorstep, knock and run away, but that didn't feel right. I was about to knock on the door when it flung open.

"You come to steal something else from me, boy?" Mr. Luckadoo asked.

"I'm sorry, sir." My whole body shook, and I started to hiccup. "I didn't mean to take it." *Hiccup.* "I was just . . . *hiccup* . . . looking at it." I pulled the purple rock out of my pocket and held it out to him in my palm. *Hiccup.* The stone fell out of my hand.

Mr. Luckadoo laughed. But it wasn't a friendly laugh. More like a mad scientist. "Just keep it," he said. "I don't want it no ways, now that you've had your grubby little hands on it." He slammed the door in my face.

"What was that about?" Brother Steve asked, but when I started to explain he just rolled his eyes. "He wasn't always like that. Just a few years ago, he was one of the nicest people you'd ever meet. Even a deacon at church. But after his wife died, he was just never the same."

I picked up the stone and put it in my pocket. I hoped that it would cheer up Grandpa.

Brother Steve and I visited more shut-ins until about 4 p.m. It wasn't as much fun as I thought it would be. Not a single one lived in a bubble. But I could see how much they each enjoyed our visit.

When we got home, Grandpa was sitting at the kitchen table. His face was all red, and his eyes were all puffy. Kleenexes were piled in front of him. He grabbed one of them and started wiping his eyes.

"Sit down, Benji," he said.

"Where's Mee Maw?" I asked. "Is she upstairs napping?" I asked the question, but I knew that she wasn't home. I could see in Grandpa's eyes everything that he was about to tell me.

Grandpa took a sip of his coffee. "Have a seat."

I backed up into Brother Steve and was about to run out the door, but he gently pushed me towards the chair beside Grandpa. I twisted out of his grip. I didn't want to sit down. On TV, people were always telling others to sit down right before they said something bad. I thought if I didn't sit down, then maybe it wouldn't be real. I pinched the scar on my arm, but this wasn't a bad dream. I was awake.

"What's wrong with Mee Maw?" I shouted. I was angry. Mad at Brother Steve for trying to make me sit down. Mad at Grandpa for not letting me be with him and Mee Maw all day. And maddest at God.

And the little voice agreed with me. *How can he do this to you again? You don't deserve this.*

"Where is Mee Maw?" I asked, pounding a fist on the table.

"Benji, it's okay to be upset," Grandpa said. He scooped up the wad of tissues and shoved them into his pocket. "I was mad that they didn't let her come home, but the doctors wanted her overnight."

"What's wrong with her?" I asked Grandpa, and then looked at Brother Steve. "Do you know what's wrong with her?" He didn't respond.

"Do you want me to go?" Brother Steve asked.

"No," Grandpa said. "Would you mind staying for a bit?"

"No problem," he said, and sat down.

Grandpa put his hands in mine and looked me in my eyes. "Benji, Mee Maw has . . ." His voice trailed off. He looked at Brother Steve, his eyes pleading for help.

I looked at Brother Steve.

"Your gramma has cancer," Brother Steve said.

"Cancer?" I repeated the word like I had misheard. Maybe this was some new form of cancer that was only as bad as a cold, but the way Grandpa squinched up his face I knew it was very bad. "Is she gone die?" I asked.

He leaned over and hugged me. "We gone do everything we can to keep that from happening."

I could feel hot tears on his cheeks, and I held him tight. I could feel his heart throbbing in his chest, and he cried like I hadn't seen since Momma died. My throat tightened, and I had trouble breathing. I felt like I was gonna choke, and started coughing. Grandpa patted me on the back, and my coughs turned to hiccups.

"I'm sorry, Benji," Grandpa kept repeating after he let me go from our hug. Like it was his fault. *Hiccup.* "The doctor said that they caught it early. They need to do surgery tomorrow. To get rid of the cancer."

Hiccup. His green eyes looked black and the whites were red.

Hiccup. I tried to swallow to get rid of the hiccups, but they kept coming. *Hiccup.*

"When . . . *hiccup* . . . can I go visit . . . *hiccup* . . . her?" I asked.

"We'll go tomorrow first thing. Let's get you some warm water," he said. "It'll stop those hiccups right up." He got up and ran the faucet.

"I need to get going," Brother Steve said.

"Thanks for everything," Grandpa said. "I appreciate your taking care of him today. We might need to impose on you again."

"No problem. I was happy to have Benji come with." He came over and messed up my hair. "Benji's better at ministering than most pastors I've worked with." He started to laugh but then stopped. "I'll call you tomorrow and check in."

Grandpa had me drink a glass of warm water. And then another glass standing on my head. We tried sugar on my tongue. Grandpa scared me. Nothing worked until he went over to the cupboard above the fridge and took down a brown bottle. The stuff that he would mix with lemon and honey every time I got a cold or cough. He poured a small amount in a glass. "Just drink it fast," he said.

I smelled it, and just a whiff about burned my nose.

"One gulp," he said. He took another juice glass out of the cabinet and poured it half full. "Now don't tell your Mee Maw about this." He picked up the glass and poured the whole thing down his throat in one motion.

I followed him and drank the whole thing. It felt like my tongue and throat had caught fire, but in a couple moments I didn't have the hiccups anymore. And in a little bit, I got really sleepy.

Grandpa helped me up the stairs to my bedroom. He hadn't dressed me in my PJs in years, but that night I didn't feel like

I could lift my arms. He took off my shirt and then I stepped out of my pants. When he folded them, the stone that I'd gotten from Mr. Luckadoo's fell out.

He picked it up. "What's this?"

"One of the shut-ins gave it to me." I felt a sharp pain in my heart. I hadn't meant to tell Grandpa a lie, but it was sorta true. I had tried to give the stone back, and Mr. Luckadoo said to just keep it.

Grandpa held it out to me so that I could look at it. "It's amethyst."

It was deep purple, and I remembered why it was familiar. "That's the state gem of South Carolina," I said.

"I got a good story for this one," Grandpa said.

I felt so tired that even though I wanted to hear the story, I couldn't keep my eyes open. He tucked me into bed and kissed me like he did when I was a little boy. But I didn't mind.

"Why don't we save the story for when we visit Lilly tomorrow?" he asked.

I nodded.

"I've never told you about my first days as a hobo."

August 13, 1983 (Saturday)
Grandpa

When Benji and I got to her hospital room, Lilly was on the side of the bed praying. Her fingers were clasped together, and I could see her lips moving. I didn't want to startle her so I cleared my throat. She turned around and opened her eyes, smiling only when she saw Benji come out from behind me.

He ran up and hugged her, and then we helped her back into the bed.

"Grandpa is gonna tell us a story about the time he was a hobo," Benji said, and handed the piece of amethyst he'd gotten from Mr. Luckadoo to me.

I took the gem, sat on the edge of the bed and held Lilly's hand. "After Maw kicked me out of the house, I had no idea where to turn. I prayed real hard to Jesus to show me the way, but with the Great Depression going on, the Lord had more important matters to tend to. I figured if I couldn't get the Big Boss Upstairs, I'd at least check with one of his workers, so I went to the church and found Pastor Jacobs. He suggested I try to make my way up north to the factories. He'd heard they might be hiring. The only way to get there was by train, and I didn't have nearly enough money for a ticket. Pastor Jacobs said he could give me two dollars, but I figured that wouldn't even get me to the Alabama / Georgia state line. But Pastor Jacobs had a plan. He said as a hobo, I could make my way up North or anywhere else I wanted by riding the rails. He said that he'd learned all about hobos because they often came by the church looking for work and a square. He then went so far as to drive me to the jungle, near Mobile, Alabama."

"There's a jungle in Alabama?" Benji asked.

"No," I replied and laughed. "A hobo camp is called a jungle. After spending the night sleeping under the stars, I got up with the sun. One of the hobos shared his breakfast of some tinned meat and poured me a cup of coffee. After breakfast, all the hobos laid out stuff they wanted to trade. This fellow named One Cup Clem saw that I had some shaving soap. He had razor blades and offered to exchange one for some soap. In the jungles, mirrors hung from trees so people could shave and clean up before heading to town for a job. I hadn't shaved in my whole life and didn't have any kind of beard but my sideburns looked like caterpillars.

"We boiled up some water, and Clem helped me attach the blade to the razor and showed me how to swish the blade around in the hot water bowl between strokes. I'll never forget the minty smell of the Colgate shave soap and the pull of the razor against my sideburns. Still the best shave of my life, and I felt like a man ready to start a new life.

"Clem was new at being a hobo too. A jungle buzzard had told him there ain't nothing better than riding possum belly on the top of a train while it's going through a tunnel. So along with a couple of others, we scrambled up to the top of one of the cars. The wind blew through our hair as we rode probably seventy miles an hour. Every now and then I could taste the smoke from the engine, like licking the bottom of an ashtray. I reckon trains in those days ran on the smokiest coal they could find.

"A tunnel was coming up in about a mile so we positioned on our bellies and held on. When we got in that tunnel, the smoke no longer went up. It just went straight back, coating me like paint. I almost suffocated from the coal dust, even though I breathed through my shirt.

"The air that had whipped around and blowed through my hair now pressed down on me like someone was standing on top of my whole body. The screeching of the wheels against the tracks pitched higher, and when the train sounded its whistle, I thought my eardrums was gone split. The air grew hotter and heavier, and then when I feared I was gone be crushed, we popped out the tunnel. I was born again.

"The wrens chirped and danced in flight overhead. The air tasted like snow and smelled like Christmas morning. For a few miles, the train tracks ran alongside a creek, and Clem and I sat beside each other on the top of the train and just soaked in the view.

"After getting off the train, we walked the few miles to the next jungle, and when we got there, every hobo in the place got a good laugh. I didn't know why at first. And then I checked myself in one of the mirrors hanging from a tree. I was black as midnight from the coal dust. I realized that I'd been tricked. That was my baptism day as a hobo. And the last time I rode possum belly through a tunnel."

When I finished the story, I could taste the coal. I even started to cough a little bit. A nurse in head-to-toe blue scrubs had been waiting in the doorway for a few minutes, listening to the story. "We need to get Mrs. Phelps to surgery."

I helped get Lilly from the bed to the gurney. "Take good care of her," I said.

"I'm going to be all right," Lilly promised. "I've got the good Lord watching out over me."

I didn't want Lilly out of my sight. Fifty years ago, I had lost the first great love of my life, and I wasn't about to lose another. I looked at Benji, as if the poor boy could do something.

He rushed over and grabbed Lilly's hand. "Let's say a prayer first."

We circled up, and even the nurse joined us. Benji prayed, "Jesus, if it be your will, please help Mee Maw get better. And I'm not asking this for selfish reasons. I'm coming to you because of Grandpa. I don't know what he'd do without her."

"Amen," I said, and looked up.

But Benji's eyes were still closed, and he had a serious look on his face. His brow was furrowed, and his eyebrows pushed together. "Lord. If you heal Mee Maw, I'll do anything."

He hesitated. Again, I said "Amen" and looked up.

But the boy's eyes were still shut tight. He gripped my hand so tight that my knuckles was turning purple as amethyst.

"Jesus, if you heal Mee Maw, I'll give my life to you. I'll be a pastor. But not like Preacher Dale. I'll be like Brother Steve. Somebody who helps people."

And this time, Lilly was the one who said "Amen."

6

December 10, 1983 (Saturday)
Grandpa

I sat at the kitchen table in a monkey suit drinking my second cup of Sanka. I could hear the click of the minute hand on the kitchen clock. It was 6:26 p.m. The Palmetto Junior Cotillion started in an hour, and we needed to get a move on. Benji and Lilly were still getting ready, and I knew better than to rush Lilly. That would just cause her to take more time.

I needed to be smart about it.

I went into our bathroom, and Lilly was standing at her sink, wearing just a slip. She was painting on her society makeup, a whole different face than the one she puts on for church. A fog of Aquanet filled the room. She'd lost her upper curves after the double mastectomy, and the bouts of radiation and chemo took her bottom ones, but the cancer was gone. Benji's prayer had been answered.

"Benji ain't even close to being ready," I said, not sure whether it was true or not.

"Well, don't just stand here keeping me from getting ready. Tell him to hurry on up."

"I hate to rush him. His nerves are already tore up."

"It's his first dance," she said. "And you've seen him. He's got cause to be worried." She sprayed another blast of Aquanet.

"He's had six weeks of ballroom dancing."

"If you'd seen him at the classes, you'd know why he's nervous." She laughed, coughing a little on the hairspray that still swirled around her. "Jon did his best, but Benji looks like he's solving a math problem when he's out there. You can see him counting the whole time. 1-2-3-4, then turn and 5-6-7-8."

She took her dress off the hanger and stepped into it. I zipped up the back.

"Why don't you go and check on him?" she asked. "Just see if you can help him. I'll come up in a minute." She went back to the mirror and started to pick at her hair. I grabbed Mighty Tim, my favorite hat for fancy occasions. It was a gray Homburg with a black Petersham ribbon.

Upstairs, Benji was standing in front of his mirror, fumbling with his thin tie.

"If you don't hurry, poor Kristy's gone be dancing by herself." I stood behind him and took over. My fingers fumbled to get the rabbit around the tree. "Why's this blame tie so skinny?"

"Mee Maw says it's the style," he said.

"I like a wide tie," I said. "Keeps my shirt clean."

"Do I have to go to this, Grandpa?" he asked.

I finished with his tie, and the front part hit just above his belt. "You gone have fun, Benji."

"Call me 'Ben,' Grandpa. 'Benji' is a name for a kid."

I stepped back and looked at him. The boy had grown three inches in the past few months. We'd had to buy him a new suit and new pair of shoes just after Thanksgiving, and I swanee the britches already seemed short on him. I was glad I'd picked Mighty Tim as my hat because it added a couple inches to my height.

"Ben," I said. "The girls ain't gone know what to do with you." I had tried to make it sound like a compliment, but I was a mite worried poor Kristy wouldn't survive half a dance. According to Lilly, she needed to wear shin guards and steel-toed boots.

I got Lilly and "Ben" together, and took a few photos of them in front of the Christmas tree. And then we got on our way.

At the dance, we watched as the daughters waltzed with their fathers. When it was time for Benji to cut in, I held my breath. Benji's dance instructor, Jon, came over and stood next to me and Lilly. He was as nervous as me.

"I'm just hoping that Ben remembers some of the things I taught him," he said. He grimaced as "Ben" moved forward instead of backward and stepped on Kristy's toes. "I should have spent more one-on-one time with him."

"I'm sure you done the best you could," I said.

"He's just at that awkward age where his body is bigger than his brain thinks it is."

Kristy tried to get back in sync with Benji, but he kept going the wrong way. She pushed him away and then went to find another dance partner. Benji sulked over to us.

"Mr. Jon, sorry to let you down," he said.

"Ben, you're going to be a great dancer one day," he said.

"Ben" looked at him like he was plumb crazy. "I don't think so."

"Don't give up. I've never seen anyone work harder than you do. Just try to count more with your body than with your head." Jon put his hands on Benji's shoulders and turned him around.

He pointed to a group of girls sitting at a table right off the dance floor. "You should get back out there. Those girls are waiting for a handsome guy like you to dance."

But Benji just stood there, and I could see his career as a wallflower beginning. "I'm just gonna go and sit down for a minute," he said, and turned away from us.

Jon grabbed him by the elbow. "Not so fast. We focused too much on ballroom dancing. I'm going to teach you a basic step you can use to dance to anything." He started bobbing his head to the beat of the music and then waited for Benji to follow. Once they were in sync, Jon took a step to the left, slid his right foot so that he was centered again and then repeated with a step to the right. Benji mirrored him.

"Now, snap or clap to the beat."

Benji started snapping his fingers and was almost in rhythm with the music.

"Now just throw in some shoulder action," Jon said.

I could see Benji going back to counting steps and then he lost the beat.

Jon stopped him. "Just start with moving your feet back and forth in rhythm. You can throw other stuff in later." He pointed again to the group of girls. "Take a deep breath. Tell yourself you're a stud and walk over there and ask one of them to dance."

Benji did as he was told. And even though he didn't dance much better, he had confidence, and that made all the difference.

Lilly and I even danced to a couple slow songs, and Benji didn't even take a break. He asked girl after girl to dance.

Before we left, Benji thanked Jon for the extra help. "I'm very proud," Jon said to him, and I could tell the compliment meant a lot to Benji.

Poor boy was so exhausted he went straight to bed when we got home. Lilly and I had a good laugh about "Ben" and his dancing. "I'm just glad he didn't break anyone's bones," I said.

The next morning Lilly made a cabbage casserole for our neighbor whose husband had just passed. Lilly and Claudette Stevenson hadn't been on speaking terms for years, but that didn't keep Lilly from doing what was proper. When Benji got up, Lilly made him take the casserole over. There were limits to being a good neighbor.

While she tidied up Benji's room, I made some coffee and settled in to enjoy some quiet and the funny papers. I'd just finished the latest *Peanuts* when I heard Lilly shriek. "Charlie! Get up here." I ran up the stairs expecting to find a dead body.

And walking into Benji's room, it kind of smelled that way. Okay, maybe it was more like armpit. Puberty was not being kind to the young man.

Lilly waved a magazine at me. "What is this?" she asked, like she had no idea what she was holding. It was opened, and she pointed to an ad for a workout machine showing a shirtless guy on a bench.

I took the magazine and closed it. "Looks like the latest issue of *Sports Illustrated* to me. It's natural for a boy to be interested in sports."

She had three more magazines, each creased and opened to pictures of muscular guys without shirts.

"And the rest of these?"

"The boy's a little pudgy. He probably just wants the magazines so he can get in shape." I hadn't realized Lilly was gone change his sheets. I usually went up and hid the magazines so she wouldn't find them.

"If they're just for exercise tips, then explain this." She pulled out a wad of Kleenex, some crunchy and used. "You don't think he's. . ." And she paused. Her lips pulled tight across her teeth and started quivering. Her eyes watered, and she was about to burst into tears.

I wasn't quite sure what to say. "The boy just hit puberty. He don't know which way is up."

Her brain was working in so many directions that it took her a while to realize why the tissues were so crunchy. The moment she did she threw them like the time we went fishing and I gave her a worm to put on her hook. She plopped down on the bare mattress, still fighting back a full-on crying spell.

I grabbed the trash can and scooped up the Kleenex. "When you're his age, you're curious about your body and it's natural to look at others."

She looked at me with her brow raised and her top lip pulled up. She wanted to believe me so I told her more things I thought she might want to hear.

"I used to look at other boys' bodies when I was kid. I remember our high school quarterback went skinny-dipping with us one time. He looked like a Greek statue who'd just walked off his column base. I'm sure Ben's just going through a phase."

"A phase?" she asked. I'd meant to calm her, but my words had the opposite effect. "What are you saying?"

I'd seen the way that Benji had looked at his dance instructor. Jon was in his early 20s, tall and muscular. He had a mustache like Tom Selleck from *Magnum, PI*. "I'm just saying that it's okay for him to be a little interested in the appearances of other guys right now."

Lilly yelped a little, like a dog that had been kicked.

"Are you saying he's that way?" She waved her hand sideways.

I shook my head no, but she wasn't convinced. "I expected we might have this trouble." She rolled up the magazine she had in her hands and started pacing. "Poor boy. I worried this would happen since he doesn't have a strong father figure in his life."

I was a mite perturbed at that, but I just let her rant until she'd blown off enough steam. "I don't think we have to worry," I said.

That made her angry, and she threw the magazine at my feet. "How can you not worry? If he's that way, he's going to end up. . . I just can't bear to think."

"I'll have a talk with him."

"You do that," she said, picked up the magazines and handed the stack to me.

"I think you should say a prayer," she said, and got down on her knees by the bed. Despite my rheumatoid, I knelt beside her.

"Dear Lord," I prayed. "We done our best to raise Benji, and he's a good boy. Please watch over him." I paused because I couldn't think of nothing else to say. I opened my eyes and Lilly cut me a look. She gripped my hand so tight I thought she was gone crush my fingers. My mind was blank, and I tried to conjure up a prayer. Before she broke bones, I prayed the first thing that popped into my head. "Give Benji the courage to change the things he can, the serenity to accept the things he can't, and the wisdom to know the difference. Amen."

"What was that prayer?" She jerked her hand away from mine. "Accept things he can't change?"

"I couldn't think of nothing. Besides, I've always liked that prayer."

She squinted. "Charlie, the boy needs more discipline in his life. Now that Brother Steve is heading to Chicago, we're going back to Preacher Dale's church. Benji needs some hellfire in his life right now. Otherwise, we might lose him forever and he'll never be a pastor."

We heard the front door slam, and Benji was calling for us. It was time for breakfast, and I bet he was hungry.

"Now don't you say nothing about this to Benji," I said. "I'll talk to him." She went downstairs to make breakfast, and I tried to think where to put the magazines. I didn't want him to realize we'd found them so I stuffed them back under his mattress.

When I came downstairs, she was adding cheese and butter to a bowl of grits. "You're going to have a conversation with him, right?" she asked.

"I promise." But I didn't have the talk. I didn't know what to say. I didn't want to embarrass him about his magazines. I thought I'd just let him live his life. And see what happened.

But years later, I would regret yet again my decision to avoid conflict.

7

July 4, 1991 (Thursday)
Ben (21 years old)

I looked out at the congregation, and even though it was 7 a.m. on July fourth, about three hundred were in attendance. I concluded my sermon. "Two hundred and twenty years ago, our forefathers declared independence from rule by an English king. Today, as Baptists, we have won our freedom from an earthly religious leader. Each of us has the ability to interpret the Bible, and this is a freedom that we should not take for granted."

The moment the "Amens" had died down, the choir director handed me a note. I felt the sharp edges of the folded piece of paper but waited until the organist began playing "God Bless America" before I looked at it.

I drove the twenty miles to Greenville Memorial Hospital in fifteen minutes. Mee Maw was asleep in her hospital bed, her mouth was open, and she was snoring louder than Grandpa ever did. The light was off in her room, and the blinds were closed. Grandpa hunched in the crimson vinyl chair. He had his face in his hands, and the brown felt fedora he called Lucky Pete had fallen to the floor amidst crumbled tissues.

When I walked over to pick up the hat, I startled him.

"Good lord, boy," he said. "You about scared me to death." He wiped a tear from his eye.

"How's she doing?" I whispered.

He shrugged. "Even after they told us a month ago the cancer had spread, I kept hoping for a miracle." He reached over to grab a tissue, but the box was empty.

I looked in the large bottom drawer of the table beside her bed, but the only thing in there was a stack of newspapers. *The Greenville News* had written a story about me for the front page of the Religion section. My academic advisor, Pastor Hardy, had brought Mee Maw two dozen copies of the paper, and she'd given them out to every doctor or nurse that saw her.

I bent over to kiss her forehead and was surprised her skin was so cool. I looked over at Grandpa.

He put his hat back on and mumbled, "There ain't nothing they can do for her at this point."

The blood pulsed in my temples, and my head was about to explode. A dam of tears was about to burst, and I needed a Kleenex. I searched in the bathroom, but there wasn't even toilet paper. I grabbed two cotton hand towels and gave one to Grandpa. I put my arm around him and hugged, but he tensed up, like the only way he could hold it together was to push down what he was feeling.

Grandpa had never been scared of anything. My nose started running, and I sniffled. A sharp, sour smell attacked my nose. For two days, Grandpa had never left Mee Maw's side. I wiped my face on the towel.

"Pastor?" Mee Maw asked, in a voice that quivered like she

was only able to make half-sounds.

I rushed to her bedside and held her hand. She opened her eyes. "You're calling me pastor already?" I asked.

"Ben," she said, and blinked a few times, like she was trying to get me in focus. "I thought you were Pastor Hardy."

"He was here earlier," Grandpa said. "Helped Lilly use her bedpan. Even emptied it."

Mee Maw stirred in the bed. "You . . . preaching?" Each word was a struggle.

"I came right after the sermon," I said.

"How'd it go?" Grandpa asked, and sat on the other side of the hospital bed.

"Even better than when I practiced it yesterday," I said.

Mee Maw had just enough strength to upturn the corners of her mouth. "I'm . . . proud." She reached up towards Grandpa's face. He leaned over and she wiped away a tear. "Charlie. Breakfast."

"I'll ring the nurse and see if I can get them to bring something," I said.

"No," she said. "Him." She pointed to Grandpa.

"When's the last time you had something to eat?" I asked.

He looked at me. I could tell he didn't want to leave her side for even a moment, but at the mention of breakfast, I had heard his stomach rumble.

"I'll be here," Mee Maw said. And I knew that Grandpa believed her. She could do anything. And if she wanted to hold out ten minutes, a few hours, or even a week, she'd be able to.

"Ben's here now." She patted my hand.

"Go ahead, Grandpa. You could use the fresh air," I said, and pinched my nose.

He smelled his armpits. "I reckon you right about that." He laughed. "I rode the rails from Atlanta to Boston one time and went two weeks without a shower and I don't think I smelled this bad."

He leaned over and kissed Mee Maw. He looked around like he was forgetting something, but then felt the top of his head.

"I won't be gone long," he said. And even though he didn't want to leave, I could tell that he needed a break. The stress was wearing him down.

After he had left, Mee Maw pointed to the blinds. "Open . . . please."

I cracked them a little, and a beam of light hit across her face. We sat there for a few moments in silence. She began to transform. The pain and worry that had lined her face and deepened her wrinkles seemed to lift. She had this glow about her.

"Sermon . . . go well?"

"It went really well. Not too many people know Baptist history. And the concept of the 'priesthood of the believer' is foreign."

"I failed . . . you," she said.

"What are you talking about?"

"Charlie . . . me . . . not good parents."

I grabbed her hand. "That's not true at all. You were the best parents anyone could have asked for."

She pulled away. "Magazines."

"What magazines?" I spit out the question before I realized what she meant. And once I did, I acted like I had no idea what she was talking about.

"Ben . . . Please."

"I just . . ." I started to concoct a lie. To give her a valid reason why I had all those workout magazines, a reason she might not believe but one that would be credible enough. Something for her to hold onto.

Grandpa would welcome it, but Mee Maw would never accept a lie instead of facing the truth.

"I pray every day for Jesus to heal me," I said.

"You're . . . good. . . . Not your choice." She grabbed my hand now and held it to her lips. "God . . . can cure." She let go of my hand and then touched where she'd been cured of breast cancer eight years ago.

I wasn't sure what to say so we just sat there. My deepest, darkest secret. Something that I hadn't told anyone. Ever. I thought they'd found out when I was thirteen, but no one had ever said anything.

I pulled away from her and stood up. I was about to run away and pretend this conversation had never happened.

But I had promised Grandpa I wouldn't leave her alone.

"Pastor Hardy . . . will help . . . you," she said.

I sat back down on the bed beside her, reached over and kissed her. And I could feel her spirit. All the goodness and warmth that she possessed washed over me.

She grabbed me. And I could tell that it was a struggle for her to hold me so tight. I could sense her pain, but she wasn't letting go.

"Promise me. . . Get help." And then I felt her grip loosen as she took a deep breath. "Be a pastor," she said, and then exhaled.

I held onto her as I felt her spirit leave her body. And I saw the look on her face. She was smiling. Joyous. A look I'd never seen before.

I pushed the call button. "Nurse!" I yelled.

And then Grandpa was at the door.

"What's the matter?" he asked and rushed in.

I leaned in and hugged Mee Maw, like maybe I could bring her back. But I felt the cold creeping in. Into her and then into me. I got chills, and the room was all white. And too bright.

Beeps and chirps from the machines made it sound like I was in an arcade. The noise became too much, and I wanted to scream, to drown it all out.

The nurse came in and checked Mee Maw's vitals and consulted the chart. Grandpa and I just stood on the sidelines watching. The nurse looked at us and shrugged. We all knew this was the end. There was nothing left for anyone to do.

Grandpa wrapped his arms around me, and I leaned back into his embrace. "Mee Maw is gone," I said, and then felt a shortness of breath like she'd taken all the oxygen with her on the way to Heaven.

The nurse said she'd be praying for us and then left.

My heart had been Hoovered out, and I was falling. Into a pit of blackness. Grandpa's sobbing shook me, but I closed my eyes and shut out all of the activity in the room. Mee Maw had been proud of me. I knew that I'd continue on while she watched me from up in Heaven.

I let go of Grandpa and went back over to Mee Maw's bedside. I sat on the edge and leaned in to whisper, "I'll be a pastor." I kissed her on the forehead. "I'll help people, Mee Maw. Even people like me."

8

July 18, 1991 (Thursday)
Ben

Academic asphyxiation was the best way to describe the design style of Pastor Hardy's new office. An oily finish covered the cherry paneling on every wall, and the low pile carpet smelled like the basement floor of the SJU library where they kept old books no one ever used. His old office was clustered with three others at the end of a short hallway that was sandwiched between the men's and women's restrooms in the Vandiver Humanities Building. This new office occupied the southwest corner of the administration building and had views of Little Sorrel Lake in the foreground and the Blue Ridge Mountains in the distance.

The trappings of the office seemed ill-suited to the man who'd been my mentor and friend since I'd started my freshman year, but he'd been promoted to Dean of the Faculty a few weeks ago. I guess this perk came with the job.

Another benefit was his full-time summer intern, Monica. She was a fellow religion major, and we competed for top grades in our classes. She was smarter and studied more, so I always came in second.

"How's it going, Monica?" I asked as I walked into the reception area.

She rushed at me with open arms. "I'm so sorry to hear about your grandmother." She gave me what Grandpa calls a "shadow hug," keeping an inch of space between us so that we weren't even touching. It was over before I had a chance to hug her back.

"Thanks," I said, and went towards the door to Pastor Hardy's internal office.

She stopped me. "He's still in his meeting with Phillip Matthews."

"Phillip Matthews? Why is that name familiar?"

"He was a religion major who graduated a few years ago. Dirty blond hair. Was on the swim team. Totally dreamy."

I chuckled. "Not the way I tend to remember guys." I pretended to be confused, but the physical description was enough for me to know who she was talking about. "Anything interesting about him other than his looks?"

She bit the nail of her pointer finger. "He was the student who gave the Founder's Day invocation his senior year."

"That's right," I said, and then nodded like I'd just realized who he was. "That was our freshman year."

She snapped her fingers. "Bingo!" She pointed to a huge stack of textbooks piled all over the love seat opposite her desk. "You mind helping me a little bit?"

"Are you opening up an annex of the campus bookstore?" I asked.

"You'd think, right? All related to my internship. I spent this summer working for the Christ-ify Curriculum Committee."

"The Christ-i-what Committee?"

"Christ-ify Curriculum Committee. They have to figure out how to make our classes more 'Christ-centric.' Not too hard when you're talking about New Testament class, but try doing that for Advanced Calculus."

The phone rang, and she answered. "Gotta run to the President's office. I can't wait to find out all about your summer as a preacher."

While she was gone, I sorted through a stack of magazines that coated a mahogany coffee table that had the same oily sheen as the walls. I skimmed the pile until finding a recent issue of *South Carolina Baptist Ministry*. On the cover in bold red letters: "TWO CHURCHES EXPELLED FROM CONVENTION." It was the first time in history the Southern Baptist Convention had expelled churches.

I'd always been a speed-reader, and blazed through the articles. One church had ordained a gay pastor. Another had allowed two guys to get "married" in their church, or at least have a commitment ceremony.

I'd gotten too engrossed in my reading to hear that Pastor Hardy had finished up his meeting and was standing in front of me. With his salt and pepper close-cropped beard and slight belly, I always thought he looked like a middle-aged Santa Claus.

"Interesting reading?" he asked.

He so startled me that I tossed the magazine too hard. I had aimed for the coffee table, but it hit his shins.

He crouched down and noted the cover before returning the magazine to the table.

Pastor Hardy tilted his chin to the side and frowned. I figured he was wondering why I had been reading that particular magazine. I was about to explain when Phillip came out of Pastor Hardy's office.

"Ben, this is Phillip Matthews. He's in his last year of Saluda Seminary. Phillip, Ben is our top religion student."

"Pastor Hardy has talked about you so much. It's nice to finally meet you," Phillip said. I had never been this close to him and from the few times I'd heard him speak, he always had such a large personality that I thought he was taller. He was a couple inches shorter than me and was probably no more than five foot seven. "I hear you're interested in Saluda Seminary."

"I'm interested in their ancient languages program, especially Greek," I said.

"It's number three in the country. After Harvard Divinity School and the Unitarian seminary in Chicago," Pastor Hardy said.

Phillip looked at his watch. "I'd best get going." He tried to leave, but Monica was back and had blocked his exit. She had an obvious crush on him. And I couldn't blame her.

Pastor Hardy looked in her direction and coughed. "Monica, I'm going to need that outline of courses this afternoon instead of tomorrow."

Monica seemed perturbed at having to end her conversation with Phillip, but she obeyed and went back to her desk.

"How you holding up, Ben?" Pastor Hardy asked. He grabbed me and embraced me so hard that I would have thought I couldn't breathe, but he knew exactly how to hug so I felt both safe and loved.

I put my arms around him and rested my head against his shoulder. I could feel wetness on his face. He was crying.

"You know how much I loved your grandmother," he said.

"It meant so much to her to have you visit as much as you did," I said. "And I know she would have appreciated all the wonderful things you said at her funeral."

"I'm not sure I ever met a finer Christian woman." He unpeeled from our hug and grabbed a tissue from Monica's desk.

He put his arm over my shoulder and then ushered me into his private office.

"Getting used to the new digs?" I asked.

"Not really," he said. "Half the time I walk in, I think it belongs to someone else, and I apologize to Monica for intruding."

I chuckled.

He pointed to an area with two club chairs overlooking the lake. "Let's sit there." He swung shut the ten-foot-high door to his office and sat in the chair across from me. I noticed that the latch on the door hadn't caught, and the door opened a crack.

"I'm glad you scheduled an appointment to meet with me," he said.

"Why?"

He looked at me for a moment, like he was about to say something, but then stopped. He pulled a pack of Juicy Fruit from his pocket. "Gum?" He handed me a stick.

"Thanks," I replied. I unwrapped the gum, popped it in my mouth and started chewing.

"Ben, go ahead. Talk to me."

Every time I got nervous, the scar on my right arm felt like a five-inch nail. That morning I had practiced saying "I have same-sex attractions" a dozen times in the mirror, but I wasn't sure I could tell him. I took a deep breath and was about to start, but the office door was swinging open inch by inch. I hoped Monica couldn't hear us. Her only flaw was that she was a gossip. People routinely shared their most intimate secrets with me and could trust that I'd never tell a soul. But if they had something they wanted the world to know, Monica was the only person they needed to tell.

I stood up and walked around, pretending to check out Pastor Hardy's office, but I was really trying to see if Monica was in earshot of our conversation. She was kneeling at the coffee table, straightening up the magazines. When she saw that I was watching her, she went back to her desk, farther away from Pastor Hardy's door.

I stopped behind his desk and stared at the wall, plastered with photos of famous people, including many SJU alum: the current governor of South Carolina; an unsuccessful Republican presidential candidate; and the *Saturday Night Live* actress who had dropped out during her first semester.

"Very impressive," I said, and pointed to a picture of him and Ronald Reagan.

"I hate that wall. The SJU Director of Alumni told me to hang up every photo of me with anyone famous." He got up and pointed to one blank spot. "I'm saving that space for you." He smiled and raised his bushy eyebrows. "In that photo I see me with my arm around Dr. Ben Stark, the pastor of one of the largest churches in the Southern Baptist Convention."

I took a moment to savor that thought and scanned the other photos, stopping on a picture of Pastor Hardy standing between a beautiful blonde-haired woman and a good-looking guy of about thirty. The guy looked familiar.

"Who's that?" I asked.

"That's my wife and son," he said. "Our thirtieth wedding anniversary was a few years ago."

I was about to ask more questions, but before I had a chance, Pastor Hardy put a hand on my shoulder and turned me around. "Ben, talk to me."

He looked into my eyes, and I was about to tell him my secret until I realized the door had gotten to the pivot point where the weight on one side was heavier than the other so it had swung all the way open. Monica would be able to hear anything I said, even from her desk.

"Could we shut the door?"

"Sorry." He closed the door and then pulled up the handle until he heard a click. "Better now?"

I sat down in the wingback chair opposite his desk this time, and he sat in his desk chair.

I was about to tell him that everything was okay, but then I thought about my promise to Mee Maw to get help.

"I think I might be attracted to guys."

I expected the ground to open up and swallow me. I held my breath waiting for a response, but he didn't say a word.

"But I don't want to be," I said.

He leaned back and rubbed the gray patch of beard covering his chin. "I know," he said.

"You know? That I don't want to be this way or that I have these feelings?"

"Your grandmother mentioned her concerns."

I wasn't sure how to handle that news. Mee Maw had talked to Pastor Hardy about me? Did that mean that Grandpa knew? I felt my throat tighten. My palms got super sweaty, and I rubbed the scar on my right arm as if I could wipe it away.

Pastor Hardy leaned in. "How long have you had these feelings, Ben?"

I hadn't prepared my detailed history of same-sex attractions. "Several years."

"Have you ever acted on these feelings?"

"No," I lied before I could even stop myself. I thought back over my college years, from my attraction to the diver in my physics class to the baseball player on my hall in the freshman dorm. I thought back to junior high when I'd started buying *Sports Illustrated* and workout magazines for masturbation material, and to eighth grade when I jerked off for the first time, with a friend at a sleepover.

"At least you haven't started down that path," he said, accepting my lie without question. "You said that you want these feelings to stop, right?"

"I pray to God every day for deliverance."

Pastor Hardy sighed in relief. "You're very brave to get help."

He turned around in his chair and studied the picture of his wife and son. His eyes glassed over.

"I don't tell many people this." He got up from behind the desk and sat in the chair next to mine. He scooted his chair over so that our knees were touching. I could smell the Juicy Fruit gum on his breath. His eyes were red, and he didn't bother to hold back the tears that streamed down his face. He whispered, "And I would ask that you keep this in confidence."

He sat back and tugged at his beard. "My son has suffered from same-sex addiction."

I felt such an overwhelming rush of emotion that I broke down into sobs. I couldn't believe that Pastor Hardy had helped someone else with the same problem. "I'm so thankful, Pastor Hardy. You don't know what a relief this is. To know that a cure is possible."

We sobbed together for a few minutes and went through half his box of tissue. He blew his nose, wiped his eyes and sighed. "I wish I could tell you that my son has been cured."

I stood up and backed towards the door. I'd been afraid to come and tell Pastor Hardy because I thought he'd reject me. But this was worse. If Pastor Hardy's own son couldn't fight this, what hope did I have?

"Are you saying I can't be cured?"

"My son told me too late," he said. "He'd already embraced the homosexual lifestyle." He stood up and went over to the large window and stared out to the distant mountains.

I went over beside him. "But a cure is possible, right?"

His tears had stopped, and he wiped his eyes. I hugged him, but this time his body stiffened. He didn't even raise his arms. After a moment, he pulled away.

The little voice in my head started its chatter. *He's afraid to even touch you now. You made a huge mistake telling him this. You could have just managed this on our own.*

Pastor Hardy put a firm hand on my shoulder. "I'm not going to lie to you. This is going to be a difficult process, but through the transformative power of Christ, a complete cure is possible."

I didn't care whether he was uncomfortable or not. I wrapped my arms around him and gave him a bear hug. This time, he reciprocated. Halfway.

"You're a much stronger Christian than my son," he said. "After all you've been through, you can handle this. And I've got something that will help you."

"What?" I asked. We stepped apart.

"I've been working on a program the past couple of years, but I haven't been able to put it into practice." He smiled and was as excited as a kid on the first day of summer holiday. "It's a seven-step program to freedom from homosexuality. The HomoNoMo program."

"Homo-what-o?" I asked.

"HomoNoMo. Homosexual No More."

That was exactly what I had come to him for. Mee Maw had been right. Pastor Hardy could help me.

"When do I start?"

"I need to do a little bit more work on the kit, but you can go ahead and commence Step 1."

I was eager to try anything that would cure me. "What's Step 1? I'm ready."

"You need to get closer to God," he said. "Read your Bible and pray more than you ever have. The closer you are to Him…" He pointed up to Heaven. "The further you are from him…" He pointed down towards Hell.

"Will do," I said, and planned on stopping by the Christian bookstore and picking up a couple new daily devotional books.

I had the biggest grin on my face I could remember. "So you're saying that by the end of the program I'll be cured?"

He nodded. "We'll make sure you're cured by March first. Don't you worry."

"March first?" I asked. "Why that date?"

"That's the final application deadline for seminary."

I did the quick math and counted the months on my fingers. "But that's only seven and a half months away."

"You'll need to work really hard, but that gives us a month for each HomoNoMo step," he said, and then he got a look of worry on his face, wrinkling his forehead and creating little lines around his eyes. "But I don't know what we'll do if you're not cured by then. There's not a single Bible-based seminary that will accept a homosexual."

9

August 9, 1991 (Friday)
Ben

During the past few weeks, I'd scheduled eight counseling sessions with Pastor Hardy, but he had canceled five—all at the last minute when I was already at his office.

And when he did show up, he was usually late. He hadn't completed the HomoNoMo program, and we hadn't even discussed my same-sex attractions since that first time I told him. We'd spent all our time focused on Step 1—Getting Closer to God. I had less than seven months until I needed to be cured, and I was spending most of our sessions talking to Monica.

I worried that he was having second thoughts on treating me. Had he already given up? Did he think that I was a lost cause and that he wouldn't be able to help me? Was a cure even possible?

I thought back to Sunday night services at church, and how we'd often have a guest speaker. We had people who used to be alcoholics and drug addicts. One woman had been a hooker and even confessed to having an abortion. Yet, each time, the church was supportive, and members would always stay after for the "meet and greet." I heard Mee Maw tell the prostitute that she was very brave and that her courage was inspirational. But I never heard anyone talk about being gay. We never had a man or a woman get up and speak before the church about same-sex attractions and how God had healed their brokenness. I wondered if this was something that I was going to have to keep secret, even if God cured me. Was homosexuality a super sin?

I wished that I could have discussed these issues with Monica. She was the smartest person I'd ever met, and her grasp of the Scripture and religious issues was unparalleled, but I wasn't about to discuss my same-sex addiction with the biggest gossip at SJU.

Not that I minded spending time with her. I'd always seen her as my rival in classes so it was nice to get to know her and learn about her family and her plans for the future. We talked about everything I had been going through after Mee Maw died, and what was happening with Grandpa.

Pastor Hardy seemed delighted that Monica and I were becoming better friends, and he arranged for us to lead a Bible study group together at a weekend retreat at Mountainview Baptist Conference Center, about an hour and a half drive away. The retreat was Friday night, all day Saturday and most of the day Sunday. He'd selected our theme: "Christian Relationships in a Secular World." Monica and I had broken down the topic into different segments, focused on relationships with family members, friends, and of course the most important—romantic relationships.

It was Friday morning of that weekend, and I worried because it would be the most time Grandpa had been alone since Mee Maw died. He'd sent me to the Piggly Wiggly to buy a selection of frozen meals and some Sanka. I was unloading my buggy full of Salisbury steak, meatloaf, and turkey dinners onto the conveyor belt when I noticed the woman behind me only had a bag of Funyuns and a two-liter of Coke. I was gonna tell her to just go ahead of me, but I got distracted by her getup. She was one of the few people in South Carolina I'd seen in full grunge attire. Her hair was frazzled platinum, like she'd done a home rinse and left the peroxide on too long. The knees of her jeans were ripped out, like she'd been dragged behind a tractor.

Plus, she was buying Funyuns. I always wondered who liked the taste of onion powder.

The cashier finished ringing up the person in front of me and grabbed the first stack of TV dinners. The woman behind me started tapping her foot, like she was in a hurry.

"Sorry," I said to her, "I was gonna let you check out first since you just have the two items, but I got distracted by the Funyuns."

"Pardon?" she asked. She hadn't heard a word I said.

"I was just apologizing. I should have let you go in front of me."

"Why?"

"You seem in a hurry."

"I am. To go across the street to the ABC store and buy some rum."

"Okay, then," I said. She looked at me, and I could see judgment on her face. Her nose upturned like she'd just smelled something bad, and I could hear her thinking, *I may be an alcoholic, but what kind of person eats only Swanson TV dinners?*

"I don't know why I told you that," she said. And then I realized she was judging herself, not me. "I don't know what I'm doing." She put her groceries on the conveyor belt. "I haven't had a drink in two months. I'm just so stressed." Her lips quivered. She looked past me, and I turned around to see if anyone was there, but she was just staring at nothing.

The little voice in my head started up. *You should talk to her. You want to be a pastor. Here's your chance. Isn't this more important than some retreat?* I tried to shut out the voice. I needed to get home, unload the groceries, water the plants, make sure Grandpa had clean underwear for the weekend, and finish packing my bags.

We stood in silence another minute, and I noticed her eyes had glassed over. She was about to burst into tears.

"Do you want to go somewhere and talk?" I asked. "I'm studying to be a pastor. I've been trained to be a pretty good listener."

She nodded but didn't say anything. I waited for her to check out, and then we went to the diner right beside the grocery store.

I checked the time. It was later than I'd thought. I'd spent too much time deciding among Stouffers, Banquet and Swanson frozen meals. Even if we wrapped this up in a half hour, I'd be late to the evening worship service.

It wasn't the best way to start a weekend where I was supposed to be working on HomoNoMo Step 1—Getting Closer to God, but I took my three grocery bags inside the diner. We sat at a booth and each ordered a coffee.

"I'm Karen," she said.

"I'm Ben."

We shook hands, and then she told me about her past with alcohol.

"I had my first beer when I was seven. My dad would watch football all day Saturday and Sunday. I'm one of five kids, and he never gave us any attention, so I think that I felt privileged or something to bring him a beer. I'd watch him pop open the top, hear that crack sound, and then he'd turn to me and smile, one of the few acts of affection I received from him."

"That's a nice memory," I said. "I can see why you'd associate alcohol with something positive."

She looked down and rubbed her upper lip over her lower. "One day, he took a sip and then told me to take a swallow. It tasted like Dr. Pepper left out in the sun all day. Warm and bitter. I went to hand it back to him, and he reached over. But instead of taking the beer, he slapped me."

"That's terrible," I said. My throat tightened, and I could almost see her as a little girl with the red handprint on her face. I reached across and patted her hand. "You were just seven years old?"

She nodded. "After he slapped me, he told me to pour the beer down the drain, but when I got to the kitchen sink, I decided to take another swallow."

"Why?" I asked.

"I thought it would make me feel better. When Dad came home from a bad day at work, beer was the first thing he wanted. After downing a couple, his mood seemed to change. Like the stress of the day was gone.

"So I drank a little of the beer. It tasted terrible, but I kept drinking it. Little by little until I felt light-headed. And for a bit, I didn't care that my father had slapped me. I drank about half the beer and then puked my guts out for the next two hours, but in those initial moments, when the alcohol first hit, life seemed okay. Despite everything."

I grabbed a handful of napkins from the metal holders and dabbed at my eyes, and when she finished I wasn't sure what to say. From my training in Christian counseling, I knew I should have offered her something from Scripture, but the only thing I could think of was "Honor thy father and mother" and that was not situation-appropriate.

I checked my watch. It was getting so late that I'd probably miss the worship service altogether.

She noticed. "I'm sorry. I don't mean to keep you."

I signaled for the waitress to bring us the check, and we sat there taking final sips of our lukewarm coffees.

You're gonna leave her now? So you can get to church? Getting closer to God means helping those who need him.

"I'm sorry," I said. "I'm here for you as long as you want." When the waitress came over with the check, I ordered a piece of pecan pie and asked for more coffee. "At the grocery story, you said you'd gone two weeks without a drink. Why start now?"

"My kid was sick the past week, and I haven't gotten any sleep. He's with his father for the weekend, and it's the first time I've had to relax. What's the harm in having a rum and Coke while I catch up on my *General Hospital*?"

"It's not very Southern Baptist of me to say this, but one drink won't kill you."

She shook her head, and tears formed in the corners of her eyes.

"You can't stop at the one drink, can you?"

"It's more likely I'd finish half the bottle," she said. "I don't know how I'm gonna get through this weekend."

I sat up real straight and remembered something from my childhood. "Don't worry about the rest of this weekend. Just don't drink tonight."

"How's that gonna help? I can't drink tomorrow because then I'll drink Sunday. I can't be drunk when my husband brings my son home or I'll lose custody."

"Let me tell you a story. When I was a kid, my dad had a job working for a beer distributor. He'd won an incentive trip of a weekend in Pigeon Forge, Tennessee. I'd only seen mountains from a distance, but as we climbed higher and higher into the Blue Ridge Mountains, I decided that I wanted to climb to the top."

"You wanted to climb a mountain?" she asked.

I nodded.

The waitress brought over the pie and two forks. I offered Karen the first bite.

"How old were you?" she asked.

"I was six, so you can imagine how once I had it in my head, I wasn't gonna let it go. Every time we turned a corner on those windy roads, I told Momma and Dad, 'I want to climb a mountain.' Momma kept telling me that I could when we got to Pigeon Forge, probably thinking I'd forget all about it. But the entire weekend, I bugged them. And I was a persistent kid. Drove them crazy. On Sunday, when we were leaving, going downhill, I started crying. I hadn't climbed a mountain. My dad was yelling at me to shut up, but Momma told him to pull over at this service station where they were putting in extra gas tanks. There was a huge pile of dirt about fifteen feet high. She told me that she'd been waiting until we got to this very special mountain, because it was named 'Mount Benji.' I stopped crying and dried my eyes. I got out of the car, and in the time it took Dad to fill up, I climbed to the top of that hill.

"Momma cheered and clapped. In my mind, I'd climbed a mountain.

"For a year after that, when I got scared or there was something I didn't think I could do, Momma would remind me that I had climbed a mountain. I could do anything I set my mind to."

Karen pulled the plate of pecan pie in front of her and took a big bite. "Good parable, pastor, but what does that have to do with me?"

"Every mountain in life is just a series of small hills. You don't have to get through the weekend without drinking. You just need to not drink tonight. And then you need to not drink tomorrow morning. And then tomorrow afternoon. And then tomorrow night. Sometimes, if we look at the mountain range, we can get overwhelmed, but if we focus on just a small task, like climbing the first hill, we can do it."

There was one bite of pie left, and she pushed it across the table.

"Can you get through tonight without drinking?" I asked.

"I can get through tonight."

I ate the last of the pie, and Karen smiled for the first time since I'd met her almost an hour ago.

When the waitress brought the bill, I asked her for a pen and piece of paper.

I told Karen, "My church has Alcoholics Anonymous meetings every week. It's Calvary Baptist, just down the street." I wrote down the address and times.

Karen insisted on picking up the check, but I refused to let her pay. I pulled out money and set it on the edge of the table. She was gonna get up, but I asked if we could pray together first. She prayed for the courage to get up the first hill, and I prayed that the accomplishment of getting through that one night would give her the confidence to get through the next day and then the next. I walked her to her car, and I watched her drive out of the parking lot. She turned in the opposite direction from the ABC store. She had climbed the first hill.

Thinking about hills and mountains, I realized that I needed to get to Mountainview. I checked my watch. I was gonna be very late.

When I got home, I was putting away the groceries when I heard a thump—thump—thump from the foyer. Thinking Grandpa had fallen down the stairs, I raced to the entry. Grandpa was dragging my suitcase out the front door.

"Ben, you need to get going or you gone be late for your Bible retreat."

"I know I'm running late, but I'm worried about leaving you," I said.

"You're the one I'm worried about," he said. He pointed to his wrist like he was wearing a watch and then waved his finger at me. "Now, don't you speed. The Lord's got a sense of humor, and he might think it's funny if you go to Heaven because you're in a wreck on your way to lead a Bible study group."

The Lord must have found laughs in other places that day because I made it to Mountainview Conference Center without incident. I'd missed registration and the evening worship service. I didn't know where I was sleeping that night, but at least I'd made it to my Bible study group with five minutes to spare.

The worship service must not have been over because no one was there. A large manila envelope with name badges for me and Monica was on a table in the room. In the packet, I found general housekeeping instructions about the weekend. I skimmed them and then went through my notes.

I was so focused on my preparations that I didn't hear anyone come in until a rough voice interrupted. "You're Ben Stark."

I looked up and saw someone that I thought I recognized, but only because he looked like a guy in one of my workout magazines. I stared at him with my mouth open.

After I hadn't said anything for probably a minute, he asked, "Ben?"

I blinked, but he was still there. "I'm Ben." I stood and held out my hand. How did he know me?

"I'm Derek Ridge." He shook my hand, gripping it a little lower than I expected so that I wasn't able to get a good hold. Instead of a firm grasp, he had just my fingers. I hated when that happened because it reinforced my fear that with every introduction I was giving away my deepest, darkest secret.

"I've seen you around SJU," he said. I wracked my brain trying to think how I knew him. The more I looked at his square jaw and hazel eyes, the more he looked familiar. And not because of the magazines. He said, "I heard you the time you spoke about abstinence at the Fellowship of Christian Athletes meeting last semester."

So that was where I knew the guy. He was an athlete.

Then it all clicked.

Derek Ridge was the quarterback of the SJU Lemonheads.

"Nice to finally meet you, Derek." I shifted my grip so that I had a firm hold on his hand. I pumped his arm twice really hard, like my dad had taught me when I was just six.

"Are you leading our group?" he asked.

"I'm here all weekend." I gestured for him to have a seat across from me, but he put his book bag on the chair beside mine. Grandpa was right. God did have a sense of humor, and he was having fun today, putting the hottest guy on campus in my Bible study group.

Derek reached into the front pocket of his book bag and pulled out a form. "Could you sign this for me?"

SJU had requirements for extracurricular religious studies, so I'd seen the form many times before. I initialed for the Friday session, and then handed it back to him.

"You don't want to go ahead and initial the rest of the dates? Save you the headache of having to sign each time."

"I'll do it each time," I said. "I don't mind."

He folded the paper in half and then returned it to his bag.

Within a few minutes, every seat was occupied, and the chapel bell chimed eight times. Our group consisted of four girls and four guys, myself included. I usually felt confident at this stage in leading a Bible group, but Derek's presence had shaken me. I couldn't even think how to begin. I looked at my notes and saw I'd written "Introduction" as the first bullet point. But I could not remember what we were going to do. Monica picked up the slack.

"I'm Monica, and I'm lucky to have my good friend Ben as my co-leader this weekend." She paused, giving me a chance to jump in, but I was still too unnerved, so she continued, "We're gonna go around and introduce ourselves, but I think all Bible study groups should begin with prayer. Ben, could you lead us?"

She grabbed the hands of the people sitting on each side of

her, like we always did when we prayed, but I had hoped to leave out the hand-holding part. But Derek grabbed my hand, and I took the one of the blonde girl sitting next to me.

I'd prayed in groups a hundred times, but I could think of nothing to say. Derek nudged me with his elbow and squeezed my hand. His hand was muscular and rough, so different from the girl's hand I was holding. He squeezed my hand again, and I squeezed back. Then I realized that I hadn't started praying. My heart bounced in my chest, and I took a shallow breath.

"Dear Jesus," I began. My palms got so sweaty. Fragments of prayers exploded like fireworks in my mind. "We come to you in a moment of silence." I shifted in my seat. "Thank you for the gifts that each of us brings to this group." I cleared my throat. "Bless us this weekend as we study your Word." I noticed that I was squeezing Derek's hand really hard so I let up. "Thank you Lord for bringing all of us here. . . . Please guide us and lead us. In your name's sake, amen."

"Amen," everyone said. The red-head sitting beside Monica smiled at me. Somehow my nervousness made her feel more comfortable in the group.

I picked up my Bible and put it on my left knee so that it separated me and Derek, like he was some demon whose path could be stopped with Scripture. "Let's go around and introduce ourselves. Say your name, where you're from, and what you hope to get out of this weekend." I pointed to a skinny guy with a bowl cut sitting to Monica's right. "Why don't you start?"

"I'm Allen," he said. "The past couple years, I hung out with the wrong crowd and started drinking. My parents told me that unless I got right with the Lord, they wouldn't pay for college anymore. I've been sober for two months."

"Thank you, Allen." I was a little surprised, but glad that he'd been so honest.

Monica patted his knee. "That was very brave," she said.

Ted went next. His girlfriend, Lisa, was sitting next to him. Ted talked about abstinence. "My friends think I'm crazy not to have sex. But I'm at seminary. Sex outside of marriage is prohibited."

"Anything that you'd like to share?" I asked Lisa, but she didn't look up. She shook her head and slouched back, resting her hands on her stomach. Derek was next.

"I'm Derek. I'm gonna be a sophomore this year at Stonewall Jackson University. Go Lemonheads!" He pumped his fist in the air, and Allen followed with the customary, "Suck it!"

Derek continued, "I'm starting quarterback this year, and I think we can make the Division I-AA playoffs. But Coach thinks something is standing in the way of my full potential. He made me come here this weekend. I don't wanna talk about the reason, but let's just call it a 'secret sin.'"

At the utterance of the phrase "secret sin," I felt like my whole body had been thrown into an icy river. Derek was struggling with the same thing I was. I wanted to get up and hug him, but I just sat there and stared at the other faces in the prayer circle. No one seemed to have any clue what he was talking about. Everyone looked to me because it was my turn to introduce myself. But I sat. Paralyzed.

"Ben seems to have lost his tongue," Monica said, prodding me, and I said my name and then something about being grateful to be there. Monica fed me a couple lines, and soon she was telling me every word to say. Every moment was a minute. I don't know how I knew, but I was confident. Derek had same-sex attractions.

We finished up the circle of introductions. I didn't listen to anything the blonde girl sitting next to me said. I heard the word "bulimia" but nothing else.

The red-headed girl was next. She seemed nervous to be there. She had barely looked up from the floor the entire time. "I'm Becca, and I'm not a Christian."

I thought I heard someone gasp, so I jumped in. "Becca, we're glad to have you here."

She looked up and then around the circle. Her gaze stopped on me. To try to comfort her, I nodded and took a deep, purposeful breath.

She mirrored my actions and then continued. "I feel like I need a higher power in my life right now. I've had a really rough year, and I'm hoping that I can find something here that can help."

"You've come to the right place," I said. "With God, everything is possible." I meant it to be sincere, but the words fell flat. After Derek's confession and how I'd felt holding his hand, I wasn't sure that I believed them at that moment. I wasn't sure that God could save me.

Monica finished up the introductions while I gathered my thoughts.

When she finished, I read my notes. "It's tough being a Christian in this day and age. There are so many things that we have to deal with that prior generations didn't. Drugs, alcohol, premarital sex. . . ." I continued reading my prepared material.

After a couple paragraphs, I looked up. No one was paying attention. Even Monica was staring at the ceiling. I cleared my throat and then tucked my notes into my Bible. "Y'all have been so open with me. I feel like there's something that I want to share. I'd like to tell you why I'm here today." Derek shifted in his chair so that, for a moment, our knees touched. I scooted my chair back.

"It was 1976. I was six years old. My dad and I were watching the Macy's Thanksgiving Day Parade while Momma cooked a huge dinner. Turkey crisped in the oven, and the sweet potato casserole and cornbread stuffing were already on the counter. That year, she'd said I could help her with the gravy.

"Momma poured in the flour-water mixture while I stirred, and she told me to keep going until it started bubbling. My grandpa and Mee Maw showed up, and they brought some pies. Momma got everything together, and then we were ready for dinner. We all made our plates, and then we sat down. After saying grace, we started eating, and it was our tradition to go around and say what we were thankful for.

"Grandpa started. He said that he was grateful for the gravy because it was the best he'd ever had. And he said the normal things about family and health. My dad was sitting beside him so he was next.

"I'll never forget the look on his face. I'd never noticed before, but he had four or five deep lines crossing his forehead. He wouldn't look at me or my mother. He just stared at his untouched plate of food and didn't say anything.

"Finally, he turned to my mother who was sitting right beside him, and said, 'I can't do this anymore. I can't pretend that this relationship is working for me.' He looked across at me, and said, 'Sorry.' I had no idea what was happening. He got up from the table and went to my parents' bedroom. The rest of us sat there in silence, completely stunned.

"Momma picked up her fork and took a bite of stuffing. When she was done chewing, she said, 'Now, it's my turn to say what I'm thankful for. Ben, I agree with Grandpa. This is the best gravy that I've ever had. And I'm thankful to the Lord for giving me you as a son. You are a special boy. And I'm thankful for my mother and father, who are the most wonderful, loving and supportive parents anyone could ask for. But most of all, I need to thank Jesus for giving me the strength that I know I'm going to need in the days ahead.'

"She was so calm and reassuring that it was like nothing had happened. We never saw my dad after that day, but because of her unwavering faith in God, Momma and I got through it.

"My mother believed that God has a special plan for each of us. And that although we might not understand it, and we may question it, and we may get angry when we don't agree with it, in the end we need to believe that through Him, all things are possible.

"I know what it's like to be abandoned, to lose the people most important in your life, but through it all, even as a kid, I knew that Jesus was there with me always." I looked around the room at each person. "And whether you're dealing with alcoholism, bulimia, other issues, or a 'secret sin,' know that Christ is with you."

I smiled at Derek, but he was petrified. His confident macho athlete demeanor crumbled, and he moved his chair so that there was as much distance as possible between us.

The church bells struck nine. "That's our time today," I said. "Let's conclude with prayer. Would anyone like to lead?"

Allen volunteered, and I realized that we had to hold hands again. I could tell that this time, Derek didn't want to. I tried to hold onto him, but he kept slipping his fingers out of my grip. I let go so that we were barely touching, but I could still feel the calluses on his knuckles.

Allen prayed. "Thank you Lord for our Bible study leaders, and for Ben's amazing testimony. Please help us to share your love with each other this weekend. In His name, we pray, amen."

The second that Allen said "Amen," Derek jerked his hand away, grabbed his Bible and started to head towards the door.

I got up to go after him. I wanted to talk to him, but a woman came into the room with a large envelope. "Is Ben Stark here?"

"That's me," I answered.

"I have something for you." She stood between me and the door.

"Could this wait until tomorrow?" I watched Derek exit.

She chuckled and handed me my registration packet. "Not unless you want to be homeless tonight. Your room key is in the envelope. We had a lot of last-minute cancelations and new registrants so we had to shuffle rooming assignments."

"Thanks." I grabbed the packet and tried to get around her, but she blocked me. If I didn't leave soon, there would be only a 50/50 chance I'd be able to find Derek. Mountainview had two men's dorms on opposite ends of the campus. I'd see him all weekend in our Bible study group, but after feeling alone my entire life, I didn't want to wait one more minute to talk to someone else struggling with same-sex attractions.

"It's so nice to finally meet 'The Ben Stark.'" She stepped back and looked me up and down. "The way Pastor Hardy talks about you, I thought you'd have wings."

"Nice to meet you," I said, and then pushed past her. I realized that I didn't even know her name, but I didn't care.

I bolted down the hall, darting between groups huddled outside their classes and squeezed through the throngs of people headed to their dorms. Outside, it was so dark, I didn't see Derek at first. But then a hundred yards ahead, he passed under a lamppost. I ran in his direction and grabbed the back of his arm, almost tackling him because of my forward momentum.

"Derek . . ." I was panting and could barely breathe.

"What do you want?" He pursed his lips.

I didn't know what to say. Sweat dripped into my eyes. We stood there and looked at each other, and I felt a connection. God had given me this special opportunity. Here was a chance I had never had before. I touched Derek's shoulder and stepped close to him so that no one else would hear. "I, too, have a secret sin."

Derek's face went white. He looked to make sure no one had heard. "I don't know what you're talking about."

"Can we find a place to talk?" I asked. I was still holding his arm.

Derek pulled away and flipped his long black hair from his face. I saw the fear in the whites of his eyes. He looked at his watch like he was late for an appointment. "I need to get to my room before curfew." He took off. I thought about going after him, but what was I gonna do? Really tackle him this time?

I was shaking, and I held onto the lamppost for support. I needed to talk to him more than anything. I wanted to know when he first started having these feelings and how he had coped with them, but I let him go. I knew I'd spend most of my night lying in bed, racking my brain, and trying to come up with excuses for why he and I needed to be alone together. But that night I had no option but to head to my room.

I headed the opposite direction from Derek, but then remembered I had no idea where my room was. The lamp hummed above, and I could see the mosquitos buzzing. One whizzed past my ears, and then I felt the biting sting on my neck. I smacked at it and dropped the yellow packet containing my key. I bent down and picked up the envelope. The room key slid out along with a piece of paper that contained not only my room number but also the name of my roommate for the weekend. Even in the dim light, I could make out the large black handwritten letters.

I stood up and felt my heart thump in my chest. God did have a sense of humor, and he must be really cracking up. I shut my eyes and then opened them in case I wasn't seeing right. But there it was. The name of my roommate for the weekend.

DEREK RIDGE.

10

August 9, 1991 (Friday)
Ben

It was one thing to have a conversation with Derek about our same-sex attractions. It was quite another to share a room with him all weekend.

As I got my suitcase out of my car, I thought for a moment about sleeping in the passenger seat. In the room with Derek, I would lie awake all night thinking about the stud in the bed next to me. But then I realized that in my car, I'd either suffocate or be one big mosquito bite in the morning. I had no real choice.

I stood in front of Room 117 with the key in my hand, not sure whether to just go on in and act surprised that he was there or to knock.

Don't knock. Just barge right in. You've got a key. It's your room. Besides, maybe Derek will be undressing or even nekkid. Don't you wanna see that?

I pushed the thoughts out of my head and decided to knock, but I made sure that I knocked the way a straight guy would, like I was hitting a punching bag.

KNOCK-KNOCK-KNOCK.

I paused for a few moments and was about to knock again when Derek yanked open the door. He was in boxer shorts, the baggy kind that I always imagined football players would wear to bed. It took every ounce of control I had to stay focused on his eyes and not look down.

"What are you doing here?" he asked.

"Looks like we're roommates for the weekend." I showed him the piece of paper that had his name on it.

"Did you just follow me and then write my name on that paper?" he asked.

I wished that his name were typed and not handwritten, so I felt the need to explain. "I didn't have anything to do with room assignments," I said, and showed him the room key. He stepped back into the room so that he was no longer blocking the door. "I got here late so the woman said they had to find a room for me."

"A teammate of mine was supposed to be here, but he bailed," Derek said.

I carried in my suitcase, set it on the desk on my side of the room and started to unpack. I took off my tie and shoes but left on my pants and long-sleeve dress shirt.

He took out a Bible that I could tell was brand new. It had a black hardback cover, and the spine wasn't bent at any spot. But he focused on it like this was something he did every night.

I hung up the dress shirts I'd brought for Saturday and Sunday and unpacked socks and T-shirts. I wanted to talk to Derek about my feelings. I was exhausted from carrying this burden alone. Maybe Derek could help me, and I could help him. I stopped unpacking and sat on the edge of my bed, looking at him.

He closed his Bible and put it on the desk. He sighed, and his face collapsed into his hands. I got up and went and sat beside him on his bed.

Derek turned his head so that he looked into my eyes. The voice whispered in my ear. *Touch him. Kiss him. Know him.*

I could smell mint on his breath. His head moved towards mine, and then I had a flashback to sitting on the edge of the hospital bed when Mee Maw died. I had made a promise to her, a promise I intended to keep. I was at Mountainview to help people, to learn how to become a better pastor and to be a witness to others.

I jumped off the bed and started repacking my suitcase. I decided it would be better to sleep in my car.

"Ben." Derek stood up, grabbed my elbow and turned me around. Standing in front of me, this close, he seemed even bigger than I had realized. He was at least six foot three and probably weighed fifty pounds more than I did. The air conditioning kicked off, and I could see a bead of sweat forming at his right temple. We stood face to face, each waiting for the other to act.

Kiss him! You can't imagine the difference between kissing him and the few girls you've kissed. That stubble will feel so good rubbing against you.

I was so tempted. I took a deep breath and exhaled. Derek stepped back.

"Sorry, man," he said. "Just my hormones are so out of control these days. You can't imagine how difficult it is for me." He adjusted himself in his boxers, and I couldn't help but look down. He was getting a hard-on. "Girls basically throw themselves at me, and I'm a guy with normal urges."

I repeated the word "normal."

"I think I gave you the wrong idea," he said, "with this talk about a 'secret sin.' It's just that I don't want anyone to find out about this. It's done all the time, but it's still frowned upon by some."

I sat on his bed, and he sat on mine. He rubbed at the stubble on his chin and flared his nostrils.

"I'm not sure if I should even tell you this," he said.

"Go ahead. I'll hold everything in confidence," I said, and nodded.

He cleared his throat. "I've been taking steroids." He smiled. "So now you know my 'secret sin.'"

I could see sweat forming at his temples, and he rubbed his palms on his boxer shorts. I knew he wasn't telling me everything. If I had any hope of sleeping that night, I needed to know the truth. I was at the brink of finding someone I could talk to, someone I could share my frustrations with, someone who was dealing with the same thing I was. I had to get him to open up.

In my training as a Christian counselor, we were taught that some people need to be pulled and some people need to be pushed. You can pull someone if you share something about yourself. Some people will reciprocate your openness. With others a more confrontational approach works, and you need to coax them a little to get them to confide in you. With Derek, I knew that I wanted to tell him about my struggles, but I realized that he needed to be pushed first.

"How is doing steroids a sin? I can see it's not the best thing for your body in the long run, but I don't see why your coach would think you needed to go on a Christian retreat because of that. What's the real reason you're here?"

He started sweating even more, and I could see him looking around the room, at everything except me. His gaze stopped on his book bag. He started nodding and then looked right at me for the first time since that moment in Bible study when I referenced his "secret sin."

"OK. Here's the full story. A couple months ago, I did my first cycle of steroids, and they made me really horny, even more so than usual. I was supposed to go out with this chick I was dating, but the coach made me stay late. We'd had a scrimmage against another school, and we'd been creamed. The score was 42-0. The center kept snapping the ball to me too low so I kept fumbling or throwing bad passes. Coach was furious. He made the two of us practice for an hour after that game. It was super-hot that day so we had taken off our pads and our shirts." Derek paused for a moment, almost like he was thinking back to that day. "After Coach was satisfied we'd improved, he told us to hit the showers."

Picture Derek naked in the shower. Think about him soaping up those muscles.

I wanted to scream for him to stop his story, but he kept going.

"I wasn't paying attention to the guy in the shower, but then I saw movement out of the corner of my eye. He had this raging hard-on, but his dick was really little. I made fun of him. He said that mine wasn't any better. I'm more of a grower so I wasn't gonna let him insult my manhood. I made him turn around so he wasn't watching me beat off a little. He had this nice little butt, and it didn't take me long to get hard."

He paused and then realized what he'd just said about another guy's butt.

"I got a boner really fast because of the 'roids. And then I told him he could look. Before I realized it, he was on his knees in front of me. My testosterone was raging so much that I was blinded. I didn't even see who was in front of me."

Think about what that looked like. Derek with his thing in a guy's mouth.

I felt so flushed I thought that I was going to pass out. I tried to push the images of Derek from my mind.

"A mouth is a mouth, isn't it?" Derek said, and I realized that I was still nodding, like Pastor Hardy had trained us when listening to someone. I should have interjected, to make clear to him that I thought it was wrong to let a guy suck your thing, but I wanted to hear the rest of his story. And then I wanted to share with him what I was struggling with.

When he saw that I was nodding at his "mouth" comment, he paused. He was no longer fearful. He no longer felt the discomfort he'd had in our Bible study room. His swagger was back.

"I let him suck me off. And it felt good. It took care of the urges. I realized it was better than messing around with chicks because I didn't have to worry about getting a girl pregnant. After practice sometimes, I'd let him do it again. One day Coach walked in on us while the guy was blowing me in the locker room. Coach said he wouldn't tolerate sexual perversions on his team and that we need to get right with God. This conference is part of our punishment. The guy was supposed to be here, but instead he quit the team."

I moved off his bed. "Thanks for sharing that with me." I extended my hand. "It's nice to finally meet another person struggling with same-sex attractions."

"I'm not struggling with anything." He pushed my hand away. "I'm not like you!"

He stood up and clenched his right fist.

I closed my eyes.

I waited for the punch.

My heart pumped so fast I could hear blood rushing inside my head.

And then I felt the impact.

But it wasn't his fist. He was kissing me. His lips were firm. The stubble of his five o'clock shadow scratched my upper lip. He reached his hand behind my head and pulled me in, kissing me hard.

I could taste his Colgate toothpaste. I hadn't brushed my teeth since the morning. Not even after dinner. I pulled back, but he held me with my arms pinned against my side. I felt his body against mine. The heat. A strange sharp funk, almost sulfur-like. Sulfur. Brimstone. Hell. I wanted to stop, but he was getting hard, and I could feel it against me. All the fear and worry and anticipation of this moment melted, and I relaxed. And then he stopped kissing me.

And pushed me away.

Hard.

So that I almost fell back onto my bed.

"Be right back," he said. "Gotta take a leak." He slipped on cheap flip-flops and left the room.

The temperature in the room seemed to be rising a degree a minute, so I stripped down to my underwear. I looked in the mirror on the back of the door. My stomach spilled over the sides of the tighty whities. A patch of hair circled my belly button, making me look even fatter.

I was about to put my T-shirt back on when he came back in.

He looked at me and grinned. He raised his eyebrows at me a couple times. "This is better than I expected." He pulled his book bag from under the desk and started rummaging through it.

I could feel my head swirling with ideas. *He wants you. He's looking for condoms. You're gonna have sex.* I tried to picture Mee Maw, but I couldn't stop looking at Derek's muscly back, his lats flexing. I pushed the image of my grandmother out of my head because I was starting to get a boner.

What was he looking for? Did he have condoms in there? If you gave a guy a blow job without using a condom could you get AIDS?

You don't need to worry about that. Look at Derek. Does he look like he has AIDS?

Derek found what he was looking for and stood up. He turned around and presented it to me.

It was the form that I'd signed earlier when I first met him at the Bible study. The attendance form.

"So here's what's gonna happen," he said. "You'll sign off that I was here this weekend, and I'll head home tomorrow and enjoy my Saturday and Sunday."

I felt like Adam in the Garden of Eden. The shame of standing there almost naked smothered me, and I put on my T-shirt and a pair of gym shorts. Derek positioned the form on the desk along with a pen. "I think you need to initial here for Saturday and here for Sunday and then sign." He pointed to spots on the paper.

"I can't do that. That's a violation of the honor code." It was an automatic response. My brain didn't process what I was saying.

He laughed.

"Good thing you're concerned about your honor. Because the alternative to signing this is that I'll tell the whole school how I roomed this weekend with Mr. Preacher-about-Campus and how when I went to sleep, he tried to get into bed with me."

He turned on the desk light, shining a spotlight on the attendance sheet. "I'll give you the night to think about it." He turned off the overhead lights and then got into his bed. "But if you don't sign, I'm not only gonna tell people you got in bed with me, but also that when you tried to kiss me, you had the worst breath ever. You really ought to brush those teeth."

He turned so that he was facing the wall. I just stood there staring at the paper while his breathing slowed.

I turned off the desk light and grabbed my toiletries and headed to the bathroom. In my four years at Stonewall Jackson University, I'd never done anything that would be a violation of the honor code. But did I have any choice?

August 11, 1991 (Sunday)
Ben

The moment I'd gotten back from the bathroom, I had signed the form, and when I'd woken up on Saturday morning, Derek had left.

He hadn't returned.

Not that I was surprised. In many ways, I was glad. By the conclusion of that weekend, my Bible study group had gotten closer than any other group I'd ever led or even been involved with, even those that lasted an entire semester. I felt a joy in my heart because we had shared things with each other that we'd probably never told other people.

Monica talked about the pressure she had dating in college while abstaining from sex.

Ted and Lisa shared that she was pregnant and that they had discussed her having an abortion.

I was fortunate to have had a childhood of traumatic events to discuss so that I didn't have to mention my same-sex attractions.

But I also felt some sadness. I had not gotten the courage to talk about my same-sex attractions, and Becca had barely said two words. I could see the pain in her eyes, and I knew that although she carried a burden as bad or worse than anyone else's, she had stayed silent.

After group prayer requests, and everyone said goodbye, Becca asked if we could chat for a bit. I pulled two chairs over to the side of the room away from the door. Becca perched on the edge of her seat. We sat in silence for a few minutes. She shifted her weight in her chair and then got up to see if anyone was outside.

"I don't want Monica to know about this," she said.

"Anything you share with me is in strict confidence," I said.

She took a deep breath and began.

"Last year, I started dating this guy. He was so good-looking. From a good Southern family. He used to bring me flowers. Like a single rose or something. I realized that he tore it off one of the bushes at my apartment complex, but it was the thought.

"And he was the perfect gentleman. At first." She paused and rifled through her purse until she found a package of tissues. I reached over, and she handed me one.

"In the beginning, our physical relationship was limited to kissing. But after a couple dates, I let him feel my boobs. One time, he tried to slip a hand into my pants, and I pulled away.

He went down there again, and I told him to quit. He didn't, so I slapped him. He stopped. And apologized. A lot. He even sent me flowers the next day. Ones that were delivered by a florist.

"After that, everything was okay because I made sure we weren't alone again. We went out with friends or on double dates, and after a few weekends, I got comfortable with him again, so I invited him over. Monica was out of town, and he said he would cook dinner for me. I imagined wine, candles, and steak. But he just brought over Dominos pepperoni pizza and a six-pack of Coors." She looked at me and nodded like she was convincing herself of something. "It was still a sweet gesture. We watched a movie. I can't remember what the movie was. But everything else I remember like it just happened."

She stopped and dabbed her eyes with a tissue. I put my hand on her shoulder.

She leaned in. "Why can't I remember the movie?"

"It's okay," I said, and she let me hug her. I wasn't sure that I wanted to hear what happened after the movie. I wanted to counsel her, but already I was at a loss. Pastor Hardy had always told me that the hardest part of counseling someone was adopting the right amount of detachment, and I just wanted to crawl up into a ball and cry. It was so terrible what she'd been through. What could I say to help her in any way? I realized that I was holding onto Becca as if I could stop her, but she was ready to go on, whether I wanted to hear it or not.

"He guzzled down the entire six-pack while we watched the movie. After the movie, he said that he had a present for me. It was wrapped really nice. I imagined some clerk at the store making sure all of the paper was cut perfectly and the corners were folded just so. Once I'd unwrapped the box, he took it from me and opened it up. Inside was red tissue, and I went to unfold the tissue, but he snapped the box shut. I jumped because I was startled, but we chuckled.

"Inside the box was a pair of red and black lace panties and a matching bra. They were very risqué, and I felt uncomfortable because no boyfriend had ever bought lingerie for me. It was inappropriate, and I told him that. It made him a little angry. He said I was ungrateful. I said I was sorry, and he said I could make it up to him if I modeled it for him. I went to the bathroom and put them on. I stared at myself in the mirror for a while. I liked how I looked in them. I felt very sexy. I came out and pretended like I was on a runway. I strutted towards him and then turned to walk away, but he grabbed me. Told me I was his little whore."

Her voice quivered, and I wasn't sure that she would finish her story, but she wiped her eyes and then continued.

"I thought he was joking. He always did juvenile stuff, like prank-calling people, so I laughed. But he jerked me around so that I was facing him. 'Don't laugh at me,' he said. Then he kissed me rough. His stubble rubbed my chin raw, and he forced his thick tongue down my throat. I tried to push him away, but he just held me. 'I know you sleep around, so you don't need to pretend,' he said."

Becca paused for a moment and looked up at me. She was at a point in the story where she didn't have to continue. I knew how it ended. I reached over to touch her hand, but she pulled it away. She grabbed her hair with both hands and pulled at it. She paused, sucked in a deep breath, and in a slow whisper, she exhaled the rest of her story.

"He forced himself on me. I tried to struggle, but he's a big guy. Taller than six feet. Really muscular. At some point, I stopped fighting him, and then he said something. Something that I can't stop thinking about. He said, 'That's it. Relax. Just enjoy it.' Despite my initial protests and saying no, from that point on, he thought that I wanted it."

She stopped, and I knew that she had said all that she wanted to. It was my turn to react. To comfort her. Tangled jumbles of Scripture filled my head, but in that moment, she didn't need me to quote Bible verses. I put my arms around her and hugged her. I needed to say something to help her, but I couldn't think of anything. She reminded me of my seven-year-old self, and I understood why adults had been so uneasy around me during that time.

I had no idea what to say, and the only thing that came to me was the same false promise that I'd heard too often in my childhood.

"You gone be okay," I told her. "You gone be okay."

11

August 14, 1991 (Wednesday)
Grandpa

Last weekend had been rough for me. I hated being alone more than Tim Taggert hated sobriety. Ben had always been busy with schoolwork and preacher stuff, and I'd never thought much about it. But for fifty-seven years, I'd had Lilly to keep me company.

And even though we had found out her cancer had returned in March, right before Easter Sunday, I had never for one second believed that she was gone die. I had watched her get sicker and sicker during her three months of chemo. I knew it wasn't working, but I just kept living like she was gone get better.

If I lost faith, she'd die for sure.

So I had forced myself to keep believing that God would heal her, and when he didn't do it, I got angry. There ain't much you can do to God when you're angry, so I took it out on everyone else. I got into an argument with the funeral director about the color of the lining inside her casket. I bickered with Ben about what songs would be sung at the funeral. I yelled at Preacher Dale because I didn't want him to preach a full sermon at the gravesite.

"A funeral is for the living, not the dead!" I told them all when I wanted to do things my way instead of following Lilly's instructions. But Ben convinced me otherwise.

The first couple weeks after her funeral, I didn't get out of bed. I told Ben that I had a summer cold, and either he believed it or just didn't want to deal with me. Neighbors and our church family brought over food, and Ben and I must have gained ten pounds. But after a few weeks, the casseroles and fried chicken platters had stopped coming.

I had learned to cook as a hobo during the Depression, so for a few weeks, Ben and I ate a lot of beans and rice. With Ben praying and reading his Bible all the time, it was like I was living in a monastery.

At some point, we discovered TV dinners, but if I had Salisbury steak, peas and carrots and mashed potatoes one more time, I was gone start praying for the good Lord to reunite me with Lilly.

And so I did something that I'm not proud of. Something that probably caused poor Lilly to roll over in her grave. I called the Widow Stevenson and invited her to come over. My heart fluttered just talking to a woman on the phone. And when she said that not only was she gone come over, but she was gone bring me a coconut cake, I got so anxious I about had a heart attack.

The day of our "date," I spent near about an hour getting ready. I shaved for the first time in a few weeks and asked Ben to help me with a certain situation.

I sat on the chair in front of Lilly's makeup mirror while

Ben wiped down some tweezers. He held back my head and looked up my nostrils.

"How long I had these nose hairs?" I asked.

"Not long," Ben said with sarcasm in his voice. "I started noticing them sometime during Reagan's second term."

He grabbed ahold of a hair and yanked it out. I about cried it hurt so bad, and I worried whether we was just putting lipstick on a pig. But after Ben got done, I looked in the mirror. I was a catch. I had a full head of hair, could remember things half the time and was pretty sure I could still dance if ever given the opportunity.

I made Ben answer the door when the Widow Stevenson came over. I was sitting at the kitchen table reading the funny papers, acting like I hadn't even remembered she was coming over. The widow handed Ben the cake, and he sliced two pieces and made some Sanka. After he served us, he grabbed his Bible and a stack of devotional books.

"Don't you want a piece of cake?" Widow Stevenson asked him.

"Looks good," he said. "But I've got a lot of work to do. Maybe later." He went upstairs.

"He's a very studious boy," she said.

"He wants to be a preacher so I reckon it takes a lot of work."

"I read that article in the paper about him," she said. "He starts his senior year of college next month?"

"Yep. And then seminary for four years. After that, I reckon it'll take him a decade before he'll finally get to preach in front of a big church."

"That's a lot of schooling and work."

"He's dedicated." I finished up the piece of cake. "This sure is good cake." I got up to cut another piece.

Although it seemed like a betrayal to my wife, I admitted to the widow that she made the best coconut cake I'd ever tasted.

She started questioning me about what I was gone do now that Lilly had passed. And I didn't have real good answers. Lilly had been my best friend and constant companion for fifty-seven years. I didn't have a plan or any clue what to do. The past month, my decisions had been limited to deciding whether to get out of bed or just sleep all day.

Between the earlier torture by Ben with the tweezers and the widow's interrogation, I felt like a prisoner of war. While she started suggesting all sorts of activities we could do together, I yelled upstairs for Ben to come down to say goodbye to the Widow Stevenson. I thanked her for coming over. She suggested we do it again, and I said that I'd call her.

I cut me a little piece of the cake and hacked off a chunk for Ben. I knew he wasn't gone like our conversation, and Ben always responded to bad news better over dessert. I let him get a good amount of sugar in him before I said, "Ben, I'm ready to move on in my life."

"Move on?" he asked. "What does that mean? You wanna date the Widow Stevenson?"

"Lord no! Lilly would leave Heaven to come back and haunt me if I ever dated Claudette Stevenson. But I need to be around people my own age. You know how many times I've come home the past few weeks and called out to Lilly, forgetting that she's gone?"

He put his hand on mine. "What are you saying?" he asked.

"I want to move into a senior home."

He sat back in his chair. "But I want to be here to take care of you. I was already planning on living here next semester."

"I appreciate all the attention, but Lord help, you getting on my nerves a mite." Ben looked offended so I leaned in and explained why. "I can't take a nap in front of the TV without you checking to make sure I'm still breathing."

He laughed. "Sometimes you are so still while you're sleeping that I worry." He stopped smiling and grabbed my hand with both of his. "I just don't want to lose you."

"Well, I'm worried you gone scare me to death coming at me with a hand mirror all the time."

Ben let go of my hands and held his arms open wide. "What about our house?"

"The wiring is so old in this place that I'm surprised it ain't burned down already. And with the economy stalling, we gone do better selling now than waiting."

Deep down I knowed that Ben had already come to the same decision, but that he would never have brought it up. He ate a huge bite of cake and then smiled. "Then I guess it's settled. Let's find you the best senior living spot in the Upstate."

August 17, 1991 (Saturday)
Grandpa

Three days later, we was in the car with three stops on our itinerary.

First up was Hickory Pines. It was located in the wrong part of town. Not because of the people who lived there, but because it would be an extra twenty-minute drive for Ben to visit. We slowed down as we went over the rail tracks, and they made a thump-thump sound. I closed my eyes and imagined I could see a train in the distance. I heard the high pitch of its whistle as it barreled towards me and then the lower tone as it passed. I felt the swooshing rush of the train, and by instinct I grabbed the brim of Classic Stan, my gray bowler with the red feather, to keep it from blowing off my head.

Ben nudged my arm. "Wake up, Grandpa. We're here at Hickory Pines."

He wanted to drop me near the door, but I preferred to walk as much as I could.

"You sure?" Ben asked. "It's super hot today."

"I'm walking," I said, and opened up the car door before he'd even pulled all the way into the space. But I should have listened. In the two hundred yards between the parking space and front door, I was sweating so much my undershirt got soaked.

"Hell's gone be a relief for some people," I said.

Ben tilted his head, scrunched up his face, and squinted. It was the look he gave me when I said something kooky.

I figured I'd better explain. "If you die in South Carolina in August, Hell's probably cooler."

He rolled his eyes. I cackled. I loved messing with that boy sometimes. He was too serious.

Inside Hickory Pines, I felt the relief of the cold AC . . . for a second. Then the smell— combination of piss and Clorox— about knocked me out the door. The cold air was no longer a relief. The chill made me shudder and I put my arm around Ben. He itched at his nose.

I was about to ask him about the smell when a young black woman greeted us. "Welcome y'all to Hickory Pines. I'm Shona."

She ushered us through the security doors and down the hallway to the newest wing. The fluorescent lights hummed.

The air-conditioning rattled as it kicked on and off. The halls were littered with medical equipment. Some of the machines were attached to people. Others were just left with cords dangling. Made me wonder what happened to them who'd been hooked up to those empty machines.

Most rooms was shared by two people with just a window that looked onto the wall of the building next to it. In one of the rooms, a guy wearing garnet sweatpants and a Gamecock sweatshirt waved at me. He was bald, with only a few long black hairs circled into a pile on the top of his head. I waved back and was about to smile, but then I realized he wasn't being friendly. I saw the look in his eyes. "Help," they begged.

Shona must have noticed my reaction because she grabbed my arm. "Your room would be in the other section of our facility."

"What are these rooms?" Ben asked.

"These are for people who just have Social Security," she said. "With that little bit of money, they can't afford the level of care we can provide your grandpa."

We walked out of the older section of the building and toured the communal room and the cafeteria. I lost focus as Miss Shona told us about all the history of the place and described the programs for residents. Was no way I was living at Hickory Pines. I wouldn't wish that on no one. Maybe Tim Taggert, but no one else.

On the way out, Shona tried to hand me a manila folder crammed with brochures and pamphlets, but I didn't take it.

When we was back in the car, Ben asked, "So what did you think?"

"Like I said. Hell's gone be a relief for the residents of Hickory Pines."

And this time, Ben didn't chide me. He nodded.

Second on the list: Magnolia for Seniors!

"Magnolia was built just three years ago," Ben said as we pulled up to a steel and glass structure that looked like some fancy office complex. Inside, it smelled like new carpet, and we was greeted by a bony white woman in her fifties. She wore two strands of marble-sized pearls, certainly fake.

"I'm Mrs. Kenneth Babcock," she said, "but you can call me Ruby."

"Nice to meet you, Mrs. Babcock," I said, and extended my hand.

"Please call me Ruby," she said.

I knew a Ruby one time, and I was not going to call just anyone by that name.

"Don't I know you?" she asked Ben, and stepped back to take a gander at him in full. "You're that boy from the paper! The preacher."

Ben blushed. "Yeah. That's me."

"Well, it's quite an honor to meet you," she said, and took Ben by the arm.

We started with the residential portion of the facility. Each bedroom had the same brand new furniture: a writing desk; a red couch with a floral print; a solid vinyl recliner; and a huge 27-inch TV.

"Each room has its own VCR," Mrs. Babcock said as she finished the tour with what would be my room for the rest of my life if I moved into Magnolia. It smelled sickly sweet, like a roll of cherry Life Savers.

"I could see your living here," Ben said to me. "It's real nice."

I wasn't quite sure and was gone ask a couple questions, but

Mrs. Babcock grabbed Ben again and led him away before I could say anything.

For the rest of the tour, she acted like I wasn't even there, until an incident when we was in her office. On the edge of her desk, she had a ceramic frog, its mouth stuffed with Halloween candy. I reached to grab a mini Hershey bar, but Mrs. Babcock jerked the frog away from me.

"Is it okay if he has one?" she asked Ben, not even looking at me.

"He can have what he wants," Ben replied. "He's not a child." He reached over Mrs. Babcock's desk and grabbed the frog and put it in front of me.

I tore the wrapper off a mini Snickers and crammed it in my mouth. "I'm taking these for later." I stuffed my pocket with mini Butterfingers and two full-sized Kit Kats.

She looked at Ben and harrumphed. She moved the frog to the shelf behind her.

"I'm not sure your grandpa would be a good fit here," she said, still talking only to Ben.

"You'd be lucky to have my Grandpa here. And if you'd spoken to him for even one minute during the entire tour you might realize that."

Mrs. Babcock looked like she'd just been cussed out. "It's just that he was taking all my candy."

Ben stood up. He pulled a couple dollars from his wallet and tossed them onto Mrs. Babcock's desk. "For the candy," he said, and walked out.

Now, when I was young, I woulda stormed out of the room and slammed the door, but at seventy-six, the best I could do was an angry shuffle.

The whole way walking to the car, Ben kept saying that he couldn't believe how Mrs. Babcock had treated me. He loved the facilities, but he wasn't about to have me live in a place that would treat me like that. When we was in the car and about halfway to our final stop, he'd calmed down a little bit and said maybe he would talk to her supervisor. The facilities at Magnolia were so nice. Maybe the rest of the people who worked there didn't act like that.

We decided not to cross Magnolia off the list, but I sure hoped we had a better experience at the last place: Dogwood Assisted Living Center.

Dogwood was a two-story, red-brick building with black wood shutters flanking each window. It looked like an old Georgian mansion instead of a place for old folks. Inside, we was greeted by a young white woman with outstretched arms. She was on the heavy side and wore a checked top with a striped skirt. Looked like she'd gotten dressed in the dark.

"Welcome to Dogwood," she said, and grabbed Ben and gave him a hug. "I'm Judy, the director of resident activities." She then hugged me.

As I let go of her embrace, I got a whiff of alcohol.

I leaned back in.

Was I mistaken?

Nope.

As someone who had spent a few years around stills and moonshine, I knew the smell of a good whiskey. When I let go of her, she weeble-wobbled a little bit so I held her shoulder until she steadied.

"Your grandpa is very affectionate," she said to Ben, and laughed. One of the laughs that's so genuine and infectious you have to join in. "He'll be very popular here."

I laughed. "I'm popular everywhere I go."

As we finished our tour of the east wing of the facility, Miss Judy's beeper went off. "I'm sorry. I've got to attend to an emergency." She waved to a woman sitting at a table reading a large-print copy of a Danielle Steele novel. "Daleah! Could you show Mr. Phelps and his grandson the west wing? I just got paged."

"I'd be delighted." The woman butterflied her book on the end table. "I'm Daleah Ashford," she said, and Ben and I introduced ourselves. This lady exuded class. She had on a triple strand of real pearls and wore a ring with a diamond the size of a marble.

"I love Dogwood, especially this part of the facility," she said. "Here we get to furnish the rooms ourselves. Makes it more like home than 'a home.'"

She showed us around, saving her place for last. She had taken three rooms and turned them into a large master suite with sitting area. Her place could have been a room in an antebellum mansion. I'm talking oriental rugs, a four-poster bed, sofas and chairs in front of a fake fireplace.

"I admit this room is a bit much," she said, "but my grandson is a designer."

I was about to ask her about her grandson when Judy stumbled into the room.

"Hello again!" she said.

The whiskey on her breath was even stronger, and I reckoned the poor woman had a serious drinking problem. Ben must have noticed it too because he stared at her like he'd figure her out if he just squinted hard enough. He kept trying to whisper something in my ear, but I evaded him.

We made our leave of Daleah and finished our tour at the administration offices.

"My work here is done," Judy said. "Now y'all get to meet Kevin Cross. He's finishing up his master's degree in nursing home administration."

She winked at Ben. "You'll like Kevin a lot."

I was wondering how she picked up on Ben's feelings so fast, but then wondered if maybe everyone else did too. They just wasn't drunk enough to mention it.

Before Judy left, she pulled me in for a final hug. "I appreciate y'all coming out for a visit today. I do hope that we've made a good impression."

She started to let go, but I held onto her. "It's obvious that you do a wonderful job making the residents here happy," I said, and then whispered, "and it's even more clear that you've got yo'self something of a drinking problem."

Judy stepped back, and I could see the shock in her eyes.

"Listen," I said loud enough for Ben to hear as well, "it's okay with me if you drink more than a Clemson fan on game day." She started to protest, but I held up my hand. "So long as you planning fun activities and ain't driving me nowhere, you and I gone get along."

Before Judy or Ben had any time to react to what I'd said, Kevin came in. He was a real looker, and I knew that what Judy had said was true: Ben was gone like him.

August 17, 1991 (Saturday)
Ben

Kevin introduced himself, and we shook hands. The tips of our fingers lingered. Not even for a second, but just enough for me to see a flash in his eyes. The little voice in my head started up where Judy had left off. *Now that's a good-looking guy. Tall. Handsome. And are you seeing those gray eyes?* I tried but couldn't look away. Kevin was six feet tall with shaggy black hair, and his eyes were the color of the winter sky before it snows.

I'd gotten so distracted by him that I'd just processed that Grandpa had told Judy she was a drunk. I wanted to apologize on his behalf, but Grandpa must not have offended Judy too badly because she was laughing as she ushered us into Kevin's office.

"Y'all are in good hands." She winked at Grandpa. "We are gonna have some good times if you decide to join us here."

Grandpa chuckled and then proceeded to empty his pockets of the candies he'd swiped from Magnolia. He arranged them on the edge of the desk as Kevin went through his presentation. Kevin pretended not to notice and focused on me.

I didn't want to stare at him while he spoke, so I looked around his office. It was so tiny. You couldn't open the door without hitting the chair I was sitting in. On his wall was a recent diploma from SJU.

I was about to mention something about his being a fellow Lemonhead, but my stomach grumbled, and I realized that Grandpa and I hadn't eaten lunch that day. Grandpa must have heard the growling because he handed me a piece of a Kit Kat.

He munched on one, and then broke off a piece for Kevin.

"Thanks," Kevin said, and smiled.

He had dimples.

"Y'all care to stay for dinner?" he asked.

He must have heard my stomach. "It's only 4:30 p.m."

"It's prime dinner time here," Kevin said.

"We need to get going," I said. "The Braves play tonight. We never miss a game."

Grandpa unwrapped and ate a Butterfinger. "The game don't start until this evening."

"Then you've got plenty of time." Kevin stood up. As he went around his desk, he had to brush past me to open the door.

"We really should get going," I said, "because . . ."

Grandpa interrupted me. "Ben, I need to try the food here. You know that on your deathbed, there's only one thing that matters: How many good meals did you have?"

We walked down the hall towards the dining room with Grandpa leading the way like he already lived there. He had a spring in his step I hadn't seen in a while. I followed behind with Kevin telling me more about the active life that seniors enjoyed at Dogwood.

I heard the voice muttering. *I think this is the first of many meals you and Kevin will share.* Pretending to rub my sideburns, I pressed my hands against my ears. I needed to quiet the voice. *He's really good-looking, even better than Derek.*

At the thought of Derek, I felt like I was standing in the sun. It was cool in the building, but sweat blanketed my brow. I slowed my pace, allowing Grandpa to get even farther ahead. I stopped for a second in front of an open door. A man in a wheelchair was inside.

Kevin put his hand on my shoulder. "You okay?"

"Just a little warm." I fanned myself with my hand and bumped his arm, hoping he'd take his hand off my shoulder. "Warm or overwhelmed."

"Maybe both," he said. He squeezed my shoulder, and I felt a flash of excitement.

I hadn't noticed the guy in the wheelchair was rolling out of his room. He came at us, and Kevin had to jump out of his way.

The man shouted at Kevin. "Stay away from me, you queer!"

The word "queer" reverberated up and down the hall, and I looked to see if anyone else had heard. Grandpa turned around, but then he picked up his pace and kept walking.

"What you looking at?" The guy pointed at me with a crooked finger. "You queer too?"

I wanted to run away and make sure no one had heard, but Kevin just smiled and leaned down to talk to the guy. "Mr. Ritter, are you jealous I might have a new boyfriend? Don't worry. I'll never find anyone as charming as you."

He turned the guy's wheelchair around so that it was pointed towards his room. "I think that *Wheel of Fortune* is on. You don't wanna miss that."

The anger lines on Mr. Ritter's face receded, and he seemed to have forgotten his outburst. "You right. That Vanna White's a looker." He rolled himself towards his room with the same speed and determination he'd come at us with in the first place.

As Kevin and I walked to the dining room, he explained. "Mr. Ritter has advanced Alzheimer's. Judy tells me he used to be the sweetest old man, but now he has these sorts of outbursts almost daily."

Grandpa was waiting for us in the entryway to the dining room. "I'm gone get a seat," he said. "I've walked more today than I have in a while, and my dogs is hurting. Ben, you know what I like, and get me at least one thing the doctor says I'm not supposed to eat."

I grabbed two trays and waited in the line. Kevin got behind me but didn't have a tray. "You're not joining us?" I asked.

"I'll help you with your grandfather's tray, but then I've got paperwork to do."

"That's too bad," I said, feeling a combination of relief and disappointment.

Behind the steam tables, a black woman who looked old enough to be a Dogwood resident stirred a mess of collard greens. She was the thin shape and light tan color of a cinnamon stick. "How y'all doing?" she asked each of us before taking our order for a "meat and three."

"I'm doing very well," I said. "How are you, ma'am?"

"I praise the good Lord every day he gives me on this earth," she replied with the conviction of a revival preacher.

"Amen," I said on instinct. Her head seemed lopsided, and I realized it was her wig that was slipping.

"You look real familiar," she said.

"I'm Ben Stark. I don't recall that we've met."

"Well, I'm Viola. What y'all having tonight?"

I ordered our meals, and Kevin carried Grandpa's tray over to the table for me.

"Ain't you gone join us?" Grandpa asked Kevin.

"I've gotta get back to work," Kevin said.

By now, I felt only relief that Kevin was leaving. The more time I spent with him, the more I felt a sense of unease. Temptation gnawed at my insides.

"But you can't go now," Grandpa said. "I have a lot more questions about this place."

Kevin smiled and looked at me. "The paperwork can wait if you need some more information."

Grandpa gestured to the empty chair beside me, and Kevin sat down. Grandpa took his napkin, put it in his lap, picked up his fork and was about to take a bite of his sweet potato casserole when I realized we hadn't said grace first.

"If we could pray?"

Grandpa stopped eating. "Of course," he said. "Food smelled so good I couldn't wait. Let's join hands."

Grandpa and I hadn't held hands while we said the blessing in years. Grandpa reached over and grabbed Kevin's hand. I had no choice but to put my hand on top of Kevin's. His hands and fingers had soft black hairs, and I fought every urge to caress them.

The Lord is really being good to you. You're getting to hold hands with every hot guy you're meeting.

I shut out the voice and said a quick blessing. "Dear Lord, thank you for this food, use it to the nourishment of our bodies and us to thy service. In Jesus' name, Amen."

"That was a short one for you," Grandpa said. "But I really appreciate it." He started back into his sweet potatoes.

"So what others questions do you have about Dogwood?" Kevin asked.

Grandpa mopped up juice from his collard greens with cornbread. "What do you think is the best thing about this place?"

"Definitely the residents," Kevin replied. "We have a great mix of people from different backgrounds and for the most part, everybody gets along."

"I reckon Judy's got a lot to do with that," Grandpa said.

"She is unconventional in style, but we all love her," Kevin said.

"I'm already partial to her," Grandpa said. "She's a big Braves fan, and she promised we'd watch all the games together on the big TV in the rec room."

"How long have you been a Braves fan?" Kevin asked Grandpa.

"I've supported baseball in Atlanta since 1932, but at that time, the Braves were in Boston. Because of crazy thinking, whites and coloreds weren't allowed to play ball together so Atlanta had two teams: the Atlanta Crackers and the Atlanta Black Crackers. The funny thing is that the whole community supported both teams, but whites had to sit in one section and the colored folks in another. A thin rope separated us, but it might as well have been the Great Wall of China."

"You're joking, right?" Kevin asked.

"My grandpa jokes about a lot, but never about baseball."

Grandpa pulled a piece of pink quartz out of a pocket. He held it between his fingers, and I could see that it was the arrowhead. "This here is my good luck charm. Ben found it . . ." He paused, not mentioning that I'd found it in a mound of dirt that was gonna cover Momma's grave. He handed the arrowhead to Kevin.

"This was part of a grand tradition between me and Ben. He'd give me a stone, and I'd tell him a story."

"Grandpa's stories got me through a whole lot of tough times."

Kevin held the arrowhead between his thumb and forefinger with the point down. "So what story did you get for this stone?" he asked.

I turned his hand over so that the arrowhead pointed upwards. "That was the logo for the Atlanta Crackers." I froze for a moment with my hand on his.

Feels good, doesn't it? Just close your eyes and enjoy this moment.

Grandpa cleared his throat and winked at me. I jerked my hand away.

"The Atlanta Crackers was one of the best minor league baseball teams of all time," he said. "And you won't believe the baseball park where they played. . . ."

Grandpa had a certain way he spoke when he told a story. Real soft at first so you had to lean in to listen.

"The year was 1932," he said. "The Atlanta Crackers was playing the Birmingham Tigers at Ponce de Leon field, or 'Poncey,' as we locals called it. For the first eight innings, nobody done nothing right except the pitchers. In the bottom of the ninth, one of the Crackers singled. That's when they called in their secret weapon. A pinch runner named Climax Clinton."

"That sounds like a made-up name," Kevin said.

"That was the boy's name," Grandpa said. "Climax used to be a pretty good hitter, but he got real scared after he stepped into a fastball, and it knocked him in the mouth and he lost about half his teeth."

"He refused to bat after that," I said.

"You can hardly blame him," Kevin said.

"He wouldn't hit, but he would still run the bases," I said.

Grandpa held up his hands. "Y'all gone let me tell this story or keep interrupting?" He took a swig of tea and lowered his voice again. "With Climax on first, our best batter, Pete Thompson, stepped up to the plate. The crowd got real quiet, and you could see the pitcher shaking his head as the catcher signaled to him. Finally, the pitcher nodded, and then wound up. He sent a fastball right over the plate. Whoosh . . . then

CRACK! The baseball soared towards the magnolia tree."

"Magnolia tree?" Kevin asked.

"I know it seems far-fetched, but I am sho 'nuff telling the truth. At 421 feet from home plate, they was a magnolia tree, smack dab in center field. The Tigers' center fielder ran back and back and back, until he hit the trunk of that tree and fell down. He looked up, and we all watched and waited. The ball must have bounced around in the limbs and branches of that tree for a full minute before falling right in the middle of his glove.

"Everyone, including the center fielder, was surprised. The few Tigers fans cheered and the Cracker Backers booed. I think I was the only one that noticed that Climax had run back to first base, touched off and then was heading towards second. The guy who caught the ball was so shocked by his luck that he blame forgot about Climax. The crowd realized what was going on and started cheering, which confounded the center fielder. The second baseman was waving his arms and yelling. That got his attention, and the center fielder throwed the ball with all his might—too hard in fact—and it sailed towards home plate. Climax rounded second, and the third-base coach waved him on. The pitcher snatched up the ball and throwed it to the third baseman. The coach motioned like mad for Climax to slide . . .

"We all held our breath while the cloud of dust cleared. The umpire waved his arms and shouted 'safe.' The crowd roared and then Climax squealed. Like a mouse. Or like a woman who seen a mouse. He jumped up off the base and started running around in a circle shouting and rubbing his behind.

"He settled down after a couple minutes, but the rest of the game, we was all abuzz in the stands speculating on what had happened. No one could figure it out. After a line drive towards right field, Climax Clinton ran home, scoring the sole run for the Crackers."

"So what happened to Climax?" Kevin asked. "Why did he react like that?

"After the game, I was sitting in my car listening to the radio. I always hung out afterwards to take liquor orders. It was a Friday, and people wanted to stock up for the weekend. While I waited, I listened to the radio, and after the game commentary, a reporter was interviewing Climax about what happened at third base. I turned up the radio and opened up the Co-Cola that I had bought after the game.

"Climax explained that he liked to play pranks on his teammates, and that they'd gotten him back one day when they put his false teeth in the bottom of the tobacco spittoon.

"Climax told the reporter, 'I had to soak my teeth in cleaner for a week, so after that, I always kept them with me. I didn't wear them because I couldn't afford another pair if I got hit in the mouth. I thought I had the genius idea to keep them in my back pocket, but when I slid into third, the bicuspids of my false teeth sunk into my rear.'

"Climax Clinton bit hisself on the butt with his own teeth!"

Kevin laughed, and I did too.

"That is a crazy story," Kevin said. "You didn't make that up?"

"I swear it's all the truth," Grandpa said. "Ruby J and I laughed so hard I spilled my Co-Cola all over my order sheets."

"What?" I asked. "I've never heard that part."

"You've heard that story a hunnert times by now, Ben. You know that I used to bootleg moonshine and because I ruined my order sheets tons of folks got sober that week thanks to Climax Clinton."

"I know you spilled your drink on your order sheets, but you've never mentioned this Ruby person. Who is that?"

Grandpa put his hand over his mouth and squeezed his eyes tight like he could make the moment go away. He waited and then peeked with one eye. I was still staring at him.

"I'll give you two a minute." Kevin pushed back from the table and took our empty trays away.

"Ben, they's some stories in my life I ain't ever told you, and it's high time you heard them. For starters, Ruby J was the first love of my life." His eyes began to water, and he picked Classic Stan off the table and fanned himself.

"But why haven't I heard anything before now?" I asked.

He sniffled a little and rubbed at his eyes. "I couldn't exactly tell you about Ruby J in front of your Mee Maw, now could I?"

Kevin was gonna head out the door, but Grandpa waved him back over. "Where's the bathroom?" Grandpa asked him.

Kevin pointed in the direction of the men's room.

"Keep Ben company while I'm gone," he said to Kevin. "At my age, stuff just goes right through me. May be awhile." Grandpa got up and Kevin sat back down.

I shook my head, and we sat for a moment. The woman who served our food had been going around the dining room filling people's glasses with iced tea or water. She had avoided our table during Grandpa's story, but now she came over. She had a pitcher filled to the brim with tea. "Y'all need anything over here?"

"Why thank you, Miss Viola." I handed her my glass. She held the pitcher sideways so that I'd get both ice and tea.

"That was a crazy story," Kevin said, and picked up the arrowhead. "A guy biting himself in the butt with his own teeth? That's hysterical."

I felt splatter on my pants and realized that Viola was overfilling my tea.

"Pardon me," she said. "I just couldn't help but overhear your story. You said a guy bit hisself with his own teeth."

"It's a story my Grandpa likes to tell. I'm not sure that it's even true. About a baseball player named Climax Clinton."

Viola dropped the plastic tea pitcher on the floor, and it splashed all over me and Kevin. "I'm so sorry," she said. "Let me get something to wipe that up."

"I'll help you." Kevin left the arrowhead in the center of the table.

I wasn't sure what to make of this twist in Grandpa's story. He hadn't been exaggerating. I'd heard about Climax Clinton a hundred times, but it had never ended with another woman.

I picked up the arrowhead and felt its rough, knife-like edge.

Apart from the fact that she'd gone to a baseball game with him, I knew nothing about this Ruby person. What had happened to her? What had happened to their love? It had been years since I'd traded Grandpa a stone for a story, but it was time for me to restart our barter system.

I needed to find a new stone.

12

September 12, 1991 (Thursday)
Ben

I had asked Grandpa about Ruby a few times over the past weeks, but he wasn't ready to talk about her. And I wasn't ready to press him. Our house and the land had sold quickly, and we were going to have to move out by the end of the month. We'd spent the past couple weeks sorting through a lifetime of his and Mee Maw's stuff, and it had been a very emotional time. Halfway through, Grandpa said he'd had enough. He told me to pack his hats and throw away the rest.

I'm not sure I could have gotten through it without Becca's friendship. After Mountainview, she had asked me over to her apartment for dinner. Monica was there each time, and given how keen Pastor Hardy was for me and Monica to get together, I thought that Becca was just trying to set us up.

But then the past couple of times when I went over to their place, Monica was out on a date. And each time I'd gone to see Pastor Hardy the past two weeks, Monica had been all about Brad, Brad, Brad, Brad, Brad.

So I sort of had my first girlfriend.

I had invited Becca out for dinner, our first "real" date, but she'd insisted on helping me finish packing. Plus, she'd heard Grandpa say he wasn't gonna make it if he had to eat more TV dinners, so she was bringing over lasagna.

I was surveying everything that Becca and I needed to pack in Grandpa's office downstairs. It was full of family photos that needed careful wrapping, and I'd avoided that until the last minute because somehow it made everything seem too final.

The other thing that I wasn't sure how to pack was the old five-gallon pickle jar filled with the stones I'd given Grandpa in exchange for stories over the past ten years. I figured it was time for us to restart our barter system. He might not tell me a story about Ruby, but maybe there were other stories he'd never told me because he didn't want Mee Maw to know.

I unscrewed the pickle jar and took out a rock. Grandpa probably wouldn't remember I'd given him that one already. The doorbell rang.

I opened the door to find Becca with oven mitts, holding a glass tray covered in tinfoil. "So this is your mom's world-famous lasagna?"

"Yep. It's right out of the oven so it's very hot," she said. "I'll just put it in the kitchen and then get the rest of the groceries out of the trunk."

"I'll get the groceries," I said, and invited her in. "Grandpa's been excited all day to see you."

While Becca chatted with Grandpa, she directed me how to make the chopped salad. Becca pulled out plates, and soon the oven timer dinged. Mozzarella cheese bubbled on top of the lasagna, and I could almost taste the garlic and the tomatoes.

We sat down, blessed the food and started eating.

"How's the packing?" Grandpa asked me.

"Becca is gonna help me wrap up all the photos, and then I just need to figure out what to do with all your rocks," I replied, and then felt a pain in my side. The same feeling I'd get before exams. Anxiety. Like a knife twisting.

"Everything okay?" Becca asked me. "You've seemed out of sorts ever since I got here."

"I'm fine. I think this is just hitting me all of a sudden. I can't believe that Grandpa moves into a home in less than two weeks."

"Has he decided where yet?" she asked.

"No," I said. "We thought that Dogwood was the only real choice, but the senior administrator at Magnolia had called to apologize, and they've offered us a premium room at a reduced rate. Magnolia has been named the best nursing home in the Upstate for the past three years, so it's been a difficult decision."

"But it's a decision that I'm ready to make," Grandpa said. He stopped eating his second piece of lasagna, wiped tomato sauce from his mouth and announced, "I'm moving to Dogwood."

I dropped my fork, and red sauce splattered all over the place. "The facilities are so much better at Magnolia," I said. I got up, wet a paper towel and dabbed it on my shirt. "Your room would be so much nicer there."

"I don't care if they're a branch of the Mayo Clinic, I prefer Dogwood."

I truly believed that Magnolia would take better care of him, and I worried that between Mr. Ritter and Kevin, I would be afraid to visit as much as I wanted. "Let's not be hasty in our decision," I said.

"Ben, I appreciate all you've done for me. But this decision is mine to make. We're in escrow on this place, and once we close, we gone split the proceeds fifty-fifty. Your half goes towards your schooling. My half goes towards my living. I think you can serve the Lord just as good as a doctor or lawyer, but you don't hear me trying to talk you out of seminary. Let me use my half to do what I want."

I sat there stunned. It was not like Grandpa to be so direct. Usually, he avoided conflict so that nobody would ever have an excuse not to like him. But I guess he didn't ever have to worry about that with me.

Becca put her hand on mine. "Ben, we've talked about this. You're just arguing to avoid the decision so that you don't have to deal with his moving into a senior home."

"I like her," Grandpa said. "She's as smart as she is purdy."

Becca held out her hand to Grandpa. "Aren't you nervous about all this too?"

Grandpa took her hand and chuckled. "At my age, nerves are the only thing that keeps your heart beating. Besides, I've had bigger changes in my life."

I saw this as the perfect lead-in for a story about Ruby so I took the stone from my pocket and placed it on the table. "What changes?" I asked. "Like when you met Ruby?"

"Her name was Ruby J," Grandpa said, and picked up the stone and studied it. He flipped it over and over and rubbed it between his fingers. He even smelled it and touched it to his tongue. He set it back down on the table.

"Ben, you found this down by the creek back when you was fifteen. I told you a story about the time me and my buddy Clem got arrested."

Trapped in my deception, I froze for a moment. I didn't think Grandpa would remember every stone I'd ever given him. But that story was an important one. What happened had changed Grandpa forever. And it all started with his spending a night in jail.

"You got arrested?" Becca asked him.

"Wasn't for murder or nothing. During the Depression, I rode the rails going from town to town trying to find work. My buddy Clem and I got drunk on an overnight train from Atlanta to New Orleans and fell asleep. We didn't get off the train before it got into the station so the bulls arrested us."

"Doesn't sound too crazy," Becca said.

"You won't believe it, but. . . ." Grandpa started to say, but I interrupted him.

"I've heard that whole story before," I said. I didn't want Grandpa to get into the part about after he got arrested. He and Clem had spent six months tracking down and bringing to justice a rapist. It was one of Grandpa's best stories, but one that would probably upset Becca.

"I want a new story," I said.

"Ben, you don't get a new story for an old stone." He handed it back to me. "I think I'm gone get me another piece of that lasagna."

When he sat back down, Becca had pulled out a rock that she had in her pocket. It wasn't from Grandpa's collection.

"Mr. Phelps. This is pink granite. I'd like to hear about how you met Ruby J."

Grandpa picked up the stone, studied it for a moment and then smiled. "This is called Kershaw Pink Granite. It's quarried right near Columbia." He handed the stone back to Becca, who pretended to inspect it. Grandpa settled in his chair, like he often did before starting a story, and I listened as he told me and Becca about the wedding of Ray Linda Pickens, where he first met Ruby J.

June 25, 1932 (Saturday)
Grandpa (17 years old)

I'd stopped riding the rails and was bootlegging moonshine and other libations in north Georgia. A buddy of mine died from consumption so I became the proud owner of a 1928 Model A.

Because I could tell good moonshine from the kind that'd make you blind and because I could deliver, I became the supplier of the best moonshine, liquor and wine in Rome, Georgia.

One of the richest men in the town, Ray Bill Pickens, wanted me to supply liquor to his daughter's wedding. So on the Friday before the big day, I headed out to his place, about three miles up Highway 17 from the town square. It was one of them rare summer days where it's warm but not too hot.

Ray Bill must have had a team of a hunnert people working to get ready for that wedding. They had fresh-painted the picket fence. A large wrought-iron gate was splattered with white flowers, and four colored boys were hanging swathes of cream-colored ribbon everywhere they could reach from their ladders.

I had to weave my car around workers who carried tables and chairs and enough wood and scaffolding for a barn raising. When he saw me pulling up, Ray Bill Pickens raced towards me waving a newspaper. He was dressed in tuxedo pants and a white undershirt, drenched in sweat.

"Lord, help us all. This wedding will be the death of me yet."
He pulled a rag from his pocket and mopped his brow.

He shoved the newspaper at me. "Here ya go, Charlie. Here's
the order."

In the margins of the *Rome Herald*'s society paper were
scribbles that took me a while to decipher. I read the list aloud
to make sure I was reading it right. "Two cases Turbo Stomper
moonshine, three cases Confederate huckleberry liqueur, and
six cases of scuppernong wine."

I looked up. "You sure that gone be enough? You expecting
the Union Army?"

Ray Bill snatched the newspaper out of my hands, turned to
page two and pointed to a photo. "That is my oldest daughter,
Ray Linda. Today is her wedding day. My wife has invited
more than a hundred people. And they are going to require
libations."

I stared at the picture of his daughter. To call Ray Linda
"ugly" would have been an insult . . . to ugly. Her eyes were so
far apart that she could probably look forward and backward
at the same time, and you could have used her underbite to rest
your cigar.

He shoved the paper back at me. I reckon Ray Bill was
gone need to get the groom pretty drunk to make sure the
wedding happened. "I'd add an extra case of Turbo Stomper,"
I suggested.

Ray Bill nodded and smiled. "As a special thank you, why
don't you join us for the reception? One of our field hands is
smoking two whole pigs, and we have a colored band coming
all the way from Atlanta. Plus, there's liable to be some single
gals here."

I could see my place moving up in society with these introductions so I decided I'd attend, provided I could find something appropriate to wear.

I only had a few other customers that day— seemed like half of Georgia was attending the wedding—but it took me so many stops to get that much wine and liquor, I'd forgotten all about finding a suit. On the way home to wash up, I stopped by a farmer who was about the only person I knew who was as skinny as me. He said he had an old tux that belonged to his daddy I could wear. He must have kept it stored in a closet full of mothballs, and although I noticed the odor when I first tried on the suit, I figured the smell would dissipate . . . after a while.

But I was wrong.

An hour before the wedding started, I showed up at the party and saw my old buddy Clem organizing the tables. I offered to help, but when I got within three feet of him, he turned up his nose.

"Lord help us all, Charlie. You smell like you got sprayed by a polecat. You need to air yo'self out."

It was a little windy that day, so I walked around, hoping the smell would go away, but the wind died down, the air got still and then heavy. The smell seemed to concentrate.

The sky was getting darker to the south, and I thought about leaving, but then the music started, and I could hear people hollering and having a good time. There were so many gals sitting at the tables I figured at least one of them would dance with me. A pretty strong breeze started blowing. Downwind I was sure to have better prospects.

This approach almost worked when I was talking to this redhead, but the wind shifted, and I had to circle her. I think that spooked her because after a couple of times, she walked away without as much as a goodbye.

I was gone try with an uglier girl when I heard the yelling.

"Look up!" someone shouted. The sky was black, like nighttime, even though it was barely four o'clock in the afternoon. The hurricane lamps on the tables blew out and then some of the tables started to topple.

Ray Bill grabbed his daughter and son-in-law and announced that everybody needed to head to the cellars. He said they was a cellar in the barn and another under the house. He headed towards the house, and I saw that the guests was following him. The wind died down, and then stopped.

I froze.

I could distinguish every sound: people's shoes banging against the hard ground as they ran; the snap of the cases as the musicians packed away their instruments; a man's low voice trying to calm his wife. The door of the hayloft had stopped slamming, and I could hear the squeak of the hinges as it rocked back and forth.

Then silence. The air pressure dropped, and it felt like someone was standing on my chest. My ears hurt like I was in deep water. And it was tough to breathe.

"Charlie! Hurry up!" Clem was yelling, and I realized that I needed to run. The house was too far away so I headed to the barn. One of the musicians had just finished packing up his accordion and was having a hard time carrying it along with all of the music that they had. I grabbed the other side of the case and some stacks of sheet music, and we headed towards the barn. They was about to close the cellar door when I heard the tornado. People say that tornados sound like freight trains.

Well, even possum belly on the top of the train in a tunnel wasn't nothing compared to that noise.

But as soon as the door shut, it got quiet. And I could hear nothing except for the breathing of everyone in the room. I looked around. Someone had lit a couple lanterns, but it was dark and my eyes took some time to adjust. I could only make out a few faces I recognized, mainly the musicians and the colored folks who was helping at the wedding.

Clem pulled out a pocketful of cigars he must have grabbed from one of the boxes that Ray Bill had. He passed them around. Someone else had the forethought to bring a couple jugs of the Turbo Stomper. The accordionist grabbed one of the jugs and started passing it around. I took a seat on the floor beside one of the purdiest women I'd ever seen. She had some weight to her, which I liked. Seemed like people had got skinnier and skinnier since the Depression, so she reminded me of better times. She had a magnolia blossom in her hair, and I could smell the subtle sweetness of the flower, 'twas even more powerful than my mothball scent. We made eyes at each other for a couple seconds until they was a sound like someone banging on the door. One of the fellows got up to see who it was, but then everything got so loud we realized it was the storm. Wood and metal scraping. Wind screaming like a girl who seen a snake. Went on for what seemed like hours but was probably just a couple minutes. Then I didn't hear nothing. But my heartbeat.

And even though I didn't even know her name at the time, and even though it probably wasn't even legal for a white man to hold hands with a colored woman in public, I reached over and grabbed Ruby J's hand.

August 29, 1991 (Thursday)
Ben

I'd been listening so intently to Grandpa's story that it took me a while to process what he had said.

"Ruby J was black?" I asked.

"Yes she was," he said.

"You have an issue with that?" Becca asked me.

"No," I said, and paused. "I just didn't picture her as black."

"Not that I cared one way or the other, but her skin tone was paler than yours or mine. . . ." Grandpa said.

Before I could ask any more, the phone rang and I jumped. Normally, I would have let the machine answer, but I'd packed it the day before.

The cordless phone kept ringing so I answered.

"Hey, Ben." The voice on the other end was raspy and deep. "You don't know me, but I saw your picture in the religion section of the paper a while back. About how you were gonna be a preacher."

I walked from the kitchen into the family room.

"Who is this?" I asked.

"Rick." His voice made my heart stop. I imagined a guy with a bushy mustache, like my dance teacher Mr. Jon used to have.

"What is this about?"

"From your photo, I thought you might want wanna hook up for a coffee or something." The way he said "something" sounded like he wanted to do more than just hang out.

"Why?" I asked. My heart rattled sideways in my chest. "I don't know you."

"You don't know me yet, but I think you'd enjoying meeting me."

This guy must be a homosexual, and he wants to take you out. If he looks anything like he sounds, you'll have a good time. I was so busy fighting with my internal voice about whether or not to go out with the guy, I asked the guy on the phone, "Where would we go?" before I could stop myself.

"What kind of food do you like?" he asked.

I was seconds away from detailing my culinary preferences to Rick when I thought I heard someone laugh in the background on the other end of the phone. I felt a pang in my stomach. "Is this a joke?"

"Not at all," Rick said. "I just thought you were hot. I liked your bleached-blond floppy hair. The article talking about how you listen to Broadway show tunes for inspiration when writing a sermon. Don't you want to go out on a date with me, Benji?"

I could feel the phone shaking in my hand, but I couldn't feel any part of my body. I was numb. *Say yes!*

I wanted to plop on the coach and talk to Rick more, staring at a picture of him, like a teenage girl in a movie. But the first photo I saw was one of Grandpa, me and Mee Maw, right after I'd given my first sermon at a real church. The look on her face reminded me how proud she'd been. And how disappointed she would be now.

"You still there?" Rick asked. "I know we'd hit it off. We have a lot in common."

"I'm not like that. I'm not like you," I said, and hung up. I looked at the picture. Thanks for being there, Mee Maw.

My heart pounded as I put the phone back in the cradle on the kitchen counter. My mind blazed with questions. Why would he think I was gay? How had he known? How had he even guessed? Why would he call me out of the blue and ask me out?

"Who was that?" Becca asked.

"Just a call from Hickory Pines," I said. The lie came too easily.

"Which one was that?" she asked.

"The one that smelled like piss and Clorox," Grandpa said. "I feel sorry for anybody who has to live there."

"I told them that we had picked another place," I said. "She asked which one, and I told her 'Dogwood.'"

Grandpa smiled because he took this as a sign that I'd accepted his choice, but Becca seemed anxious. Had she seen through my lie? I felt that at any moment she would ask, "So when are you and Rick going out on a date?"

But instead, she picked up the piece of pink granite and leaned in to Grandpa. She just wanted to hear the end of his story. "So what happened next? You're in a cellar with a group of people, there's a tornado and . . ."

June 25, 1932 (Saturday)
Grandpa

We waited. We could hear the wind howling, and the banging and slapping and clanging started back up. We figured we was safe so long as we stayed in the cellar, so we decided to make the best of it.

Ruby J was staring at me, and I realized that I had not been much of a gentleman, so I took off my hat and introduced myself.

"I'm Charlie Phelps." In this tight space, my mothball smell was stronger than before, and I felt the need to legitimatize my presence at that shindig. "I'm a friend of Ray Bill's."

Ruby J held out her hand. Short fingers, but the softest hands I'd ever felt. "Everybody calls me Ruby J."

"You Clem's sister?" I asked.

"No, that's Ruby B. I'm his cousin."

"So two Ruby's in one family?" I asked.

"Actually, there are four of us. In addition to Ruby B, I have two other cousins named Ruby."

The guy with the accordion tapped me on the shoulder and lit the cigar I'd been handed. I turned to face Ruby J and took a long puff. I was trying to be dapper, but I'd never smoked a cigar before. I didn't realize you're not supposed to bring the smoke into your lungs. I started to cough. My attempts to stifle it made me sound like a Model A sputtering to crank as I stuttered to talk to her.

The moonshine had made its way around the circle. Ruby J took a sip from the jug and handed it to me. We could hear the commotion overhead as the storm sounded like it was ripping apart the barn. I had never needed a drink more at any other moment in my life, but I paused. It was one thing to hold Ruby J's hand, but I had never drunk after a colored person.

My whole life I'd been taught that I'd get all sorts of diseases as a result, and I was about to pass the bottle to the next person when I noticed the look on Ruby J's face.

Disappointment.

Like you ain't never seen in your life.

Just one look from her like that could make you feel like you were being damned to Hell for all eternity.

The fella to my left had his hand on the bottle, but I jerked it back and took a small swig. At that moment, I expected life to change, all my preconceived notions about colored and whites to shift. But it was just a drink of moonshine, like any other. I took another swallow. That was the best sip of

Turbo Stomper I'd ever had. It coated my whole insides with a calmness, and I smiled at Ruby J and passed the jug to the next fellow.

We spent the next hour or so waiting for the storm to calm. After a while, the musicians pulled out their instruments and played some music to lighten our spirits. Clem grabbed Ruby J's arm and they started spinning around and dancing. Others followed, and soon I was the only one sitting down. Ruby J came over and grabbed my arm.

"You too good to join us?" she asked.

I got up and started moving my feet side to side and forwards and backwards.

I tried a fancy move, and almost fell over. Ruby J laughed, and I can still hear the sound. Sounded like a chicken being strangled underwater. But it was the most joyous laugh I had ever heard. I thought that if I could spend the rest of my life making her laugh that I would die a happy man.

September 12, 1991 (Thursday)
Ben

Grandpa untucked his napkin from his shirt and dabbed at his eyes. Looking into the windows of his soul, I could see in him a deep pain I'd only seen twice before, at Momma's funeral and during Mee Maw's last bout with cancer. Grandpa, Becca and I finished our meal in relative silence, just making small talk about the weather.

Over the next couple of weeks, I never mentioned Ruby J again. I hated seeing Grandpa in such pain, and even though I knew that he had stories to tell me that he needed to get off his chest, I couldn't be the one to force the issue.

I'd have to let him tell me about Ruby J on his terms.

With Becca's help, I finished packing up the photos, Grandpa's collection of stones, and the rest of my things. When the movers came, it was difficult watching them separate our boxes, knowing that his were going one place and mine another.

13

September 19, 1991 (Thursday)
Ben

While Grandpa moved into his more permanent home at Dogwood, I moved into the carriage house on Pastor Hardy's property. He and his wife had offered to let me live there rent-free.

I'd unpacked all of my things in the last couple days except for one box labeled MAGAZINES. I had intended to throw those away, but Becca was with me while I was packing so I just threw them all into a box, expecting to sort through them later. Other than a couple copies of *Southern Living,* the magazines all had photos of guys in various stages of undress, working out. I was gonna just toss the whole thing, but the voice convinced me otherwise. *You're supposed to treat your body like a temple. Keep the workout magazines. You've gained so much weight these past few weeks. Get rid of them later, but right now, you need them.*

I opened the box and took out my favorite: *Men's Exercise: For Men Only.* The cover promised "Seven Ways to Cut the Flab," so I flipped through, figuring I ought to at least rip out the diet article.

But I never got past page 3, featuring a shirtless guy with a serious look and some horrid free-verse poetry about how concentration yields results. I was so focused on the guy's abs and the thick vein that ran down the length of his arm, snaking down his bicep, that I jumped when the doorbell rang. Pastor Hardy had mentioned he might stop by to make sure I was settling in at the carriage house, so I took the stack of magazines and put them on the coffee table, making sure the two copies of *Southern Living* were on top of each pile.

Pastor Hardy didn't bother to wait for me to answer the door. "It's finally finished," he announced as he walked in. He handed me a white plastic box, which looked like a first-aid kit except that it had a rainbow-colored cross on top instead of the normal red one.

"What's this?"

He beamed with pride, grinning so wide I could see top and bottom teeth. "The very first HomoNoMo kit. A cure in seven simple steps."

"I'm glad this is simple and easy because I've got only five and a half months left," I said. I wasn't sure if he could hear the frustration in my voice that it had taken so long for him to get me the cure.

"I never said it's going to be easy." He set the kit on the coffee table. "The steps are simple but hard. But I know you can do this."

"Wow," I said, but not because I was impressed. I didn't understand how this could help me. I undid the plastic clips and opened the box. Inside, I found some kitchen-sized trash bags, a stack of trifold pamphlets and a black rubber band by itself in a small Ziploc. And an envelope with instructions and some paper inside.

Pastor Hardy took the pamphlets from the box and arranged them on the coffee table. I picked them up one by one and read the titles.

Choosing God on the Straight Path.
Don't You Want a Family?
AIDS as God's Punishment for Homosexuals.
What Does the Bible Teach about Homosexuality?

The last thing in the box was a booklet. I opened it to the table of contents.

> SEVEN STEPS TO A CURE
> Step 1—Get closer to God
> Step 2—De-gay your life
> Step 3—*Ipsa scientia potestas est*
> Step 4—Snap away the gay
> Step 5—Watch sports
> Step 6—Straight-ify your life
> Step 7—Say goodbye to your same-sex addiction

I went back through all of the items a couple of times. I'd been waiting two months for this? I didn't see any hope for a cure with this. I was about to say something, but Pastor Hardy jumped in.

"Of course, we'll continue with our weekly meetings," he said.

The mention of "weekly meetings" was too much for me. I stood up. "We haven't had weekly meetings! You scheduled them, but you missed most of them."

He looked at me as I had just slapped him. "I missed those appointments on purpose," he said. "I wanted you to spend time with Monica. I think that she would make the perfect preacher's wife."

I was gonna tell him that I thought she'd make the perfect preacher, but I wasn't about to derail my cure for an argument on the role of women in the Baptist church. "How is this supposed to cure me?"

"Trust me, Ben. I've spent a lot of time working on this, distilling this treatment into its fundamental and critical parts. You've already completed Step 1. I can tell from the meetings we'd had that you've never been more focused on Bible study and prayer." He grabbed the white plastic trash bags. "Today, we commence Step 2 — De-gay your life."

I was about to tell him that I might have already completed Step 2 because I had recently turned down a date with a guy, but he opened one of the trash bags and set it on the edge of the coffee table, three inches to the left of the box full of the workout magazines.

"What's the trash bag for?" I asked.

He bit his lower lip, flared his nostrils and ignored my question. "Patti and I are so happy to have you staying with us."

I sat up straight because he'd gotten so serious all of a sudden. "I'm so grateful that you offered me this place. I didn't realize you weren't going to let me pay rent."

"We don't need the money." He put his arm around me. "Besides, you're like a son to me."

I rested my head against his shoulder, but he pushed me away. "And like good parents, Patti and I need to establish some rules that we expect from someone living in our home." He scanned the room like he was a policeman looking for clues. He saw the box with MAGAZINES written on the side and the stack of them on the coffee table. He rummaged through until he found the copy of the men's workout magazine I was just looking at. Why did he choose that particular one? Was it still somehow warm?

"This is a stumbling block," he said, and opened the magazine to a random page where a shirtless twenty-something guy was showing the proper form for squat thrusts. "We need to get rid of some things in your life that may be holding you back. You know the Bible verse about plucking out your eye."

"Of course. From the Sermon on the Mount." I had memorized more Bible verses than anybody else at my church seven years running so I quoted the verse: "'If your right eye causes you to sin, tear it out and throw it away! It is better to lose one of your members than to have your whole body thrown into hell.' Matthew 5:29."

"Exactly." Pastor Hardy started sorting through the rest of the magazines. "So that's what I'm here to do."

"Pluck out my eyes?"

"Of course not. Or at least not yet." He raised his eyebrows to make clear he was joking, but there was an ominous tone in his voice. "You and I are going to de-gay this place." He flipped to another page in the magazine. He pointed to the photos of a guy wearing skimpy shorts and nothing else.

"This is homosexual pornography." He flipped through pictures. "Every page, shirtless guy after shirtless guy."

My throat tightened. I felt like I was on trial, and the prosecutor had just presented to the jury the murder weapon with my fingerprints on it. But I wasn't about to rest my case.

"It's a workout magazine." I grabbed another issue from the coffee table. "See?" I pointed at pictures of two guys who were working out together at the beach using only a towel. "This article is really practical in case I'm somewhere with a friend, and we want to lift weights but don't have access to a gym."

I turned the page, and one guy was straddling the other one with his crotch in his face while they each pulled on ends of a towel. I was losing my case.

"Why are they always shirtless?" he asked.

I had not been captain of my high school debate team for nothing. I laughed like the answer was obvious. "That way, you can see what muscle group is the focus of the exercise."

I threw down the magazine and grabbed a different one. This one had more articles than pictures. As a result, I'd only bought that magazine the one time. I opened it to the table of contents.

"This one's clearly for straight guys. It has lots of articles about sports and sex with women." I handed it to him, and he skimmed the table of contents.

"This magazine may be less homo-centric, but be honest, Ben. Did you buy it for the articles?"

In my quest to find some jerk-off material, I had skipped past the article about finding a woman's G spot and seven tips for satisfying your partner. But I wasn't ready to give up so quickly.

"These guys have shirts on, or tank tops at least, and they're showing the proper form for all sorts of exercises." I turned to a page near the back of the magazine. "See. Here are instructions for bicep curls, dumbbell raises, even preacher curls. These magazines are sort of like the Bible for working out. You need instructions or you'll fail."

Pastor Hardy sighed like he was preparing for a bigger battle than he had anticipated. He tugged at his beard as I rubbed the scar on my arm in a duel of our nervous tics. At least I wasn't hiccupping.

He broke first. "When was the last time you actually did a preacher curl? Or any arm exercise for that matter?"

I could have answered with the truth. Last night, I did quite an extensive arm workout, even using the pictures of those guys, but that would just prove his point.

"I only bought those magazines so I could get in shape. Isn't my body supposed to be a temple?"

"You're one hundred percent correct. A temple, not a playground. What do you think your grandma would say about these magazines? Do you think she would approve?"

How dare he bring Mee Maw into this? What is he thinking?

I was about to yell at him. To tell him to get out of my house, but then I realized that it was his house. I stammered to say something in response, but he kept going.

"I spoke to her the day before she died. She said that she was worried about you and asked me to keep an eye on you. I'm here because of a promise I made to her." He started to put the magazines into the trash bag. "And I believe that you also made a promise to Mee Maw."

His words hit me so hard I thought I would fall down. I couldn't believe that he was using her against me. My vision got blurry, and the room started to spin. I sat down on the couch. My legs were numb, and I wasn't sure I could get up again. Mee Maw had said Pastor Hardy would help me.

I took a deep breath. He was right. I needed to de-gay my life. I grabbed the copies of *Men's Exercise*.

"I'm dedicated to this one hundred percent," I said.

He opened up the trash bag, and I dropped them inside.

"That's the spirit. And Ben, I'm here because I love you. Before you're ready to start seminary, you're going to need to be on solid footing." He took out the two *Southern Living* and threw the rest away. "Any more in the bedroom?"

"I'll get them." I had stashed under my mattress a couple issues of *Men's Workout* and one copy of *Honcho* I'd found in the bushes at a service station.

"Take this trash bag with you in case you find other things," he said. I left the room and went upstairs.

Pastor Hardy seems very controlling, coming in here and throwing away your stuff. Nothing wrong with a few aspirational photos. Becca's not gonna want some flabby boyfriend. You need to keep at least a few magazines if you want to keep a girlfriend.

I ignored the voice and threw all the magazines into the trash. When I came back downstairs, Pastor Hardy was perusing my collection of tapes and CDs, stacked in a six-foot spinning tower right beside the brand new stereo system Grandpa had bought me as a housewarming present. On top of the CD player was the jewel case of Madonna's *Erotica*. Pastor Hardy held it with only his thumb and forefinger like it was biomedical waste.

"Madonna?" he asked. "We'll need to rid you of her."

I could barely argue with him on that. Every time I listened to Madonna, I thought about writhing on a dance floor with one of the shirtless men who populated her videos.

He worked his way through my CD tower, and I sat on the couch watching him separate my life into "gay" or "straight." What I assumed to be the "gay" pile was three times larger than the other. As he stacked Madonna's entire music catalogue onto a pile of ABBA and Queen CDs, I realized how far I had to go on my quest. He spun the tower a quarter turn and started to add CD after CD of Broadway show tunes to the discard pile.

I jumped up off the couch. "Hold on. You're making a mistake here." I grabbed the CD of *Les Miserables*. "This may not be Amy Grant, but it's hardly gay music."

He started to protest. "Soundtracks to musicals?"

I corrected him. "They're original cast recordings. What do you expect me to listen to? Grunge? Nirvana is too depressing."

At that moment, the doorbell rang, and I dropped the CD jewel case. I rushed to the door and opened it to find Becca.

"What are you doing here?" I asked.

She looked over my shoulder and saw Pastor Hardy. "Sorry, Ben. I didn't realize you weren't going to be alone." She stepped back outside the door as if waiting for an invite. "Remember, I asked you about coming over and printing out a paper."

I'm sure my face was redder than Becca's hair. I had forgotten I had told her she could come by this morning to use my daisy wheel printer.

"Of course. Come on in," I said. I stepped over and picked up the *Les Miz* CD. "Pastor Hardy, this is my girlfriend, Becca."

Pastor Hardy stood frozen like he didn't know how to act.

Becca walked over to introduce herself. "Nice to meet you, Pastor Hardy. My roommate, Monica, has said very nice things about working for you."

Pastor Hardy stepped back and tugged at the patch of gray hair on his chin. "Ben didn't mention that you were his girlfriend."

"We haven't been dating that long," she said.

"But we're really in love," I said, and went over and held Becca's hand. She squeezed mine and then pulled it up to her lips and kissed it. Neither of us had ever said, "I love you" to the other, and this was the least optimal time, but she was supporting me. Maybe I did love her.

She looked at the trash bag, CDs and the pile of magazines. I could see the "What are you doing?" question forming in her mind. I thought about my philosophy class and what Professor Eisenberg had taught us about moral relativism. "I agreed to donate some CDs and tapes and magazines for a back-to-school party we're having for some underprivileged kids. Pastor just stopped by to pick them up."

Becca accepted my lie and let go of my hand. "Okay, I'll just be in the bedroom using your printer." She left and went to my bedroom.

Pastor Hardy moved to the movie soundtrack section of my CD collection. I had everything from *Breakfast Club* to *Pretty Woman*. "What are you thinking?" he asked, and started moving them into the pile I hoped were the ones I could keep.

"Soundtracks are a great value," I said. "You get songs from a lot of different singers."

"I'm not talking about your taste in music! I want to know why you're dating that girl and not Monica? Haven't you and Monica been hanging out?"

"Only when I went over to have dinner with Becca. But most of the time I'm there, Monica works on other things. To be honest, Monica is interested in someone other than me."

"But the two of you are perfect for each other. She'd make an ideal pastor's wife. Is this Becca girl even a Christian?"

"She acts more Christ-like than most Christians I know."

He shook his head and then continued his assault on my music collection. "That's not what's important." He started tossing more CDs into the trash bag, bypassing the process of separation. He stopped for a moment and turned around. He tilted his head and raised his eyebrows. "Have the two of you ever . . . ?" He paused and looked down at my groin area.

"Of course not!" I said. "Premarital sex is a sin."

He put down the trash bag. "Patti and I are glad to be able to offer you this place, but as I mentioned, this is part of our home. There are rules that we expect you to follow."

"What rules? No loud music after 10 p.m. No parties. That kind of stuff?"

"Those are obvious. You need to abide by special rules, given your situation."

"Like what?" I asked.

"First, we aren't comfortable if you have a visitor over."

I wasn't sure that I understood what he was talking about. "You're saying that I can't have a friend over?"

"You can have friends over. Just not only one friend. Girls don't count, but I don't think you should date this Becca girl."

Anger felt like sunburn across my shoulders. "Becca is the perfect person for me to be dating right now, and I hadn't realized that there would be rules for living here."

"You live in our house. You follow our rules."

He didn't say anything about rules before you moved in here! Is he renting you an apartment or is this a prison?

I looked around the carriage house. It was much nicer than I could afford otherwise. It had a newly updated kitchen and a small eating area where I'd been able to put our old dining table and chairs. The living room fit a sofa and a chair. It had a large bedroom with a desk and lots of bookshelves. It even had a walk-in closet. But still.

Pastor Hardy returned the stack of CDs he was holding to my CD tower. He also took *Phantom* and *Les Miz* out of the trash bag. "I think we've made some good progress today. You can keep your original cast recordings." He put his arm around me. "These rules are for your own good."

"I really appreciate all you're doing for me, Pastor Hardy. It's just all a little overwhelming."

"What's overwhelming?" Becca asked as she came back into the room.

"That was fast," I said. "Normally, it takes forever to print."

"Oh, it's gonna take a while," Becca said. "I just figured I'd come back and help you two out."

Pastor Hardy handed me the trash bag. "We actually just finished up."

This time, Pastor Hardy acted normal towards Becca. He held out his hand. "It was nice to have met you."

They shook hands and he left.

"Wasn't he taking that stuff to a party for underprivileged kids?" she asked.

The trash bag felt heavier and heavier, and I worried that one of the CD cases would split open the bag, and my collection of men's workout magazines would spill all over the floor.

My neck seized up, and I felt like I couldn't move any part of my body other than my lips. "To be honest . . . we weren't finished." I set the bag on the floor. I felt an immediate release from the weight. "Pastor Hardy likes you so much. He thought he should leave and that I should spend some time with you. Alone."

"So spending time with me alone is overwhelming?" she asked.

"No." My heart started pounding, and I had to sit down. I'd told more falsehoods in the past ten minutes than I'd told in the last year. I wasn't used to lying at this rate. I started to feel the hiccups kick in at the pit in my stomach. I didn't know whether these were caused by the lies or all the stress of having Pastor Hardy criticize my magazines, taste in music and choice in girlfriends. I couldn't do anything right.

"It's overwhelming going through all of my stuff," I said. "Reminds me of how difficult it was when we went through all of Mee Maw's and Grandpa's things."

One thing that did have me upset was the fact that my carefully organized CD collection was now in disarray all over the floor. "He misunderstood what CDs I said I was donating," I said, trying to explain the mess. I went over and started the process of re-sorting all the CDs.

"What can I do?" Becca asked. I handed her CDs to hold. "Ben, it's an adjustment living on your own for the first time, but I'm sure that Grandpa is doing well at Dogwood."

"I hope so. I can't wait to see him this Saturday." I spun around the CD tower and had the column of movie soundtracks almost complete. "Could you find the soundtrack to *Pretty Woman?*"

Becca looked through the stack of CDs, picking up a few that were covering the rest of the stack. She gasped, and then dropped them all, their jewel cases clacking on the wood floor.

All the color drained from her face, and she backed into the couch until she sat down. Her expression was blank. Her eyes stared into the distance and she crossed her arms in front of her chest and squeeze-hugged herself, rocking back and forth.

"What's wrong?" I sat beside her on the couch and put my

hand on her shoulder to comfort her, but she recoiled and moved to the other end. "Becca, what's the matter?"

"That was the movie. . . . That was the movie."

"I don't know what you're talking about," I said.

She looked at me and started crying. "*Pretty Woman* is the movie I watched the night I was raped."

I sat paralyzed. I had all this training in Christian counseling, but I couldn't think of anything. Anything to say. Anything to do. I was in shock and could only just repeat, "I'm sorry, so sorry . . . so sorry."

She stopped rocking and leaned in towards me so that she was right in front of my face. "I see him on campus all the time." I could feel her anger, like frostbite. "Every time I see him, he smiles at me. It's like he is oblivious that he did anything wrong."

I shook my head in disgust. "That just makes it worse."

"Right?" she asked. "I could understand if he cringed from me. But he just says, 'Hey, how's it going?' as if we will just get back together." She scooted back over so we were sitting side by side. She looked down into her lap. "Except for the fact that I've kept the earring, I sometimes don't even believe that it happened."

"The earring?" I asked. "What earring?"

"I forgot I hadn't told you the end of the story. A couple weeks before that night, he'd gotten his left ear pierced with a gold hoop, like George Michael.

"I told you that I had blanked out for the most part while it all happened, but I really just focused all my attention on his earring. Did it hurt when he got it pierced? Did he flinch when the needle pricked his ear? Did he feel pain as he got it done? It looked a little red still. I hoped that it had gotten infected.

"I don't know how long he was inside me, but at some point his pace quickened. He moaned, and I saw the look. I didn't tell you before, but I wasn't a virgin. I'd had sex twice before, and I knew when a guy was about to come. His eyes rolled back in his head, and his mouth gripped into a tense O. And all I could think about was not wanting to get pregnant. And he started to moan. 'Oh yeah. That's it.'

"And then all of sudden, I decided to fight back. I'd been staring at that earring so I reached up to tug on it a little. I thought it would distract him so that he couldn't come, but my anger exploded. Into a single burst. And I yanked the earring right out of his ear.

"He pulled out and reared back his hand, like he was going to slap me. But then I guess his ear hurt too bad because he ran into the bathroom. 'Get me some ice,' he demanded, but I couldn't move. Not even to cover myself up. He took one of my pink floral towels and held it to his ear. I was motionless while he put on his clothes, but as soon as I heard the door slam, I pulled all the covers on top of me and over my head. I just lay there for probably an hour crying and holding onto the earring."

She had been balling up her fist more and more while she told her story, and only when she finished did she uncurl her fingers. I looked into her hand, half expecting to see the earring, still bloody.

"Do you want to tell someone at school?" I asked. "I'm sure he'd be expelled or even go to jail."

She shook her head. "I've thought about that. Many times. But what is anyone gonna do?"

"We should go to the police," I suggested.

She got up from the couch and starting pacing. "It's he said/ she said. He'll say that I wanted it. And until the end, I really didn't fight him as much as I should have. I keep thinking I could have stopped the whole thing before it happened if I'd just ripped out his earring at the start."

I got up and stopped her. I wanted to hug her, but she pushed me away.

"Becca. You can't blame yourself for what he did to you. The guy is gonna get what's coming to him."

"But that's just it," she said, and buried her face in her hands. "Nothing's gonna happen to him." She started sobbing, and I didn't know what to say.

I wasn't about to tell her what I'd been taught as a Christian counselor: "Don't worry. He'll be judged in the next life." I wished that I could do something, but she hadn't even wanted to tell me who her rapist was, and I wasn't about to pressure her on that.

She was right: Nothing was gonna happen to this guy. And I sobbed along with her. I felt an emptiness like I'd never felt before. I wanted to go to the bathroom and throw up.

Nothing was gonna happen to this guy.

And he might even do it again.

14

September 28, 1991 (Saturday)
Ben

Grandpa had promised to tell me more about Ruby J if I brought him a new stone, but I was forbidden from visiting him during the two weeks after he moved into Dogwood.

Kevin had explained, "It's important for residents to develop their own place here in the Dogwood community. Without family and friends visiting, it encourages them to socialize more."

I had no doubt that Grandpa would be the unofficial mayor of Dogwood within three days, but I did heed the advice.

The morning after Pastor Hardy had made me throw away all my magazines and Madonna CDs, I'd gotten a muffin basket on my doorstep. Inside was a card from him and Mrs. Hardy that said, "Welcome to our home and congratulations on completing Step 2."

After de-gaying my life, I'd spent the past two weeks on HomoNoMo Step 3: *Ipsa scientia potestas est.* Translated from Latin, it means "Knowledge itself is power."

Step 3 required me to learn all I could about homosexuality. Every other day, Pastor Hardy showed up unannounced at the carriage house with another pamphlet, article or book on the dangers of the "gay lifestyle." According to all the information, the gay lifestyle had basically three stages. Sickness. Death. Hell.

I read about the devastating impact of AIDS in the gay community, and the increased rate of depression and suicide for homosexuals. After all the stuff I'd read, I didn't notice any reduction in my attraction to guys that I saw around campus, but I certainly had less desire to act on those feelings. I guess Step 3 had accomplished its purpose.

Step 4 promised to reduce my desires through the time-tested principle of negative reinforcement. I had to wear a rubber band on one wrist, and whenever I had an impure thought about a guy, I was supposed to snap the rubber band. Pain and same-sex attraction became one.

It had been two weeks since I'd seen Kevin, and I was so worried about running into him that I wore a rubber band on each wrist when I went to Dogwood.

My fears were valid because Kevin was hanging out at the entrance waiting for me. He was studying but put his textbook down when I got there. He looked up and smiled, but as far as I was concerned, he was Medusa, and I wasn't about to stare at him directly.

"Your grandfather said you were coming today," he said. "He said to tell you he's in the main rec room."

Kevin was about to get up, but I beelined for Grandpa, snapping both wrists each step of the way. By the time I got down to the rec room, my arms hurt so bad that I started to cry a little.

Grandpa held court at the main table. When he saw me, he came over to hug me.

"You miss me that much?" He stopped and wiped my tears. We walked back to the table together, his arm around my waist, and mine on his shoulder.

"Ben, meet my friend, Mr. McGee."

Mr. McGee wore a ten-gallon hat with a garnet hatband and a large black raven feather. He looked to be in his mid-seventies and had a tanned and weathered face like he'd spent most of his life outdoors.

"My friends call me 'Cowboy,'" he said, and tipped his hat to me.

"Nice to meet you, Cowboy. I'm Ben Stark."

I circled the table to look at their cards. Grandpa and Cowboy each held three cards, with a card face up in the middle and the rest of the cards down in a pile. "What y'all playing?" I asked.

Cowboy answered, "Your grandpa calls it Scratch the Queen, but it ain't no game I ever heard of before."

I looked at Grandpa's and Cowboy's hold cards, and couldn't tell who was winning.

"How do you play?" I asked.

Grandpa said, "The basic objective is to get two cards adding up to ten points that are the right suit to scratch the Queen you're holding."

"Who's winning?" I asked.

"Your grandpa," Cowboy said. "I ain't won a single hand. Every time I think I'm about to win, he teaches me a new rule."

Cowboy drew a card and then discarded the three of spades. Grandpa sucked in air through his teeth like Cowboy had just gotten a card that was either really good or really bad for him.

Grandpa picked up the three of spades, discarded a one-eyed Jack, knocked three times and then announced that he'd scratched the Queen. He turned over his cards: Queen of Hearts, Seven of Clubs, and Three of Spades. He then explained, "That Three of Spades you gave me along with my seven add up to ten points. Black cards scratch red Queens."

"No wonder you're losing," I said to Cowboy. "I don't understand anything he just said."

"A jungle buzzard outside of Augusta taught me this card game in 1932. I had forgotten almost all about it, until I saw Cowboy's plaid pageboy hat." Grandpa sat back in his chair, beamed and said to Cowboy, "Speaking of which, you owe me that hat."

"You're playing for hats?" I asked Grandpa. "Don't you have enough?"

"Ben, you can never have too many hats. They keep your head warm, the sun out of your eyes and the rain off your face. If you ain't got time to fix up your hair, you can just throw on a hat. You can show respect by tipping your hat or taking it off during meals and church. You can disrespect somebody by keeping it on and flicking the bill. It's a whole other language."

"It's a whole lot of bull," Cowboy said. He stroked his mustache and curled the waxed edges. "But I ain't that nonplussed. I never really wear that hat anyways."

"Wanna join us for a game?" Grandpa asked me.

"Y'all can count me out," Cowboy said. "I've got family visiting this afternoon, and I need to clean up right quick." He got up from the table. "The seat's all yours."

Grandpa started to deal, but I stopped him. I dropped the stone I'd brought onto the stack of cards in front of me. "You promised me a story about Ruby J if I brought you a new stone. I found this by the SJU lake."

Grandpa picked up the stone and studied it. The pebble was the size and thickness of a half dollar. "I like how smooth and flat it is," he said. "I guess the cards can wait. Let me tell you about my first date with Ruby J."

July 17, 1932 (Saturday)
Grandpa (17 years old)

Saturdays were short workdays for Ruby J, so she had arranged for me to pick her up in the alleyway behind the courthouse. During the workweek, the place was jam-packed with lawyers and their clients, but on the weekend, they wasn't nobody there. We was gone drive to a secluded spot near where I kept my best still.

In the two years that I had been bootlegging, I had never seen anyone on the dirt road that led to the birthplace of Turbo Stomper. Years back the road led to a good fishing spot, but during a heavy storm, the dam holding back the water broke and the pond drained. The coons and the crows had picked clean the fish so now it was just a dry bed of fish bones. Kind of looked like some abandoned architectural site. Or at least that's how I was gone explain it to Ruby J.

When the truth is ugly and a little white lie don't hurt nobody, a decent man will lie every time.

I'd only been parked behind the courthouse five minutes, but I was already worried she wasn't gone show. In that little bit of time, I'd gone through a hundred reasons why she and I couldn't date, but then I saw her. And none of them mattered.

She wore the prettiest summer dress you ever seen. It was

yellow as a canary and flowed like a choir robe. Now, I wasn't prone to nerves, but at that moment I felt my heart pounding in my chest, and I just knowed that she was gone be able to hear it when she got in the car.

I turned on the radio. I probably should have gotten out of the car and opened up the door for her, but it was 1932, and I could get arrested or worse if people found out I was going on a date with a colored woman. I didn't want Ruby J to think I had white-trash manners, but that was better than jail I reckoned.

She was wearing a wide-brim hat and a scarf. She always kept herself covered to keep her skin white-looking I think. And although she would normally have taken the hat off in the car, she kept it on. She had to scrunch her neck up so that her hat wasn't crushed.

We drove out of town, passing a couple cars, but no one noticed anything. I was speeding a mite. I think we was both nervous cause neither of us said much. Once we got off the main road and onto the windy dirt road, I felt more comfortable and tried to chat with her. She didn't say nothing, and I looked at her. She was green as a cucumber.

When you by yo'self and driving down a bumpy road for work, you don't really think that much about the way that your innards are being churned up. When you on your first date with a lady you want to impress, you really don't want her to upchuck.

I apologized and slowed down the car as we headed towards the dead pond. It was probably 90 degrees that day, with humidity about the same. I got out the blanket and basket of food my landlord had prepared. Between my nerves and the heat, so much sweat rolled down my face that I worried I might drown. But Ruby J was like a Tennessee morning glory, opening up to the heat of the day to show its radiance. Fine drops of perspiration made her glow, and the sun just made her all the more radiant.

I flung out an old olive-green army blanket. Now, for men, sitting in a chair or on the ground ain't a big deal, but for women folk, it's an art. Something that separates one class of woman from another. I've seen women sit in a chair with they legs spread so wide it's like they ready to give birth, and I've seen ladies sit with they ankles crossed like they waiting in a room right outside the pearly gates for Saint Peter to call their name and welcome them to Heaven.

You should have seen the way Ruby J sat. It was like she had strings attached to her from above, and God was slowly lowering her to the blanket. And once she was on the ground, she situated her skirt in the most demure way, covering her legs and even her ankles.

In that moment, I rebelled against a lifetime of teaching and preaching about how blacks were inferior to whites. They wasn't a white woman of any class who could have sat down like Ruby J.

I was sho 'nuff glad that I had spent the extra nickel and bought a block of ice because everything was still cold. I laid out pimento cheese sandwiches wrapped in waxed paper and some deviled eggs. I even had some tater chips, but they'd gotten so smushed they wasn't fittin to eat.

A bobolink sat in a white oak tree that shaded the spot where I had laid out the blanket and serenaded us with a couple of songs. I was so nervous I couldn't stop talking.

I started with my birth. I told her how even though Maw was pregnant with me, she still worked the fields cutting okra. She'd filled half her bushel when she felt a sharp pain and her water broke. She went under a maple tree and gave birth to me. She clipped my umbilical cord with the shears she was using to cut the okra. She handed me to a friend and told her she'd come get me in a couple hours to feed me. You see, Maw hadn't picked her full bushel so she wasn't gone stop or she wouldn't have got paid.

"You're pulling my leg," Ruby J said.

"I'm telling the truth," I told her. "Excepting maybe it wasn't okra. May have been tomatoes."

Ruby J laughed. That time it sounded like a turkey making love to a coyote.

And then I heard a rustling in the bushes. She hushed up real fast.

"Who's there?" I asked, but not loud enough for anyone to hear that wasn't five feet away. Had we been followed? Had someone been watching me sitting there with a colored girl eating a meal?

More movement in the bushes and then nothing.

I wished that I had a weapon of some sort.

Ruby J drank the rest of her Cheerwine and stood up prepared to face danger with a six-ounce bottle. "Who's there?" she shouted.

We heard more rustling in the bushes. A big black nose broke through. And then a tongue flicking back and forth. And finally, the horns and head of a cow. She started towards us and then mooed but it sounded more like a cry for help. She was in real pain. You know how you can just look in a person's eyes and know exactly what he's thinking? Same's often true for an animal. Well, I knowed that cow was hurting. She stumbled out of the bushes and collapsed. She just lay there, and I seen that she was giving birth, and the calf was breached. All we could see was its tail.

I had never helped a cow give birth, but Ruby J had growed up on a ranch. She comforted the cow and told me what to do. I tried my best to get that calf turned around inside and then get it out of there. Took us about two hours, but we did it.

I thought that only bad things would come from dating a black woman. But if me and Ruby J hadn't been on a date together, that mother and baby woulda died.

September 29, 1991 (Saturday)
Grandpa

When I finished my story, I picked up the stone and put it in my shirt pocket.

"That's a pretty cool story," Ben said. "I can't believe I've never heard that before."

"Like I told you. Hurts me a little to even talk about those days." I rubbed at my eyes. "I just wonder how things might have been if me and Ruby J had lived in a different time. I loved Lilly more than anything in the world, but each time you love somebody it's different. And I just don't think you ever get over your first love."

Ben's eyes went glassy, like he was gone, and he slouched over, like he had a heavy weight on his shoulders. I bet he was thinking about how he was gone find his first true love. I worried about that quite a bit myself. As much as I liked Becca, I knew that she wasn't the right one for him. I could relate to his predicament. I was in love with a colored woman at a time when it was illegal. I know what it means for society to judge you for the person you love. I wanted to say something to Ben, but I just didn't feel like I could so I did what I do best and changed the subject.

I shuffled the cards. "Now Ben, don't you get yo'self all six ways to Sunday thinking about things too much. Let me teach you how to play Scratch the Queen." I dealt each of us five cards and then told him a little bit about how to play.

What I didn't tell him was that the whole point of Scratch the Queen is to make up rules as you go along. But once you've set a rule, you can't change it, and you can't come up with a conflicting rule. Ben was smarter than Cowboy, so I had to keep changing the rules every hand. At one point, I got confused, and I saw Ben looking at me sideways.

"Let's just play blackjack," I said. Ben squinted his eyes and stared at me. He knew.

"No. Let's keep playing this game," he said. "I think I've got it figured out."

I chuckled and shuffled the cards, even adding back in the half dozen cards that I'd pocketed for when I thought I might need them.

Dogwood resident Mary Jean Stribling came in, and I introduced her and Ben. She sat at the other end of the table. She spent most of her time gardening, and I seen her out in the rose bushes earlier in the day. She must have just showered because her hair looked like a drowned rat.

"What card game you playing?" she asked, and unpacked her box of green rope, red wooden beads and the partially completed macramé Christmas tree she'd been working on for the past three days.

"Scratch the Queen," Ben said.

Mary Jean raised her eyebrows like she was trying to flirt with me, but at her age maybe it was just a tic or something. "I don't believe I'm familiar with that game." She unspooled some of the green rope, twisting the ends and making a knot.

"It's something a jungle buzzard taught him," Ben said.

Mary Jean's face contorted, and now I thought she must be having a stroke. "A jungle buzzard?"

"A buzzard is the person in charge of a jungle," Ben said. "A jungle is a hobo camp."

"I'm proud to say that I was a hobo for a couple years in the early part of the Great Depression," I said.

She pooched up her lips at me. "You were a bum?"

I pushed back from the table. "Now wait just a minute . . . ."

Ben put his hand on my forearm, trying to calm me down. "Grandpa, I'm sure she didn't mean anything."

"I was a hobo," I said. "Hobos are not bums."

"Hobo. Bum. All the same to me," Mary Jean said.

"You don't know the first thing about hobos." I raised my voice not only because Mary Jean is hard of hearing but also because I wanted to make my point. "Hobos are a noble people. Bums just sit around and do nothing, begging for handouts. Hobos ain't nothing like that. We wasn't lazy. We just didn't like to be tied down. We'd go from town to town looking for work, trading our time or things we'd made for a square meal."

"Hobos even have a code of ethics," Ben added.

"The cardinal rule," I said. "Live life by your own rules. Don't let another person rule you."

While Ben and I was schooling Mary Jean on the hobo code, Daleah Ashford had walked up to the crafts table carrying a large cardboard box. "I never realized I was a hobo," she said. She started emptying her box and spread out two three-foot by six-foot panels, one in a deep purple cotton duck cloth, and the other in a yellow poplin fabric. "I've lived my life according to the philosophy of setting my own rules."

A bit of the cloth fell into the area where Mary Jean was working, and Mary Jean pulled back like Daleah had just put a snake on the table.

"Well, I've always lived my life by God's rules," Mary Jean said. "Ben, I read that article about you in the paper awhile back. I know you agree with me. We all need to follow the Bible."

I saw Ben shift in his chair. "I do live my life by God's rules," he said, and cleared his throat. "But as a Baptist, I get to interpret the Bible for myself and decide what God's rules are." He smiled, hoping that had settled the argument and that we could all get on about our business.

Mary Jean started to say something back but she stopped when a man, either in his forties or later-seventies, came in and put his hands on Daleah's shoulder. He had thick brown hair like a young fella, but he was all bones and skin like an old person.

"I see you've already started, Nanna," he said, and leaned down to kiss her forehead.

"This is my grandson, Jon Michael," Daleah said.

"Grandson?" I asked. Up close, I could tell the guy was younger even than I'd thought, probably only about thirty-something. I squinted. He looked familiar for some reason. I got up to shake his hand. His fingers was bones.

I pointed across the table. "This is my grandson Ben," I said.

Ben got up but then just stood there like he didn't quite know what to do. The guy started to step back, but then Ben held out his hand. I had taught that boy manners. He better know how to act in social situations.

"I'm Ben," he said. "Nice to meet you, Jon Michael." They shook hands and then I noticed that Jon Michael gave Ben a look. Held his hand a second longer than I thought would have been normal.

"Hold on," Ben said. "You're Mr. Jon."

Certainly that couldn't be Ben's old dance instructor.

"Benji Stark!" Jon Michael said. "You've grown up so much that I didn't recognize you."

"And you've. . ." Ben stopped himself. He didn't want to say that he didn't recognize Mr. Jon because he'd lost fifty pounds and looked like a totally different person. "You've shaved your mustache."

Jon Michael rubbed his upper lip. "I shaved that about five years ago." He took cutout fabric letters from the box, and Daleah placed them on the yellow poplin.

"What y'all making?" I asked Jon Michael, and dealt the cards to Ben.

He hesitated for a moment and looked at Daleah. She nodded, so Jon Michael answered. His voice broke as he explained, but I could hear the courage in it. "It's a quilt panel for my lover. He passed away last month from AIDS."

I'd read some stuff about that sickness, and I knowed that it was terrible. And then I realize it explained why Jon Michael looked so bad. "I'm sure that your lover must be looking down from heaven and smiling," I said.

I was so focused on the other cut-out letters Daleah was

taking out of the box that before I had a chance to stop him, Ben had asked, "So what are you going to put on the purple fabric?"

I kicked him under the table.

"Ow! Why'd you do that, Grandpa?" I stopped dealing the cards.

Jon Michael pointed to the gold glittered Mylar letters J-O-N-M-I-C that Daleah had placed on the table.

"The other panel is mine."

Ben's face dropped like a stone off a railroad trestle. My heart sank in the pit of my stomach, and I felt so sorry for Jon Michael. Ain't nobody deserve nothing like that.

Mary Jean went back to doing her macramé with the focus of a surgeon, as if any distraction from her red beads or twisted green knots might cost a life.

"How are you doing today, Mrs. Stribling?" Jon Michael asked.

Mary Jean didn't respond at first so he asked her again louder.

"I'm fine," she said, "but all this chatter makes me lose my count."

She shoved her half-completed Christmas tree into a large sewing bag, scraped up her beads, and jammed the rest of the green rope into it as well. Some of the beads rolled across the table and a couple fell onto the floor.

"Here, let me get those," Jon Michael said, and started to help her pick up the beads.

"No, it's okay. Just leave them. I need to get going."

"Have a nice day, Mrs. Stribling," Jon Michael called out to her, and I really think he meant it.

She slung her bag around her shoulder and run out the place as fast as I'd ever seen anybody in Dogwood move.

I couldn't understand why Mary Jean wasn't more Christian in her ways. Her daughter came here every Saturday with her children, and that woman wasn't even married. Didn't see none of us treating her kids any different because they was bastards. The little one and I had spent thirty minutes playing peekaboo just last week.

"Let's get back to our game," Ben said, and shuffled the cards. After a couple hands, I noticed Mary Jean had rolled Harold Ritter from his room and was pointing him at our table. As we played the hand, Harold edged his wheelchair closer and closer. He'd put his feet in front of him and then shuffled them a little bit. Inch by inch, he came at us. Mary Jean stood in the corner of the room, and as Harold got closer to us, her smile got bigger and bigger.

Ben and Jon Michael couldn't see Harold coming, but I could. And he was mumbling something, but I couldn't make out what he was saying.

We finished up the hand and Ben won for the first time. "I think I'm getting the hang of it."

I was so focused on Harold that I'd forgotten to change the rules that time.

Ben picked up the stack of cards and shuffled. Harold rolled up to the empty space at the table where Mary Jean had been sitting.

"You want me to deal you in, Mr. Ritter?" Ben asked, and started dealing the cards.

Harold looked at Ben and squinted his eyes. He then turned his head to look at Jon Michael. "You a queer?" Harold asked.

"No!" Ben answered.

"I ain't talking to you, boy," Harold said, and started poking his bony finger into Jon Michael's arm. "You one of them queers with AIDS?"

Jon Michael moved his chair to the right so that Harold couldn't reach him anymore and grabbed some fabric, cutting it up into small pieces.

I wanted to say something. To tell Harold to stop. To say something comforting to Jon Michael. But I just sat there, staring at my cards.

The whole room got quiet, and then Ben pushed his chair away from the table. The scrape of the metal sounded like thunder on the tile. He went over behind Harold and rolled him away from the table.

"Where you taking me, queer?" Harold yelled.

His voice calm and comforting, Ben said, *"Wheel of Fortune* is on. You don't want to miss Vanna White turning those letters."

Mary Jean went over to Ben and was about to say something, but Ben held up his hand and stopped her. In a commanding but soft voice he said, "Mrs. Stribling, one day God will judge us all, but in the meantime, he does not need your help."

Ben rolled Harold out of the room and down the hall.

15

October 1, 1991 (Tuesday)
Ben

I hated Step 4. My wrists were to the point of bleeding from snapping the rubber band so much, and the worst part? Pastor Hardy said that I had to keep wearing the bands until I was cured of my same-sex addiction. The only good news was that I could go ahead and start on Step 5—Watch Sports.

That one seemed easy.

I loved sports, baseball in particular, and at least once a week, Craig Allen Vandiver and I would get together and play catch. We'd been friends since kindergarten, and we'd played high school baseball together. He had made the Lemonhead baseball team, and although I could pitch fast enough for college, I didn't have the required accuracy.

That Tuesday afternoon, we met up at the practice fields, and while we were pitching, we talked about the Atlanta Braves and how they'd gone from last place to within a few games of first.

"You gonna watch the game tonight?" I asked.

"Of course," he said. "If they want a real shot at winning their division, they've gotta do well tonight," he said. "Wanna watch the game together?"

"Absolutely," I said. "I just got my place in order. Would love to have you over." The words of invitation were out of my mouth before I remembered that I was forbidden from having just one friend over. "Maybe you could bring a friend or two?"

I was thinking about how to ask permission from Pastor Hardy in case only Craig Allen could come, but he interrupted. "I'm watching the game with some frat brothers at Troy Xanthus' apartment."

"I don't wanna go to a frat party," I said.

"It's not a party. Just some guys watching the game. You should come."

"I'll be there," I said. Watching sports with frat guys sounded very straight. Step 4 wasn't doing much to reduce my same-sex attractions, but Pastor Hardy would be proud of how quickly I was progressing through Step 5. After another half hour of pitching, I called it quits. I kept mixing up the signals, and when Craig pitched, I couldn't catch the ball. I couldn't stop stressing about what I ought to wear to Troy's and what I ought to bring.

What to wear? When Becca and I had packed up my old bedroom, I'd found the Hank Aaron baseball jersey Grandpa had bought me when I made the cut as a starting pitcher on our high school baseball team. It was one of my most treasured possessions. I wasn't sure if I should wear it to Troy's, but once I'd started wearing it for a couple of months while Grandpa and I watched games, the Braves had started winning. I didn't want to jinx anything so I decided to wear it anyways.

What to bring? Momma would roll over in her grave if I showed up empty-handed to a party. Becca had given me an oatmeal and chocolate chip recipe I was dying to try, but showing up with a plate of homemade cookies seemed a little gay, so I stopped at the Highway 29 Bait Shop to get some store-bought snacks.

The front part of the Bait Shop smelled of cigarettes and minnows, and I had to walk past two aisles of rods and reels and the magazine section to the snack wall at the back of the store.

A hundred different Frito-Lay products paralyzed me. I picked up a bag of plain potato chips, but then wondered whether BBQ chips would be the snack that would tell Craig Allen's fraternity brothers that I was definitely one of them and not a homosexual trying to pass as straight.

I was drawn to the red can of Pringles, but I realized that wasn't a good option. The name "Pringles" sounds like the name of a gay chip, made worse by their inherent neatness all stacked in that phallic can. Plus, with his twirly mustache, the Pringles man looks like a '70's gay porn star.

I picked up a bag of Ruffles and noticed that Frito-Lay had a 1-800 number for product questions. Would the woman who answered the phone be able to tell me what snack product would most strongly announce my undeniable straightness to a group of college guys watching a baseball game?

I put it back on the shelf.

My Momma's disapproval from the "beyond" notwithstanding, I had almost decided to show up empty-handed, when Jesus intervened. Grandpa always said that "God ain't a personal concierge service," so I don't ask for small favors. But it must have been a slow day because when I backed up, I knocked off the end-shelf a box of Cracker Jack.

The perfect baseball snack.

Gene Kelly and Frank Sinatra even sang about Cracker Jack in their 1949 MGM musical *Take Me Out to the Ballgame.*

I grabbed a couple large boxes and headed to pay. Walking to the front of the store, I saw Phillip Matthews, the Saluda Seminary student I'd met in Pastor Hardy's office the day I first sought help for my same-sex addiction. He was in the magazine aisle, and I almost didn't recognize him because he looked less like the hot swimmer I'd lusted after my freshman year and more like a guy who was dressed for shoplifting. He was wearing a sweatshirt and had the hood pulled over his head.

"Hey Phillip," I said. "What's up?"

He jumped a little bit, like I'd startled him. "Nothing." He held a magazine. It was wrapped in brown paper, almost like a safety seal that couldn't be opened until you bought it. He glanced at his watch and his brows furrowed.

"Am I keeping you from something?" I asked.

He gripped the magazine tight in his hand, crinkling the brown paper. "I'm late for a meeting. Wish I had time to talk, but I need to go."

He stumbled backwards down the aisle and put the magazine in the Home & Gardening section. He left the store without buying anything.

I stepped over to the aisle where he had put the magazine between *Southern Living* and *House & Garden*. On the brown paper that wrapped the magazine, someone had written in black Magic Marker, *Honcho.* I'd found a copy of that magazine in the Bait Shop parking lot a few months ago. It had naked guys inside with hard bodies and hard other things.

I could hear the blood rushing past my temples. What would Phillip be doing with a porno? I checked to make sure no one was watching, and then picked up the magazine to put it back in its proper place, in case some poor housewife found it when she went to buy *Southern Accents*. On the shelf above the magazines with the hidden covers, I saw familiar names: *Playboy, Hustler, Penthouse*. And magazines just dedicated to the letters those magazines got from their readers. I figured that they probably had a lot of complaints from people who actually bought the magazine for the articles.

On the bottom shelf were the brown-covered magazines. More black-marker titles. Copies of *Honcho* and then other magazines I'd never seen. *Torso. Inches.*

You should take a look. No harm in just taking a peek. It's really a good way to see if the therapy is working. You might not find them interesting. Maybe Step 4 is working, and you can stop wearing those rubber bands.

I grabbed one of the magazines wrapped in the paper bag and peeked through to look at the cover without opening it. Staring at me shirtless and wearing just underwear, a hairy muscly guy, early 20s. The bulge in his underwear undeniable. No wonder they called it *Inches*. I dropped the magazine and stepped back.

I snapped the rubber band on my wrist a couple times and then took another look. I felt a twinge below the belt, so I pulled the rubber band back so hard that I yelped a little from the pain.

"What's going on back there?" the cashier called out to me.

"Just getting some snacks," I said.

"Snacks are over in the next aisle." He shook his head and then went back to watching the little black and white TV he had at the register. My heart was pumping all my blood to the wrong place, and I put the boxes of Cracker Jack on the shelf and picked up the copy of *Inches*. I slid my fingernail under the edge and untaped the brown wrapper. I opened up the magazine to a picture of a guy with a hairy chest. He was nekkid. I heard the jangle of the bell at the front as another customer walked in. A cold wind blew right through me, and I shivered and dropped the magazine. The cashier looked up from his TV show again.

I picked up the magazine. The tape on the brown paper had adhered to the cover, and it ripped when I tried to pull it off. I couldn't put it back on the shelf that way. Plus, the cover was all bent. The other customer was heading in my direction so I tucked the magazine into the front of my pants. My Hank Aaron jersey covered all traces.

I grabbed my boxes of Cracker Jack and on my way to the front of the store, grabbed the latest *Southern Living, Southern Accents*, and a few hunting magazines to balance out the mix. I could barely look at the cashier as I set my items on the counter.

The cashier looked away from his program as he tallied up my total for the Cracker Jack and magazines. "Anything else?" he asked me.

I felt like he knew that I had the copy of *Inches*. I'm sure he could see the look of terror on my face. I was shivering. I took a deep breath. I wasn't about to add theft to my list of sins. "The other day when I was in the store I had some magazines, and I noticed when I got home that the clerk hadn't charged me for all of them."

"Was it Betsy?" he asked. "If she keeps making mistakes, I don't think I'm gone be able to keep her on."

"It definitely wasn't a woman. Look. Just charge me another $5.95, and that's what I owe you."

"You're a fine Christian," the guy said. "Most people wouldn't have said anything."

I felt less like a Christian than I had at any other point in my life, but I thanked him and paid for the magazines.

When I was in my car, I looked around to make sure that no one was watching and pulled *Inches* from my pants.

I sat for a minute before starting up the car. I'd been cold in the store, but having gotten away with my crime, my face burned like I was under a heat lamp. I turned on the A/C and just sat there in the parking lot.

You've got the magazine. You might as well just have a little peek.

I turned on the overhead light and was about to open the magazine when a guy knocked on my window.

I threw the magazine onto the passenger floorboard and rolled down the window. The guy bent over and put his elbows on the window. He was good-looking, with a muscular build, blond wavy hair and a close-cropped beard that was a much darker color than his hair.

He smiled, two rows of perfect white teeth. "Are you Chad?"

I torqued my body towards the passenger side. "No."

"Are you sure you're not Chad?"

"I'm certain I know my name." I don't know how I knew, but the guy was gay and somehow he knew that I was too. I had no idea why I didn't just drive away. Instead, I moved back towards the open window so that our lips were just a few inches away. "I'm not Chad, but can I help you?"

He stood back up and grabbed at his crotch. "I don't know?" he asked. "Can you?"

Taking the porn magazine must have started some chain

reaction because for a moment, I thought about turning off the car, getting out and going wherever with this guy.

And then I realized that "wherever" probably meant going behind the store or in the filthy bathroom. The guy must have written his name on the stall in the men's room, and whoever this Chad guy was had called him for a hook up. What was I doing? I rolled up the window and backed up the car, almost running over the guy's foot.

I peeled out and headed towards Troy's. My mind was racing with possibilities about what might have happened if I had pretended to be Chad, but with each thought I snapped the rubber band. The pop-pop sound finally drowned out the thoughts. But when I arrived at Little Sorrel Manor, a group of apartment duplexes near the campus, I had a pit in my stomach.

My evening had started off bad, and I felt like it was gonna get even worse.

I arrived at Troy's a little after 8 p.m., just before the game was set to start. On the front door, a sign on a cardboard pizza box read, "Party inside!!! Come on in!!!"

I could hear the announcer calling out the roster for the game. I wanted to find out who was pitching for the Braves, but Craig Allen stopped me at the entrance. He stood near the kitchen door with a red plastic cup of beer.

A tray of lime-green Jell-O shots accented the kitchen table. Less than a dozen were left. The counters were littered with tiny plastic cups with flecks of lime green still stuck on them and paper plates with pizza crusts.

"Ben, I know you don't drink," Craig Allen said, and pointed to the tray of Jell-O shots. "Those things have alcohol in them." I guess he thought I was really naïve, but he was right. Other than when my father would give me a sip of his beer, I had never had alcohol. People say that Jesus' first miracle was turning water into wine, but in my Greek classes, Pastor Hardy had taught that Koine Greek doesn't distinguish between fresh and fermented grape juice. As a Southern Baptist, we believed that Jesus turned water into grape juice.

"I saw some Cokes in the fridge earlier," Craig Allen said, and grabbed a shot.

"Hey, give me a couple more of those," a familiar voice behind me ordered. I turned around. It was Derek Ridge, Mr. Quarterback. I hadn't seen him since the retreat at Mountainview when he kissed me on the lips and then blackmailed me.

"Who's your friend here?" Derek asked Craig Allen, as if he had no idea who I was. I had to keep my lower jaw from cracking on the floor. Was he really going to act like we'd never met?

"This is one of my best friends," Craig Allen replied. "We go way back. Ben Stark, meet Derek Ridge."

"Could you hand me a shot?" Derek asked me.

I didn't understand why he didn't just get it himself, but I guess he thought he'd get a rise out of me. I could play his game. I picked up the whole tray and offered it to him, like I was a waiter at a cocktail party offering hors d'oeuvres. He grabbed a shot, stuck his tongue into the side of the cup and spun it around, loosening the Jell-O from the sides. He flipped his tongue underneath and freed the shot from the container. He sucked it down, and I watched as Craig Allen performed the same act. The smell of lime from the bright green Jell-O reminded me of Grandpa's Old Spice.

"Aren't you gonna have one?" Derek asked.

I hesitated for a moment, wondering how it would taste and how I would feel, but I needed to stay focused on Step 5, so I lied. "I'm driving, and I have to study for a huge test tomorrow." A small sin to keep me from bigger ones.

Derek grabbed another shot and made a point of cleaning it out with his tongue. He was definitely trying to mess with my head. I grabbed a Diet Coke and went into the living room. We watched the first several innings in horror. In the bottom of the fourth, the Braves trailed the Cincinnati Reds 6-0. The Braves scored a few runs after that, but going into the seventh inning, they were behind 6-3.

But then the Braves started playing ball. When they scored two runs, all of the guys were off the couch, pumping their fists, high-fiving and straight-hugging. I could see why watching sports was Step 5 on the HomoNoMo program. This was the healthy male interaction that I was missing. It was gonna set me up for Step 6 when I focused on straight-ifying my life.

For the seventh inning stretch, I went to the kitchen to get a bowl for the boxes of Cracker Jack. On the way back into the living room, I almost tripped on a long phone cord that snaked from the kitchen phone jack to the coffee table.

The volume on the television was turned down, and everyone was gathered around. Our host, Troy was bent over the speakerphone on the coffee table. He dialed, and a voice that was all too familiar to me answered.

"May I speak with Monica Greer?" Troy asked, but in a high-pitched nasal voice that sounded like Dana Carvey doing the Church Lady from *Saturday Night Live*.

"This is she," Monica replied. "Who is this?"

Troy said, "This is Nurse Cook from the Greenville County Health Department."

"What's this about?"

I wanted to tell Troy to stop, but I froze.

This is what straight guys do. It's funny. Just relax and have some Cracker Jack.

"I am sorry to have to tell you this, Miss Greer, but someone with whom you've recently had sexual relations has been diagnosed with gonorrhea."

One of the guys had to run from the room and could be heard laughing from the kitchen. I should have stopped it, but instead munched on some Cracker Jack and listened.

"Is gonorrhea serious?" Monica asked.

"Gonorrhea is treatable, but you will need to set up an appointment with your doctor."

"Who gave me this?" Monica's voice mixed fear with anger.

I wanted to stop it, but everyone was gathered around and snickering. This was straight male bonding.

Just think of it as getting an early start on Step 6 and straight-ifying your life.

"Miss Greer," Troy continued, "we cannot identify the person who gave us your name. On a confidential basis, we just take the names and then call those individuals and inform them."

"Well, how many people are you calling that this guy slept with?" Monica asked. I could hear her voice, getting higher in pitch.

Most of the guys were bent over double laughing. "Let's see. One . . . two . . . . three . . . four . . . four pages of names."

"Four pages! I am going to kill that Brad Abernathy."

One of Troy's friends was about to press the button on the speaker to hang up, but Troy slapped his hand. He gestured that he wasn't quite finished and mouthed, "Wait. Wait." Then he continued, "Ms. Greer, we need the names of everyone with whom you've had sexual relations the past three months."

"Is this confidential?" she asked.

"Of course," Troy said, letting his voice fall in its cadence a bit. "Of course," he repeated back up in the high pitch. "We need the name of anyone you've had sexual relations with."

"Does a blow job count?" Monica asked. A couple guys started laughing out loud, and that snapped me out of the fog I was in. This had gone on long enough. Step 6 could wait. I went into the kitchen and unplugged the phone jack.

"What the fuck?" Troy asked, looking around to see what had happened. I plugged the phone back in, went into the living room and stood in front of the TV.

"Call her back now and tell her the truth," I said. "Tell her it was a prank call."

"Don't come to my house and tell me what to do."

"If you don't call her back, I will," I said, and went for the phone.

Craig Allen stepped in between us. "Ben, just let it go. Calling her back would be worse. Then she would know that it was a prank call and that she just told a room full of guys she's the campus BJ Queen."

"Monica isn't like that," I said to him and the rest. I wasn't backing down. I pushed Craig Allen aside. "Troy, call her back and tell her it was a mistake. Tell her you just got notice that an entire batch of tests had been false positives and that you are so sorry."

"Or maybe I should call you again." Troy picked up the phone and pretended to dial.

"What?" I asked.

"Hey there," he said in a mock sexy voice. "This is Rick. You want to go out with me, Benji?"

For a moment the room went black, and then everything was polka-dotted. Lights flashed over images. Even though I hadn't had a shot, I felt what it must feel like. I was light-headed and dizzy.

Then I got scared. Who had been there when he called me? In each direction, a guy was laughing at me and pointing at the butt of the joke. My heart pressed against my chest so hard and my breathing became so shallow, I thought I'd pass out. I tried to recall what I'd said on the phone and remembered that I'd asked him where we'd go on the date.

Craig Allen stepped in front of me, and I realized that he thought he was keeping me from going after Troy. "Just let it go, Ben."

I knew that even with all my rage, I wouldn't be able to hit Troy. Violence wasn't my strong suit. Grandpa had always taught me that the better man never threw the first punch. He would always find a way out of a situation.

But I thought of Jesus and how he acted in the temple. Even Jesus got angry. Anger is not a sin.

Wiggling free from Craig Allen's grasp, I grabbed the bowl of Cracker Jack that was on the table just behind the couch and poured it over Troy's head.

Troy tried to stand, but then fell back down. He was drunk, but on the second try, he was able to stand. He feigned a punch, and I flinched. "That's what I thought," he said.

Craig Allen let me go, and I took a couple steps back.

"That's it!" Troy shouted. "Walk away, you little queer. You're not gonna do anything." He pushed his hands through his long hair to get out all the Cracker Jack pieces.

And that's when I saw it.

His left ear lobe. Split in two pieces. As if someone had yanked an earring out of his ear.

Troy was the guy.

The one who had raped Becca.

Adrenaline shot through my system so fast that I had lunged at Troy and punched him in the face and in the gut before anyone realized it. Craig Allen grabbed me and pulled me off.

Troy came after me and punched me in the stomach a couple times while Craig Allen was holding me.

"Stop it," Craig Allen said, and let go.

I fell to the ground and Troy screamed at me. "Get out of here, you faggot!" He started kicking me.

Craig Allen was yelling at him to leave me alone and other guys tried to get him to stop, but Troy was a football player and much bigger than any of them. I protected myself as best as I could and prayed that he was too drunk to keep going.

After a few more kicks, he stopped and stepped on my face with his bare foot.

"Who brings Cracker Jack to someone's house?" he asked. "What did you think? That there would be a ring in there?" He pressed his foot onto my face and then reared back with the other. I choked on the rank odor while I braced for impact. I closed my eyes and tensed my entire body. I waited. And waited.

And then Troy's foot wasn't on my face.

And he was flying across the room onto one of the sofas.

I opened my eyes to see Derek standing there above me. "Leave him alone," he said to Troy.

Troy jumped up off the couch and stood in Derek's face. As big as Troy was, Derek was bigger.

Craig Allen helped me up and took me outside. I had to sit on the steps leading down to the parking lot. The air was cold, but I was sweating. My stomach hurt, but I couldn't really feel the pain over my anger. My heart pushed so hard against my chest that I thought I would be able to see it. My ears rang, but I could hear Troy's deep voice saying, "This is Rick." I imagined that he'd used this same voice when he'd said to Becca, "You like that, don't you?"

I threw up on the sidewalk. The Diet Coke burned the back of my throat. I coughed up and spit out brown popcorn kernels. I wanted to go back inside and punch Troy at least one more time.

"You okay?" Craig Allen asked.

"I'm fine. I just need to get home."

He helped me to my car. I turned on the engine and cranked up the heat. On the drive over, I'd been listening to the pregame show, so the radio was still tuned to the Braves broadcasting station. The score was 6-5, and the Braves were up at bat. I backed up and was headed out of the parking lot when Derek stumbled in front of my car. I slammed on the brakes and watched him make his way to his car. He fumbled with his keys and couldn't get his door unlocked.

I pulled my car into a parking space just a couple down from him and got out.

"You okay?" I asked. He started leaning to the left, and I thought he was gonna fall so I held him up.

"I'm fine," he said. "Just a little wound up from all the excitement." He unlocked his car and plopped down in the driver's seat.

I kept him from closing the door. "Derek, you can't drive home."

"I just live nearby in Lemonhead Village."

"I can drive you," I said. "It's on my way home." That wasn't the truth, but I couldn't let him drive drunk.

He tried to start his car but couldn't get his key in the ignition. "Maybe I should let you take me home," he said.

On the drive, we didn't say a word and listened to the game. When we got to his house, he put his hand on my knee before he got out of the car. "Thanks for the ride."

"Thanks for helping me out at Troy's," I said, and put my hand on his. He pulled it away.

"I owed you one." He got out of the car and staggered a little as he walked away. I was about to back out when he turned around and came over to the window. I rolled it down.

"You wanna come inside?" he asked. "Watch the game?" It was the second time that day I'd been propositioned by a guy at my car window.

I should have said no again.

But your house is fifteen minutes away. The game will be over by the time you get there. Don't you want to see it! Plus, Step 5 is watching sports.

"Sounds like fun," I said, and got out of the car and followed him inside. I could still taste the combo of Diet Coke, Cracker Jack and vomit in the back of my throat so I went to his bathroom and used some toothpaste to finger-brush my teeth.

By the time we were settled on opposite ends of his sofa, it was the bottom of the eighth. When the Braves held the Reds and got a man on base in the top of the ninth, we started high-fiving and kept jumping out of our seats.

We watched the end of the game standing up and cheering and screaming. The Braves' right fielder Dave Justice hit a home run with one man on base, and the Braves scored their seventh run to put them ahead. The Braves held the Reds scoreless in the bottom of the ninth.

"I can't believe we won!" I said. I had pushed to right field everything that happened at Troy's and even with Derek at Mountainview.

The program went to commercial before the post-game commentary and interviews. And Derek turned the TV on mute.

"I can't believe we're alone together again," Derek said. He grabbed the back of my head and kissed me. But not like before. This time, I could tell that he wanted more.

16

October 1, 1991 (Tuesday)
Ben

I could taste the bitter flavor of beer on his breath.

"Let's go upstairs," he said, and grabbed my hand.

His bedroom was sparse. Just a mattress on the floor and two piles of clothes, one clean, the other dirty. He started to take off his shirt, but I grabbed his hands and stopped him.

I had a flashback to that moment at Mountainview where, the last time we went down this path, he mocked me and then blackmailed me.

He stepped back and took off his shirt. He sniffed the pits, folded the shirt and then tossed in onto what I assumed was the clean pile. I stared at his eight distinct abs.

My thoughts about everything that happened before were erased by one overarching concern. I hated my body.

He came over to me and pulled off my jersey. I could feel my fat one-pack ab. I crossed my arms over my stomach as I stood there in front of him. I backed up, but the temptation was too strong.

Don't worry about that. I don't know why either, but this guy wants you.

Derek kissed me again, and this time I tasted more of the lime Jell-O than the beer. Time slowed down. Our hands rubbed over each other's private parts, grabbing, squeezing. I'd never touched another guy's thing before. He moaned. A jolt of excitement shot through me. My mind blanked. Lightning stormed inside me. Nothing existed except that moment.

And then he asked, "What's with your wrists?"

I looked down and realized that my wrists were bright red. I took off the rubber bands and shoved them in my pocket. "Nothing."

Derek shuffled back, and I followed him. I was afraid to allow any distance between us because while our bodies touched, he couldn't see how unattractive I was. We fell down onto his bed, but it was not graceful, like I'd seen in so many movies. With his bed on the floor, I misjudged my positioning and kneed him in the groin.

"Ow," he said, and pushed me off him.

"I'm sorry. I didn't mean to."

He rolled over on top of me, and I could feel all 210 pounds of him. "You need to make it up to me."

He moved to the head of the bed so that his chest and stomach went past my face.

"Kiss it and make it better," he said, and then positioned "it" right in front of my mouth.

I closed my eyes tight. I couldn't breathe. I felt him pushing down his underwear so that his flesh touched mine.

I pushed him off and moved up to kiss him again on the lips, trying to make love like I imagined it should be: two bodies intertwining and folding into one.

But with Derek it was not like that. I was conscious of everything. The separateness of my body and his. Everywhere he touched me, my thoughts critiqued that body part. I had never realized how inferior I felt. I wanted to enjoy it, but my brain wouldn't shut off.

He tried to get me to do more, but I felt like he was rushing things. I wanted him to just lie there and let me take my time exploring his body. I wanted to find a way to enjoy this moment. I wanted to kiss him more, so I did. So much that his stubble started to irritate my face.

He kept trying to position me, but I was determined. For a while, we just wrestled, rolling over and over on the bed. This time, I was glad that his bed was on the floor because we kept falling off.

After a couple minutes, he stood up. "So, you wanna wrestle?"

I got up and ran at him like a linebacker trying to tackle him. He was the quarterback, so he easily moved out of my way and grabbed me from behind. He squeezed tight, pinning my arms to my body.

"Ouch!" I said. I was sore from my tussle with Troy.

He loosened his grip, so that it didn't hurt anymore, and I bumped him with my backside hard so that he fell back down onto the bed.

He leaped back up, and then came at me. He grabbed me this time and flipped me up so that I was hanging upside down. I could feel him erect against the back of my head.

"So, you think you can take me?" he said.

I was starting to feel the pain from where Troy had kicked me, so I relented. "All right, Mr. Quarterback, you win."

He rested my head on one of the pillows that had fallen off the edge of the bed and then lowered me down.

He lay down beside me, and for the first time since we'd gotten into his room, I felt comfortable.

We were in bed together, and in that stillness, I felt a connection. The desire that both of us wanted to be there.

But then the bed started moving. He was stroking himself, so I jerked off also. A decade of practice got me to the edge quicker than I had hoped, and I was getting close when Derek rolled over and got on top of me. Every muscle in his body stiffened. The bicep in his right arm looked like a baseball, and I could see the blood pumping through the veins in his arms.

Because of his position, I couldn't wank off anymore, so I moved my hands behind my head and just watched. A perfect patch of curly black hair blanketed the space between his pecs, and a thin black line went from his belly button down to his pubes. I reached up and starting tracing the outline of his abs. With his free hand, he moved my fingers up to his nipples. I circled the hair around them and started to put my hands back down. He grabbed them and moved them back up.

"Work my nipples," he said. I had no idea what he meant by that. I took my pointer finger and pushed on them like I was sending Morse code. This must not have been right because he kept saying, "Harder, harder." I started rubbing them, like I was polishing tarnish off silver, and that must have been more effective, because he started moaning.

"Oh fuck," he said, and I stopped. I don't think I'd heard that word other than on a Richard Pryor comedy record that Craig Allen's dad had.

"Jesus Christ, don't stop!" he yelled. It was one thing to be having sex, but to invoke the Lord's name in vain. I couldn't cross this many lines at once. I put my arms back behind my head.

It didn't matter because Derek grunted and then came. Before all of his stuff had even landed on me, Derek had jumped off and run to his bathroom.

I lay on the bed feeling him on my chest. I could hear the water running in the bathroom. I thought about finishing off, but the image of him on top of me jerking off had been burned into my brain. It was a visual I wanted to enjoy. I grabbed one of his pillows and buried my face. It smelled like sweat. Like he hadn't washed these sheets in a month, but I inhaled. The smell was intoxicating, and I wanted to savor it.

I would have lain there for hours and was about to smell his pillow again when a towel landed on my stomach. Derek was standing over me. He pointed to the clock radio on his dresser. "It's late," he said.

I took the towel and wiped off. "Could I use your shower?" I asked.

"I've got an early day tomorrow. It's probably better if you just go ahead and leave. There's a washrag in the bathroom. Just use that."

I went into his bathroom and found the washrag on the back of the shower door handle. It was still a little soapy so I rinsed it off in the sink and then used it to clean off my chest. I didn't look in the mirror because I didn't want to see my body. I wanted to believe that I was worthy of being with Derek. But I felt that even Derek realized the mistake he had made. I splashed water on my face to hide tears.

Derek opened the bathroom door and threw my underwear, pants and jersey at me. "Here you go."

He had on the loose boxer shorts like he'd had on when I'd first knocked on his door at Mountainview. He stood there while I dressed. I wasn't sure how to read the look on his face. He scratched at his chest and rubbed his chin. He shifted his weight back and forth.

Then I recognized it.

Revulsion.

He wanted me gone.

I swallowed down a bout of hiccups and splashed more cold water on my face. I dressed so fast that I didn't realize I'd put my sweatshirt on backwards so that the hood was in the front. "Goodbye?" I said, more like a question.

He had maneuvered around me and was scouring his mouth with his toothbrush. Dribbles of foamy Colgate ran down his chin. He looked at me like he hadn't realized I was still there. He spat in the sink and a "Bye" at me.

I went down the stairs and was almost at the door when I heard him behind me. I felt a sudden lift in spirits. Like he'd realized that he wanted me to stay the night. He was going to apologize for how he had reacted, and we would lie there beside each other until his alarm went off in the morning.

"Lock the door on your way out," he yelled and then went back to his bedroom.

Outside was much colder than it had been earlier. I felt a chill in the air and in my soul. I walked past a guy and a girl that I'd seen around the campus dining hall. They both stared at me, and I wanted to pull the hood over my head, but then realized it would cover my face. I almost did it anyway so they couldn't see my shame. I ran towards my car. When I reached into my pocket, I pulled out the rubber band along with my keys. I put the rubber band back on my wrist. I pulled it to the breaking point and then let it whack my wrist.

But it didn't work.

That night when I tried to go to sleep, I could only think about kissing him. The way that his stubble rubbed my bottom lip. My face was raw, but I cherished the pain.

Isn't that what you've always wanted? Derek is kind of a jerk, but remember how natural it felt. Right at the beginning.

And in that one moment when Derek had been lying next to me, in stillness, it felt natural.

But all I could think about was the pamphlet, *What the Bible says about Homosexuality:* to lie with another man is an abomination. I had a meeting with Pastor Hardy in the morning. I knew that I'd have to tell him, but then I worried that maybe I shouldn't. What if he thought I was a hopeless case? What about my dream of going to seminary?

I thought about the promise that I'd made to Mee Maw on the day she died. More than anything, she wanted me to be a pastor. She had been so proud of me. I thought about what she must think of me now. Watching me from up in heaven. Shaking her head in disgust. I reached over to the box of tissue beside the bed and wiped away my tears.

I'd given myself to Derek, and lost myself in the process. I'd destroyed everything I'd worked for, breaking the promise I'd made to God and to Mee Maw.

A cure never seemed further away.

17

October 2, 1991 (Wednesday)
Ben

Last night when I went to bed, the emotional pain from how I was treated by Derek was worse than the physical pain from my altercation with Troy. But when I woke up, I felt like I was gonna throw up. My body was scrunched into the fetal position, and I ached all over.

I slid off the bed, stumbled to the bathroom mirror and examined myself. My stomach had black globs with blue shadows. I was about to get back in bed and sleep for another hour, but my alarm went off. It was 8:15 a.m. I had an appointment with Pastor Hardy at 9 a.m., but I decided to call up to his house and cancel.

I opened my front door to see if his car was still in the driveway. It was gone, but there was a note taped to my door.

Where were you last night? You got in after 1 a.m. I expect to see you in my office at nine o'clock this morning.

Yours in Christ, Pastor Hardy.

I didn't want to go to see him. The physical pain was bad enough. The emotional pain from Derek was too much already.

I didn't need Pastor Hardy tacking on the spiritual wound of eternal damnation.

I picked up the phone to dial his office, but if I claimed an illness, Monica would tell Becca, and I'd have to cancel our date that night. Becca was cooking for me, and she'd been excited all weekend about having me over.

I didn't want sex with Derek to create a ripple effect of deception and disappointment.

I had no choice but to go and face Pastor Hardy.

It took longer than normal to get ready because the stomach pain limited my movements. I was ten minutes late to my appointment.

"Sorry I'm late," I said to Monica, who hadn't even looked up when I walked in.

"I almost called to move your appointment to this afternoon. We've had to put out a few fires this morning." She was organizing papers that she had spread all across her desk. I could tell that she hadn't slept much last night. Her eyes were red and puffy, and she was slumped, propping her head up with her hands.

I thought about telling her about the prank call, but Craig Allen had probably been right. As bad as she felt now, it would probably be worse if she knew that she'd told an entire room of guys that she'd had sex with Brad and given at least one other guy a blow job.

I sat down on the love seat and, after waiting for about five minutes, I asked, "Should I reschedule?" I tried to temper my enthusiasm at the prospect of coming back another time, but before she could answer, Pastor Hardy called out from his office.

"Is that Ben? Send him in."

I stutter-stepped into his office and stood just inside the doorway. Pastor Hardy was never someone who thought cleanliness ranked near godliness, but that day it looked like he'd been bombed with reams of paper. He hunched over his desk, focused on his work and didn't bother looking up over his reading glasses.

"I pray your day is off to a better start than mine," he said. His brow was so pinched together that the deep lines on his forehead looked like ravines. He made some notes on the pages in front of him. "We are announcing increased support from the South Carolina Baptist Convention, and I have three different drafts of the same press release." He rummaged through a stack of thin thermal fax paper.

"Monica!" he yelled. "Where's the fax we got yesterday from the audit committee?"

I still stood in his doorway, so she had to squeeze past me to hand him the fax he wanted. He skimmed it and scribbled notes in red pen.

"I hope the faculty rubber-stamps my proposal," he said, but more for his benefit than mine. "But the main thing is to get approval from the board of trustees." He finished marking up the faxes and walked them out to Monica. He barked orders at her for a couple minutes, and I thought she was gonna cry. I'd never seen him or her like that. I stood frozen in the doorway.

He went back into his office, and I thought about just running away. It was not the day to tell him about Derek. "I'll come back another time," I said, and started towards the outer door of the waiting room of his office.

"No," he said. "Come on in. We need to chat." He came over

and put his arm around me and escorted me to his office. He squeezed my shoulder, just hard enough to press against the bruises on my stomach. I flinched and pulled away.

"What's the matter?" He glared at me like I had a big scarlet H on my chest. "You look like Adam after he took a bite out of the apple. Where were you last night?"

I couldn't think of anything to say so I kept quiet. But three words rumbled around in my head, and I couldn't stop them before they had rolled down the back of my throat and across my tongue. "I had sex." I looked behind me to make sure Monica hadn't heard, but she must have walked down the hall to the fax machine. I shut the door.

I thought he'd be angry, but Pastor Hardy smiled and went to cleaning up the papers on his desk. "You and Becca hadn't had sex yet?" He sounded surprised.

"Wouldn't that be a sin?" I asked.

"Ben, premarital sex would not be the worst thing you could do." He pulled off his reading glasses. "Especially given your circumstances."

I was too stunned to respond. He'd been upset at first that I was dating Becca and not Monica, and now he seemed unfazed and maybe even proud when I told him I had sex. The lack of any disapproval in his voice made me angry. I couldn't believe what he was telling me. According to the Southern Baptist Convention and every sermon and Sunday School lesson, premarital sex was a sin.

I slouched in the wingback chair opposite his desk so that I felt the least amount of pain. My anger shifted into relief that he wasn't upset at what I'd told him, but then I remembered. I'd had sex with Derek.

He thinks you've had sex with Becca. Give him a high-five and walk away. You don't need to tell him about Derek. Look how bad his day has been already. He needs a win.

"Becca and I didn't go all the way," I said, which was the truth but also completely misleading. I felt like my heart was going to stop. My throat got so dry, it was like all the moisture in my body went to my palms.

"How far did you get?" He shifted his focus from all the paperwork to me and pinched his eyes together. "Third base?"

I shrugged. I didn't know what he was talking about. Third base? I wiped my hands on my pants.

"Second base?"

When I didn't answer this time, his concern became palpable.

"How can you say you've had sex when you don't seem to have done anything with her?" he asked.

"I'm not even sure what second base is."

"Then we will need to remedy that," he said. When he was deep in thought, he would tug at the couple of gray hairs in his otherwise white beard. I never could understand how he could tell which ones were gray and which ones were white, but he only seemed to pull at the gray ones. "Has your grandfather told you nothing about sex?"

"He told me stuff," I said, but I really couldn't remember a time when Grandpa and I had talked about sex.

"So you're not familiar with the bases?" he asked.

"Like baseball?"

He nodded.

I thought back and seemed to remember that Grandpa had told me the basics of intercourse, but it had never involved baseball. Grandpa wouldn't have missed any opportunity to teach me a point with a story. Especially one about baseball.

"Grandpa taught me about the birds and the bees but never about sex and baseball," I said, trying to make a joke.

But Pastor Hardy just tugged at his beard. "First base is kissing."

"Just any kind of kissing?" I asked. "Or does it need to be French kissing?"

He leaned back in his chair. "It doesn't really matter what kind of kissing."

"It would seem to me to matter," I said. "Kissing on the cheek or on the lips is very different from using tongue."

He shook his head, and clucked his teeth like he often did when he was getting frustrated with me. "Let's say that first base is kissing. Then second base is feeling a girl's breast."

"Through her shirt or does it have to be direct contact?"

His eyes got wider, and he snorted. "It's not important."

"You're saying that I don't know anything because my Grandpa never taught it to me, and you're not doing a very good job telling me what's what." I'd started to get frustrated with Pastor Hardy. I felt like he'd promised me a cure, and after I'd started seeing him, things had only gotten worse.

"Ben. I'm on your side, remember? I'm trying to help you."

"Sorry," I apologized, and meant it. I was blaming him for my mistakes. I decided to just listen and interpret the rules of sexual contact for myself, like how good Baptists read the Bible. "So what's third base?"

"Third base is touching each other's genitals. It can involve just hands or even oral."

I didn't say anything, and I realized that he was waiting for me to either tell him how far I'd gotten with Becca or ask him about home plate. But all I could think about was how to apply it to what I'd done with Derek. We'd gotten to first base before we'd even gone upstairs. And I'd rubbed his nipples really hard so I'd gotten to second base. I'd brushed his thing a few times and grabbed it and held it at one point, so I figured we'd gotten to third.

Home plate obviously involved intercourse, and we hadn't gotten there.

He grew tired of waiting for me to answer the question he'd implied, so he asked directly. "How far have you gotten?"

I was about to answer third base, but then I figured I better limit this to things I'd done with Becca. "I've gotten to second base with Becca if that includes brushing my hands against her breasts through her shirt."

"That's definitely not second base." He stood up and walked over to the window to stare out at Little Sorrel Lake. "Ben, this next step of the HomoNoMo program is a little unorthodox. And it's not something that I would recommend for just anyone, but it's the only way that I think someone with same-sex addiction can truly change. In order for you to straight-ify your life, it's time for you to get past second base and move at least to third." He pulled at three gray hairs that were just under his chin. "And in your case, I'm going to suggest that you even try for a home run."

I traced the thick skin of the scar on my arm and let his words reverberate in my skull. Everything that I'd ever been taught about premarital sex was being thrown out the window.

I was over the analogies and needed to hear him tell me outright. "At first, you didn't even want me to date Becca and now you're telling me you think that I should have sex with her?"

"Ben, I've talked about this with my wife, and she had a different view on your dating Becca. She reminded me that she wasn't a Christian when we first started going out. And we both agreed. It's more important that we cure you of your same-sex addiction. March first is coming up fast. You need to replace your unhealthy attractions to guys with normal attractions to girls."

He nodded, like he did when he felt like we'd accomplished a lot in a session, but I continued to rub my scar. The scar was so hard it felt like a pencil on my arm. I pushed at it, like I could make it go away. My head pounded and I felt short of breath. I wasn't any closer to a cure than I had been when I first told him I was attracted to guys. In fact, I was worse off.

"There are a lot of rules in the Bible," Pastor Hardy said, "but I like to focus most on what Jesus taught. He never said that premarital sex is wrong." He tugged at the gray hairs in his beard. "And in your case, it's something that you should try. I think it's the only way for you to heal your brokenness and become whole."

I left his office, more confused than I'd ever been. The President of the SJU faculty, my mentor and a role model for everyone on campus, was the third-base coach telling me to leave second, round third and go home. I felt a pain in my gut, but it wasn't from where Troy had kicked me. My entire value system was being called into question.

But more than anything I wanted to be cured. And in order to get to Step 7, I had to accomplish Step 6.

The list of sins I'd committed while on the HomoNoMo program was long and growing. I'd developed a crush on Kevin. Stolen a porn magazine (even though I did pay for it). Almost accepted a date with Rick. Nearly propositioned a guy in the Bait Shop parking lot. And gotten to third base with Derek.

But according to Pastor Hardy's logic, the score was still tied: Gay-0, Straight-0.

But if I wanted to straight-ify my life, I needed to score with Becca.

18

October 4, 1991 (Friday)
Ben

When I arrived at Becca's apartment, she greeted me with a glass of red wine. I jumped back like she was Eve handing me a bite of the apple in the Garden of Eden. I'd already decided that I was gonna need liquid courage that evening so I was prepared to drink, but Step 6 was straight-ifying my life, and sipping a glass of wine didn't seem all that manly. "Cheers," she said, and we clinked our glasses together. I thought about asking for a beer, but I feared she'd see through the request, throw the wine in my face and blurt, "Oh my god! You don't really want a beer. You're gay, aren't you?"

I took my first sip of red wine. It was bitter and made my mouth feel dry. I looked at Becca and smiled, and then realized that I was holding the glass by the stem, and my pinkie finger was pointing out like an old lady at teatime, so I gripped the glass and chugged the rest of it.

"Good shit," I said, something I'd heard people say in the movies about alcohol.

Becca stared at me. I don't think I'd ever used a cuss word in front of her before.

"Glad you like the wine," she said. "It's a California Merlot." She opened up the oven door. "Dinner still needs an hour or so." She picked up her glass and took a sip. "This is good, isn't it?"

We both smiled. It was that rare moment in a relationship. We were the only two people in the world that understood how good this wine tasted.

She put down her glass and moved so that she was standing just in front of me. I'd been so preoccupied with acting straight that I hadn't noticed what she was wearing: tight jeans and a low cut sweater top as white as a wedding dress. A straight guy would probably have commented on his girlfriend's outfit first thing.

"Don't you look sexy tonight," I said, but my words had no conviction. To prove I found her sexy, I leaned in and kissed her.

Her lips and skin were soft. So different from kissing Derek with his hard lips and stubble. I rolled my tongue against hers. She put her hands on my waist, just above the bruised places where Troy had kicked me. I wondered what it would be like to be with her in a sexual way and moved closer. Her hands lowered, and I flinched.

"What's the matter?" she asked. I wasn't sure I should tell her about Troy. I didn't know whether it would upset her. But I didn't want her to think that I had pulled away because I didn't want to be with her, so I opened up. While I told her about the prior night, she didn't say anything, but I could read her facial expressions. Her jaw tensed and her lips pulled tight across her teeth. Her eyebrows rose and lines wrinkled her forehead. Her face went blank and doll-like. She was withdrawing into her safe place.

I explained about going to Troy's house to watch the Braves play. How he'd prank-called Monica, but before she could detail her sexual history to a room of frat guys, I'd unplugged the phone. I left out Troy's prank call to me, but I told her I was so upset over how he treated Monica that I had dumped a bowl of Cracker Jack over his head. When he'd run his hands through his hair, I'd seen that his left ear lobe had been torn. And I'd known that he was the one. I went on to tell her about the fight, and by the time I'd finished, I realized that I'd made a mistake.

It would have been better to just let her think that I was pulling away from her in that moment. After I got through with the story about the prior night, a chasm had opened up between us.

I couldn't think of anything else to say, but then I had an idea. I lifted my shirt. The bruises looked even worse than they had that morning. Swirls of yellow, red and purple had added to the prior blue and black marks.

Becca's eyes refocused. Her face softened. Her lips pushed together. "You did that for me and Monica?" she asked, and approached me. She held up her hand to touch my stomach, and I stepped forward. She used such great care, but not just because I might be sore. It was like she could heal my wounds. And the warmth of her hands made me feel better. She put her arms around my shoulders, careful not to press against me too much. And she whispered in my ear, "I love you, Ben Stark. You're my knight in shining armor."

And then she led me upstairs to her bedroom, and I understood why she was ready to be with me, even after all she'd been through. It was the same reason I'd so easily followed Derek upstairs after he had rescued me.

She had loosened up, but I felt a tightness in my body. I'd never been with a woman before, and I wasn't sure how far Becca wanted to go. I stopped at the doorway to her room. I hesitated, while she removed the seven throw pillows, in patterns of pink and red roses with green leaves, from her bedspread of mauve and Kelly green. Her room was straight from a Laura Ashley catalog. Once she had stacked all the pillows in the corner, she lay back on the bed and motioned for me to join her.

I said a quick prayer and then heard the voice inside my head. *Step 6—Here you come!*

I lay down on other side of the bed, and we rolled over to face each other.

We kissed deeper and harder than we ever had before, and I moved my right hand up and touched her breast. I realized I was handling it like a bomb that might explode so I tried to think about them as if they were Derek's abs. I caressed her breast, and she moaned, in a good way.

I groped here and there, trying to get my hands on her body in a natural way. But I was conscious about everything. Should I touch both breasts at the same time? Should I rub her inner thigh? Are there certain places I should kiss her? With Derek I had wanted to touch him everywhere, but with Becca I worried that lack of experience would reveal my gayness.

She kissed my neck so I kissed hers in a few places. I thought about giving her a hickey. Physical proof that I did more with my girlfriend than just talk. Then people would know that I wasn't gay.

I went back to the same spot and starting sucking on her neck, but she grabbed my head and kissed me back on the lips. She pulled up my shirt so I did the same with hers. I touched her stomach.

She flinched.

"Sorry," I said. "I'm rushing things."

"It's not that. Your hands are freezing."

I held my left hand up to my face. My hand was like snow.

She doesn't think that you like her. You need to pick up the pace. Blood ought to be flowing everywhere in your body. Your hands are cold and you're not even hard. She's gonna think you're not into her. You need to prove to her you want her.

I rubbed my hands together and was going to start kissing her again, when she grabbed my right arm.

"Did Troy do that to you?" she asked. Her jaw dropped, and her eyes widened.

I sat up on the bed and twisted around to see if there were marks I hadn't noticed.

"Your wrists?" she asked. "They're redder than your other bruises."

Step 4 had been brutal. I'd never realized how much I thought about guys all the time, and my wrists bore witness to that. I couldn't tell her the truth so I tried to laugh it off. "That's just negative reinforcement," I said.

She was a psych major so she knew all about that. "And what bad habits are you trying to break?" she asked.

I didn't know why I hadn't foreseen that question, and I didn't have an answer, but when I'd turned around to look at my backside, I'd realized how much weight I'd gained since Mee Maw died.

"Just trying to stop eating so much," I said, and pinched my flab.

"I think you're just perfect," she said, and sat up beside me. She put her hand behind my head and pulled me in to kiss her. And this time, I stopped trying to kiss her like I had with Derek.

Everything didn't have to be hard. It could be soft. And I kissed her with a passion I hadn't realized I felt for her.

And then not everything was soft. It got hard.

Hallelujah! I got turned on.

That gave me hope that a cure was possible.

"I love you, Becca," I said, and then hiccupped.

"I love you, Ben."

Hiccup. . . . Hiccup.

"I always get hiccups when I'm nervous. Just give me a minute." I tried to stifle them, but that just made it seem like I was having a convulsion.

"Can I get you anything?" she asked.

"Just a glass of warm water."

I lay there while Becca went to the bathroom. I could hear the water running. Was I doing the right thing? Having sex with Derek had been wrong. If I had sex with her, would that be right or wrong? Or would it be wrong, but just not as wrong as sex with Derek?

Have sex with Becca. You pretty much got to third with Derek. If you want to straight-ify your life, you need to go all the way with her.

Even Pastor Hardy had told me that it was the right thing to do, and he and the little voice never agreed on anything. But deep down, I knew that I shouldn't.

"Two wrongs don't make a chicken a rooster," Grandpa had

always said, and even though I'd never quite understood the expression, in this case, it seemed to make perfect sense. I wanted to have sex with Becca, but not for the right reasons.

By the time Becca came back with the glass of warm water, the hiccups had stopped.

I knew that I wouldn't go all the way, but that didn't mean that we couldn't fool around. I felt her boobs. And not just through her shirt.

And then I went down on her. I had no idea what I was doing. It was just folds of flesh that I didn't understand, but she must have liked what I was doing because she moaned. A lot. She squirmed a little and tried to move, letting me know that she was getting close.

"That feels so good, babe," she said. "I don't want you to stop, but I want you inside me." I could feel the tremor in her lower legs, and I doubled-down on my efforts. I was going to finish her up. Better than giving her a hickey, I was gonna give her an orgasm. That would prove that I was straight.

She gripped the sheets and threw her hands over her head. She grabbed a pillow and held it over her mouth as she climaxed.

And I got hard. Very hard. When she had stopped writhing in ecstasy, I moved up to lie beside her on the bed. I started jerking off.

She lay there beside me, telling me how amazing I was. How great I made her feel. How much she loved me, but I really just wanted her to be quiet. I needed to focus and her voice was throwing me off my game. I wanted to hear Derek's voice. Kevin's voice. Even Rick's voice, even though Rick wasn't real.

I thought about giving up, giving her a kiss and telling her that

I needed to leave, but I wanted her to know that she had turned me on. That it had been great for me too. That I wanted her.

So I tried to think about her. About how her body had felt. About kissing her. But that made me start to go soft. I didn't want her. I wanted Derek, and I went back to fantasizing about him. How his muscles felt. The hardness of everything about his body. I started pumping it harder and faster and then I felt the buildup. Unlike anything I'd ever felt in my life. And then I looked at Becca, and I knew that I didn't love her. She was beautiful. And special. But she wasn't the person I wanted.

And then I couldn't get my concentration back.

I didn't love her.

And . . . then I just stopped. "I'm sorry. It's just so painful."

She pulled back and got a weird look on her face with her lips pursed together. "Painful?"

"My bruises. Where I got kicked."

Her expression softened, and she snuggled into me, careful not to press against my sore places. I closed my eyes and reached over and grabbed her hand. After about ten seconds, she rolled over, facing me. Our lips were almost touching. And for the first time since I'd stood in her doorway while she was lying on her bed, I was comfortable.

I took a deep breath.

The tension of the past couple days eased up.

I was about to tell her how nice it felt to be next to her, but she spoke first. "Hopefully, you'll feel better by Homecoming. I can't wait to go to the dance."

"What?" I asked. My tiny bubble of contentment burst and little bits splattered all over the room. "There's a dance?"

19

October 26, 1991 (Saturday)
Grandpa

For the past two weeks, Ben had talked about nothing but the Homecoming dance. And it wasn't because he was excited. The boy was all nerves. And I reckoned he needed to be worried. Lilly and I had chaperoned a dance when he was about thirteen, and I seen chickens scratching at meal bugs that had better moves than that poor boy.

But I had a plan. I was gone change all that. I'd talked Jon Michael into taking another stab at teaching Ben how to dance. Surely the boy had developed some coordination in the past eight years.

As anxious as Ben was about the dance, I was a mite nervous myself that day. I was gone introduce him to my new girlfriend at Dogwood. I'd been standing in front of my closet for ten minutes trying to figure out which hat to wear. Picking a hat is an art and a science. You got to balance comfort and style. Mighty Tim and Major Jack made me too tall for Viola, and Lucky Pete and Classic Stan didn't stay too well on my head when I was moving. I settled on Cowboy 1. It used to belong to my new best friend, Cowboy McGee, but I'd won it during our first game of Scratch the Queen. He'd asked me what I was gone name his old pageboy hat. I told him that I was gone call it "Cowboy 1," because it was gone be the first of many hats I'd win from him. That brag did me wrong because Cowboy has made a big point of strutting around in "Charlie 1," "Charlie 2," and "Charlie 3" the past month. I'd taught him to play Three-Eyed Sally and a couple more games I learned from my hobo days, but I reckoned Cowboy was a better cheater than me.

I'd just finished getting dressed when I heard the knocking on my door.

"You ready to dance?" Jon Michael asked, and he and Kevin tangoed into my room, holding each other cheek to cheek. Jon Michael's grandmother came in after them. Daleah wore a white and black Chanel suit and carried the boombox and had a handful of CDs.

"New move for you," Kevin said to me, and then dipped Jon Michael, picked him back up and spun him around.

"Y'all crazier than a rabid dog," I said. "You know if I tried to dip Viola, one of us would break a hip."

"You ready for your big debut?" Daleah asked.

"I reckon we ought to practice one last time," I said.

Kevin got the music all going while Jon Michael got into position with his left hand on my shoulder. I put my right hand on his lower back, and then we clasped hands, my left in his right. Kevin and Daleah got in a similar position. When I'd first tried learning, I'd started with Daleah as my partner, but it was too hard for me to figure out whether to follow Jon Michael or Kevin, and Daleah didn't know how to correct my form. So Jon Michael became my dance partner, which worked out pretty good. He was a great teacher and as frail as Viola, even if he was a head taller. To music from *Swan Lake*, we waltzed around the room.

"You've got it!" Jon Michael said as the song ended.

I smiled and gave him a hug and was about to give him a peck on the cheek, when Ben walked in.

His mouth dropped like a striped bass mounted over a fireplace. "What's going on?"

"We gone learn you to dance," I said.

October 26, 1991 (Saturday)
Ben

I looked at Kevin, Jon Michael, Daleah and Grandpa. I felt like I'd walked into an intervention where they weren't quite ready for me. I imagined that Grandpa and Jon Michael were gonna tell me that I'd disappointed them with my poor dancing ability since I was thirteen, and that Daleah and Kevin would interject how they were worried about me because I couldn't dance.

But no one said a word. I felt my throat close up, and I was about to just run out of there. But Grandpa was shaking his head.

Daleah ushered me over to the couch. "Let's have a seat."

I thought the intervention was about to start, but they had other plans.

Kevin positioned Grandpa's arms so that he was posed like a statue. Jon Michael fiddled around with the CDs and the boombox. Soon, I heard the opening strains of Madonna's "Vogue." Kevin grasped his hands behind his back and contorted his body so that his torso twisted away but he still faced us. Jon Michael joined them and stood in the middle with his back to me and Daleah. They all started snapping to the music. The beat picked up, and when Madonna said the first words of the song, "Strike a pose," Jon Michael spun around with his hands framing his face, and Kevin and Grandpa followed his lead.

The music got louder, and Jon Michael and Kevin performed a choreographed number from the video. With the precision of a drill team, they moved in sync while Madonna name-checked celebrities. Grandpa followed them as best he could with his own hand motions. Daleah laughed so hard, tears were streaming down her face. It was comical, but I found no humor in it. I was worried that I was about to be forced to join them.

The second verse started, and Grandpa came over and grabbed my arm. "Come on."

"Show us what you got," Kevin said.

I got up and followed Madonna's command to "Strike a pose," when a pounding on the door jolted all of us.

Mary Jean Stribling stormed in. "It's been bad enough, y'all blasting that 1-2-3 stuff all week. But I'll be damned if I will abide listening to this Satan music."

Grandpa went over and turned off the music. "Sorry, Mary Jean."

Mrs. Stribling was about to say something, when Judy, the Dogwood social director, popped into the room. "I could hear y'all all the way down the hall."

"We're just teaching Ben how to dance," Kevin said.

"The Homecoming formal is next weekend," Jon Michael added.

"And he's got a girlfriend," Grandpa said, and then either smiled or smirked at me. I wasn't sure which.

Judy bit her lower lip and stared at the ceiling for a moment. "We definitely can't let the poor boy leave here without knowing how to dance," she said. She scratched her head. "I planned an ice cream social for this afternoon. No reason why we can't start it now with a dance party."

"Well, you can't have it here!" Mrs. Stribling shouted. "Christmas is two months away, and I'm way behind on my macramé trees. Y'all make so much noise a person can't even think."

"I'm not sure she could think in a library," Grandpa whispered to me, and I tried not to laugh.

"Let's take this party to the auditorium," Judy said. "Kevin, go ahead and get set up. I'm taking Mary Jean back to her room and see if there's anything I can do to help with her work." Judy put her arms around Mrs. Stribling, who was trying to think of some way to protest.

Kevin grabbed the boombox and started firing off orders. "Ben, grab the CDs. Jon Michael, help me get things set up in the auditorium. Daleah, round up the usual suspects. And Charlie, why don't you run and get your girlfriend?"

I had picked up the stack of CDs, but then shoved them into Jon Michael's arms.

"You have a girlfriend?" I asked Grandpa.

Everyone froze at my question. I think they thought that Grandpa would have already told me about her, but he never liked to be proactive on anything.

"Mrs. Viola Chapman," he said. "She's the purdy black woman . . . works at the cafeteria. . ."

"The woman that almost spilled a pitcher of tea on me?"

"She's the one," Grandpa said.

"But Mee Maw hasn't been dead a year. Isn't it a little early?"

"Lord help, Ben. At my age, I might not have a year."

Everyone laughed. Except me. I did not find the prospect of Grandpa's imminent death amusing, but before I could say anything else, Grandpa grabbed me and dragged me out the door. His pace was quicker today than I'd remembered. I guess because we were on our way to meet his girlfriend.

Mrs. Campbell's room was in the other wing where the residents had smaller living areas and the furniture was all standard-issue.

When we got to the door, Grandpa knocked. "Viola?"

Mrs. Chapman was asleep in the hard vinyl chair next to her adjusta-bed. Whereas Grandpa's living quarters seemed more homey, hers felt like a hospital. Equipment surrounded her bed, and she had standard-issue furniture, all in vinyl.

Mrs. Chapman's wig had slipped down and partially covered her face.

In a sing-song voice, Grandpa called out, "Knock, knock, Viola."

This time, she stirred. She lifted her head and repositioned her wig.

"That you, Charlie? Let me get my specs on. You knowed I can't see a blame thing." Mrs. Chapman felt around on the table next to the chair. She put on her glasses and then reached up and grabbed my chin, turning my face so she could study my profile. "You and your grandpa favor so much, it's almost like I'm staring at a young Charlie." She chuckled. A laugh that started like a cough, like she had phlegm in her lungs, and then just petered out into a squeak.

"Let's git out of here, Viola," Grandpa said. "I got a surprise for ya."

She pushed herself out of the chair and went over to her dresser. She took off her wig and then put on a wig that had a hat already attached to it. Without the wig, Mrs. Chapman didn't have a stitch of hair.

Grandpa was so excited he was soon ten feet ahead of us, but Viola was moving a little slow. She grabbed my hand, and I escorted her down the hall, as if I was going to present her at a cotillion.

Kevin and Jon Michael had assembled a line of Dogwood residents, and they were teaching them some moves to MC Hammer's "U Can't Touch This."

We entered the auditorium, and I became the one moving slow. "Let's dance. I do like me this song," she said. Viola had to pull me to join the rest of the group. "Now, show me what you got."

"I've only got one basic move," I said. "Mr. Jon—I mean Jon Michael—taught it to me."

I demonstrated. Wide step to the right, follow with a step to the left, slight bounce and snap. Then step to the left, follow to the right, slight bounce, snap.

"Lord help us all." She shook her head. "You ain't got none of your grandpa's moves." She grabbed my arms and jiggled them. "You need to let loose."

She went over and grabbed Grandpa. He didn't care how he moved but was just enjoying the music. He bobbed his head and clapped a lot, but never on the beat.

"Now you see how good yo grandpa dance?" Viola asked me. "You gotta do that."

"I don't understand," I said. "My dancing is at least on beat."

"Child. You ain't getting my point," Viola said. "You can't just listen to the music like it's a clock you got to keep time to." The song ended and Kevin put on Crystal Water's latest CD, *Surprise*. The first track was *Gypsy Woman (She's Homeless)*.

Viola raised her arms up in the air like she was at a revival. "Bring all that joyful noise into yo'self." She pulled down her hands and then pushed them down. "Let the music flow out through the rest of yo' body."

Most of the residents got tuckered out before the song ended, but Kevin, Daleah, Grandpa and Jon Michael kept going.

Viola took my hand. She was frail, but her hands were warm, and she radiated an energy I'd never felt before.

"Now close your eyes," she said. "Don't think about nothing."

I shut my eyes and just focused on the music. Angelic voices. Synthesized music in the upper registers. I moved my shoulders and let go of Viola. "I think I understand."

I shook my hips and then spun around.

"Now you got it!" she said. She and Grandpa sat down in one of the chairs on the edge of the stage, but I kept moving to the "La da dee, la dee da. La da dee, la dee da" until I realized that Kevin and I were the only ones still dancing. I looked at him and he smiled.

I immediately stopped—dancing and smiling.

"Keep going, Ben," Grandpa cheered me on. "You're just getting the hang of it."

"Isn't it time for ice cream?" I asked Judy, who had rejoined the party at some point.

"I reckon we better shut it down before someone has a heart

attack," she said, and turned off the music. "Ice cream will now be served in the cafeteria."

The residents followed her to the cafeteria, but Kevin asked me to help put chairs away.

"You're a pretty good dancer," he said.

"Not really. Viola said my Grandpa is a better dancer than me."

"I've seen his moves," Kevin said. "Yours are better."

He grinned and I shuddered. All my energy had drained into my chest, and it was concentrating into a single point. Like I was gonna implode.

"One last dance before we ruin all this good exercise with ice cream?" he asked.

"There's no music," I said.

"I hear music when you're around," he said.

It was the sweetest thing anybody had ever said to me, but I had to get out of there. "Another time?" I asked when I should have just said no.

"I'll hold you to that," he said, and smiled.

We joined the others in the cafeteria, and I ate my bowl of vanilla ice cream, avoiding Kevin the entire time.

After the ice cream social, Viola, Grandpa and I ended up in his room. With all the excitement, he was worn out, so I suggested that we relax and watch TV. He and Viola sat on the love seat, and I sat in Grandpa's recliner. In a few minutes, both of them were snoring, and Viola's wig was about to fall off.

I kicked back in the recliner and closed my eyes. I wished that I could have taken a nap, but I had a lot to worry about the next week. Spirit Week was coming up, and I had to show up to school Tuesday in a dress.

People who aren't from South Carolina may not understand that Football is as important a religion as Christianity. And like any religion, Football has its own set of rituals. At Stonewall Jackson University, these included participation in Spirit Week, the holy week leading up to Homecoming. Each day had a theme where students had to dress up to show school spirit. Monday was Nerd Day. Tuesday was Cross Dress Day. Wednesday was Foreigner Day, where you'd dress like someone from another country. On Thursday you wore pajamas. And of course Friday was School Colors Day.

My ethics professor, Dr. Eisenberg, decided that Spirit Week would be the perfect opportunity for us to write about society's acceptance of deviant behavior, but only in the confines of everyone doing it. In three days, I was supposed to show up at SJU in women's clothes, and I hadn't even started planning my outfit.

Viola's hat-wig combo was lying on the pillow beside her at this point. I figured there wouldn't be any harm in just trying it on. I moved the recliner to its upright position as stealthily as I could. I crept over to her and Grandpa. Viola had shifted her position, and the wig was wedged a little bit between her and the end of the love seat. Inch by inch, I extracted the wig. She snorted, and I froze, not really sure what I'd do if she woke up and I was standing over her. But then she went back to snoring, and I had the hat-wig in hand.

I crept to the bathroom and stood in front of the mirror. I'd tried on every hat Grandpa had ever owned, but I couldn't get this hat-wig thing to look right. I adjusted it a little bit, checking myself out at different angles.

From my right profile, I realized I lacked the jaw line to make it work.

When I left the bathroom, Viola was awake and running her hand over her bald head. "If you wanted to try on my wig, you could have asked."

"I'm sorry," I said. "It's not what you think."

Viola chortled. "You can't tell this from looking at me, but I been on this earth for seventy-nine years. I don't bother to try and figure out people. Giving folks the benefit of the doubt will save you a lot of grief."

"It's just that we have this dress-up day at school," I said. "The guys are dressing up like girls, and the girls are dressing up like guys."

"Well, you should have just told me that. This ain't the wig you want." I handed the hat-wig back to her and she put it back on her head. "Help me up." She held out her hands, and I pulled her off the couch. She was so thin, the hat-wig doubled her weight.

"Ever since my chemo, I've had about every friend from my old church bring me some cast-off wig. I've got about a dozen for you to choose from. And maybe even an old dress or two. You may not believe this looking at me, but I was quite plump in my day."

I looked at Grandpa, who was still snoring.

"He'll be like that for another hour or so," Viola said. "Always takes him a little nap this time of day. Ain't he cute." She leaned over and pinched his cheek. His head shook a little but then he went back to sawing ZZZs.

"Let's us go on down to my room and we can get to know each other better while I'm helping you pick out a wig and a dress."

For a minute, I smiled, thinking about how funny it would be to waltz around SJU in a dress, a wig and a big hat, but then I remembered that Tuesday I had my appointment with Pastor Hardy. I had been excited to tell him that I'd gotten to third base with Becca, but my news wasn't gonna have the same impact if I said it while wearing a dress.

But then I realized that there was one thing that I could tell him where he wouldn't care if I showed up nekkid. I'd been through Steps 1 through 6. It was time for me to tackle Step 7, saying goodbye to my same-sex addiction.

20

October 28, 1991 (Monday)
Ben

Pastor Hardy had said not to rush Step 7. He said that I should only undertake that last step when I knew that I was ready. But I needed to say goodbye to my same-sex attractions. When I was with Becca that night, and I couldn't be with her the way that I wanted to, I felt like I needed to try my best to get through Step 7. I saw it as the only way for me to be with Becca the way that I should. I'd felt guilty about thinking about guys while lying there beside her. It felt like I was cheating on her, even more than when I'd had sex with Derek. I loved Becca, and I wanted to be straight. I needed to be cured.

From my nightstand, I got out the HomoNoMo kit and opened it. The plastic hinges were so worn that they had started to tear. I'd broken the first rubber band in a couple days, and I'd bought a bag of rubber bands that I kept in the box. The pamphlets had been so crisp and black and white when I'd first opened the box, but now the pages were tattered and marked up with red ink and yellow highlights. Pastor Hardy had given me another trash bag to put in the box just to remind myself to throw away anything that could become a stumbling block. I took all of those items out of the box and looked at the last remaining item. An envelope with SAME-SEX ADDICTION on the front. Inside was a set of instructions and some note paper. I needed to write a note to my homosexuality. A goodbye letter to my same-sex addiction.

> Dear Same-Sex Addiction,
>
> I want to thank you for teaching me to be humble. For showing me that I need Jesus in my life. That without him, I can't accomplish much, but through him all things are possible.
>
> It's been a long road. I remember how when I was eleven years old I would stand in front of the mirror, looking at my body. The pudgy round belly, skinny arms and chunky legs. I felt so terrible about myself. And then I saw "him" for the first time. Grandpa had bought me the baseball-themed special issue of *Sports Illustrated*, and halfway through, there it was. The Soloflex guy. He was sitting on the edge of a workout bench and was shirtless. His left hand held the wrist of his right arm, and he was flexing his biceps.
>
> I wanted to be like him.
>
> And I confused wanting to have a body like his for wanting his body. I corrupted things in my brain because of how I felt about myself.
>
> I wasn't masculine enough, and I thought that by being with a guy like that, his manliness would rub off on me. So my mind got messed up. Even though I knew it was wrong to look at those pictures, it felt right for me.

But I didn't want to be that way. I prayed for you to leave me alone. I read my Bible and devoured devotional books. I begged for forgiveness. Pleaded. But you stayed around. Usually in the background but sometimes you'd show yourself. Like at Mountainview with Derek. And then at his apartment. My feelings about Derek confused me even more. I wanted him so much, but he didn't care anything about me.

And you don't care about me.

You've made me feel so bad about myself that I've wondered at times whether my life has any value. I've believed at times that God doesn't love me. That he wouldn't care if I didn't exist. That no one would care if I just ceased to be. That the world would be a better place if I'd never been here.

So I'm asking that you go away. I need you to leave my life. There are so many things that you've done to put my life on the path to ruin.

You separate me from being the person I want to be, the person I need to be, the person I promised I would be. When I was thirteen, I promised God that if he would heal Mee Maw, I'd be a preacher. On her deathbed, Mee Maw made me promise to get help in fighting you, and I've kept that promise and recommitted myself to being a pastor.

You might say that I'm just asking you to leave because of those commitments. But don't you understand I've never felt like I had to follow this path out of obligation to that commitment? More than anything else in the world, I want to be a pastor. But how can I if you're there in my way? I need to have a wife and kids. You need to go away.

But before you go, there are some things that I need to tell you. First, thank you for helping me grow stronger in my relationship with the Lord. Thank you for helping me to understand what real struggle means. Because I better understand sin and the control it can have over people's lives, I can be a better pastor.

But I've learned everything I can from you.

I need you to understand that our time is done. I can't follow you anymore. My heart and my head and my body reject you. I don't want you in my life. I want you to leave. And I don't ever want to see you again.

No longer yours,
Ben

I took the letter and folded it in the envelope as called for in the instructions. I tucked the envelope into the passage of the Bible in Leviticus where the Word calls homosexuality an abomination. At that point, I felt like I'd been shot and gutted, and I was hanging from a tree while all my blood drained. I was so exhausted that I just wanted to crawl into bed for a week, but there was one last thing I needed to do if I was to have any hope of being cured.

I needed to pray.

I sat in the place that was most special to me, at the small dining table and chairs that Mee Maw and Grandpa had in their house for fifty years. I'd squeezed it into the tiny eating area just off my kitchen. I could see watermarks from the glass of cold milk Mee Maw had every night. I traced the scratches where Grandpa laid out his collection of stones.

I rested my arms on the table and prayed until I couldn't think of anything else to say to God. The clouds had darkened the sky since I'd sat down to write the letter, but after I finished praying, beams of sunlight streaked through the clouds, creating a halo effect, like God was speaking to me from above. It was a scene that looked like a poster that would be hanging in a Sunday School class. I took this as a sign from God that he was responding to my prayer.

Do you believe it's true that with God, all things are possible?

I took a deep breath and let this notion flow over me like water.

Isn't it possible that God made you this way? That he doesn't want you to change? That by trying to be someone you're not, you're dishonoring God's creation?

I shut out this thought. The voice in my head needed to quit. I sat at the table, trying to focus, but memories of childhood flowed through as if they were stored in the oak table. Like the rings of a tree trunk. I remembered sitting at the table listening to Brother Steve talking about being a preacher. And then hearing about Mee Maw's cancer. I remembered the day we got the phone call that she was cancer free. I remembered how every night she and I sat at the table and read the Bible together. But most of all, this was the place where I'd most often bartered Grandpa a stone for a story.

Now, sitting in the darkness, I let my mind become clear. And I made space for God. In my heart.

My breathing slowed. I could feel the air filling my lungs and going down into my belly. An energy coursed through my body, and for a moment, I was above my body looking down. And I could see a shining white light at the top of my head. And then I was back in my body, feeling the energy flow into me, healing my soul.

And then in the midst of all of that, I wanted to sing. And so I did. *How Great Though Art.* My life sounded like violin strains. And I heard the birds chirping.

I was cured.

October 29, 1991 (Tuesday)
Ben

I no longer cared about moving my appointment with Dr. Hardy to a different day that week, and I was proud to show up at his office in a sunshine yellow Sunday-go-to-meeting dress, a long blond wig with orange-can curls, and Viola's biggest hat, with a brim so wide it barely fit through doorways.

Viola had insisted I take that particular hat. "It depresses me," Viola had said.

"How can that be?" I had asked. "It looks like it's been attacked by a thousand canaries who left all their feathers behind, but it's not one bit depressing."

"I've worn it to seventeen funerals, and I'm ready to get rid of it."

When I got to Pastor Hardy's office, Monica wasn't at her desk, and the door to his office was closed. I caught a glimpse of my reflection in the glass of one of the photos on the wall. I looked like Big Bird dressed as Dolly Parton.

I changed my mind. I couldn't let Pastor Hardy see me like this, no matter how excited I was to tell him about being cured and getting to third base with Becca. I turned around to leave and bumped into Monica.

"Looks like someone is embracing Spirit Week this year," she said.

"Go Lemonheads," I replied and raised my fist halfway.

She had two armloads of folders. "Could you please help me?" she asked.

I grabbed one of them, and she made room on her desk for the rest.

"Is that Ben?" Pastor Hardy called from his office. "Send him in!"

I stood there, still wondering whether to just run away.

"Go on in," Monica said. "They've been waiting for you."

"They?" I asked.

"Pastor Hardy and Phillip Matthews."

I hadn't seen Phillip since I ran into him in the porno aisle at the Bait Shop. I figured this meeting would prove to be interesting. The wig felt a little crooked on my head, so I adjusted it and then stepped into Pastor Hardy's office like I was navigating a mine field.

"So how are things go . . ." Pastor Hardy asked, but his voice trailed off at the end, like he had answered his own question. He was behind his desk, and he turned his head to the side and looked at me like maybe he was just seeing me at a bad angle, and that if he just squinted enough, somehow I'd be wearing jeans and a Mountainview Conference Center T-shirt.

Phillip stood up from the chair and came over to shake my hand, a strong and assertive shake, very different from how he'd slinked away from me after I caught him hiding a copy of *Inches* in the aisle of Southern lifestyle magazines.

"I guess it's Spirit Week," Phillip said. "Great costume."

"And you chose to participate in this particular day?" Pastor Hardy asked.

"I'd like to ask why you aren't dressed up?" I sat down in the wingback chair next to the one where Phillip had been sitting. Phillip sat back down. "It's Spirit Week. As the President of the Faculty, shouldn't you be showing some school spirit?"

Pastor Hardy treated my question as if it were rhetorical and changed the subject altogether. "Are you wondering what Brother Phillip is doing here?" he asked.

"I assume he's here for counseling, like me."

"Heavens no," Pastor Hardy chuckled and replied. "He runs the Straight Path at Cavalry Baptist. They're the organization that helps . . ." Pastor Hardy paused and looked back and forth between me and Phillip. His gaze stopped on me. "He helps people like you, Ben."

"I don't need help anymore," I said. "I've been cured."

I tried to lean back, but the thick rumpled polyester fabric of my dress was uncomfortable, so I sat forward with my legs spread wide apart and put my hands on each knee with my elbows out, like a baseball player in the dugout.

I'd expected Pastor Hardy to push back on my announcement a little. I thought he'd question me or have even a slight bit of doubt, but he jumped up and came over to give me a hug. "That's amazing news!" The hat toppled off my head, and an explosion of yellow flowers followed when it hit the floor.

Pastor Hardy let me go and raced over to one of the large metal filing cabinets. He navigated through a pile of books on his floor. "I've been waiting for this day," he said. "I've got something for you." He seemed like a kid wanting to show his favorite toy on Christmas morning. It took him a minute or so to find what he was looking for.

I didn't take my eyes off Phillip. He wouldn't meet my gaze anymore, and after a while he got up to stare out the window at

Little Sorrel Lake. I'm sure he worried that I would "out" him to Pastor Hardy, but in the glass house of a dress I was wearing, I wasn't about to throw stones.

"Here it is!" Pastor Hardy exclaimed and came at me with a letter-sized manila folder. He grinned and pulled a two-page letter. It was addressed to the dean of the Saluda Baptist Seminary.

I skimmed the letter. Scholarship. Full room, board, tuition.

"SJU is gonna pay for me to attend seminary?" I was too stunned at that point to be excited.

"I've spoken to your professors in the religion department," Pastor Hardy said, "and we'd like to award you the Vandiver Medal."

Although I hadn't seen Craig Allen since he helped me after Troy beat me up, he'd been one of my best friends since kindergarten, and I was well aware of his family's charitable contributions to the school. The Vandiver Medal was given to the top student in the religion department.

"But shouldn't this be going to Monica?" I asked.

"No doubt her grades are better than yours," Pastor Hardy said. "But we're not awarding the scholarship to someone who doesn't want to be a pastor."

"She would love to be a pastor," I said, "but as a woman, she can't."

Pastor Hardy ignored my comment and launched into details about how the scholarship worked, but I wasn't listening. Monica was the smartest person I knew. It didn't sit quite right with me that she wouldn't be considered for the scholarship. He noticed my distraction and stopped the description of the benefits.

"Ben, you know that the Bible is very clear about the role of women in the church." He quoted 1 Corinthians 14:34. "As Paul wrote in one of his epistles, 'Let your women keep silent in the churches, for they are not permitted to speak; but they are to be submissive, as the law also says.'"

"I know the Scripture," I said. I wanted to challenge him: In 1 Corinthians 12:1-10, Paul wrote a diatribe on the importance of women covering their head when they pray, and I didn't know a single Baptist church that insists on that passage.

But I kept silent. I wasn't about to challenge Pastor Hardy on the inerrancy of the Bible, but getting the scholarship still didn't sit quite right.

Monica knocked on the door. "Pastor Hardy, you're needed immediately in the Trustee's Board Room."

"Sorry," he said. "I thought we'd have more time before the meeting. We're still negotiating the terms of the increased endowment from the Convention." Pastor Hardy grabbed half a stack of papers from his desk. "Monica, could you get the rest?"

She came in, and I tried to see if she was looking at me any different or if she knew anything about the scholarship. But I couldn't tell, and she and Pastor Hardy left.

Phillip closed the door after them.

"Ben, I need to tell you some things before Pastor Hardy comes back."

"Like explaining what you were doing at the Highway 29 Bait Shop?"

Phillip stood up and looked me dead set in the eyes. "I was there trying to recruit guys for the Straight Path meetings that I run. I slip flyers into the magazines that men might buy. Let the guys know that there's a support group for them."

I didn't believe a word of what he was saying so I stared him in the eyes, daring him to turn away. But he held my gaze, and eventually I was the first to blink. Maybe he was telling me the truth.

"I want them to know that the Straight Path is there for them if they want to change," he said.

"Who wouldn't want to change?" I asked. This thought hit me harder than thinking that Phillip might also have same-sex attractions. "Why would anyone not want to change? Who would choose these—I mean those desires?"

"It's not that simple. I've read all the scientific research I can find. There's not a lot out there. But there's no evidence that people can actually change. People can modify their behaviors, usually just for a short period of time. There's nothing to suggest that they can actually change the deep-rooted attraction to someone of the same sex."

This hit me like a punch in the gut, and I knew because I'd been hit there before.

"But I've been cured."

"Ben. This is where Pastor Hardy and I diverge in our beliefs on same-sex attractions. He wants to call it an addiction, but it's not a disease. There's not a cure. God made you this way. You can accept that or you can fight it."

"But I've been cured!"

"It may feel like that now, but the feeling is only temporary. I've seen it too many times."

I'd never felt such rage in my life. Not even at Derek when he blackmailed me, or at Troy when he beat me up.

I'd been cured.

I knew it.

"How can you know anything that I'm going through?"

Phillip plopped down on the window seat. Before, we'd almost been shouting at each other, but now his voice was so low that I almost couldn't hear him. "Because I used to pray to be cured," he said. "I used to be like you."

One part of me wanted to run to him and throw my arms around him and comfort him, but that would grant some credence to what he was telling me. I couldn't do that. Instead, I ran out of the office.

I was cured. I had to be.

And I would prove it.

To Pastor Hardy. To Phillip. And to myself.

After the Homecoming dance, Becca and I would have sex.

21

November 2, 1991 (Saturday)
Ben

For SJU Homecoming weekend, the alumni association had rented out ballrooms at seven different hotels, with each one playing different styles of music. The older alumni danced to '40s and '50s music at the Holiday Inn. There was a Beatles-themed party at the Ramada, but the biggest party was at the Howard Johnson's. Attendance at this event was limited to current SJU seniors and graduates within the past five years. Whereas the other places had bands, our party had a DJ spinning dance music.

When I walked into the Howard Johnson's all alone in my gray tux, I felt about as comfortable as I had in the yellow sunflower dress, Dolly Parton wig, and canary feather hat. I had wanted to pick up Becca at her apartment. It seemed like the gentlemanly thing to do, but Monica was getting a hotel room, and she and Becca and some friends were all gonna get dressed together. Their desire for a grand entrance meant I was solo. My silver lamé bow tie and cummerbund would have made perfect sense if I were standing next to Becca in her matching dress, but by myself, I looked like the geeky character in a John Hughes movie.

One of Becca's friends was operating a check-in table. "Have you seen Becca and her friends?" I asked.

"I don't think they've gotten here yet," she said. I put a twenty-dollar bill down in front of her. She handed me two soft drink tickets. "Hang out by the flocked tree to the left of where the DJ is stationed. I'll tell Becca to look for you there."

I started to walk away, but she called out. "I almost forgot." She handed me a golden ticket.

"What's this for?" I asked.

She pointed to a table across the way. "Don't forget to pick up your commemorative snow globe on the way out. The theme this year is Winter Wonderland."

I went over to the table and picked up one of the snow globes. It was a glass globe about the size and heft of a baseball. Inside, there were tiny models of prominent SJU buildings, including the bell tower and library. Etched on the glass was *Stonewall Jackson University-Homecoming 1991.*

"These are really nice," I said to the guy manning the table.

"Yeah. The yearbook company donated them. Sort of a payback for the screw-up with last year's yearbook where half the pages were printed upside down."

I shook up the snow globe and watched until the tiny bits of white plastic settled back down at the bottom. I put it back on the table and walked into the real winter wonderland set up in the ballroom. White plastic bits covered the entire room just like inside the globe. Strobe lights flashed our school colors, purple and yellow. Beats boomed. A song I didn't recognize thumped like a heartbeat. At first, it seemed like everybody was on the same vibe and dancing in unison. I envied them because they were so comfortable, but then I noticed a few guys who were like me. They bounced in place, moving only their shoulders and trying to find the beat.

Viola was right. The main thing was not to have any preconceived notions about how to dance. But just to feel the music. I closed my eyes for a moment and started to let the music wash over me.

I made my way over to the large tree to wait for Becca. For a few minutes, I did my old-school side-to-side toe tap, snap, bouncy head moves. But then a Madonna song came on, and I closed my eyes to get a sense of the beat. I rocked my hips around and tried another spin and accidentally kicked a girl.

"Watch it!" the girl's date yelled over the music.

"I'm sorry," I said. I turned my back on them and went back to my basic moves. Halfway through the song someone tapped me on the shoulder.

"I said I was sorry." I turned around, but it was Kevin. He wore a tux that looked much nicer than my rental.

"I'm glad to see you here," he said. "Where's Becca?"

"She's coming with her friends. You didn't mention you were coming."

"Some friends invited me last minute." He grabbed one of the guys who was dancing near him and spun him around. "Ben, this is David. David, Ben. And this is Stan, his boyfriend."

Over the music I thought that maybe I had misheard and that he had just said "friend." But the way the two guys were dancing near each other, you'd have to be blind not to realize that there was chemistry between them. I was surprised that they would be so open about their feelings for each other. Stonewall

Jackson University was a Christian school, and their behavior at its Homecoming dance seemed somehow disrespectful.

The music changed, and then a song came on that I knew. "You owe me a dance," Kevin said, and started dancing near me, like when we were at Dogwood.

Tiny hairs on the back of my neck stood up. Kevin got a little closer, and I could smell his cologne. It was woodsy and smoky.

Just one dance won't hurt. It's not like dancing with a guy is gonna un-cure you. Look how much fun his friends are having. You just need to relax. Practice for when Becca gets here. Better to stomp on Kevin's toes than hers.

Kevin danced a little bit closer to me, and I inched back as if an invisible force field separated us. But then he spun away from me, and I went towards him. I raised my arms over my head and danced closer to him. I wanted to inhale his smell. His friends had sort of circled around us so that we were dancing in the middle of a group. I felt a sense of lightness and freedom. And then . . .

I saw Becca. She made her grand entrance and moved through the parting crowds as if she were royalty.

Kevin turned around and saw her. "She looks like a princess."

Her red hair was teased up and sprayed, Pat Benatar-style. She was wearing a silver dress that was a little tighter and shorter than outfits I'd seen her wear before. The strobe lights started back up, making it seem like she was moving in slow motion towards me.

"You look amazing!" I said, a little too emphatically because I wasn't sure what she was gonna make of my dancing with Kevin and his friends. But she'd visited Dogwood a couple times, and she and Kevin had become instant friends.

"I love how your outfits match," Kevin said to us. "Your idea?" he asked me.

"Actually, it was Becca's," I said, but then realized he was just kidding.

"Thanks for keeping him company," she said to Kevin. "But I'll take over from here."

Kevin went back to dancing with his friends, leaving me and Becca standing on the dance floor.

She put her hands on my shoulders. "Ready?" she asked.

I nodded. She pushed my right shoulder back and then my left shoulder, and we repeated that for a couple of beats, but I was ready for more. I pulled away from her grip and then did a few hip swivels and bopped my head in tune to the music. The music crescendoed, and then the strobes started flashing like cameras popping off everywhere. The room went black, and then all the lights came on. I planted my right foot forward and then spun around like a Madonna backup dancer.

"Wow," Becca said. "Where'd you pick up those moves?"

I didn't want to tell her that Kevin and Jon Michael had helped me with these steps, so I replied, "Viola."

"What?!"

I yelled over the music. "You know Viola from Dogwood, she's Grandpa's new girlfriend."

"I love it," Becca said, and then she started busting out some new moves of her own.

We laughed and danced, and then grooved on to a couple more songs before the DJ went into a slow song.

"Time for a break?" Becca asked, but I wasn't ready.

I pulled her close to me. "This was what I was waiting for."

I leaned in and kissed her. She put her head on my shoulder while we danced in each other's arms.

This was what being cured felt like.

I could sense our hearts beating in unison, and I inhaled the smell of her hairspray and Beautiful perfume. I pulled her in even tighter and was about to kiss her again when she pushed me.

The shocked look on her face stopped me cold. "What's the matter?" I asked.

"Is that Troy talking to Monica?" she asked.

I asked her to repeat what she'd said. Not because I didn't hear her, but because I didn't want to believe it. My brain needed time to process what was being said.

She turned me around so that I could see. Troy was dancing with Monica. Becca had never told Monica why she had broken it off with Troy. That was her decision, but I should have told Monica that Troy was the jerk who had called her, pretending to be from the health department. I'd had the chance, and I hadn't done it.

Becca's face went blank. I could feel her slipping away from me, retreating into the void that was her safe space.

"Troy. . . . Monica . . ." she said, and then went limp in my arms.

Kevin was nearby, and he had been watching us ever since we stopped dancing. He saw that I was struggling, and he came over to me.

"What's up?" he asked.

"Becca isn't feeling well," I said. "Let's get her off the dance floor."

We helped Becca to the side, and I lost sight of Troy.

People stared at Becca. "Is she drunk?" one of her friends asked. "Is she okay?"

We helped her get to the entrance to the dance, and she was panting like she'd just run a marathon.

"I need air," she said. "I need air."

"Kevin, can you take her outside?" I asked. "I've got something I have to do."

Someone else might have asked "Why?" but Kevin just knew that I needed his help, and that explanations would come later. I watched as he and Becca went outside, and then I went back into the ballroom. It took some time to make my way through the crowds. The seas had parted when we took Becca off the floor, as if everyone could understand the situation and felt bad for her. But when I was by myself, it was different. I had to fight my way upstream. Excusing myself as I bumped into one couple after another, I finally made my way back to where Troy and Monica had been dancing.

I hadn't worried too much about Monica until that point. I'd just focused on not stepping on any dress hems. I never doubted for a moment that they wouldn't be there.

But they weren't. I didn't see Troy. I stood on my tiptoes, trying to scan the room for him. Nothing.

I felt my heart vibrate in my chest. Where could they have gone? Kevin's friends were still dancing in that area.

"Did you see a tall guy dancing near here?" I asked either David or Stan; I couldn't remember who was who.

"How tall?"

"Over six foot. He was dancing with a blonde in a sequined dress."

"That's not really narrowing it down," David or Stan said.

I looked around again, hoping maybe I'd just missed Troy or Monica.

"What does he look like?" I was asked.

And I knew that I had to say it. "Really good-looking. Muscular. Square jaw. Long hair."

"Oh yeah," one of their other friends said. "He pushed through here a couple minutes ago. Stepped on my toe and instead of apologizing, said something as if it were my fault."

"Where did they go?" I asked.

"That way." He pointed to the side of the ballroom. Not the main entrance/exit, but the doors leading directly to the hallway where the elevators took guests to their rooms.

Surely Monica wasn't going up to Troy's room.

I tried to decide whether to find Becca and Kevin. Would they be able to help me? Then I realized I had to go after Troy first. I needed to get to him before he had a chance to do anything to Monica.

I rushed over to the side exit and saw Troy and Monica getting on the elevator. I shouted Monica's name, but she didn't hear me. I couldn't stop them and had no idea what floor they were headed to. The hotel was six stories tall. I raced up the first flight of stairs and then looked out onto the hall of the second floor. I didn't see anyone. Then I went up the next flight of stairs. They hadn't gotten off the elevator on that floor. I was breathing heavy and went up to the top three floors, but they would have had plenty of time to get to Troy's room if they were on those floors.

I took the elevator back down and stopped at every floor in case they might be in the hall. But I'd lost them. Monica was alone in Troy's room and at his mercy. Each moment I couldn't find her gave him more time to do to her what he'd done to Becca.

I went back down to the lobby and found Kevin and Becca at the entrance of the ballroom. I could tell by the look on Kevin's face that Becca had filled him in on why we were so concerned.

"Where are they?" Becca asked.

I shrugged.

She grasped my arm. Rings of white rimmed her eyes. "Where's Monica?"

"They left the dance floor," I said. "They got on the elevator."

Becca usually withdrew into herself in times of severe stress. I'd seen it several times before, but this time, her nostrils flared, her brows pressed together. Short rapid breaths punctured her words. "We need to find her."

"Let's try calling up to his room," Kevin said.

"That's not gonna work," Becca said. "What are we gonna do? Ask to speak to Monica?"

"I'm pretty sure they're not on the second or third floors," I said, but after that I didn't know what to do. There were three other floors.

"Let's just ask the front desk for his room number," Kevin said.

"They won't give out the room number," Becca said. "When I got here, I asked for Monica's room, and they wouldn't tell me."

"We've got to find her," I said. "We've got to do something."

"We'll find her," Kevin said in the reassuring tone I'd heard him use with families of Dogwood patients. "It's still early so there's probably not too many people in their rooms. Let's start on the top floor and just go from room to room, knocking on doors."

"He's not gonna answer," Becca said.

And then I had an idea. I went to the clerk at the front desk.

"Could I get my room key?" I asked.

"Sure. I'll just need to see some ID," he said.

"That's the thing. My ID is in my room."

"Well, without ID, I can't give you your room key."

"Come on," I said. I pointed over to Becca. "See that girl over there? This is a special night for us, and I really need that key."

The clerk looked over at Becca, who was pacing back and forth and mumbling under her breath. She didn't look ready to go up to her boyfriend's room. She looked like she was fearful for her life.

"I'm sorry," the clerk said. "Without an ID, I can't give you the key."

"Well, could you just call up to my room?" I asked. At this point, I hoped that maybe I could see the number the guy was dialing or do something. "Maybe my friend is there."

"What's your name?" he asked.

"Troy Xanthus."

The clerk punched at the computer and then bit his lower lip. "How do you spell that?"

"Xanthus. X-A-N-T-H-U-S."

The clerk went at the keyboard again. "Is this a joke? We don't have you as a guest in our hotel."

I laughed out loud and shouted, "Gotcha! Made you look!" I turned around to where Becca and Kevin were. "I got him!" I yelled to them. I could see they had no idea what I was talking about, but at least the hotel clerk wasn't gonna call security on us.

I ran over to Kevin and Becca. "No luck. Troy doesn't even have a room here."

We all stood there. A pit of dread burned in my stomach. I tried not to think about how long Troy and Monica would already have been alone in the hotel room. How were we gonna find them? Where could they be if Troy didn't have a room?

And then it hit me. "They must be in Monica's room!" I said.

Becca opened up her clutch. "I've got a key."

While we waited for an eternity for the elevator and then took what seemed like the longest ride in history, we talked strategy.

"Let's just get Monica out of there," I said. "Troy can be violent. We don't want to engage him."

"There's an army of cops outside hoping to catch some underage drinker, so we can get them involved if we need to," Kevin said.

"I'll stay with Monica," Becca said. "I just hope she doesn't need a shoulder to cry on."

Once the elevator door opened, we ran down to Monica's room.

On the other side of the door, we could hear Monica shouting. "Let me go!"

Becca fumbled with the key but she was shaking too much. She handed it to me, and I unlocked the door. We opened it, and there was Monica with Troy.

Troy had his back to us. Monica was standing in front of him. He had pinned her arms to her side. "Now get down on your knees. Just like you did for Brad and . . . " He noticed that Monica was no longer looking at him but over his shoulder. He let go of her and turned around. The three of us stood in the doorway.

Monica ran over to Becca. "Let's get you out of here." Becca pulled her out of the room. Troy raced over to grab Monica, but I got in front of him.

"You're not gonna get away with it this time," I said.

I could smell alcohol on his breath and feel the heat from his body. "And what are you gonna do?" he asked, and laughed.

I was trying to think of something to say when he body-slammed the door, pushing Kevin, Monica and Becca outside.

I was trapped alone.

In the room.

With Troy.

Kevin threw himself against the door, preventing Troy from locking the deadbolt.

After a few seconds, Troy gave up with the deadbolt, and just latched the chain. They couldn't get in so he didn't care. He turned to me and started popping his knuckles. "Time to finish what we started."

He pushed me, and I stumbled.

Kevin, Monica and Becca had reopened the door but couldn't get in because of the chain.

"Stop it!" Kevin yelled as he tried to batter open the door.

Troy grabbed me by my lapel and pushed me back so that I landed against the desk. He was coming towards me, but then Monica and Becca started yelling at him to leave me alone. I'd hit my head and felt a little woozy. I tried to get up while Troy went back to the door.

He bellowed at them. "You bitches know that you wanted it! You just have to say 'no' because that's what's expected. It allows you to be the Madonna and the whore. I get what I want. A good lay. You get what you want. A real stud!"

Becca yelled, "You're not a stud! A real man wouldn't treat women the way you do."

"You want to talk about who's not a real man?" Troy asked

her. "How about your so-called boyfriend? Did he tell you about the time I prank-called him?"

Using his deep "Rick" voice and using a falsetto to represent me, Troy then acted out the conversation we'd had on the phone while Grandpa and Becca had been in the other room eating lasagna. "'Benji, would you like to go out with me?' I asked him, and then he answered, 'Oooohhh . . . sounds fabulous . . . where would we go?'"

Becca and Monica got quiet, and he shut the door and latched the bolt. He took a step towards me, and then another. It was like he was in slow motion.

My heart thudded. I started sweating. I could feel myself shaking.

Another step.

"I'm glad to get another crack at you."

Step.

"You come to my house, mess with my phone, attack me, and walk away to tell about it."

Step.

I felt along the desk for something I could use as a weapon: a paperweight, a letter opener, but it was a cheap hotel. There wasn't even a pad of paper. And then I saw it on the TV stand, and I grabbed it.

I wound up for a pitch, holding up my left knee.

Troy shook his head. "What are you doing? Some karate kid move?" He laughed, but only for a moment. From the pivot, I pushed off my right foot, rolled my right arm around, snapped my wrist coming over the top, planted my left foot down, and then followed through. The Homecoming 1991 commemorative snow globe hit him right in the groin, and he went down.

Hard.

And didn't get up.

I went over and undid the chain, unlocked and opened the door. I hugged Monica and Becca and held them until Kevin showed up at the room with a police officer. Troy was still on the floor writhing in pain. The police officer picked up Troy and took him away.

Monica went downstairs with them to give a statement, and Kevin said he'd better get back to his friends. Becca and I were alone in the room. She had picked up the snow globe and was staring at it. I went to put my arms around her, but she pushed me away.

"Why didn't you tell me about the prank call?"

22

November 2, 1991 (Saturday)
Ben

The fear I'd felt being alone in the hotel room with Troy was less than what I felt now. I didn't respond to her question at first, so she asked me again. "What did he mean about your wanting to go on a date with him?"

"Nothing." I put my hands on her shoulders and looked her in the eyes. "He prank-called me, and he used that really sexy deep voice . . ." I stopped and realized that I shouldn't have characterized it as "sexy." I felt the hiccups coming on. My voice was shaking. *Hiccup. Hiccup.* I tried to continue. "He asked me out on a date. *Hiccup.* I told him that I wasn't like that."

She put her arms around me and hugged me. "You're the type of guy that I could see spending the rest of my life with." She stepped back but held onto my shoulders. "You're gentle and kind and not like any guy I've ever dated, but I don't know. I just feel like there's something you're not telling me."

"*Hiccup.* I need to get some water," I said, and went to the bathroom. A bottle of tequila rested on the counter, and I took a big gulp. I think paint thinner would have gone down easier on my throat, but it stopped the hiccups. Becca had taken off her high heels and was lying on the bed. I lay down on the bed beside her.

I was looking up at the ceiling when I said, "I love you, Becca."

"I love you too, Ben." She rolled over on her side so that she was facing me. "But I feel you're not being honest with me. From the moment we met, I've told you everything about myself, about my past, about Troy. Why didn't you tell me about the prank call from Troy?"

I rolled over to face her. This was my chance. If I didn't tell her about my same-sex attraction now, then I would never be able to tell her in the future. She would always look back to this moment and question why I didn't tell her. And if I didn't tell her, I would have to live my life always knowing that I was lying to her. I sat up on the edge of the bed.

"I had a disease," I said. "But I'm cured now."

"What?" She got up and went to stand in front of me.

I could see her mind racing, thinking back to any point in our relationship or in any discussions we'd had. Any hints that I might have something wrong with me.

"Was it an STD? Were you the one with gonorrhea?"

"It wasn't gonorrhea," I said. I got up off the bed and paced the room. I wasn't sure how to tell her or if she'd understand. I just knew that I had to tell her. "I had a same-sex addiction."

"What? What does that mean?"

I didn't want to say the word she needed to hear to understand. I never liked framing myself in those terms. But I knew that I had to say it. "I'm gay."

"What?" Becca asked. Time slowed to a pace like an hourglass dropping grains of sand one at a time.

And then I realized that wasn't what I wanted to say at all. "I mean, I'm not gay. I used to be, but I was cured. I no longer have a sinful attraction to guys."

"I cannot believe this." She laughed but just a burst, like it came from a rifle. "You're gay?" She dug her fists into her hair and tugged, pulling her auburn curls into her face. She doubled over on the side of the bed like she was gonna throw up.

"Not anymore. I was cured so I'm not gay." I got up to comfort her, but before I could put my hand on her shoulder, she slapped it away.

"Don't touch me!" she screamed, and stumbled back from me. "How could you lie to me like this? Pretend to be in a relationship with me?"

"I'm not pretending anymore. I've changed," I said.

The color drained from her face. I could see the look in her eyes. The same one that she had when she first told me about her rape. "So you're using me just like Troy."

"What?"

"Taking from me what you need, and discarding me when you're done."

"No. It's not like that at all. I love you."

And then she slapped me, hard across the face. "Don't you dare say that to me." She sat down on the edge of her bed and started crying.

I wasn't sure whether to stay and comfort her or run away. Or throw up.

I was starting to feel the tequila I'd drunk, and the room

was spinning. I didn't get a chance to do anything before Monica came in through the door.

"They're taking him away in handcuffs!" she announced, and gave us a thumbs up. But her arms dropped to her sides when she saw Becca. "What happened?

Becca pointed at me.

The initial sting from where Becca had slapped me faded, and I felt a red warm burn on the left side of my face. And tingly from the tequila.

"Ben, what did you do to her?" Monica yelled, and when I didn't answer, she charged at me. I could see the red blood vessels streaking across the whites of her eyes. I pulled back and held up my hands, like I was a kid playing dodgeball.

"I didn't touch her," I said. "I swear. I just told her something."

She grabbed me by the shoulders. "Why is your face so red?"

"Becca slapped me," I said, "and I might have had something to drink."

I wiggled out from her grip.

"Ben. You need to tell me what happened. And don't lie to me. Or I'll go back downstairs and get an officer to come up and arrest you."

My breathing stopped, and my face felt like someone was holding an iron to it. I looked over at Becca, and she got up off the bed and came towards me.

"He's gay," Becca said.

"I'm not gay," I said. "I've got same-sex something . . . addiraction"

"What are you saying?" Monica asked.

"He's got same-sex addiction or attraction or whatever he wants to call it."

Monica smiled like she'd figured out something that had bothered her for a while. "I knew there was something," she said. "I never expected that, though." She seemed satisfied. A mystery solved.

"And he's been using me to try to make himself straight," Becca said.

Monica turned to me and shook her head. "Wow. Ben Stark is gay."

"I'm not gay," I said, and the room spun faster.

"Ben, you think that you can change who you are?" Monica said. "That through some Christian counseling and prayer, that you can make yourself straight?"

"But Pastor Hardy cured me!"

"Pastor Hardy couldn't even cure his own son," Monica said.

"How do you know that?" I asked, and the spinning stopped. Even through the haze of the alcohol, my focus had become razor-sharp.

"I know everything that goes on at SJU," she said. "Or at least I thought I did until today."

I grabbed Monica by the shoulders. "Promise me you won't say anything around campus about me," I said. "Promise me."

"Don't worry. I know people think I can't keep a secret, but I've only told about one-tenth the things I know."

I stepped around Monica and went to Becca, but she pulled away. "I'm s-s-s-sorry, Becca. I understand if you need time."

And then Becca started laughing, like she'd never heard anything funnier in her life. I froze, unsure what to do, until she continued, "Ben, we don't need time. We're done. I'm not gonna continue to date you. Where do you think this will lead? Marriage? Kids? You leaving us for some guy that you picked up at the gym?"

I wanted to slap my hands onto my ears so that I didn't hear what she was saying. That couldn't be right. I wouldn't do that to her. To our kids. I had to get out of there.

I ran to the elevator. How could Becca not support me? I'd been there when she needed me. I had helped her deal with all of the Troy stuff. As much as I could.

Why couldn't she at least be a friend?

Did I even have friends anymore?

And then I realized that I did have one friend nearby. Someone who cared for me. And I cared for him.

I needed to find Kevin.

23

December 28, 1991 (Saturday)
Grandpa

I'd seen Ben at the lowest points in his life. After his dad abandoned him, after his mother died, and during Lilly's cancer. But I had never seen him as depressed as he was after Becca broke up with him.

I felt bad because I was having the time of my life. Viola and I was seeing each other six times a week (her idea to have a day apart). We even had a real date every Wednesday night, when Judy planned a trip to the movies or some other social outing. It was like we'd knowed each other for years, and I couldn't believe that I had found love again.

But I just couldn't be happy while Ben was so down. I needed to cheer him up.

I had thought Christmas would improve his mood. I got him a baseball signed by twenty-seven Braves' players on their World Series team, but he just looked at it and then went back to watching TV.

I tried to get him to join us for caroling. He loved singing, but he wouldn't budge from my couch.

Ben was in a pure-T funk, and they was nothing I could do to help.

My next big idea was to take him to see the 1976 version of the movie *King Kong*.

Ben and I had seen the movie before, on Christmas Eve in 1976. Ben's mom was in her own state of depression because her bum husband had walked out during Thanksgiving dinner, and she had ruined Christmas for poor Benji. But after seeing *King Kong*, Ben's whole mood changed. For weeks afterwards, all he could talk about was how the big ape had jumped from one tower of the World Trade Center to the other, and about how the whole thing looked so real. It had been a turning point for him in getting over his dad, and I hoped that fifteen years later, the movie would work its magic again.

Yep, Ben was smarting because Becca had broken up with him, but as much as I liked the gal, I knew that she wasn't right for him. For that matter, I didn't think Ben was gone be happy with any girl. I wanted to say something to him, but it felt like a betrayal to Lilly for me to talk to him about this. She'd wanted me to talk to him eight years ago, and I hadn't done it then, so it didn't feel right for me to have a conversation now. Ben would have to sort this one out on his own, and I had to support whatever choice he made.

But just because I'd decided I wasn't gone talk to him about it, that didn't mean I couldn't help things along a little bit. And that's why I'd invited Kevin to join us for the movie.

I'd heard from Jon Michael that after Becca broke up with Ben at the Homecoming dance, Ben had gone down to find Kevin, and that they'd danced a little bit together. Word had it that Ben was enjoying hisself.

Because Becca was no longer in the picture, Ben had been visiting me more often, and he and Kevin was spending a lot more time together. But they'd never gone on a proper date. I was gone change that.

I checked the clock on my VCR. Ben was gone be here in about ten minutes, and I needed to make sure Viola was about ready. Usually, she was pretty quick because she'd done her wig earlier in the day and could just plop it on her head and go.

I walked down the hall towards her room, and I could hear the shouting from a few doors down.

"Nana, we're going to pay you back! We just need the money for a few months." It was her daughter.

I stood outside the door. I wanted to barge in and say something to her daughter and let her know how much she was upsetting Viola, but I just listened in.

"I just worry," Viola said.

"You always said family was the most important thing to you," her daughter said.

"It is, but I've already given you most of my savings."

Her daughter stormed out the room and brushed past me, almost knocking me down.

I peered into the room to see what kind of shape Viola was in.

"Did you hear that?" she asked.

"Maybe a little."

"She swears that with just a little more money, her boyfriend can turn his business around."

I wanted to remind her that the economy wasn't doing that well, but I just kept my mouth shut.

"I've got so much money invested already. If there's a chance I can get it back . . ." Viola's voice trailed off.

I wasn't gone lecture her about how to raise her daughter. Nothing worse than somebody offering you parenting advice after you done made up your mind. So I just changed the subject.

"You need to get dressed," I said. *"King Kong* don't wait for no one."

She was doing a final tease of her wig but then stopped. "That's the movie we gone see?"

"It's got everything you could want in a movie. Big ape grabs the girl, climbs up a building, gets shot at by airplanes."

"I know. I've seen it." She pulled her wig off her head. "I don't wanna go."

"But Ben needs this. He's been so depressed. This is gone be our big double date night. Don't you wanna help poor Ben get over Becca?"

Viola came over and stood in front of me. I still hadn't gotten used to her being bald-headed.

"Are you sure you want to push this whole thing between Ben and Kevin?" she asked.

"You've seen how Ben is when he's alone with Kevin, and he don't think no one's looking. Can't you imagine them sitting in the theatre together, holding hands and sharing a tub of buttery popcorn." I smiled because I could see the look on Ben's face.

Viola had her wig in hand and was trying to decide what to do. "Come on, sweetie." I nestled up close to her and stood behind her. "Ben's loved this movie since he was six. I just knowed it's gone work." I kissed her on the neck. "Besides, you love that actress Jessica Lange. She was in that movie *Cape Fear* we saw a couple weeks ago."

"Jessica Lange's in *King Kong*?" Viola stepped back from me. She looked at me sideways.

"It was her first role," I said. "She's the beauty."

Viola shook her head and exhaled a strong burst through her nose. "You done a good job selling this as something we gotta do for Ben so I reckon I ain't gone be able to say no. It will be interesting to see the updated version," she said. "How much time we got?"

"We should really get going," I said.

"I was gone glue my wig, but I don't reckon I got time," she said. "Just give me a couple minutes to tape it. I'll meet y'all at the entrance."

When I got back to my room, Ben had already settled on the couch and was halfway through a pint of Ben & Jerry's chocolate chip cookie dough ice cream. It had taken me more than a decade, but I'd finally got the boy to enjoy something other than just vanilla. "Get up," I said. "We're going to a movie."

"I don't care about going to the rec room and seeing some black and white movie back from your days," he said. "I'll just sit here and watch *Golden Girls*. And I think there are new episodes of *Empty Nest* and *Nurses*."

"We're going out."

"Out?"

"Yep. They're playing *King Kong* at the movie theatre downtown. I figured we could go see that again. It's been fifteen years. I forgot how it ended."

I got the reaction that I'd hoped for. Ben smiled and then put down the ice cream.

"I reckon you gone need to do something about yo' hair," I said. It was standing up every which away. I followed him to the bathroom and gave him a little Brylcream. He finger-combed his hair a couple times and managed to tame the worst of it.

"Looking good," I said. "We're all set for our double date."

"Double date?" Ben asked. He squinted at me and pinched his brows together.

"Viola is going with us, and Kevin's gone meet us there," I said.

"How does that make it a double date?" His eyes widened and his mouth dropped open. A look of fear and excitement.

"Just a figure of speech," I said, and chuckled.

He bought it, and away we went.

I had planned to arrive plenty early so we could get good seats, but even though it was thirty minutes before the movie started, the line was much longer than I'd expected. The line wrapped around the building like King Kong wrapping his arms around the World Trade Center. We got out and went to wait, but then heard someone shouting our names. Kevin was already there, and he was near the front of the line.

Thanks to Kevin, we got into the theatre in five minutes. Kevin and Viola got us seats while Ben and I got popcorn. While in line for the concessions, I noticed the movie poster of King Kong on top of the Empire State Building.

I grabbed the edge of Ben's jacket and pointed out the poster. "Ben, didn't King Kong climb the World Trade Center?"

"Yeah," he said. "He was holding onto one of them and then jumped to the other when the airplanes attacked."

I studied the poster more closely and instead of Jessica Lange, the movie starred Fay Wray. They were showing the original version, set in 1933, not the 1976 version that Ben and I had seen.

I felt my knees buckle, and I thought I was gone faint. "I gotta run to the bathroom," I said to Ben. "Y'all go ahead and sit down."

I ran away from Ben, Kevin and Viola as fast as I could. I felt like I'd drank seven pints of Turbo Stomper. My head pounded and my throat was so dry I couldn't speak. I went to the bathroom and into the stall and sat down. I felt the first tears on my cheek, and I yanked a couple squares of toilet paper from the dispenser. The roll kept going, and I watched the paper pile up on the floor.

Ben knocked on the stall. "You doing okay in there, Grandpa?"

"Let's find someplace to talk," I said. I grabbed up all the paper and flushed it.

We went outside where the smokers congregated, a gravel-covered patio with concrete benches. I sat down on one of the benches and Ben sat across from me. And I told him a story I'd never told him or anyone else.

March 21, 1933 (Saturday)
Grandpa (17 years old)

They's a new movie over at the cinema in Fulton County," I told Ruby J when I met her at Conroy diner for our weekly lunch together. I'd sit at the table by the window inside, and she would sit at the outside table by the same window. With the window open, it was like we was together, even though we wasn't.

"What kind of movie?" she asked.

"Something called *King Kong.* About a big Gorilla that terrorizes New York City."

"That sounds interesting," she said.

"Would you like to go?"

She laughed her snort of indignation. "You know well enough we can't go to no movie together. You gone sit downstairs, and I'll sit up in the balcony with the other colored folks. We gone wave to each other every now and then?"

"Ain't gone be no big deal. You light-skinned enough. Just wear some powder and your scarf and hat."

I looked at her and could see that she was considering it so I kept it up. "I think people probably won't have any idea you colored."

Ruby J protested and refused and turned me down for a month. Good thing the movie was doing so well because it was still playing by the time she said yes.

The movie was unlike anything I'd ever seen. From the first scene, when they was on the boat, I was transported to the remote island where King Kong lived. Ruby J and I held hands, laughed and then cried together when King Kong got killed. I think we both understood a little bit about not being able to have love because of your differences.

We'd made it through the movie without anyone even noticing us. The woman beside Ruby J had even said something white trash about how noisy the colored people were in the balconies. I chuckled because the woman didn't even realize that she was saying that to a black woman.

I got real cocky afterwards and suggested that we go to a diner and sit together. On the inside.

Ruby J didn't think it was too good an idea, but I think she was a mite inspired by King Kong and his pursuit of love at all costs, so she agreed. At the diner, we got seated in a booth and were chatting about the movie. Without thinking, Ruby J removed her scarf. I heard a few rumblings as folks noticed her kinky hair.

The waitress came over, her eyes glued to her order pad. I ordered and then she noticed Ruby J for the first time. I could see how her expression hardened when she realized that Ruby J was black. Her eyes squinted and her cheeks sucked in. "I'll be right back," she said, and went over to the man at the cash register.

She didn't even hide the fact that she was pointing at our table. Then the man pointed. He was skinnier than me and had a wiry mustache. He looked like the villain in half the movies they showed at the time. When he got to the table, he took off his hat. He ran his hands through his oily black hair. His eyes were dots of coal.

"Now, I'm sure y'all ain't wanting no trouble, but we ain't serving y'all."

He turned around and gestured to a sign behind the register. Written in a fancy script. Like you'd write *Happy Birthday*. Or *Welcome Home*. The sign—*No Coloreds Served*.

And then he pointed to Ruby J. But looked only at me. "Now you and your nigger gone need to leave."

I wanted to start a scene. To pick trouble. To jump up and punch that man out, like a hero on the silver screen. But I just stood up and headed towards the door. I didn't want any trouble. He could have called the police instead of just telling us to leave. I had two cases of Turbo Stomper in my trunk. I didn't want to go to jail again.

But I regret to this day that I didn't even help Ruby J out of the booth. I just stood at the door, with my head hung low. But I did watch Ruby J. She scooted out of the booth, stood up, folded her scarf on the table and then tied it over her head. She made eye contact with every one of the diners who were staring at her. She said good evening to a couple of the ladies and smiled.

I ain't never seen no one with more class in my entire life. And I'm including Daleah Ashford in that.

December 28, 1991 (Saturday)
Grandpa

When I finished telling the story to Ben, I felt about three inches high. All this time, I been telling Ben how he needed to live his life without worrying about what other people think, and I'd acted like a coward in front of the woman I loved. I put my head in my hands and just sobbed.

"What do you want to do, Grandpa? Do you want to leave?" I asked.

"No," I said. And then I realized that this time was gone be different. I could have the date with Viola that I wasn't able to have with Ruby J. "Ben, I'm fixin' to do what I should have done almost sixty years ago. After watching a movie with the gal I have a fancy for, I'm gone take her to a diner. I'll order a cup of soup or something that's not gone tear up my stomach tomorrow. And then me and my girlfriend are gone share a piece of pie."

I marched into the theatre like a soldier doing battle. The lights were already off so I had to call out for Viola. Kevin stood up, and I could see that he and Viola had saved two seats between them. I think they was the only seats left in the whole theatre.

The movie followed a different story line from the 1976 version, but I think Ben enjoyed it. I know Viola enjoyed it because every now and then she would tell me in a too-loud-for-the-movies voice how much she liked a particular scene. At the end of the movie, the whole audience took a while to get moving. Like we was all just wanting to enjoy the stillness and magic of the movie a little while longer.

After a couple minutes, people got up and started heading towards the exit at the back of the theatre. We all stood up and shuffled towards the end of the aisle. Kevin was telling Ben something funny that had happened at Dogwood last week. I was listening to the guys in front of us talking about how cool the movie was. One guy didn't say too much so his friend asked him how he liked it.

The guy replied, "It was pretty good, except for that nigger in front of me who kept talking."

By that point, we were at the end of the aisle, and the guy was right in front of me. Ben grabbed my arm. I realized that he had heard the guy. And so had Viola. Her entire person invalidated with a single word.

I didn't know what to do. Kevin hadn't heard and was making some joke and laughing. At first, I stood frozen like the moment before a skunk sprays you.

Then I turned around and pointed my finger at him and then at Viola. "Would you please apologize to the lady here for your rudeness?" I asked, but my tone made it more of an order.

"Whaddya mean?" the guy asked, and looked at his buddies.

"You knowed what you said, and you knowed that word ain't acceptable." I grabbed him by his jacket, and he tried to push me off, but I kept my grip.

"Let go of me, old man."

"Don't play dumb with me, boy. It don't suit you." I pushed him a little, and he stumbled. He started to come at me, but his friend held him back.

I didn't care at that moment if he punched me in the eye. I got right up in his face where I could smell popcorn, and I said more to that one kid than I'd said to a lifetime of bullies.

"Now, you can apologize or you can go through the rest of your life regretting it. Believe me, I know how it is to carry something like that. I've been doing it for almost sixty years. One day you gone look back and wish you had done the right thing. I'm sure in her eighty years, she's heard that word before. So I'm telling you for your sake, not hers. Say you're sorry."

The guy stepped back and looked to his friends like a two-year old that's fallen and waits to see his parents' reaction before he starts to cry. One friend was looking at the ground, but the other smacked him on the arm.

"He's right. You don't want this on your conscience. My brother is dating a black girl. My dad said something terrible about them, and now I don't see my brother much anymore."

The guy punched his friend in the arm and was about to say something to me, but he stopped. I gave him the best stink-eye I'd given in my seventy-six years on the planet.

He looked at me and then at Viola. "I'm sorry," he said, and then hustled past us and out of the theatre.

When we got out to the lobby, we all took a minute to settle. Kevin was confused as to what had happened so Ben had to explain it to him. I stood there feeling like a valiant knight waiting for Viola to thank me for defending her honor, especially against a ruffian who could have put a whooping on me. But she came up and whacked me on the shoulder.

"Charlie, I can't believe you. Telling those boys I'm eighty years old when my birthday ain't until next week."

I didn't know what to say.

"Besides, I don't look a day over seventy-four," she said. And then laughed. The first time I'd heard her laugh when she didn't sound like she was coughing up her lungs, heart, stomach and spleen. It started deep in her belly, and this time, she got it out. It rolled up into her chest and then finished in her head. It sounded like a pig being drowned in Jell-O, but it was the most joyous laugh I'd ever heard in my life.

And it was a laugh that I knew.

I got so weak in the knees I had to sit down on one of the benches the smokers used. "But this can't be."

Viola nodded.

"But you can't be her. Ruby J was so heavy and had such a . . . full bosom."

"Right after they found my breast cancer, they did a double mastectomy," she said. "And with all my bouts of chemo, I've lost so much weight. It's no wonder you didn't recognize me."

"How long have you known that I was the Charlie you dated so many years ago?" I asked, still not believing that it was true.

"I knew it the moment I met you when you came to visit Dogwood. Ben looks so much like you I thought I'd seen a ghost. And then I heard the story about Climax Clinton."

"So that's why you spilled the pitcher of tea," Ben said.

Viola nodded again.

"When did you change your name?" Kevin asked.

"I got sick of being one of four Rubys in my family. My second name was Viola so I started going by that. My last name became Chapman when I married my late husband."

"Why didn't you say anything?" I asked, and got up off the

bench. "You let me court you this whole time without telling me who you were." I went to put my arms around her, but she held out her hand.

"Charlie Phelps, I ain't wanted to tell you because to be honest, I was still mad at the Charlie I knew all those years ago."

She stepped back and put her hands on her hips, and was shaking her head. It was a pose that I recognized. She was furious at me. "I've been pretending that you was a different person since you didn't know who I was. But now that you know I'm Ruby J, I can't help but think of you as that Charlie. The Charlie who let the owner of that diner talk to me like that without even a word in my defense. And the Charlie who wanted me to be with him but only on his terms."

"What do you mean 'only on my terms'?" I asked.

Viola wiped back tears. "Kevin, please take me back to Dogwood." She turned and walked away.

She could walk faster than me, and I couldn't catch up so I shouted out to her. "But I loved you!"

Viola whipped back around, causing her wig to fly off. "Charlie, you loved the version of me you'd created, not the real me." Even though she was bald-headed, she walked away with the same dignity, elegance and grace she'd had when I'd first met her sixty years ago. Kevin picked up her wig and headed after her.

I felt like King Kong after he'd been shot a hundred times and was falling off the building. My whole world was spinning, and I grabbed ahold of Ben.

"How could I not have known?" I asked.

"She doesn't look the same," Ben replied. "She admitted that."

"But I should have known." Ben put his arm around me, and we walked to his car. "I should have known."

I'd reconnected with the first love of my life, and even though I couldn't have dreamed for this day to happen, it had all turned into a nightmare.

24

January 13, 1992 (Monday)
Ben

I would have thought that Grandpa and Viola's relationship would have gotten even stronger once Grandpa realized that she was Ruby J, but everything had gone sideways. Something had happened sixty years ago that I didn't know about. And Grandpa didn't seem to have any idea what he'd done wrong other than not defending her at the diner, and neither of us thought that Viola would be the type of person to hold a grudge on something like that for so many years. There had to be something else.

Grandpa didn't give up though. He courted her with all the determination of a high school kid. He was failing miserably, but instead of making me more depressed, it helped bring me out of my funk. They weren't together yet, but the fact that God had given them another opportunity proved to me that the Lord has a plan for our lives. Even if we don't understand his plan or agree with his timing, we just need to have faith.

I had considered pursuing Becca with the same level of commitment, but my heart wasn't in it. And Pastor Hardy encouraged me to move on, even continuing to try to set me up with Monica. After much effort, I convinced him that Monica would never date me because it would be a betrayal to Becca, and he relented.

He was okay with my being single for a while because he was focusing one hundred percent on the fact that I'd told him I was cured. And this news had energized him. He was fighting with the faculty about the changes the South Carolina Baptist Convention wanted to make to the curriculum, and it seemed like my cure gave him the reason he needed to press on. More than ever he believed that a more Christ-centric curriculum would benefit all of the students on campus with whatever problems they were dealing with. He knew that if he could just implement his changes, he'd help generations of students.

He also didn't mind my being single because I was spending a huge amount of time preparing to replace Phillip as group leader for the Straight Path meetings. Pastor Hardy knew that Phillip had a different view on whether a cure was possible, and even though I had less training, he thought I'd do a better job. I was excited to take on the job because I knew that helping other people would keep me from slipping back into a depression.

The one thing that I did fear was telling a group of people that I had been gay. But Pastor Hardy had insisted that my story needed to be told. He said people needed to believe that a cure was possible, and they wanted to hear from someone whose life had been transformed by the healing power of Jesus Christ.

But I couldn't stop thinking about what Phillip had said. As much as I had felt like God had taken away the desires and as much as I wanted them to be gone, I kept wondering whether the cure was permanent or whether I was just clinging to the edge, and eventually I'd have to let go and fall back into the pit of homosexuality.

The night of the first Straight Path meeting, it was raining. The weather forecaster had said it was time to stock up on bread and milk because the rain was gonna turn to frozen precipitation, but I wasn't afraid because the snow would only come later that night, well after our meeting ended and I was safely back at home.

It wasn't snowing yet, but I didn't like driving in any type of bad weather so I gave myself plenty of time to get to Calvary Baptist, and arrived ten minutes early. That night all of the groups met: Alcoholics Anonymous, Narcotics Anonymous, Gamblers Anonymous, Sex Addicts and the Straight Path group. As I drove up I could see a group of smokers huddled under the shelter just outside the door of the fellowship hall, and I figured there were a whole lot more people inside.

I didn't want to mingle with the other addicts. I worried someone might recognize me, and I'd have to explain why I was there. So I waited in my car. I should have left the engine running because the temperature dropped quickly. I rubbed my arms to warm up, and I felt the bump of the scar on my right arm. It always seemed more pronounced when I was cold.

I traced its outline and thought about Momma. What would she think? Would she be proud of me for fighting these feelings or feel ashamed that I had them in the first place? Would she blame herself?

On nights like that, when the sky was gray flannel, and I felt like I could reach up and grab a piece of it to stay warm, I thought of her. And how her death was my fault.

December 26, 1977 (Monday)
Benji (seven years old)

Yesterday was Christmas. But Santa didn't get me what I really wanted.

I'd waked up and looked out the window. The trees was brown. The grass was yellow. The driveway was black. They wudn't no snow nowhere.

I had raced downstairs past the living room to my parent's bedroom. Presents were piled under the tree, but what I wanted wouldn't be wrapped. I knocked on their door. Sometimes it was locked but that morning, it wasn't so.

"Mom! Dad! Merry Christmas!" The bed looked like it had been made, but on one side, the comforter and pillow was all scrunched up. A heavy afghan that Mee Maw had given Momma last Christmas laid at the foot of the bed. The light was on in the bathroom, and the door was open a crack. "Momma!" I yelled. "Where are you? Dad!"

Momma answered from the bathroom. "One second, Benji!" I crawled into the bed and waited. A couple minutes later, she came out of the bathroom. She had on her old red housecoat and two different-colored bedroom shoes. Her normally-perfect helmet-y head of hair looked like she'd been in a crash. She wore no makeup. She hadn't even drawed on her eyebrows.

I didn't quite know what to make of her.

"Where's dad?" I asked.

"Benji, you know your dad is not here." Her eyes were red and watery.

"Yeah, but Grandpa said that he couldn't make it because of the snow, and I didn't see any snow outside."

"Well, B. It's probably really snowy in Chicago where your father is. I'm sure otherwise he would have spent Christmas with you." She pulled her housecoat around her real tight. "It's so chilly in here." She went and got back into bed and didn't wake up until after lunchtime.

Mee Maw and Grandpa had stayed over in the guest bedroom. I went and woke them up. I needed at least one adult before I could open the presents from Santa.

Santa might not have brought me my dad, but I reckon he'd tried to make up for it with presents.

"Looks like someone was a good boy this year," Grandpa said.

Momma didn't really get out of bed the whole of Christmas Day, but me and Grandpa and Mee Maw did a bunch of stuff. Grandpa had bought me a piano, and Mee Maw taught me how to play "Jingle Bells." Grandpa and I sang every Christmas song in the Baptist hymnal while Mee Maw cooked a big dinner like we had on Thanksgiving, but with ham and not turkey.

The next day started just as cold and gray, and Momma stayed in her room until lunchtime. We had leftovers, and Momma seemed to be feeling a little better. She ate a good meal for the first time in a month. And she gave me a new baseball mitt that she'd forgotten to give me the day before.

After lunchtime, the sun peeked out a little. Grandpa took me down to the lower pasture to throw balls. It was about three o'clock when Grandpa said that he was tired and needed a break. We were in the mud room wrapping string around my mitt with a baseball stuffed inside, when I saw the first flakes.

"It's snowing! It's snowing!" I shouted.

I raced into the kitchen to find Momma washing the last of the casserole dishes. "Momma, can we make snow ice cream?"

"Yeah. Better check and make sure we got everything. Check the pantry and make sure we got the vanilla and sugar."

I pulled out my helper stool. The Tupperware was full of sugar, and I spun the spice rack until I found the 'nilla extra. "We got the sugar and 'nilla, Momma."

"Make sure we got milk," she said. "I might have used the last bit for the mac-n-cheese."

I put away my helper stool and then checked the fridge. "No milk, Momma."

"Well, get your new jacket. Throw it on over your PJs and grab some shoes. We'll just run in right quick, so ain't no need for you to get all dolled up."

Outside, the snow was melting as soon as it hit the ground.

"I'm not sure we're gonna get enough snow to even make one scoop of ice cream," she said.

"Grandpa said there was a lot of snow coming this way. He said it was gone get colder later. We gone make a snowman."

On the way to the car, Momma grabbed my hand. "The sidewalk is getting a little slick."

"Your hands are like ice, Momma."

"That's why I need to hold yours, hon." She smiled. Probably her first real smile in a while. I knowed that she liked the Jean Nate cologne I got at the Five-n-Dime because Mee Maw helped me pick it out for her. Momma had given me a make-believe smile. When I gave her the Christmas card I had made for her at Sunday School, another pretend smile.

But this one was the real deal. Maybe she just needed me to warm her up a little. I squeezed her hand extra hard.

She opened the driver-side door of the Chrysler station wagon with its wood-paneled sides, and I scrambled in and across the seat. Momma got in and started the car. I switched on the radio. Christmas songs still played, and we sang a few carols on the way to the store. A few times I reached over and held her hand again as it rested on the gear shifter. Still cold. I rubbed it a little.

"I'll warm 'em, Momma."

She shifted gears and then held my hand as we sang "Deck the Halls" in our best harmony.

At the Piggly Wiggly, the milk shelves was almost bare. Just half gallons of buttermilk and big things of cream. Momma looked around for someone working there and found a butcher putting stuff on the shelves. His white apron had spots of blood on it, and curly bits of meat hanged off his sleeve.

"Y'all got any milk?" Momma asked.

The butcher shook his head. "No ma'am. Y'all know how Southerners are. First sign of snow, and the milk and bread shelves are raided."

Momma nodded.

Outside, the snow was coming down even harder and was sticking to the cars and trees. I tugged on Momma's coat. "It's okay. We don't have to make ice cream."

Momma grabbed my hand. "My son wants snow ice cream, and if we have to drive to every grocery store in town, we gone find a blame gallon of milk."

Twenty minutes to the Winn-Dixie. Same story. Another ten minutes to the A&P. A tall skinny black man said he had a few gallons stashed in the coolers in the back. "We're shutting the store down in twenty minutes if it keeps coming down like this." He handed Momma a gallon of Pet whole milk. "Y'all be careful driving home."

We paid and Momma let me carry the gallon back to the car. I slushed through the couple of inches of wet snow.

When we got back to the car, I asked, "Momma, can I drive home?" I loved sitting in her lap when she drove. Sometimes, she would pretend to let me steer.

"Not tonight. It's starting to snow real hard now, and it would be safer for you in the back." It was getting late, and I knowed that she wanted to get home. Momma hated driving at night, especially in bad weather.

The A&P was about twenty minutes from our house. Momma turned the radio down a little bit and was focused more on the road than carols. I was belting "I'm Dreaming of a White Christmas" almost in rhythm to the wiper blades clearing the snow from the windshield as she slowed to the four-way stop sign at the intersection of the two highways. The car slid off to the shoulder, and it took Momma a couple spins of the tires to get us back on the road.

She looked out the front and side windows. "It's really coming down now. Good thing we went ahead and got this milk when we did."

I put the gallon of milk on the seat beside me and leaned up and hugged Momma's neck. "I love you," I said, and sat back down.

She turned around and smiled. "I love you, Benji." She edged the car out into the intersection. "I hope that you had a good Christ—"

I felt a jolt and heard a crash like lightning and thunder when the storm is right on you. The car was spinning. Momma screamed, and I saw flashes of light.

Then nothing.

I think I'd been asleep because I woke up at some point hurtin'. Felt like someone had took a hammer to my right arm. I tried to raise it, but seemed like it belonged to someone else. Cold drops hit my face, like rain. Drops falling in my mouth. I tasted it—sweet and creamy.

I heard Momma moaning.

"Momma! Momma! Help me!" I was lying on my back. The car was upside down. The vinyl of the backseat a foot above my head. I tried to sit up, but there wudn't no room. And I couldn't. The milk soaked my hair, and I got cold.

"Benji? You okay? Benji!"

"My arm hurts, Momma."

I raised my head and followed the black plumpy jacket to the white of my Christmas jammies sticking out underneath. But they wudn't white no more. My jammies turned redder and darker the more I stared. I tried to wiggle my fingers but couldn't.

The motor was still running, the radio advertising an after-Christmas sale at Woolworths. "All Christmas ornaments and cards and winter jackets fifty percent off!!!"

I started to cry. I heard Momma moan again and then cough.

"It's okay, Benji. Momma is here."

She reached over, her fingers crawling, stretching until she grabbed my good hand.

Then silence.

She'd stopped coughing. And I heard sirens in the distance. The pain in my arm flashed white hot. So much pain. I squeezed her hand but she didn't squeeze back.

"Momma! Momma!" I called out to her.

But she didn't say nothing.

January 13, 1992 (Monday)
Ben (22 years old)

The church "bells" pealed the "Westminster Chimes," but they were just an audio recording. Six bing-bongs followed. The smokers stamped out their cigarettes and headed inside. I grabbed my Bible and notes and got out of the car. A couple pellets of sleet mixed with the rain, and I ran to the church entrance. The basement was just a cluster of small meeting rooms off a central corridor. The smell of stale tobacco and fresh-brewed coffee hung in the air.

A man came down the stairs behind me and announced, "Alcoholics, y'all need to move to a larger room again. Just take the steps up to the social hall and someone will direct you to the small chapel."

A woman with dark auburn hair wearing a plaid lumberjack shirt and dirty jeans brushed past me and bee-lined to join the AA folks. She knocked my Bible out of my hands, and my notes scattered. She bent down to help me pick up the index cards, and our eyes met for a moment. She looked familiar.

The woman handed me my notes and then raced up the stairs. I headed towards the room at the end of the hall. On the door to the room was a sign on a white piece of copy paper. Written in red ink in a jagged right-angling scrawl. Straight Path Meeting.

Tonight there were four guys and one woman. Everyone was seated in a circle staring at the floor or the ceiling.

I began. "Welcome. I'm very honored that you've come tonight. I'm Ben, and I'm your new leader." I was then supposed to say that I previously had same-sex addiction, but God had cured me. I'd been practicing in front of the mirror and with Pastor Hardy. But I couldn't get my lips to form the words.

I looked down and pretended to try to find my place in my notebook.

A guy sitting right across from me raised his hand. "I'll start," he said. He was probably about twenty. He wore acid-washed jeans with neon paint splattered on them, high-top Converse shoes and a black sweatshirt with a pink neon triangle on it. He picked at his left ring finger and bit his nails while he talked.

"My name is Johnny, and I have homosexual desires." He put his hand over his heart like he was gonna pledge allegiance. "I pray to the Lord every day to rescue me from these sins, but they're too strong. And being gay is too much of a temptation."

Everyone nodded, and the guy continued his story. "Last night, I went out to Fortress. So many hot sweaty guys dancing to a mix from Madonna's latest album. I got so drunk. I met this guy who had the best chest I've ever seen. He offered to take me home, to his place . . ."

Johnny paused for effect and looked around the circle. Except for the woman, we were all hanging on every word.

One guy was rubbing his crotch through his pants. "So did you go with him?"

Before Johnny had a chance to answer, everyone looked at the door. I turned around to see who the latecomer was.

It was Phillip. I didn't know why he was here. Had Pastor Hardy sent him to spy on me or did Phillip just show up to undermine me?

"Sorry I'm late," he said, and took the empty chair across from me. "I see that your new leader Ben has things well under control."

I nodded and didn't want Johnny to continue his soft-core porn story so I decided it was time to move on. "Thanks for sharing that, Johnny. Who's next?"

One guy raised his hand, and Phillip and I both pointed at him.

"Sorry," Phillip said. "Old habits."

"I'm Dan," the guy said, "and I'm gay."

"You have homosexual desires," another interrupted. "Being gay is a choice."

"I didn't choose to be gay," Dan said.

"None of us would have chosen to be gay," I said. "Why would we choose to go to Hell?"

Dan looked down, and I felt bad. I hadn't intended to be that sharp.

I spent much of the rest of the meeting looking out the window. It was snowing more than I'd expected, and I started to worry how I was gonna get home. The woman was the only one who hadn't spoken, and I hadn't mentioned anything about being cured. We had about five minutes left when she raised her hand.

"I'm Carla, and I'm attracted to a woman. I pray for God to heal me, but my feelings of attraction to women just get stronger. I wish I knew there was a way out."

Phillip looked at me and was shaking his head. Don't do it, he was saying. I took a deep breath and then shared my testimony.

"Carla. A cure is possible. I'm living proof." I told them about how I'd had same-sex addiction since I was eleven years old, and how these feelings had threatened to keep me from pursuing my dream of being a pastor. And how through prayer, Bible study and commitment to a healing program run by my mentor, God had cured me.

"But why hasn't God cured me?" Carla asked. "I've been trying my hardest."

"Maybe God has a different plan for you," Phillip said. I glared at him and was about to say something, but Johnny interrupted me.

"I don't understand God," he said. "He makes me this way and then tells me that I can't do anything about it. Sometimes it makes me think my life is not worth living."

Carla nodded. "I just want to be with the person I love."

Johnny said, "I just want to be loved."

"God loves you," I said.

"Doesn't God love me enough to cure me?" Johnny asked, and I didn't know what to say. My victory felt hollow. I felt a tingling in the back of my head. Like when a body part falls asleep and then wakes up. And I felt a tightness in my stomach. My cure meant nothing if others were suffering from the same thing.

The church bells chimed seven o'clock. The meeting was over.

"Before we go, let's pray," I said. I clasped my hands in front of my heart like a Precious Moments figurine and watched as everyone did the same. "Dear Lord, we come to you as humble servants. We know that you have a plan for each of us in our lives, and that although it may take time for us to understand your plan, please . . ."

My mind blanked. The gray flannel sky was falling in chunks now, and I could see the snow piling on the cars and even on the ground. And then I prayed the only thing I could think of. "Dear Lord, please give us the courage to change the things we can, the serenity to accept the things we cannot change, and the wisdom to know the difference. Amen." Although this prayer was used to close many AA groups, Pastor Hardy had been clear that it wasn't appropriate for the Straight Path. With God, all change was possible.

I opened my eyes, and Phillip was smiling. "I need to go and make sure all of the other rooms have been put back in order," he said.

As I put the chairs in the room back along the wall, I felt like I'd failed as their group leader. I'd told them about my cure and instead of being inspiring, I'd come across like I was better than they were.

And I wasn't sure how I was gonna drive home in the icy slush that awaited me.

I was heading out towards my car when I heard someone calling my name. "Ben!" I turned around and it was the woman in the flannel shirt, the one who had bumped into me earlier. I wasn't sure how she knew my name. She was waving me back over to the fellowship hall entrance.

When she got back in the light of the doorway, I recognized her. "You're the Funyuns Woman from the Piggly Wiggly."

She stared at me, and then I remembered her name. "You're Karen. How are you doing? Still climbing those mountains?"

"It's so amazing that I ran into you tonight. I started going to AA meetings ever since we had that talk at the coffee shop. I had a couple setbacks along the way . . . " She paused.

"It's great to see you." I gave her a hug and then wanted— needed—to get out of there and get home.

"I can't believe that you're here." She wouldn't let me go and hugged me tighter. She started to cry, and I just held her for a while until she had settled down.

We went into one of the side rooms, and she updated me on her life over the past six months.

"I've been trying to get my life turned around. I started night school, and my kid has had to spend more time with his dad. I didn't realize that my son had been getting picked on, and his dad had been teaching him to fight. The principal called me, and my son got suspended. So for the past week, I've had to watch him during the day, drop him off at his dad's place, and then go to school in the evenings and then study at night. I had to swap shifts at work. I've barely slept two hours in the last several days. We had a big test at school, and some of my classmates invited me out for drinks.

"I just needed a break. I couldn't imagine how I was gonna keep up that schedule for the next few months while I have this class. The bar is in downtown Greenville, and I was driving around trying to find parking when I drove past Hilltop Baptist Church. And I thought of you. I was so focused on the mountain ahead of me that I'd forgotten about the hills. I realized that I just needed to get through tonight. So I turned around in the middle of the road and headed here."

"I'm so proud that you made the decision to come here," I said.

"And I can't believe that you're here too. What brings you here?"

"This is the first night that I've led one of the other. . ." I paused, trying to think of what to say. "AA-type meetings."

"I just want you to know how much it meant when you took the time to talk to me. I owe you so much." She kissed me on the cheek. "You're like my guardian angel," she said.

"I'll always be here when you need me," I said, not really sure how to respond.

She smiled, and as she walked away, I felt better. I might have failed in my Straight Path group, but at least I was ministering to someone.

When I got to the exit, Phillip was still there.

"I overheard what you said to that woman. Pastor Hardy is right. You do have an amazing gift."

I watched as Karen drove away, her car sliding to a stop at the exit of the church parking lot.

And then I felt a wave of nausea, like a pit in my stomach opened up, spilling my stomach acids into the rest of my body, melting my organs. My lungs had dissolved, and it was hard for me to breathe. I felt like I was gonna faint. My knees buckled.

Phillip rushed over and grabbed my shoulders. I kind of fell into his arms. "Are you okay? You look as white as the snow."

"I just don't wanna drive home," I said. "I live about twenty minutes away, and I don't like this kind of weather." I wanted to be home. I needed to be home. To be somewhere warm and safe.

"I'm just a couple minutes' drive," Phillip said. "You can hang out with me. It wasn't supposed to be snowing yet, so maybe the temp will warm a little, and this will turn into rain again."

I wondered if there was anywhere I could sleep in the fellowship hall, but someone was locking up the doors.

"I have a 4x4," Phillip said. "We'll be okay."

Unless I wanted to sleep in my car, I had no choice.

"It's okay, Ben. I'm just here to help."

When he said this, I noticed a quick smile and a flash in his eyes. He had other ideas on how he could help me.

25

January 13, 1992 (Monday)
Ben

Even in Phillip's four-wheel-drive truck, we skidded on the road. I white-knuckled the grab handle until my wrist hurt. When we slid on a sheet of ice halfway through the one stop sign, I reached my left hand out and held onto whatever I could find: Phillip's hand on the gear shifter.

"Don't worry," he said. He turned his hand over so that he held mine. I gripped tighter until he said, "You don't need to crush my hand. We're almost there."

I loosened my grip but still held onto him. He went another hundred yards and then turned in to a short driveway in front of a small red brick cottage.

"We're home," he said. His moved his hand and set it on top of mine. He brushed the little hairs on my knuckles with fingertips. And even though we were safely parked in his driveway, I felt more fear than ever. I was about to embark on a course more dangerous than if I'd driven home in the sleet.

I jerked my hand from under his and ran towards his front door. I didn't see the black ice that covered the sidewalk, and I fell and landed hard on my side. I was shaking, from the cold a little, but mainly from the prospect of being alone with Phillip in his apartment. I tried to stand up, but the walkway was too slick, and I fell again, this time onto the slushy ground.

Phillip braced himself against one of the columns on his front porch and reached down to assist me. My right side was soaking wet. He helped me inside the house, and a blast of heat, hell-hot, crushed me as I entered.

"Let's get you changed into dry clothes," he said.

He took me to his bedroom and sat me on the edge of his bed while he went through his dresser drawer to find me sweats and an old SJU T-shirt.

I tried to lift my arm so that I could take off my shirt, but I could barely move. Sitting there cold and shivering, I had a flashback to the day my Momma died.

"You need help getting undressed?" he asked.

I nodded.

"Did you hurt yourself when you fell?"

I shook my head. I wasn't hurt physically from the fall, but emotionally I was in so much pain that I was comatose. The last time I'd felt this way was December 26, 1977.

After the wreck, when our car was upside down, I remembered listening as hard as I could to hear if Momma was saying anything or breathing, but the only thing I heard was the ambulance siren. It got louder and louder until my ears seemed to split. The firemen came and had to pry the door off the car to get me out. About ten minutes later, the tow truck arrived.

I was sitting in the back seat of the fire truck with a blanket wrapped around me when the fireman told me my mother was dead. Through the foggy window, I watched as they extracted her body from the other side of the car. There was no sense of urgency. It was more of an inconvenience for them. They couldn't tow the car with her inside. They moved her onto a stretcher and put a white sheet over her. The thin fabric absorbed her blood and bloomed like a red rose.

Sitting on Phillip's bed, I shut my eyes as tight as I could, trying to block out my recall of that image.

"You're getting my bed all wet," Phillip said. "Let's just change your clothes, and you can lie back." He slid off my pants and underwear and pulled up the sweats. He put his hand on my back and folded me up so that I was sitting upright. He took off my shirt and then finished dressing me.

"Ben. You okay?"

I didn't answer. All I could think about was my mother. If I hadn't wanted snow ice cream, she'd be alive today. I could still feel the wetness of the milk dripping onto my face while the sirens got louder.

I started shivering and lay back on the bed. Phillip got me a blanket, but I still shook. He got on the bed and nestled in behind me. He put his arms around me, and his body heat rolled over me like warm water.

We lay like that for a while, and I wished we could stay there all night. I was content, but then I felt him growing hard behind me. I was aroused as well, but I didn't want to move. I worried that this moment would end, and that it would proceed like sex with Derek. The connection would be gone.

For a few moments more, he held me like that and just rubbed himself against me. He rested his head against my neck and then put an arm around me and pulled me into him.

"This is nice, isn't it?" he asked.

I rolled over so that our lips were almost touching. I felt my whole body quivering. A voice at the end of a long hallway whispered "Don't do it," but it was so faint that it couldn't override the screaming from my entire body.

Now, this is what you've wanted all along. Derek was a warm-up. Becca was a mistake. Phillip is the person who's gonna make you happy.

"Oh, Phillip." I kissed him hard, but he pushed me back.

"Don't call me Phillip," he said. "Let's role play. Call me 'Chad.'"

"What roles are we playing?" I had heard about crazy things that gay guys did together. Preacher Dale had told the congregation one time that gays beat each other with whips and engaged in all sorts of perverse things. I hoped that Phillip didn't expect me to get into that.

"Just, I'm Chad and you're. . . ." He paused. I guess he didn't think that "Ben" was sexy.

"Jake," he said.

I had to agree that Jake was a hot name. I often thought about a guy named Jake who was in my ethics class. "Why are we calling each other by other names?"

"It makes it hot," and he leaned in and kissed me. Not just physical and hard, like Derek had done, but with passion. Sex with Phillip would be for both of us to enjoy. I wasn't just there to get him off.

Other than trying to remember to call him Chad, this was what I had always hoped that sex would be. That I thought it could be.

After we rubbed each other's privates a bit, he stopped and got out of the bed. He lit a candle on his dresser and rummaged around in his nightstand. In the light of the candle, I could see a shiny foil wrapper.

Silver.

A condom.

"I want you," he said, and handed it to me.

I had never touched a condom before. I could feel the round outline through the packaging.

"Come on, Jake," Phillip said. "It feels really good."

I wanted to say "yes," but I worried this would establish a pattern in my life. A guy would suggest things that I would have considered unconscionable before, and in the heat of the moment, I would do them.

But I worried that if I said no, this connection would end. And we'd never get back to the point where he was holding me in his arms.

"Can't we just make out a little bit more first?" I asked, trying to buy myself time.

"Sure," he said, and we kissed for a while, but I realized that the moment was over for him. I'd never get back into the nook underneath his arms. The passion fizzled, and soon we were just lying there beside each other.

"Well, I'm hungry," he said.

I was gonna lie there and try to figure out what had happened, but I knew if I thought about it too much, I would get upset.

I got out of the bed and joined him in the kitchen.

While he grabbed stuff from the fridge, I looked at his bookcases. Leather-bound books with gold writing on their spines lined up like soldiers on the shelf.

"What are these?" I asked.

He turned back over his shoulder to look. "That's the New Testament," he said. "The Greek texts."

"You read Greek fluently?" I picked up one of the volumes and flipped through the pages.

"That's something you'll learn at Saluda Seminary," he replied, and got out pots and pans and stuff from his cupboard.

"I've been taking Greek for three semesters," I said, "but I still have to use my dictionary most of the time." I put the book back on the shelf and noticed an entire section of titles with their pages showing instead of the binder.

"At seminary, you'll get to where you can read it like English."

"I'll look forward to that," I said, and grabbed the top of one of the books to pull it off the shelf. The well-worn book angled towards me and then fell to the floor, landing face down on the plush carpet.

"I'm making pasta," he said. "You prefer meat sauce or just marinara?"

"Meat sauce," I replied, and bent down to pick up the book. It was titled *Being Gay and Christian.* On the cover was the Jesus fish filled in with rainbow colors. The book's spine was bent, and when I opened it, clumped pages stood up in three sections. Passages were underlined, highlighted and starred.

"Would you mind giving me a hand?" he asked, and I put the book back on the shelf.

I chopped up some vegetables while he made the sauce. Once he'd set the table, he looked out the window by cupping his hands to the side of his face. "We're definitely getting some accumulation. Good thing you didn't try to drive home. I think you'll need to stay here tonight."

I could barely eat dinner, thinking about being able to sleep with Phillip. I imagined cuddling up next to him.

When it was time for bed, I followed Phillip to his bedroom, but he stopped at the linen closet in the hallway.

"You'll sleep better on the couch," he said. "I tend to thrash around a lot. I wouldn't want to keep you up."

"The couch will be great," I lied.

He got me the sheets, a thin blanket and a pillow, we said good night, and he left me all alone in his living room.

I listened, and I could hear water running in his bathroom, and then I saw that he had turned off the lights. I wanted more than anything to go and be with him. Get in bed with him. But I'd either have to do things I wasn't ready for or face possible rejection. Neither alternative was attractive. The urges of my body unsatisfied, I tended to the thoughts that swirled in my mind.

For the next hour and a half, I read the entire book *Being Gay and Christian*.

The book went through every passage in the Bible against homosexuality. The Old Testament scriptures were explained in their historical context, such as when it said it was an abomination for a man to sleep in the same bed with a woman while she was having her period. Or how it was wrong to wear gold jewelry.

The book cited Romans 7:26. "But now we are released from the law, having died to that which held us captive, so that we serve in the new way of the Spirit and not in the old way of the written code." This message means that when Christ came, he fulfilled the laws of the Old Testament, and following Christ is the substitute for following the laws of the Pentateuch.

Jesus himself said nothing about homosexuality, and nothing in his teachings would suggest that he would judge anyone. *Being Gay and Christian* went through passages in the New Testament that have been translated as condemning homosexuality, but the words used by Paul had such limited usage in Greek that their meaning is not known. At that time, Greek did have words for two men in a relationship, but the New Testament does not use them.

In the end, I was more confused than ever. My entire life, I'd been taught that being gay was wrong and that it was a sin, but that was based on one interpretation of the Bible. This book proposed an alternative. Grandpa always warned me that the Bible could be used for any purpose. When Jesus was tempted, Satan quoted Scripture.

I knew that Phillip had been right. I'd merely suppressed my feelings of attraction to guys. When I didn't have any opportunity to be with a guy, I'd fooled myself into thinking that the attractions were gone. But when Phillip snuggled into me, being with him was the only thing that felt right in the world. It seemed natural.

I was the furthest thing from being cured.

And March first was just six weeks away.

January 14, 1992 (Tuesday)
Ben

When the sun came up, I got up off the couch and got dressed. Outside, snow still covered the roads, and my car was parked at the church lot too far away to trudge. I went back to Phillip's bookshelf and flipped through more of the books that he had. I'd finished skimming my third book on

Christianity and homosexuality when Phillip walked into the room in a sweatshirt, boxer shorts, and mismatched socks.

"Hungry?" he asked. "I've got bacon, sausage, eggs and some melon that may or may not be good. It's been in there for a few days."

"Bacon or sausage sounds good. I'm not a huge fan of melon."

Phillips chuckled and then got out bacon and eggs and orange juice. "You mind cracking the eggs for me?" he asked. It was clear that he had no intention of talking about what had happened or didn't happen between us.

"Have you ever been in a relationship?" I asked, whipping up the eggs.

He hesitated and flipped over the strips of bacon.

"I was in a relationship once," he said, and forked the bacon from the pan onto a paper plate. "He wanted more than I was able to give him."

"What does that mean?" I asked.

"It's one thing for me to be physical with a guy in private, but he wanted to go out in public. He wanted to go for dinners, movies, things like that."

"He sounds horrible," I said, thinking that Phillip was kidding, but I realized he was serious. I thought about how Grandpa used to have to sneak around with Ruby J.

Phillip set the plates on the table and sat down. I poured orange juice for us and sat down opposite him.

"Do you consider yourself gay?" I asked him.

"I'm attracted to guys. I enjoy having sex with them. But I don't want a relationship with a guy. Being a minister is too important to me. I don't lead a gay lifestyle, so I don't consider myself gay."

I wondered if that was where I was headed. Maybe Becca was right. I would marry someone, have kids, and then have a boyfriend on the side.

I was reaching for a slice of bacon when the doorbell rang.

"You expecting someone?" I asked.

"No," he said.

He got up and answered the door, and to the surprise of both of us, Pastor Hardy barged in.

"Thank goodness you're here, Ben," he said. "Patricia and I were so worried when you didn't come home last night before we went to bed. And then when your car wasn't in the driveway this morning, I got a little panicked."

"It was snowing pretty hard when we wrapped up last night." I pointed to the couch where the sheets and blankets were piled up, and the back cushions of the couch were on the floor. "Phillip was kind enough to let me bunk here for the night."

"How did things go?" he asked me.

For a second I panicked that he was asking me about how bunking with Phillip went, but then he added, "You do okay with your first meeting?" I realized he was referring to the Straight Path meeting.

"It was intense," I said.

"You tell them you were cured?" he asked.

I didn't look at Phillip. "Yes. I told them."

"What was their reaction?"

"One guy wanted to know why God didn't love him enough to cure him."

"God loves all his children," Pastor Hardy said. "That guy just hasn't worked hard enough." He glared at Phillip.

Ignoring the look, Phillip asked Pastor Hardy, "Would you like anything to eat?"

"No. I have to get to SJU. We have an important vote coming up, and I've got to get materials together for the faculty." He turned towards the door, but then stopped.

"Ben, there's something that I need to ask of you. It's a huge favor, and I'll hope you'll say yes."

"I owe you everything, Pastor Hardy," I said. "Of course I'll do it."

"Let me explain first." He moved the sheets from the couch, picked up the cushions and put them back on the sofa. "Have a seat."

I never liked having to sit for news, but I did as I was told.

"The future of SJU is at stake." He held his thumb and pointer finger a short distance apart. "We're this close to getting a huge increase in the endowment from the South Carolina Baptist Convention, but we need to make some changes to the school. It will make Stonewall Jackson University one of the finest Christian schools in the country. We just need to convince some people that all this liberal arts stuff isn't as important as inculcating the right values in our students."

"What can I do to help?" I asked.

"I need you to share your story. Testify how God has delivered you from your sinful ways and made you whole."

"With whom would you want me to share the story?" I asked. It was one thing to tell a small group at a Straight Path meeting, but quite another to tell an entire congregation.

"I want you to deliver the convocation at Founder's Day."

I felt a lump in my throat. SJU Chapel was packed with 3,000 people on Founder's Day. Usually, they had one of the top evangelists or public speakers in the country speak at Founder's Day. "You mean the invocation, right? The prayer at the beginning like Phillip gave?"

But Pastor Hardy shook his head. "I want you to give the main speech. The convocation. You'll have thirty minutes to tell your story. I'll help you prepare every step of the way."

"How would what I say affect anything with the faculty or the trustees or the Convention?"

"People love a good conversion story. It's why Paul was the most famous apostle. After the article about you in the paper, you're already a minor celebrity in this town. I bet we could get a follow-up story since you promised your grandma on her death bed that you'd continue."

I didn't know what to say.

"Just think about it," he said, and got up and headed towards the door, but stopped.

"Phillip, do you mind if I use your phone? Patricia was really worried about Ben. I just want to tell her that he's safe."

"It's just there in the kitchen," Phillip said.

As he walked back to the kitchen area, Pastor Hardy scanned the living room area one last time, like a detective looking for clues. I noticed that his gaze had stopped on the end table, and the pile of books I'd been reading.

"Looks like someone is getting some reading in," he said, and went over to look at the books. He read the title aloud. "Being Gay and Christian."

I didn't say anything. And neither did Phillip. I don't think he knew that I had found those books.

Pastor Hardy went over to the phone and dialed. "Hold on, honey," he said. "I can't understand a word you're saying."

I could see the color leave Pastor Hardy's face. Like he was being erased with White-Out. "I need to leave," he said, and then put down the phone, not even bothering to close the door all the way.

"That was odd," Phillip said, and went over and shut the door.

"Absolutely," I said, and I wasn't even talking about Pastor Hardy's phone call with his wife. I was thinking about how odd it would be for me to stand up in front of 3,000 people and tell them that I was cured when I'd just had the most intimate moment of my life with a guy who wouldn't call me by my name.

26

January 14, 1992 (Tuesday)
Grandpa

Ben was talking so fast that I couldn't make out what he was saying. Something about preaching at Founder's Day in front of the whole school. I'd heard Ben preach many times, and he got as many Amens as a backwoods pastor at a Pentecostal revival. The boy could deliver a message. I was trying to figure out who I could brag about this to. I didn't feel like I could say nothing to Viola. We was barely on speaking terms, and her poor daughter was so much trouble that it just made me feel bad to talk about what a good son Ben was. I was avoiding Cowboy because he'd caught on that I cheated at cards and had gotten mad at me for accusing him of doing the same. The only person who would really appreciate this was Mary Jean. And I valued her opinion less than a good bowel movement.

Then I remembered they was one person that would be happy for Ben. And maybe even explain to me a little bit more about Founder's Day.

Kevin.

Besides, I always liked the opportunity to talk Ben up to Kevin. From the moment we'd met him, I'd thought that he'd be a good match for Ben.

The snow had kept about half the staff from coming in so all of the administrators were doing double duty. I figured I'd find him down in the east wing emptying bed pans, but he wasn't nowhere.

I went back to my room, but this time when I passed by Daleah's place, the door was ajar.

I popped my head in to see if she might know where Kevin was. He was there on the love seat, holding Daleah in his arms. Judy was sitting in the couch opposite them and was saying something, but then stopped. They all looked at me.

Something was horribly wrong. I'd never seen Daleah look less than perfect, but her face had run down onto her shirt, and her hair stuck out in all directions like she'd been electrocuted. And then when she told me what happened, I felt my own shock.

Her grandson Jon Michael was dead.

I tried to lower myself onto the couch but fell on the coffee table. My heart stopped, and my vision splintered. I thought I was gone be sick but swallowed it down. I couldn't upchuck on Jon Michael's favorite rug.

"Are you okay, Charlie?" Kevin asked. He helped me up and onto the couch beside Judy.

I grabbed Judy's hand and pulled her close to me.

"I'm gone need some of your hooch," I said.

She let go of my hand and sat up real straight. She looked at Daleah.

"My dear," Daleah said. "I think we could all use a glass of something strong."

Kevin nodded and then Judy ran off. "I'll be right back," she said.

Kevin sat beside me, and we held hands.

"How could this happen?" I said. I looked over at Daleah. "We live in a home full of old people. It should have been one of them to go. Not Jon Michael."

Kevin squeezed my hand. "It's tragic. He would have turned thirty-two next week."

I pushed Kevin away. "Don't you think I know that!" I shouted and stood up. "We'd already planned his party. He has the same birthday as Mary Jean. She said something last week about all the Mexicans working in *her* garden, like she owns the place. We was gone plaster all the walls with signs that say '*Feliz Cumpleaños.*' We even had us a *piñata,* and I was this close . . ." I held my thumb and pointer finger about three inches apart . . . "to talking Judy into letting us fill it with candy and give everybody a turn to whack at it with a stick."

I reckoned I was yelling because Kevin's lower lip shook like he was on a train riding old rails.

"I'm sorry," I said. "I'm just so blame angry. Seems like the good Lord takes the good ones too early."

I was about to sit back down when the phone rang. I was up, so I answered it. "It's the funeral home," I said, and handed the phone to Daleah.

She listened for a little bit. "Yes, but—" she said, and then stopped. She listened for a while and then raised her voice for the first time I could recall. "James Paul McDylan! I've known you since you were a baby. And even changed your diapers on more than one occasion. Your family has buried everybody I've ever been related to, and half the people I've ever known.

And you're telling me you won't take my grandson's body?"

Her hand shook as she held the phone. "I'll tell you what won't be good for your business. I live in a place where a hundred people will need your services in the not too distant future, and I guarantee you this. Not a single one of them will use your funeral home." She was about to hang up but then added, "You'll be hearing from my lawyer." She slammed down the phone.

She stood there trembling. "They won't take his body," she said, as much to herself as to us.

"What?" I asked. My anger had a new target now. "Because of. . ." I was about to ask, but then stopped. Of course it was because of that.

"Is that legal?" Kevin asked.

"Probably not," Daleah replied, "but I really don't have time to file a lawsuit."

I helped her back over to the love seat. Judy arrived with a yellow envelope. "This is all that I have left," she said, and handed it to me. Inside was a fifth of vodka.

Kevin went over to Daleah's china cabinet and pulled out three Waterford crystal tumblers. He handed me a glass and poured me two fingers worth. I took a swallow. It burned, and the feeling in the back of my throat matched what I felt in my heart.

January 18, 1992 (Saturday)
Ben

Viola had asked me to return the sunshine yellow wide-brimmed hat with feathery strands splayed out in the front. She said that it was Jon Michael's favorite, and he would have wanted her to wear it at his funeral. I asked her if she wanted to ride over with me and Grandpa to the service, but she said she was gonna take the Dogwood bus.

When Grandpa and I got there, the church was packed. We were seated about halfway back. Viola was in front of us, and to my surprise, Mary Jean Stribling was sitting beside her. They were whispering their opinions about how each thought Daleah was doing.

"She's so brave," Viola said.

"She's holding up better than I would," Mary Jean said.

Grandpa was ignoring Viola and studied the program. He'd hold it up close and then far away. On the front was a good picture of Jon Michael, taken a few years ago. He looked more like the Mr. Jon who had taught me dance lessons than the skin and bones man I'd come to know more recently.

"I forgot my specs," Grandpa said, and handed me the program. "Can you see if there's gone be an opportunity for me to say a couple words about Jon Michael?"

I studied it for a moment and then my forehead and eyebrows punched together so tight I thought my eyes were going to pop out of my head.

I had never known Jon Michael's full name until I saw it there in thirty-six point type.

Jon Michael Hardy

No! I flipped the program over to the back.

Jon Michael Hardy is survived by his parents, Ray and Patricia Hardy and his grandmother, Daleah Hardy Ashford.

My brain jolted back to that moment when Pastor Hardy called his wife from Phillip's place. He must have found out then. I felt bad enough that Daleah had lost her grandson, Grandpa had lost one of his best friends, and I'd lost someone I'd known and respected for the better part of a decade. I didn't realize that Pastor and Mrs. Hardy were suffering the loss of their only son.

I knew what it was like to lose your closest relative. I pushed past Grandpa to get into the aisle.

"The service is about to start," Grandpa said, and grabbed my arm.

"I want to find Pastor Hardy," I said, and went to the front. The preacher was about to get up, but then he saw me coming forward and stopped. I expected to find Pastor Hardy and his wife in the first row, but Daleah was sitting there with Kevin and people I didn't know. I looked to the other side of the church, but I didn't see Pastor Hardy. Or Patricia Hardy.

Kevin got up.

"You okay, Ben?"

"I'm just looking for Pastor Hardy," I said.

Kevin escorted me back to my seat. The preacher started with the benediction, so Kevin sat with us. I had Grandpa on one side and Kevin on the other. My mind raced. Where could Pastor Hardy be sitting? I wanted to be there for him.

A woman who must have been a professional opera singer began with "Wishing You Were Somehow Here Again" from *Phantom of the Opera*. I felt like I was in a trance. I didn't understand anything that was going on. Where was Pastor Hardy? I looked around. I wanted to find Pastor Hardy. To comfort him. To let him know how sorry I was. And then I remembered how emotional Pastor Hardy could be sometimes. Maybe he was sitting in the back because he didn't want to be seen crying. He did have a reputation to uphold.

Grandpa handed me a Kleenex, and I wiped my eyes. The preacher started his eulogy, and I hoped that Pastor Hardy was okay. I felt bad for him. To be such a public figure and have to worry about appearances.

The words rolled around in my head. Appearances. Public figure. Reputation.

And then I realized what reputation Pastor Hardy would be more concerned about upholding. I understood why I couldn't find him. I realized why we were at the Episcopal church and not the Baptist church that Pastor and Mrs. Hardy attended.

I felt the anger bubbling in my soul. A thick tar coated my heart. I wanted to run out and track down Pastor Hardy and yell at him. To tell him how disappointed I was. To release my anger. I must have been shaking or something because Grandpa put his hand on my knee.

I looked up and noticed that the priest had just called for Daleah to come up and speak about Jon Michael on behalf of the family.

"Jon Michael was always my special boy. I remember one moment in particular. When he was a little boy, barely four, President Kennedy was shot. It was the Saturday before Thanksgiving. The entire world stopped. Jon Michael and I watched the funeral. It probably wasn't the best thing for a boy his age. But he had this way about him. From the moment he could speak, it was like he was a little adult." Her voice cracked and she stopped. "We watched as the nation mourned. And when John Jr. saluted his father's coffin as it went past, I started to sob. But Jon Michael put his arms around me and held me."

"'It's okay, Gam Gam,' he said. 'I'm here for you. I won't let Dadda get shot.' And he was there for me in my life when I needed him. When my husband died, I couldn't do anything, but Jon Michael took care of the funeral arrangements. It was the most beautiful service I've ever attended, and I made him promise to make my funeral even better."

She looked down at the closed casket. "I never thought that he would go before me." She was about to break down but then jolted up straight. "I'm sure that some of you don't know about Jon Michael's life or want to pretend that it doesn't exist. But Jon Michael lived his life the way that God made him."

A few people grumbled in the church, but she just spoke louder.

"I know some of you are thinking that Jon Michael got what he deserved. But for the people who truly knew my grandson, you know that the only thing he deserved was the love of everyone in his life."

By the end of her speech, I was so upset that I couldn't see. I followed Grandpa to the car, and we went to the gravesite. I even let Grandpa drive.

At the cemetery, there was still snow hiding in the shadows of the tombstones. Reverend Price stood in front of the coffin and beside the Astroturf covering the mound of dirt that would fill Jon Michael's grave. The folks from Dogwood sat in gold Chiavari chairs while the rest of us stood. I wished that I'd brought sunglasses because even though it had been cloudier earlier, the sun shone bright. I counted twenty-two people, but not Pastor Hardy.

After the short sermon, Reverend Price invited Viola to sing Jon Michael's favorite hymn. Daleah had convinced Viola to sing. Grandpa told me he didn't think it was a good idea, but he wasn't about to tell Viola that.

I feared Grandpa was right because Viola looked like she didn't want to be up there. She stared at Jon Michael's friends. Viola started off but her voice was so shaky she stopped. Tears streaked her face. I moved through the crowd and went up to stand beside her. I put my arm around her and held her. She cleared her throat and then started the song again. Together we sang.

> *Just as I am—without one plea,*
> *But that Thy blood was shed for me,*
> *And that Thou bidst me come to Thee,*
> *O Lamb of God, I come.*
>
> *Just as I am—and waiting not*
> *To rid my soul of one dark blot,*
> *To Thee, whose blood can cleanse each spot,*
> *O Lamb of God, I come!*

After we finished the song, I was gonna take Viola back to where she'd been standing before, but she moved in Grandpa's direction. I helped her over to Grandpa, and I stood between the two of them, the three of us with our arms around each other. Jon Michael's casket was lowered into the grave. Even though it was freezing, and the wind was blowing right through the wool suit jacket I was wearing, I wasn't one bit cold. A fury burned inside me. I couldn't understand how Pastor Hardy could turn his back on his own flesh and blood. How could he abandon his son?

After the funeral, we went to a wake at the home of one of Daleah's friends. I didn't bother to meet the hostess, and I heard

Grandpa apologizing for my rudeness as I pushed past the mourners. I had accepted why Pastor Hardy would skip being seen in public at the church, but I couldn't believe that he wouldn't show up at the wake. I searched room by room. The dining room was so crowded that I had to circle a couple times. Friends had filled the dining table with plates of fried chicken, meatloaf, ham, biscuits and no fewer than seven different casseroles.

People trolled about with plates of food in a dream state, whispering to each other but then almost shouting at Daleah. It was like somehow hearing loss accompanied the grieving process. I remember people talking to me the same way when my Momma died. And I was grateful. It was painful enough just to exist. To have to strain to hear someone speaking would have been too tough.

I made my way to the kitchen where the table in the breakfast nook was piled with chocolate cake, peach cobbler and a million-dollar pie.

Kevin came up to me. "I've looked all over for you. It was so great of you to sing with Viola. If the pastor thing doesn't work out for you, maybe you've got another career option."

"I'm a real triple threat," I said. "Preacher . . . singer . . . and thanks to Jon Michael, dancer." I thought it would be a funny comment, but it fell flat.

Kevin talked a little about the day in the auditorium where Jon Michael was teaching everyone how to dance to MC Hammer's "U Can't Touch This." And I thought about the moment that Kevin and I had shared alone right after everyone had left for ice cream.

Kevin's lower lip quivered, and his gray eyes glassed over. His voice trailed off, and we stood there for a moment. There was a magnetic pull between us that I couldn't resist. I grabbed him, and we hugged. Our faces were close, and I could feel his breath on my lips.

And then I heard Grandpa's voice and turned to see him talking to Mrs. Hardy. I pushed Kevin away and stormed over, ready to yell at her. To tell her that I couldn't believe that she hadn't even shown up for her own son's funeral. To release at least some of the pent-up anger, disappointment and frustration I had for her husband.

I was so mad that red dots blurred my vision. But when I got up to her, and she saw me, she just grabbed me, hugged me and wouldn't let go. I stiffened, hoping that she would stop, but she just held on. Like she could get back a piece of Jon Michael if she just squeezed me tight enough.

I relaxed and then put my arms around her.

"I'm so glad you came, Ben," she said. "You have to live the life you were meant to live. Don't let my husband or anyone else tell you different. You're special, and God made you that way."

She unpeeled from our embrace, but I gripped her shoulders. "Where is Pastor Hardy?" I asked her.

She stumbled on her words, trying to think of some excuse. "Well, but he's . . ." she started, but didn't have the energy to finish.

I needed to understand. "Where is he?" My fury was building up so much that I was shaking her. "Why is he not here!" I shouted and then let her go.

But only one person could answer that question. And I needed to confront him.

27

January 19, 1992 (Sunday)
Ben

I had wanted to talk to Pastor Hardy last night, but when I got home, all the lights were off at the main house. Grandpa had wanted to stay at the wake until Daleah was ready to go, and by the time I drove him back to Dogwood and made my way back home to the carriage house, it was after 10 p.m.

I stayed up for an hour or so, checking out my window and watching for lights at the big house. At the slightest sign that Pastor Hardy might be awake, I was ready to march over. But I wasn't about to go over there in the pitch black and bang on the door. Like every good Southerner, Pastor Hardy had a pistol at the ready in his nightstand, and my anger wasn't worth getting shot over.

At some point, I fell asleep on the couch. It was light outside when I woke up to the sound of an engine revving. I raced to the window to see Pastor Hardy's car pulling out of the driveway, the wheels spinning at times on the slush. Three inches of snow coated the ground, enough to close down

Upstate South Carolina, including Sunday services at the SJU chapel. I wondered where Pastor Hardy was going, so I put on my heaviest sweater, a down jacket, and duck boots and headed up to the main house.

Mrs. Hardy answered the door but didn't invite me in. I could hardly blame her. I'm sure I'd scared her yesterday.

She did tell me that he was headed to his office.

As I walked back to the carriage house, I thought about the Founder's Day speech. At the wake, someone had told me the faculty had voted against Pastor Hardy's curriculum changes. Their vote was only advisory, but it meant he faced a more difficult challenge with the board of trustees. The future of the school hung in the balance, and he wanted me to put my thumb on the scales.

Before Jon Michael's funeral, I had considered delivering the convocation. I wasn't keen on the idea of telling the whole school that I had been gay, but Pastor Hardy had done so much for me. He'd been like a father.

But yesterday, I'd seen the type of father he was, one not too different from my own.

Looking at the snow that covered the road, I wanted to call his office, to tell him everything over the phone, but I had to deliver this message in person. I thought about waiting and talking to him tonight or tomorrow, but after sitting around for two hours, I was just getting angrier. I tried to eat, but I had no appetite. I couldn't read because I couldn't stay focused. I thought about listening to music, but Pastor Hardy had thrown out all my favorite CDs. My rage was poisoning me, and I needed to confront him. Pronto.

It was only seven miles from my house to SJU, and the drive

usually only took fifteen minutes, but the snow was really coming down. At one point, I skidded to the shoulder, almost landing in a ditch. The wheels spun out, and I couldn't get back onto the road. It was near the entrance to a subdivision, and I thought about just leaving my car there and going to somebody's house to get help. I prayed for the Lord to intervene, and I put the car in reverse and pressed the gas just a little. The back wheels got traction, and I edged back onto the road. I was closer to the carriage house than I was to SJU, and I wanted to turn around and just head back home, but I knew that I had to continue. I'd never been more scared in my life, but I kept going.

Thirty minutes later, when I parked at the administration building, I couldn't stop myself from running to the entrance. The steps were icy, and I almost fell more than once. I couldn't see straight, and by the time I stormed up the steps, my breathing was heavy.

The outer door of his office was closed.

As I stood there, I felt the same churning in my stomach I'd had when I first went to see him in July last year. I said a quick prayer, took a deep breath and knocked.

"Come in," he shouted.

I maneuvered past mountains of textbooks stacked everywhere. Chemistry, biology, psychology, European history. Papers were piled up in every chair in his office.

"It took you long enough to get here," he said. "Patti said you left the house almost an hour ago. I was getting worried." He smiled. "I'm glad you're okay."

I glared at him, taking short breaths through clenched teeth. "How am I okay?" I asked. I was pleased when his smile dissolved into a puzzled look, with his brow furrowing and his eyes focused on me, worried that I might attack. "Where were you yesterday?"

"I was here working all day," he replied without any hint of recognition that I might be asking him why he hadn't attended the funeral of his son. My breathing sharpened and I was so mad that I couldn't even form the next question I wanted to ask.

"I don't understand . . . " I said.

Pastor Hardy's pupils narrowed. "Is this about the other day?" he asked. "You want to know if Phillip is gay?"

"What?" I asked. It was like he knew where I wanted the conversation to head, but he was trying to divert my focus.

"I know that Phillip thinks he can be gay and Christian. And he does a great job compartmentalizing the two. It's a path that works for him for now."

"What?" seemed to be only question I could come up with.

"I don't agree with him on this point of course. Homosexuality is an abomination. But I haven't given up on him yet. He doesn't have your faith, and that's standing in the way of his ability to achieve completeness. To be cured like you."

At the word "cure," all of the anger that had been fomenting inside me coalesced. "But I'm not cured!" I shouted, taking him by surprise. "I thought that I was, but I still have attractions for guys." I thought about telling him that Phillip and I had sex, but we really just cuddled so I held back.

"I know you and Phillip had sex," he said. "You looked so guilty when I walked in on you. It was obvious."

"We didn't have sex!"

He leaned close to me, pulled out a fresh piece of Juicy Fruit and chewed it with intention. "It doesn't matter if you did or didn't. I'm more concerned he'll corrupt you into thinking you can be gay and Christian."

He put his arm around me and squeezed my shoulder. "Now let's talk about your sermon. I've made some notes."

He went over to his desk, and I had completely forgotten about why I'd even come into his office until I saw the wall of photos behind his desk. The ones of him with the governor, the famous Saturday Night Live actress, President Bush. But there were several blank spots.

"Where are the pictures of Jon Michael?" I asked, and stepped away from him.

"Who?" he asked, as if he'd never heard the name before.

"Jon Hardy," I said. "Your son."

He stopped for a moment and I saw the pain on his face. His eyes swelled with tears, but he cleared his throat and wiped his eyes. "I took them down," he said in a flat tone.

I could barely see or hear or even move I was so mad. My voice shook as I asked him the question I'd been wanting to ask. "Why didn't you go to your son's funeral?"

He didn't say anything or even acknowledge the question at first. He went to a box I hadn't noticed in his cluttered office and picked up one of the photos that he'd taken down from the wall. He stared at the photo of himself, Mrs. Hardy and Jon Michael. He didn't control his tears this time. "What good would that have done? He was gone, and I'd done everything I could for him."

"Did you?" I asked, and went over to him. I grabbed the photo and held it in front of him. "Did you just ever try loving him and accepting him?"

He snatched the photo back. "You see, that's where you've got it wrong. I loved him! That's the reason that I couldn't accept him."

He started speaking to the picture, as if he could talk to Jon Michael. "What was I supposed to do? Be a supportive father? Tell you that I loved you no matter what and that it was okay for you to be gay?" He paused, and I could tell that he was about to break down into tears, but he halted. He cleared his throat and wiped his eyes.

He put the photo back in the box. The harshness in his tone softened, and we were no longer in a shouting match. His voice was so soft that it was almost a whisper. "My love for him required me to call out what he was doing as wrong. I couldn't accept the life he chose. It led to death. And Hell. And it breaks my heart more than you can imagine. Don't you know that's why I'm so hard on you? Why I want you to succeed so badly?"

I could have nodded because I did understand him at that point, but my anger still bubbled over, and I couldn't stop myself from shouting again. "But why couldn't you be there for Daleah? For your wife? Why couldn't you be there to honor your son's memory?"

"Look around you, boy!" He pointed to all the piles of paper and mounds of textbooks. "I'm in the fight of my life! The faculty has revolted. They want the school to become secular. In three weeks, the trustees are going to decide between my proposal and the faculty's suggestion to break away from the Baptist Convention. The character and future of this school are at stake. I was not about to risk everything I've worked for so that I could attend a funeral."

"But he was your son!"

"He stopped being my son when he chose that lifestyle over God. I told him that, and I don't regret the decision."

"So is that how things are?" I got up and started pacing the room. "I commit a sin, and then I'm gone from your life?"

"Ben, you're totally wrong. Let me show you something." He went to the box with the photos and pulled out one wrapped in brown paper like he'd just gotten it back from being framed. He handed it to me.

I unwrapped a framed photo of me, standing behind a pulpit preaching.

"I called the newspaper and had them print that for me. It's the one from the article. I told you I'd add you to the wall one day, and with all your progress, I want your picture up there. You've accomplished more spiritually than most of the people up there." He took the photo and then hung it in one of the empty spaces on the wall. "This picture will be an inspiration to students who come to me struggling with same-sex addiction. I can point to you this and tell them that if they work hard enough, God will cure them, just like he did you."

"But I told you. I haven't been cured. I'm still attracted to guys."

"Ben. You're cured. Now that doesn't mean you're not going to have what I call 'phantom feelings.'" He cleared a space for us to sit down by the window. "I knew a soldier that fought in the Gulf War, on the front lines of Operation Desert Storm. He lost a leg. They had to cut it off right below his hip joint. And even though he'd lost the leg, he sometimes felt like it was there. He'd wake up and feel like his leg was itching, and he'd try to scratch it. But he didn't have a leg. It's a common phenomenon. Over time it goes away. These feelings are a shadow of the former ones, and eventually, just like he's come to realize he's lost his leg, you'll come to accept that you've been cured."

I sat back with that knowledge. It didn't not make sense. "But what about others like me? Why doesn't God cure them?"

"You can't have survivor's guilt. Other people are on their own path. You just have to follow yours."

"But I'm not sure that a cure is possible. For a time, I thought that I had been. Right after I wrote that goodbye letter to my same-sex addiction, I thought that it had worked. My heart felt joy and peace I'd never known before. But it was just temporary. When I got the chance, I was intimate with another guy, and in that moment, being with him was everything that I wanted it to be. And it felt natural and right."

"Homosexuality is neither 'natural' nor 'right.'" Pastor Hardy's eyes flashed with such anger that I felt like he was about to strike me. "Leviticus 18:22 says that it's an abomination for a man to lie with another man as he would with a woman."

I turned away from him and went over to the photo wall. I traced one of the spaces where Jon Michael's photos had been. "Leviticus 11 says it's an abomination to eat pork or shrimp, but we don't follow that Old Testament rule."

"So has Phillip corrupted you?" he asked. "You think you can be gay and Christian?"

"I don't know that. I just know that I'm not cured. And I'm not sure a cure is even possible." I straightened the picture of me he'd just hung on the wall.

He sighed and shook his head. "I had hoped it would not come to this," he said, and went over to his desk and pulled out a red folder and a green folder. He also grabbed some Kleenex. He sat down on the sofa and wiped the tears that rolled down his cheek. "Come sit," he said.

I sat at the other end of the sofa, but he scooted close to me. So close I could smell the Juicy Fruit. My nerves clenched. I had a metallic taste in the back of my throat, an anticipation of something bad.

"Ben, I know you've tried your best. And that's why I feel obligated to do this. It's for your own good. And even though you might not see it that way now, at some point you'll thank me. When you're married with a wife and kids and you're pastor at one of the largest churches in the South, you'll remember this moment and you'll be grateful."

He handed me the green folder first. The label read *Letter of Recommendation—Benjamin Stark*.

"Go ahead, open it," Pastor Hardy said. He smiled. "It's one of the best recommendations that I've written."

It was addressed to Thurston Perry, the head of the Saluda Baptist Seminary.

> Dear Pastor Perry,
>
> I am writing to recommend Benjamin Thomas Stark as a member of the 1992 Fall session into Saluda Baptist Seminary. In my twenty-two years as a professor, eight of those as chaplain of Stonewall Jackson University, I have not met a student who has struggled through as many trials and tribulations as Ben and come out with a stronger faith and belief in Christ.
>
> Ben's father left him and his mother when Ben was a young child. Barely a year after that, Ben and his mother were in a tragic car accident. Ben's mother died, and Ben has both physical and emotional scars of that inci-

dent that he carries with him to this day. Without any strong father figure in his life, Ben has had to adapt and work towards becoming the man that Jesus wants him to be. And that man has had some temptations along the way.

Like Job in the Old Testament, God has allowed Satan to create obstacle after obstacle in Ben's path, things that would have shaken the faith of less strong servants of our Lord. Less than eight months ago, Ben came into my office to ask for help. Help in dealing with a same-sex addiction. At the time, Ben had never acted on those feelings, but he was worried that the temptation at some point might be strong, and that he would not be able to resist. Over the past school year, I've worked with Ben on overcoming his same-sex attraction, and although he has not always been perfect—let him without sin, cast the first stone, as our Lord Jesus Christ might say—he has remained fervent in his commitment, and I am pleased to share with you the exciting news that God has cured Ben of his affliction. Ben's prayers and hard work have been rewarded. He is free of his disease.

I am pleased and proud to provide this character reference for Ben Stark. He will certainly be a wonderful addition to your student body, and because of what he's endured, he will be a compassionate and effective pastor after graduation. . . .

As I read the letter, I could feel the tightness in my chest. And the heat in the room became oppressive. I wished that I weren't wearing such a heavy sweater. I pushed up the arms of the sweater. "But this isn't true," I said.

Pastor Hardy sat at his desk. "I love you, Ben. And that's why I want you to be able to fulfill your dream of becoming a pastor. But you have to make a choice. Do you want to be gay or do you want to be a pastor?"

I'd spent so much time wondering whether it was okay to be both gay and Christian, I hadn't stopped to realize that my views didn't matter. If the Christian community in general didn't accept this view, then I couldn't have both. All of a sudden I understood Phillip completely.

Pastor Hardy took the letter from me and put it back in the folder. He stood up from his chair and then handed me the red folder. Its label read *Letter regarding moral turpitude of Benjamin Merritt Stark.*

"Ben, because I do love you as a son, I'm prepared to move forward with this approach, however much it pains me."

I feared opening this folder, and my fingers traced the edge. The sharpness of the corner sliced my finger. It was just a tiny paper cut, but it hurt. I tasted the sharp, metallic iron of the blood.

I couldn't believe my eyes as I opened the folder and read the letter.

Dear Pastor Perry,

It is with great sorrow in my heart that I write to you to tell you about the tragic fall from grace of Benjamin Merritt Stark in the past year. I can no longer recommend him for seminary because he has been corrupted by the world to believe that he can live his life as a

Christian while still embracing sin. I've watched with horror and dismay as Ben has spent the last year changing from being one of the most upstanding Christians I've ever known, into a practicing homosexual. Ben has willingly put himself in situations where he could be tempted. And it's terrible to understand that he did this after much counseling from me.

I pray for this young man every day, and I hope that at some point, God will show him the light, the error of his ways. Otherwise, I worry he will succumb to the plague that God has cast upon those who have turned their backs on him. . . .

I didn't need to read the rest of it.

"You can't send that," I said. "It's not remotely true, and I'll never have any chance of getting into seminary with that letter."

"So I guess you can see where I'm going with all of this," he said. "I've got two letters. Which one I send will depend on you." He took the two folders and held them up in front of me. "Help me help you, Ben."

For a moment, I sat in silence in his office unsure what to do. I had two options. I could give the sermon that I wanted to give, forfeit my academic scholarship . . . and then do what? I had no backup plan.

I guess there were some options. A middle ground where I could give him what he wanted while getting what I wanted. Give the sermon that he wanted me to give and continue on the path I was on. Exploring my sexuality. Finding out what it means to be gay. He'd send the glowing recommendation letter,

I could keep my scholarship, go to seminary, get a Ph.D. in religion and then decide what to do at that point.

In the meantime, I could live my life the way that Phillip did. Put on a mask and pretend to be witnessing to gay people. Help them overcome their disease, while at the same time, troll bookstores and hook up with men that I'd met at the bars.

Or I could be like Derek. Deny being gay but still have sex with guys.

I wasn't sure what to do, but I knew that I needed some time to figure it out. "You won't be needing that," I said, and pointed to the red folder labeled *Letter regarding moral turpitude of Benjamin Merritt Stark.*

"I knew you'd make the right choice, Ben." He got up and came over and gave me a hug. "You're going to be okay, son." He handed me a thick file. "Here's a first draft of a sermon that I wrote for you to give. Contact me with any questions. So long as you keep the theme, feel free to make it your own."

I left his office and went home. Classes had been canceled, so I spent time reading through what he'd written.

He only wanted the best for me. And he had done a lot to help me in my time at SJU, especially in the past six months with the HomoNoMo program. With his help, I'd gone through some significant changes, even getting to a point where I had become a different person. I'd found and embraced my masculinity. I'd had a girlfriend, I'd had healthy male relationships. I'd watched sports. I'd changed the music I listened to. And I'd used negative reinforcement to associate pain with feelings I had about guys. I had tried to become the man that I was supposed to be. I'd come to him as "broken" and he had forged a path for me to "wholeness."

He wanted me to be happy. And his draft of the sermon had some good points. Things that needed to be preached about. But the more I read through the sermon, the more uncomfortable I became. I couldn't tell people I was cured. I thought about Johnny in the Straight Path group, worried that God didn't love him because he wasn't cured. If I pushed that a cure was possible, what would that do to other students who were struggling with the same thing?

All of his efforts to help me become a "complete" person had failed. I wasn't cured of my same-sex addiction. My attractions to guys hadn't been reduced. It was true that I had become a different person, but that person was no longer me. I pulled out my Bible and worked on some changes to the sermon. I knew that Pastor Hardy wasn't going to like them.

And that he might take away my scholarship. And keep me from going to Saluda seminary. But I still had the money from when Grandpa sold the house. I had a perfect GPA. Certainly, I could find an alternate route and go to a divinity school instead of seminary.

Being a minister was more important to me than anything. Since I had been thirteen years old, it was all that I'd ever dreamed about doing. I couldn't give the sermon Pastor Hardy wanted, but I wasn't about to give up my calling and renege on the promise I'd made to God.

I looked outside. The sun was shining, the temperatures were warmer, and the roads were clearing.

Grandpa had not wanted to tell me why he and Ruby J ended their relationship. He'd said that he'd tell me when the time was right. And now that I was embarking on this new path, I decided now was the time. I needed to know the conclusion to his story.

January 19, 1992 (Sunday)
Ben

When I got to Dogwood, Judy had the residents outside, and they were making snow angels. I worried about broken hips and pneumonia, but I could tell that they were having the time of their lives.

I didn't see Grandpa, but I heard Viola laughing. She and Daleah were having a snowball fight with Cowboy. When they saw me coming up the walk, they joined forces and unleashed a barrage of snowballs. Fortunately, no one could throw very far, so most landed well in front of me.

Judy announced that it was hot cocoa time, and all the residents headed inside.

Kevin found me and said that we needed to talk. And not where any of the residents might overhear.

"Should we walk towards the lake?" I asked. "I need to find a stone."

"Let me go get a heavier coat," he said. "Just meet me at the entrance."

"I want to tell Grandpa I'm here and let him know about the cocoa," I said. "He loves hot chocolate."

While Kevin went to get a jacket. I went to Grandpa's room. He was hunched in his chair with the TV on, but he wasn't watching it. He didn't look like he'd showered or combed his hair in a couple days.

"What's the matter?" I asked him.

"Viola ain't speaking to me."

"I thought that after the funeral, you two would be back together."

"Ben, I don't know what to do." He stared at me with an

emptiness in his eyes I'd never seen. "Just this morning, I talked to her and apologized for not defending her at the diner, but she won't forgive me. She says that I still don't understand what I've done."

I put my arm around him. I could understand that Viola had been mad at him, but I couldn't understand why she wouldn't forgive him.

"Have you talked to Daleah about it?" I asked.

"She's on Viola's side and says she don't blame Viola one bit for how she's treating me."

I wasn't sure what to say, but I knew that Viola was gonna be in the rec room getting cocoa. Maybe she just needed time. "Don't worry about it anymore for now," I said. "Just put on a hat and get to the rec room. They're having cocoa."

"You can bring me one back," he said, and turned up the volume on the TV.

"You get your own. I'm going for a walk, and then I'm coming back to hear everything that happened between you and Ruby J. I feel like there's some stuff you haven't told me."

I went over and gave him a hug. "And throw on some of your Old Spice. You smell like you've been riding the rails for a month."

He chuckled, and then smiled for the first time since we'd gone to see *King Kong.*

I used his restroom, and when I left, he was standing in front of his closet, trying to decide which hat to wear. I went to the rec room, grabbed two cups of cocoa and headed to meet Kevin at the entrance. He was carrying a brown paper grocery bag and wore a big jacket with a fake fur collar.

We walked down to the lake, and I could tell that he was

getting up the nerve to ask me something because he kept trying to start a conversation.

"I'm sure you're wondering why I asked you down here," he said. He pulled a loaf of bread from the grocery bag. The rustling of the plastic was enough to cause the ducks to gather in front of us, fighting over the crusts and pieces that we threw in their direction.

"Is it because you're worried about my grandpa?" I asked, "because I certainly am."

"Your grandpa will be fine," he said, and then looked away. "I'm worried about Viola."

"What's the matter?" I asked. I panicked that her breast cancer had returned. Certainly God wouldn't allow that to happen.

"I'm sure you're aware how expensive care here is at Dogwood."

"I'm well aware. Half of our money went to Grandpa's being here."

"When she first arrived, Viola had plenty of money to afford to be here, but since then she's given everything she had to her daughter. She can't afford to live here anymore."

"That's terrible," I said.

Kevin and I sat without saying anything for a while, watching the ducks fight over pieces of bread.

"Does Grandpa know?" I asked.

"No, and Viola doesn't want to tell him."

"Where is she gonna go?" I asked.

"We've arranged a spot for her at Hickory Pines."

"Hickory Pines! That's the place Grandpa said smells like Clorox and urine."

"It could be a case study on bad senior care," Kevin said.

"The state would probably have shut it down already, but it's the only place in the Upstate that people can afford with just Social Security."

"Isn't there some way to keep her at Dogwood?"

"There is one way," Kevin said. "Now, Viola doesn't know about this, and I'm not even sure she'd accept, but I just wanted you to know the situation. And I was hoping you might want to pay for her to stay here."

"But I don't have that kind of money," I said.

"I know it's a lot of money, but you've got that scholarship to seminary and her living quarters aren't nearly as expensive as your grandpa's." He handed me an envelope and stood up. "That contains different payment plans and options to keep Viola here. It's not a decision you should rush into one way or the other. Just think about it."

"It's just that . . . " I wanted to tell him that things had changed, and that I might need the money myself in case Pastor Hardy revoked the scholarship. But if I told Kevin that, he would tell Grandpa and Viola, and they wouldn't give me the option whether to help Viola stay at Dogwood. I wasn't sure what I was going to do, but it was a choice that I wanted to make. I folded up the envelope and put it in my jacket pocket.

"When do I need to let you know about the money?" I asked.

"As you're aware, payment is required by the first of the month, so I'll need to know by then."

"But that's only two weeks away!"

"I can probably talk them into giving you a couple extra days to decide. I wish I could do more, but we have a waiting list, and it's not my call."

"Thanks for letting me know," I said, and rubbed my arms to warm them a little. "I'm gonna hang out down here for a little bit longer."

He handed me the paper bag with several more loaves. "Finish feeding the ducks. We've had a lot of snow this year, and they're hungry," he said.

My head hurt so bad that I had to lean over on the bench and press my temples together with my palms. I wanted to cry, just to have some emotional release, but I'd shed all my tears at Jon Michael's funeral the day before. I sat on the bench and balled up bits of bread. I chucked them as far as I could until my arm was sore. I wanted to talk to Grandpa, but I still wasn't sure what to say about the situation with Viola.

Instead of walking the short path back to the main building, I went the other way around the lake. The sun had gone behind the clouds, and it was getting colder so I quickened my pace. Under a black willow tree on the other side of the lake, the snow had not accumulated, so I looked there to see if I could find a stone.

I'd never noticed it before, but Grandpa had carved his and Viola's initials into the tree. I traced my fingers on the outline of the heart and then the letters. On the ground I saw a river rock, smooth and gray. It was the color of Kevin's eyes. I picked it up and walked the slight hill back to the main building.

When I got to Grandpa's room, I handed him the stone. He rolled it in his hands, feeling the smoothness, studied it in the sunlight, and then told me a story.

July 3, 1933 (Monday)
Grandpa (18 years old)

Faulkner County prided itself on having the largest Fourth of July fireworks display in the state of Georgia. Even in the midst of the Great Depression, the town wudn't gone give up that tradition. Ray Bill and other prominent businessmen had been saving up all year for that event, and none other than President Franklin and First Lady Eleanor Roosevelt planned to attend, passing by on their way to their home in Warm Springs, Georgia.

I volunteered to help, and we was divided up into six stations set up strategically around Lake Flannery. I was responsible for making sure nothing caught fire while they was fireworks going off everywhere. I was having the time of my life watching the sky blaze with red and blue and white lights, but I made sure to stamp out the cinders that landed around me.

The Faulkner County marching band was playing "The Star-Spangled Banner," and I could hear it plumb across the lake. Like every American, I put my hand over my heart and sang along, but I reckon I should have kept working because the other members of my brigade continued on loading fireworks, positioning them, and lighting them. I got carried away by the ramparts' red glare, the bombs bursting in air, and then I started to smell something burning.

The lake level was real low and an area that used to be underwater was now just dry grass. In the two minutes that my attention had been diverted, what might have been a couple sparks was now half a hillside. The wind picked up and the fire spread to where two of the stations had their fireworks piled up. They started shooting off in all directions. Was really an appropriate scene for the song, probably what Francis Scott Key saw when he wrote that poem.

With fireworks going everywhere, I took off over the hill to escape. And who do I run into but half the colored folks in town, including Clem, there with his family: Ruby T, Ruby P, and of course Ruby J. Because of the smoke, I had so much soot on me that I don't think that any of them recognized me.

"We need to get out of here before this whole hill is on fire," I yelled, and we all ran through the fields.

I couldn't find Ruby J again in all the commotion, and I walked back to the boarding house where I lived. I went to wash up and didn't even recognize myself in the mirror. My face was blacker than Clem's. My hair was all white from the ash that had fallen on my head and gotten stuck in my Brylcream.

I'd burned up all my options in that town so I figured I'd head north, like I had intended to do when I left home. I thought about the things that I'd miss, but I realized that they was nothing keeping me there except Ruby J.

I went to see her the next day to try and get her to go with me, and for reasons that I've never understood, she refused.

I never saw her again for almost sixty years.

January 19, 1992 (Sunday)
Ben

Grandpa was crying when he finished his story, and he wouldn't look at me. I could see how much pain he felt at losing Viola the first time six decades ago. I kissed him on his forehead and was about to leave when he grabbed me by the arm.

"How was your walk with Kevin?"

I looked at his face to see if I could discern any clue that he knew what Kevin and I had discussed. "It was fine."

"You two getting to know each other pretty well?"

"I guess so," I said.

"I know it's none of my business, and I've never interfered in your love life before, but I like him," Grandpa said.

"What does Kevin have to do with my love life?"

"Maybe he has something to do with your lack of a love life," he said, and chuckled. "Ben, I know that you're attracted to him. I saw it the first day you met him. It's one of the reasons that I chose Dogwood over Magnolia."

I dropped onto the couch. I had never realized that Grandpa knew of my same-sex addiction. I'd suspected, but he'd never said anything.

"I'm not that way," I said.

"Ben, I've known since you was thirteen that you liked boys and not girls. And it don't matter to me. I just want you to be happy."

"But I don't want to be that way. In fact, I used to pray every day for God to cure me."

"I know that Mee Maw believed it was wrong, and that you feel an obligation to her. And even though I ain't on my deathbed, I want you to promise me something."

I shook my head. "I'm not sure I can do that."

"Hear me out then. You keep your promise to your Mee Maw and be a preacher. I see that passion in your eyes. The joy you have when you help someone, and the joy that you bring to their lives."

He reached over and grabbed my hand. "But I also see you in so much pain at times. You see a guy you think is good-looking, and then you beat yo'self up. But it ain't gotta be that way. Try following your heart. God gave it to you for a reason."

"Is that the promise?"

"No. Mee Maw made you promise you'd be a preacher. I want you to promise me you'll be a hobo."

"What?" That's not where I thought the conversation was headed. I tried to pull my hand away, but he held onto it.

"Be a hobo."

"You want me to travel the country riding the rails?"

"Only if you want to." He laughed. "I don't mean it literally. I just want you to follow what I've taught you about being a hobo. Live life by your own rules."

I tried to pull my hand away, and again he held on tight. "Promise me," he said.

"I promise," I said, and then he let go. We sat and watched TV for a while after that, but we didn't say anything else. When it was dinner time, he invited me to join him, but I left. I needed to go home and think. And pray.

I got halfway down the hall when I heard Viola calling my name.

"Ben, I need to talk to you," she said.

I figured that she probably knew that Kevin was gonna talk to me, but I didn't want to say anything. "What about?" I asked.

"There's something you need to understand about your grandpa."

"I'm not sure why you're telling me and not him."

"Ben. Your grandpa knowed what he said to me the last time we saw each other all those years ago. Either he understands why it hurt me so, or he don't. But I can't explain it to him."

"So you're gonna explain it to me?" I asked. "And you want me to tell him?"

"No. I just want to tell you what happened. From the way you acting, I can tell you don't know the whole story."

It felt like a betrayal to listen to Viola's side of the story. If Grandpa had wanted me to know about it, he would have told me.

"I'm sorry. I need to get going."

"Ben. Just give me a couple minutes. I know you've got a lot on your plate, but I think what I'm gone tell you will help. In your situation. I think you need to hear this."

At this point, you have so many people telling you what to do, what is one more voice?

I had to agree and followed her back to her room.

And after hearing Ruby Viola Jackson Chapman tell me about the last conversation she had with Grandpa on July 5, 1933, I realized that she was right. What she said did help me in my situation. I realized that I had only one choice about Founder's Day.

28

February 2, 1992 (Sunday)
Ben

I'd spent the past two weeks meeting with Pastor Hardy and working on my sermon for Founder's Day. I thought that I'd figured out a compromise where I could please everyone, but I didn't know how Grandpa was gonna feel about it, so I came up with a dozen excuses as to why he couldn't attend. Finally, he gave up.

I'd been so nervous that morning of Founder's Day that I hadn't eaten anything at the breakfast reception. I'd just sat at the head table with Pastor Hardy and the other speakers, including Monica. She was gonna deliver the invocation. A woman had never led the Founder's Day prayer, but she'd worked so hard for Pastor Hardy over the past year that I guess he figured he ought to reward her somehow.

I'm not sure why, but Pastor Hardy had me and Monica sit on stage with him during the Founder's Day celebration. The lights were so bright that we couldn't see anybody in the audience. After welcoming everyone, Pastor Hardy called on Monica to deliver a prayer as SJU entered its 149th year as a Christian university.

I tried to pay attention during Monica's invocation, but my focus was on the sermon I was about to deliver in a half hour. I pantomimed my way through the hymns and the rest of the service until it was my turn. Pastor Hardy touched my knee and then went to the podium to introduce me.

"Ladies and gentlemen, students and alumni. As many of you are aware, this is a first for us here at Stonewall Jackson University. Usually, we have an evangelist who's spoken all over the world or a famous alumnus who's made his mark in the Southern Baptist community, but today, we're blessed to have Benjamin Merritt Stark as our speaker. He's a senior here, and we hope will start at Saluda Baptist Seminary this fall. I have known him as a God-fearing Christian, one who has had to battle his demons, but he is here today to testify how the power of Christ has helped him to overcome those demons."

The piano started in the upper treble register. Then a flute took over that melody, freeing the pianist to play only harmony, and she blocked out the main parts of "Jesus Loves Me." It was the most elegant version of that song I'd ever heard. I lost track of what Pastor Hardy was saying for a moment, but then I heard the word "Dogwood."

"If you could turn down the house lights," Pastor Hardy said, and looked back to me. "This is a surprise for Ben. We're very honored to have his grandfather here. Charles Phelps, would you please stand up?"

I couldn't believe that Grandpa was there. Along with Daleah, Cowboy, Judy, Kevin and about a half-dozen other Dogwood residents. On the opposite end of the pew was Viola. I thought I was gonna be sick, and I searched the stage for a potted plant or somewhere to throw up.

Like Evita, Grandpa waved to the crowd below him. Someone started to applaud, and then everyone did. Grandpa took a bow.

Pastor Hardy turned to me and smiled. It was the grin of a victor. It was a grand slam in the last game of the World Series. "And now I give you Ben Stark, who will deliver a sermon entitled 'Living by His Word.'"

The applause beckoned me, but my legs wouldn't carry me out of my seat and to the stage. Pastor Hardy came over, like he was going to shake my hand, which he sort of did, and I'm sure no one could tell, but he grabbed me and pulled me up.

I stutter-stepped over to the podium and stood behind the microphone. With the spotlights back on, I couldn't see anyone in the crowd.

I fumbled through my pages, adjusted the mic and coughed.

I took a sip of the water that had been set on a shelf inside the podium.

I opened my Bible, but froze.

And then I felt them. In the back of my throat. In the pit of my stomach. The hiccups. I drank another sip of water and almost belched it up. I felt my diaphragm start to spasm, and I realized I wouldn't be able to give the sermon I'd prepared. I looked back at Pastor Hardy and was about to concede defeat. He could just deliver the sermon he wanted me to give. Cut out the middle man.

I closed my Bible and put the sermon on the podium shelf. I was about to turn and walk off the stage when Grandpa yelled. "Go Ben!"

The audience laughed.

I took a deep breath.

The hiccups subsided.

"In January 1978, for my eighth birthday, my Momma gave me a King James Bible. It was black leather with gilded pages, and my full name was on the front in a fancy gold script. I remember trying to read that Bible as a kid. It was tough because the words we use today aren't the same as those used almost 400 years ago. It's ironic that later in 1978, a group of biblical scholars published an updated translation. Its goal was to provide an accurate translation of the Bible using clear English. Although some people still love the poetry of the King James Version, and I'll always treasure the Bible my momma gave me, I've grown fond of the New International Version. Today, I'd like to read a passage that I've recently discovered. Please open your Bible, regardless of what translation you have, to 1 Peter 2. It's a very small book in the Bible, so don't feel bad if it takes you a little time to find it. I'll read verses four through seven.

> 4 As you come to him, the living Stone—rejected by humans but chosen by God and precious to him
> 5 you also, like living stones, are being built into a spiritual house to be a holy priesthood, offering spiritual sacrifices acceptable to God through Jesus Christ.
> 6 For in Scripture it says: 'See, I lay a stone in Zion, a chosen and precious cornerstone, and the one who trusts in him will never be put to shame.'
> 7 Now to you who believe, this stone is precious. But to those who do not believe, The stone the builders rejected has become the cornerstone.

"I love the metaphor Peter uses here. The concept of a 'living stone.' One that was rejected by humans but that was chosen by God. I feel like I'm that cornerstone. Now before I explain my reasoning to you, I want to share something with you.

"My Grandpa collects stones. Ever since I was a kid, I'd find a stone and trade it to him for a story. He has had an interesting life, so I got a lot of great stories. He was a hobo and rode the rails during the Great Depression. I probably shouldn't mention this in church, but he also bootlegged moonshine during Prohibition. But most important to him and to me, in the 1930s, he fell in love with a woman named Viola.

"On July 4, 1933, Charlie was 17 years old. He had volunteered to help the little Georgia town where he lived with their annual fireworks show. While the band played 'The Star-Spangled Banner,' he did what every good American is supposed to do. He stood at attention with his hand over his heart and sang along. But the fireworks didn't stop, and he should have been watching for the sparks igniting the dry grass.

"His distraction led to a fire that burned down half the town. Charlie knew that he had to leave, but he didn't want to go without Viola. But the problem was that his girlfriend was black—and sixty years ago, it was illegal for a white man and a black woman to even eat in a restaurant together in the South.

"On July 5, Charlie woke up at sunrise and packed what little he had into the back of his Model A. He was gonna head north for a better life, and he wanted Viola to join him. She was mad at him, for good reason, and they weren't on the best of speaking terms, but Charlie decided he couldn't leave town without trying. Or at least saying goodbye.

"He drove over to the boarding house where she lived with her cousin. Her cousin came to the door. 'What you doing here, Charlie?'

"'I need to talk to Viola,' Charlie said.

"'She's not here right now,' the woman said, and then slammed the door in his face.

"As he walked to his car, he left pieces of his heart trailing behind him.

"He didn't know that she was watching him, but she was. And she was about to call out to him when he stopped and turned around and started yelling, 'Viola! I know you're in there! I need to talk to you.'

"He kept shouting, and in a few minutes, she came out. 'They's a cemetery just a half mile from here,' she said. 'Ain't no need to wake those poor folks up.'

"Charlie begged her to go with him. 'We can head north where it won't matter that I'm white and you're black.'

"'How we gone get to New York?' she asked.

"'I'll drive us there,' he said.

"'What we gone do?' Viola asked. 'A black woman with a white man? There ain't a hotel or restaurant for a thousand miles that'd take us.'

"'You can always pretend to be white,' he said.

"'Is that how you think this will all work?' she asked. 'My race won't matter because I can just be white if I want to?'

"Now, I'm not sure if Charlie had thought of that idea before he went over to her house, but he latched onto it. In his mind, Viola could just live her life pretending to be white. 'You pulled it off before,' he said, reminding her of the time they'd gone to the movies together. 'You can just wear a wig or do something to your hair. You're already light-skinned enough. You just have to stay out of the sun.'

"Viola saw Charlie smile for the first time since he'd come

to her house that day because I guess he figured the plan might actually work. In his mind, he and Viola could make a life together. Maybe no one would ever find out she was black.

"I'd never heard this story until just a couple weeks ago. And I didn't hear it from my grandpa. When Viola told me her side, I could see the pain and the hurt in her eyes. My grandpa was asking her to live a life that would be a lie. He wanted her to be someone that she was not.

"She told him, 'You have no idea what it's like to be black in a white world. Don't you think that sometimes I wish I were white? Don't you think that it would be so much easier? I could sit down at the counter and have my coffee and crumb cake inside instead of 'to go.' I could ride in the front of the bus instead of having to wait for empty seats in the back. I could walk down the street without men thinking less of me just because of the color of my skin.'

"But Charlie still didn't understand. He pleaded with her. 'If it means that we can be together, can't you just pretend?'

"Viola walked away, and Charlie never really understood why.

"But I think the message of this story is pretty clear. You have to live your life as who you are. You can't pretend to be someone else."

I looked over and saw that Pastor Hardy was focused on my every word, so I reached under the podium and took out the compromise–please everybody–sermon I'd prepared. It wasn't too late for me to go along with it. I could make the sermon work with the story I'd just told and the Bible verse. But that's not where my heart was leading me, so I continued:

"This is the message of verses four and five:

4 As you come to him, the living Stone—rejected
by humans but chosen by God and precious to him
5 you also, like living stones, are being built into
a spiritual house to be a holy priesthood, offering
spiritual sacrifices acceptable to God through Jesus
Christ.

"And that's why I'm here today. To offer a personal sacrifice.
To tell you who I really am. And to live my life how I need
to. After months of prayer, Bible study and reflection, I've
come to realize that I can come to God 'Just as I Am.' And
that is as a gay man. Not a man who suffers from same-sex
addiction as some would want me to believe, but someone
who was created by God to have natural attractions to men.

"For a long time, it was something that I was ashamed of. I
hid it from myself and then from others. I shared this secret
with Pastor Hardy back in July of last year. He helped me,
developing a seven-step program that promised a cure. And I
followed it religiously. I read the Bible and prayed harder than
I ever had before. I de-gayed my life, getting rid of a lot of
music and magazines that Pastor Hardy said were stumbling
blocks. I read up on homosexuality and all of the perceived
dangers. I wore a rubber band on my wrist and snapped it
every time that I had an impure thought. I watched sports and
did other things to become straight. And finally, I wrote a
goodbye letter to my same-sex attraction, calling it out for all
of the negative things that it had caused in my life."

I'd been using the envelope containing the letter as a
bookmark in my Bible, so I took it from where I'd held my

place in 1 Peter and held it for the congregation to see.

"I went back and read this letter again last night, and I realized that it wasn't being gay that had caused all of those negative things. It was hating the person who God had made and praying that God would cure me.

"I haven't yet reconciled being Christian and being with another man in a physical relationship. I'm well aware that some Bible verses seem opposed to homosexuality, but I do know that this is how God made me, and he doesn't expect me to change. I've followed my grandpa's footsteps in charting a course for my life that will cause me to be rejected by many people. But I know that I'm on the path that God has planned for me.

"I want to be a pastor more than anything else in the world, but I have to live my life by my own rules, based on my personal relationship with God. And I invite each and every one of you to do the same. Thank you, and God Bless."

I paused, expecting boos or jeers, but instead, the entire congregation was quiet for a moment. I think that they were all in shock.

And then Grandpa stood up and leaned over the edge of the balcony so that he could see Viola.

"I love you, and I'm sorry," he said. "I should have never asked you to be someone you're not."

"It's sixty years late, but I'm gone accept your apology," Viola said. "I do love you, Charlie Phelps." She stood up and scooted her way across the aisle of people towards him. "And I'm so proud of our grandson."

A large group of faculty members and some students got up and started to applaud. But then an even larger group of people stood up and started booing and shouting. People started calling me a blasphemer. And the congregation erupted in a free-for-all.

I froze, not knowing what to do, until I was pushed away from the pulpit by Pastor Hardy. Monica came and helped me off the stage, and she and I sat in a front-row pew.

It took a few minutes, but Pastor Hardy quieted the crowd. "Ladies and gentlemen. Faculty. Students. Alumni. Special guests. I asked Ben to speak today as an experiment. For the past four years, Ben has been exposed to what is referred to as a 'liberal arts' education. Students are presented with a broad range of ideas, and they are expected to have the emotional and spiritual maturity to filter through those ideas and make decisions. But we can see from Ben's sermon the dangers of bombarding young minds with all of these radical ideas. They're too immature to be able to process what's right and what's wrong.

"And without context and constraint, these ideas can corrupt them. It's important to teach different ideas, but we cannot do so in a vacuum. That's why I've worked over the past year to develop a curriculum here at Stonewall Jackson University based on biblical ideals and principles. We can create an educational model that will become the paradigm for Christ-centered schools across the country."

I sat as Pastor Hardy went through and dissected each part of my sermon. Some people left, but the majority remained, and by the end, Pastor Hardy asked, "Can I get an Amen?" and in one voice, the entire congregation responded, "Amen."

During the final hymn, I slipped out. Grandpa and Viola were waiting for me in the vestibule.

"I've never been more proud of you, Ben," Grandpa said.

Viola put her arms around me and hugged me.

My sermon had divided a crowd of three thousand people, but at least it had united the two who mattered the most.

29

June 22, 1992 (Monday)
Ben

Pastor Hardy sent the letter regarding my moral turpitude to Saluda Seminary, revoked my scholarship, and destroyed my chances of ever becoming a Southern Baptist preacher. But he didn't fare much better as a result of my sermon.

After it came to light that he'd tried to blackmail me into telling people I was cured (Monica's work, I think), he was demoted from his role as president of the faculty. He also lost his bid to change the school's curriculum when the board of trustees voted to sever ties with the South Carolina Baptist Convention. He left Greenville for a couple months and went off to a seminary in Chicago to brush up on his Greek.

I had been forced to move out of his carriage house and was staying at the home of Craig Allen's parents for a couple weeks. Craig Allen had found me after the sermon, and he said that he'd always suspected. His mom had hugged me and said that she was proud of me. I was gonna house-sit while they were on their annual summer trip to Italy. It was a little awkward because Mrs. Vandiver was constantly telling me about all the artists who were gay, from Michelangelo to Leonardo da Vinci.

I wasn't sure what that had to do with me, but at least she was trying to be supportive.

The Vandivers insisted on paying me to stay at their house, and I would have refused, but my religion degree had not opened many employment doors, especially with the economy tanking. I still planned to go to seminary or divinity school. I just needed to figure out how to come up with the funds. I'd committed most of my money to keep Viola at Dogwood, and in the fall I was gonna apply to schools and try for scholarships and loans.

My sermon at Founder's Day wasn't written up in the Greenville newspaper, but it might as well have been. It seemed like the whole town knew that I'd announced to three thousand people that I was gay and wasn't looking for a cure or a boyfriend.

I'd gotten a lot of phone calls from people telling me that I was going to burn in Hell.

I'd gotten as many phone calls from people who said they admired my courage.

I'd also gotten a couple calls from one guy asking me out. And I knew this time it wasn't a prank. Kevin and I had dinner at least once a week, and we'd taken Grandpa and Viola to the movies a few times. I'm not sure these were "dates" because I hadn't decided it was okay for me to have a physical relationship with a guy. But being with Kevin felt natural. He knew how I felt about the sex part, and he said he was fine just hanging out. He never pressured me for more.

I'd never been happier, and I thought that everything was right in my world until I got a phone call yesterday morning.

I'd never expected to hear from Pastor Hardy again.

He was in town on a break from his sabbatical, and he said that he wanted to meet and talk. He wouldn't have his old office on campus until the end of the year, so I invited him over to the Vandiver's house I cleaned up a little bit before he got there. I'd spent a couple hundred dollars of my graduation money rebuying all of my Madonna CDs, and there was plastic wrapping all over the kitchen table.

I was nervous when I answered the knock at my door, but Pastor Hardy seemed as anxious as I did. I had expected him to be standing there with the new and improved version of the HomoNoMo kit, but instead he had a stack of books in his arms. He'd lost all of the gray hairs in his beard. I'm not sure whether he'd aged that much in the past couple months or he'd pulled them all out from stress.

And even though I'd invited him over, I still didn't trust him. I blocked the door like he was a teenager trying to sell me chocolate bars so his band could go on a trip.

"You know the saying about beware of Greeks bearing gifts," he said. "Well, not to worry. I bear gifts of Greek."

He smiled, and I wasn't yet sure what to make of his visit, but I invited him in.

"Anywhere I can set these things?" he asked.

I cleared a space on the coffee table, moving the pile of magazines, mainly Mrs. Vandiver's copies of Town and Country, but also a couple of men's workout magazines. He noticed them, and my eyes dared him to say anything.

He did not.

"You know that I've been at Lincoln Theological Seminary," he said. "It's one of the best seminaries in the country for the study of ancient languages."

I nodded. I had wondered why Pastor Hardy would spend a year at a Unitarian seminary.

He handed me one of the books he'd brought, the first volume of the annotated New Testament in Greek.

I opened it to Matthew 5 and tried to read some of Jesus' Sermon on the Mount.

I stumbled. My Greek was getting rusty. "Thanks, but not sure I have much use for these," I said.

"You'll be using these every day," he said. "I've arranged a spot for you in the first year theology program at Lincoln. And you, my boy, are the recipient of the Jon Michael Hardy Scholarship. It's a full ride to seminary, with tuition, room and board. My wife and Daleah's idea."

I should have been more skeptical from the start, but for a moment I felt excited. I could pursue my dreams a year sooner than I'd even thought possible.

But then the little voice. *What's in this for him?*

He must have noticed the look on my face because he smirked. "Of course, I'll be there to make sure that you don't get too far off track."

"So you'll be at seminary, watching over my every move?"

"It won't be like that," he said. "Seminary can be a cemetery for faith. I want to make sure that doesn't happen to you." Pastor Hardy came and put his arm around me.

"And what about my views on homosexuality?" I asked. "Is this gonna be HomoNoMo, the sequel?"

"I realize that I had been pushing you too hard. I was trying to tell you how to read the Bible, instead of letting you determine for yourself what it says. At seminary, you'll get that chance."

He stood in front of me and hugged me tight. He hadn't given me a bear hug like that since I first came into his office almost a year ago.

I pushed back from his embrace. "And so you want me to study the Bible in the original texts and believe what?"

"Ben, after you study at seminary and look at the original Greek, you'll realize that the Bible is very clear. Homosexuality is a sin."

So there I was. On the cusp of getting what I wanted: Being able to attend seminary, and with a scholarship that would cover everything. But like his earlier offer of the Vandiver medal and letter of recommendation, this offer from Pastor Hardy had strings attached. And this time, they would be connected to me from above. Pastor Hardy would be watching over me, making sure that I did everything he wanted me to do. He wanted a second chance at converting me.

"Don't think I don't appreciate what you're offering," I said. "I know that in your own way, you do love me, and you only want what's best for me. But the problem is that you want to decide what's best for me, and then you want me to live out the blueprint that you've drawn."

I picked up the stack of Greek texts. They were much heavier than I'd imagined. It was like the weight was not just the paper but also the Word of God. "As attractive as your offer may be, I have to refuse. And I can't accept these."

"Those books cost almost a thousand dollars," he said. "You keep them. And you don't have to let me know about the scholarship today. I'll hold the slot for you. I'm not going to give up on you. That's the one mistake I made with my son."

I walked Pastor Hardy to his car and as I watched him drive

off, I wanted to hate him. To be mad at him. To shout after him to get out of my life and never come back, but I couldn't help but feel sorry for him. He'd lost the only son he'd ever had. And I knew that I wasn't going to be able to replace Jon Michael.

I also knew that he was never going to be a father to me. Grandpa was the only real dad I'd ever known, and I'd him made a promise.

As much as I wanted to be a preacher, I had to be a hobo first, and I needed to live life by my own rules.

I no longer worried about spending eternity in a gay ghetto in Hell. I still had an itch that I wasn't sure whether to scratch, but I knew that Momma and Mee Maw were looking down from Heaven, and they would accept my choice.

I was gone be okay.

ACKNOWLEDGMENTS

I have to start at the beginning. In April 2010, I gathered with some friends during lunchtime in a warehouse space in downtown San Diego. The greatest writing teacher of all time, Judy Reeves, told us to write about a collection. I thought about a seven-year-old kid wandering down by the creek on his grandparent's farm. He would find a stone and then trade them to his grandfather for a story. This idea of a collection of stones became the driving force behind my character's transformation in this novel. *Judy, you were the teacher of my first writing class, and you made me love writing. I love you and love writing with you. You are my muse!*

I wrote the first draft of The Wisdom of Stones in the summer of 2010, working every Tuesday night at Eclipse Chocolate and every Saturday at a local coffee shop. I owe an incredible debt (to be repaid in chocolate bars) to the Get It Done writing group of Dan, Dylan, Stacy and Phyllis. *Dan - You were my partner in crime too often and you are gonna be the next published author. Dylan - You blazed the trail with your award-winning novel, A Belief in Angels. Stacy - You are the most creative person I've ever met, and I covet your ability to excel at everything! Phyllis - You may not know this, but you are the one who recognized that my voice was distinctly Southern and told me to follow that trail.*

I worked on and off on the novel, not making much progress, until the fall of 2013 when I met Marni Freedman. I knew I had a "good" writing coach when she "loved" what I'd written and inspired me to keep going when I didn't think I could. I knew I had a "great" writing coach when she "hated" some things I'd written. Yeah, I cursed her name, but then a little time went by, and I realized that she was right. *Marni, your insight into plot changed my writing, and this book would not have been possible or 1/100 as good without you!*

Writing a novel is tough enough, but at least I had some talent and knew something about plot. Publishing and marketing a novel is a completely different set of skills. This novel would have never been completed and never been published without Antoinette Kuritz at PR Strategies. *AK - You joke that you're like a mother to me, and that's not too far from the truth. Your gentle nudges along the way helped me get to the finish line, and then most importantly made me not keep trying to run the race with yet another draft!*

I have so many fellow writers to thank for their encouragement and support during the past six years. I have to mention a few key people in Dan Blank's Mastermind group. *Amanda - You are the twin sister I always wanted. Jack - You wrote the first review of an early draft of this novel, and the review made me want to write that book so I kept working. I hope this book lives up to your review. Teri – Thanks for being you and for all of the feedback on the multiple drafts. You are an angel, and I hope you like the orchid I'm gonna send you on my launch date.*

It takes a special kind of person to be married to a writer. And with all the writing awards out there, I don't know why there's not an award for being married to a writer. I wish such an award existed because even if this book doesn't get any recognition, I know that my husband, LJ Joyner, should get an award for putting up with me the past six years while I worked on this project. Whenever I got stuck on a story problem, he was always there with the right idea about how to move on. And he created space in our busy lives that allowed me to spend thousands of hours hunched over my computer. *LJ - For suffering through hours of neglect, and the ups and downs of the creative process, I hereby establish in your honor, the LJ Joyner Purple Heart, to be given to the spouse / significant other of every writer for pain and suffering and injuries in the line of duty in supporting writers everywhere.*

ABOUT THE AUTHOR

Brian Peyton Joyner was born and reared in a small town in Upstate South Carolina. His parents were proud of him while he served twenty years as a corporate attorney. On August 1, 2016, he left his job (and disappointed his parents) to become a full-time writer, speaker and advocate for "agreeable disagreement." He lives in Palm Springs with his husband and two dogs that he'd like to trade for better ones (the dogs, not the husband. That man is a saint).

CPSIA information can be obtained
at www.ICGtesting.com
Printed in the USA
FSOW01n0612281216
28913FS